Beyond Homer

Beyond Homer

Our Common Fate

Benjamin W. Farley

RESOURCE *Publications* • Eugene, Oregon

BEYOND HOMER
Our Common Fate

Resource Publications
A Division of Wipf and Stock Publishers
199 W. 8th Ave., Suite 3
Eugene, OR 97401

www.wipfandstock.com

ISBN 13: 978-1-49825-054-2

Manufactured in the U.S.A.

Translations from German and French writers quoted in this novel are the product of the author. *Beyond Homer* is a work of fiction. Aside from historical personages and places, the novel's characters, dialogue, events, and situations are purely fictional. Any resemblance to actual persons, living or dead, is coincidental.

To
Alice Anne,
John and Bryan

I want to stretch out a helping hand to all who climb the dark
hill of Destiny, our common fate. We never climb alone,
though we often seem to do so;

belief in loneliness is the first illusion to dispel,
the first temptation to conquer.

I address myself to those who despair of ever reaching
the summit of the mountain,

or who are persuaded that there is no summit and no ascent,
and that the adventure of life

is reduced to tramping miserably about in the mists.

Gabriel Marcel, from *Being and Having*

Acknowledgments

FIRST, I WISH TO thank Libby Case of Columbia, South Carolina for the many hours she devoted to helping me prepare *Beyond Homer* for publication.

Second, as disclosed on the copyright page, the translations of the German and French poets, whose verses appear in the story, are the product of my own pen. This is true of Pascal's *Pensées* as well. Many gifted and talented translations are available, but I wanted to try my own. I would be remiss, however, not to acknowledge the sources I found most useful throughout the project. Most helpful in creating Father D'Maricio's On Solitude were the works of Thomas Merten, Thomas Moore, and Paul Tillich's theology of Being.

Baudelaire, Charles, *Les Fleurs du Mal*, édition 1861 by Claude Pichois, Gallimard, 1972. An excellent edition of Baudelaire's poems in French.

———, *The Flowers of Evil*, ed. by Marthiel and Jackson Mathews, New Directions Publishing Corporation, New York, 1989. A lyrical translation of Baudelaire's work. *Bulfinch's Mythology*, Modern Library, New York, no date. An unparalleled source.

Burkett, Walter, Greek Religion, 1985, Harvard University Press.

Goethe, Johann Wolfgang, *Das Leben, es ist gut*, Insel Verlag, Frankfurt, Germany, 1997. Contains a clear and readable German text.

———, *Selected Verse*, ed. by David Luke, Penguin Classics, London, England, 1964. Includes the German text with literal translations at the bottom of each page.

Haftmann, Werner, *Chagall*, Harry N. Abrams, Inc., New York, 1959. Assembles a collection of Chagall's paintings in full color. Werner's commentaries on Chagall's work are excellent.

Hamilton, Edith, *Mythology: Timeless Tales of Gods and Heroes*, The New American Library, New York, 1942. Indispensable.

Kerényi, C., *The Gods of the Greeks, 1951, Thames & Hudson.*

Impressionists, ed. by Antonia Cunningham, Metro Books, New York, 2000. A worthwhile collection of numerous Impressionists' works, along with able introductions.

Maurois, André, *Paris,* Fernand Nathan, Paris, 1960. A charming literary tour of the city by one of France's greatest writers.

Napoleon and Modern War, rev. & annotated by Conrad H. Lanza, Manchester, NH, 1943.

Paris: The Green Guide (Michelin), Hannay House, Watford UK, 2003.

Pascal, *Pensées de Pascal,* Intro. & notes by Ch.-M des Granges, Edition illustrée, Garnier Frères, 1964. The text from which I translate essential sections.

Penguin Book of French Poetry 1820–1950, trans. & intro. By William Rees, London, England, 1992. Again, a notable resource. French text at the top of each page; literal translations at the bottom.

Rilke, *Rainer Maria, Rilke: Selected Poems,* trans. by C.F. MacIntyre, Univ. of California Press, Berkeley, Calif., 1940. MacIntyre's work is hard to equal.

The Essential Rousseau, trans. by Lowell Pair, A Meridian Book, New York, 1983.

Third, one of the great joys that few are privileged to experience fell to me in the year 1960 and again in the winter and spring of 1970. Thanks to Professor Balmer Kelly of Union Theological Seminary, Richmond, Virginia, I was able to spend 1960 with the Community of Villemétrie—a Protestant monastery and retreat center—then located near Senlis, France. Later, the Community relocated to the vicinity of Orgement, a small town southeast of Paris. I was the Community's designated chauffeur and enjoyed the honor of driving in and out of Paris countless times. I was also emboldened to immerse myself in the culture of de Gaulle's Fifth Republic. In 1970, I returned to Paris for additional study. Somewhere along the way, the seeds for *Beyond Homer* were sown. Nonetheless, it was not until after my retirement that the precise idea for the novel took hold. The Paris of the 1960–1970 decade now lies in the past, but I have sought to recapture it as it was then. There is no city like Paris, nor country like France. I was fortunate. I shall forever be grateful to Balmer Kelly, who encouraged me to go, and to André de Robert, the Director and saint of Villemétrie. Their names do not appear in the novel, but they inspired in me a love for ideas, a tolerance for others, and an appreciation of the transcendent. I have made my share of life's mistakes, but I have never forgotten de Robert or Balmer Kelly.

1

THE MUGGY AIR HAD finally begun to cool. I could feel its dampness tingling on my face and hands. My glass of beer had long since turned tepid, but the pale libation had helped me endure the warm and limpid evening. Now it filled me with a pleasant and lazy languor.

It was April, 1970, and the brightly lighted café off the *Jardin de Luxembourg* was beginning to fill with patrons. A fashionable couple had just arrived by taxi and were escorted into the luxuriant bistro noted for its escargots, aperitifs, and dark oak paneling. A slight buzz erupted as a waiter seated the couple at a small, round, elegant, black table, pulled up against a screen of velvet green wall covering bordered by dark paneling. Heads turned in their direction and voices whispered: "*Alors! C'est M. Gibert*," or something to that effect, but his name escaped my minimal knowledge of Parisian celebrities. I had seen the man earlier at an avant-garde theatre up the street, where an array of speakers had been allotted twenty minutes each to vent their respective grievances: namely, their anti-Vietnam War sentiments.

What had struck me about the Frenchman, however, was the contradictory nature of his character. On the one hand, he displayed an aristocratic bearing in his fine-tailored, black suit and foppish red scarf; yet, on the other hand, there was a casual demeanor about him, seasoned with just a modest hint of Gallic aloofness and disdain. The strikingly beautiful woman in the café had been at his side. She was wearing a light burgundy, leather jacket, matching leather pants and beret, and pearl-covered, high heel shoes. She couldn't have been more than five feet tall.

The first speaker had been a youthful, unruffled Vietnamese, dressed in Viet Cong garb. He delivered an impassioned speech in French on behalf of the "*libération de mon pay*," or the liberation of his country. He was followed by a young hippie in blue jeans who wore a white Russian tunic and whose long blond hair flopped in his face the entire time he waved his arms and ranted knowingly about American imperialism, injustice, and jingoism. He concluded by quoting lines from Whitman's *Leaves of Grass:*

Welcome are all earth's lands, each for its kind.

It was the rhetoric and theme of the last speaker, however, that captivated my own imagination. The pudgy, red-bearded man (probably in his mid-forties), with a receding line of rusty gray hair, took to the podium as if by habit, and, taking off his watch, laid it against the folder-rest of the stand. After a brief pause, he adjusted his glasses. He was accompanied by a lithe, light-skinned black girl, with long black hair and hazel irises, set in the whites of large soft eyes. She had glanced back at me, just before her partner had struggled on stage, and smiled. I returned her engaging overture with ample recognition and interest of my own.

"I am Carl Sullivan," the big man introduced himself, "a Harvard graduate and Alabamian, whose field is, unfortunately, everything," he stated with a gruff voice. "I am currently here on sabbatical, from an ivy league school near Chattanooga, whose name I need not divulge. I teach a variety of humanities courses," he boasted, with a toothy air, "but the classics are my definitive love, my quintessential joy. If I seem overbearing or a little imperious, forgive me. Let me retell a famous story, and you draw your own conclusions. And yes, it does have to do with our purpose here." He cleared his throat.

"Phaeton was the son of Apollo and Clymene, a lovely nymph. One day a fellow schoolmate laughed at Phaeton's reference to his divine parentage, so the lad begged his mother to provide some proof of his celestial birth. She implored him to journey to India, where the sun rises in the East, and to entreat the Sun to own him as his son. The youth listened with delight and hastened toward the eastern horizon. Upon arriving, he made the ascent to Phoebus's palace, where it glittered behind lofty columns of gold and precious stones." Then, for the next twelve minutes or so, Sullivan retold the entire story of how Phaeton managed to coax his father into allowing him to drive the sun-god's chariot across the sky. Only the task was too daunting for the boy. Thereupon, seeing that Phaeton had lost control of the steeds and that the whole of Mesopotamia, Arabia, and Africa were turning black to a crisp—along with its people, Sullivan said: "Thus did Zeus take notice, call the gods to council, even grieving Phoebus, and, seizing a spear-sharp thunderbolt, hurled it at the youth. A bright flash filled the heavens and spread across the seas. Down fell Phaeton in a fiery plume, as his ashes drifted softly in the shifting winds and hot breeze. Phoebus leapt into the falling chariot and, fumbling for the reins, brought the glowing vessel back to night and evening's soft decline, against a golden sunset in the silent west."

Sullivan shifted his weight from one foot to the other behind the podium. The audience appeared stunned. A titter of light laughter crept across the room. I found myself smiling, too. I had read the story myself, but couldn't remember when or where. Suddenly, it dawned on me that I had read it in Sullivan's *own book*, that this was the man whose work on the classics I had admired for the past ten years, alongside Nietzsche's and Dickinson's.

"*Merde*!" said the hippie. "I thought you said your remarks would be relevant."

"Ah, but they are!" interjected the Frenchman, as he turned and frowned sardonically at the young man.

I was about to lift my wrist to order a second beer, when I noted another couple arriving, this time on foot, down the slight hill from the theatre. I rose to my feet. It was Sullivan and his young wife, or paramour.

"*Bonsoir*," she smiled, recognizing me. "*Vous-étiez à la petite conférence, nes' pas*?"

"Yes," I replied, in English. "I enjoyed the story. It's one of my favorites."

"Mine, too," groaned the sweating Sullivan.

"Still, you retold it with fascinating effect."

"Except on the hippie. Plus, I borrowed generous snatches from Bulfinch; and I was reciting it from my own book: *From the Minoans to Homer: The Immortal Gods and Mortal Man*."

"I'm familiar with it. I have it back home, in my own library."

"May I ask your name?"

"Clayton Rogers Clarke, from Virginia. I'm on sabbatical, too. Perhaps you've heard of my college—The Shenandoah University."

"Ah, yes! One of those 'Harvards of the South.'" he smiled painfully. He extended his clammy hand.

An embarrassed smile slipped across the black girl's mouth. "He's not always this pleasant," she grimaced. "We know a number of faculty members from your school. One's directing my graduate program, along with Grumpy, here."

"I need to sit down," said Sullivan. "May we join you?"

"Please, do!" I noted that the girl's fingers sparkled with several rings, but none on her wedding-ring finger. She caught me staring at her hands and smiled.

The professor plopped into the nearest, wire-back chair, opposite mine, while I assisted the girl, whom I seated to my right.

"Don't get any ideas," Sullivan glared. "It's a long story."

"I've plenty of time. *Qu' est que, le temps*? Anyway?"

"Don't get philosophical," he frowned. "What do you teach?"

"Philosophy and religion courses. I was a minister once, but returned for a Ph.D. in philosophy."

"Why'd you get out?"

"That's a long story, too."

"Well, we've got at least an hour," he looked at this watch. "What about you, Sugar?" he put his hand on the black girl's right thigh.

"Oh, Lord, you still treat me like a slave, don't you?"

"No. Maybe your great-grandparents were. But you're not. Besides, Professor Clarke doesn't know about our Alabama laws. Or do you?" he looked squarely at me.

"About what?"

"Incest."

"No. Your secret's safe."

They both smiled, as she put her hand over his. "It *is* a long story," she emphasized.

"*Mademoiselle et Monsieur*! What is your wish?" asked the waiter.

"Jack Daniels! You do carry it, don't you?"

"Of course, Monsieur! *Et vous, Mademoiselle*?"

"White wine! Something from Bordeaux. Sweet, but not too dry."

"*Bon*! But the wines from le-Midi; they are so truly superior."

"She said, 'Bordeaux!'" repeated Sullivan.

The garcon appeared offended, but held his head aloft, as if to signal that he was above such boorish reproach.

Just then Monsieur Gibert came out of the bistro and approached our table.

"Please, won't you join me and the Madame inside," he gestured with a gracious arc of his hand. "I was—shall I say—mesmerized by your speech. It would be an honor." His English was close to impeccable. "I'm Jacques-Maria Gibert, with *Le Miroir Français*, one of its feature writers."

Sullivan looked slightly shocked, if not annoyed. "Please, Monsieur, why don't you and the Madame join us. I'm tremendously tired. I apologize, but I am."

"And stubborn," added the black girl.

"*Eh, ma petite*, may I ask your name, Mademoiselle?"

"Well, at least, there's one gentleman in France," she replied. "Julene Sullivan. Professor Sullivan and I are cousins."

"Remarkable! I thought perhaps you were his wife."

"Not by Alabama law," she patted Sullivan's hand. "I can't speak for Virginia," she looked coquettishly at me.

"You know the answer to that. Cousins are always marrying cousins in Virginia. At least, second and third cousins."

Gibert motioned for his wife to join him. She appeared exasperated at his beckoning, but, clinching her purse in her left hand, she rose misgivingly from her chair and came toward the doorway.

Several waiters quickly brought two extra chairs to the table.

The maitre d' came out. "I'll be in charge," he informed the waiters. "Monsieur Gibert, do you wish anything to eat. *Non*?"

Gibert glanced at each of us. "Mademoiselle? Messieurs?"

"No, thanks," I said.

"Ditto!" remarked Sullivan.

"*Non*, Monsieur," replied Julene. "But thanks."

"*Ah, bon*! Then champagne for everyone," suggested Gibert. "The night is too young to waste. Darling, you do remember these fine people, *je crois*?" he directed his comment toward his wife, who had just arrived by his side and was trying her best to act pleasant.

"Certainly," she smiled, extending her right hand, first to Sullivan, as he struggled to his feet, then to me. A curious little pout formed across her mouth. She reached up and adjusted her beret. Her dark red hair glistened with strands of silver and platinum. She pursed her lips for me to kiss. It was all very charming, if not a tad affected.

I leaned down and kissed her cheek. She, in turn, kissed my neck. "Enchanted," I managed to whisper. "Thank you for joining us."

"Did I have a choice?" her eyes searched mine with a hint of a tease. "And you, Precious," she turned toward Julene. "You're not Française, I believe."

"No. I'm not from one of your former colonies," Julene stated, with abruptness.

"Now, now, Sugar, let's be civil," interrupted Sullivan. "*C'est la France.* Not Alabama."

"Oh, I rather love it," rejoined Mme. Gibert. "Really, I do. But I've never been to your Alabama; only New York and Washington," she looked inquisitively at me.

"Well, you haven't missed a thing," growled Grumpy.

"How can you say that!" retorted Julene. "He doesn't mean it, truly. We're just northwest of Huntsville, a beautiful area, like you've seen in the movies, or *Southern Living*, if you're familiar with our magazines."

Mme. allowed the closest waiter to seat her. I couldn't help but stare at her. Her skin was smooth, but ashen and pale, with a delicate hint of rouge; her lipstick glowed a green iridescence in the bistro's neon sheen. "I edit the fashion page of Monsieur's paper, here," she nudged Gibert. "We're quite familiar with your *Vogue*, but not your *Southern Living*, as you call it."

She had turned toward Julene, but I could tell that her eyes and voice were intended for me to observe, for me to hear, if not to admire. Gibert noted her behavior, but seemed more interested in Professor Sullivan than in either Julene, his wife, or me.

"Can we talk about your Phaeton and your interpretation of the myth? Would you care to know what I think?" he said to Sullivan.

"I hate to interpret my own comments. But, certainly, I'd like to hear yours." Sullivan took his spectacles off and cleaned them with his tie, then pushed them back on over his squat nose.

"Ah, Monsieur. Where to begin! *Hubris*: individual and collective! Mortal pride and immortal sorrow! An eternal balancing act that not even the gods can reverse. A miring down in the consequences of ones own undoing. *N'est-ce pas*?"

"That's as good as any," replied Sullivan.

"How France has paid that price across the centuries! 'Tis our national pastime, I regret to state. A glory in blood, revolution, empire, colonialism, grandeur and demise."

"Don't mind him," laughed Mme. "He's just building up to tell you about his own book."

"How *sauvage* !" Gibert retorted with a glimmer of pleasure that she had mentioned his book.

"Which is?" I asked.

"Well, it's still several weeks off. Actually, it won't be out till June or later."

"And?"

"*Le Futur d'un Grandeur Passé*. It's a commentary on where we French have been and what still lies ahead, politically and culturally for us."

"Sounds worthy," Sullivan remarked. "I might need to see it."

"Hopefully, you shall."

"Too boring!" chimed Mme. Gibert. "Let's return to Phaeton," she said, with a peevish roll of her eyes. "I think it all has to do with the umbilical cord. After all, it was his mother who initiated the search. She knew it was time for the boy to grow up. Plus, she was irked at his father for abandoning her. *Le batard* had it coming," she grinned mischievously. "Phoebus's fake grief and all that! Parents can never predict or foresee the fate of their children. It is the way of all flesh. I think I'm right, *non*?"

"Valid. Equally valid," smiled Sullivan.

"I like the explanation about the Ethiopians turning black. Like we blacks have to be white or brown before we can be worth anything, but owing to some stroke of ill luck, we ended up turning color. Man, that is outrageous prejudice!" Julene averred.

"Now, Sugar, let's not be so emphatic. There are frescoes on the palace walls in Crete, depicting brown girls frolicking on the backs of great fish and graceful green sea monsters, totally without any inkling of racial overtones. It's your festering Alabama past, with all its lash-whipping frenzy, and torrid oral history that's been your ambrosia too long."

"Oh, Dr. Clarke, have you ever heard such a beguiling and devilish tongue!" chortled Julene. "'Lash-whipping frenzy' my ass! Blacks are the true children of Phoebus, the descendants of that abominable, but life-giving Sun. Every anthropologist knows that."

"The poor child never sees it," Sullivan grimaced with a feigned scowl. "'Heaven and earth,' *ouranos kai gaés*, are a unity, interdependent. Neither can strive to be the other; neither can substitute for the other, neither can take the other's place. Zeus is lord of both. Even lord of the underworld and all its chthonic creatures. We have to peel back those mythic layers, if we're ever going to recover our own *ousia*, the truth about our own *beingness*."

"*Ah, mon vieux*! Now you are espousing existentialism," complained Gibert. "Please, let's not spoil the evening."

About that time, the maitre d' returned with two bottles of champagne, glasses, and a large white china dish arrayed with cheese, crispy thin French tea biscuits, and six petite lemon tarts. After a flourish with his towel and the uncorking of the bottles, he poured our drinks and placed the half-filled remaining bottle in front of Gibert.

"A toast to our new American friends! *Salut* to all!" Mme. offered.

We raised our glasses and touched each other's. "*Salut! A tout le monde, salut.*"

For a brief moment, Mme.'s eyes met mine. Her subliminal message was unmistakable. Julene didn't miss it either. Julene smiled as I clinked my glass a second time against hers. "To Mme. and Miss Alabama!" I said, with a celebratory gesture.

"Yes! I'll drink to that," affirmed Gibert. "*C'est magnifique.*"

"You romantics are all alike," groaned Sullivan. "To the gods, those restless and fate-bound immortals, enchained in their own jealousies and limited powers—to them I lift my mortal cup, and bid, 'live on.'"

"Hear, hear!" we agreed, as the soft night enfolded us in its restful ambience.

I don't remember how much longer we talked, but after a third round of champagne, Gibert said: "Ah, Professor Sullivan" (only he pronounced it 'Sue-lee-von'), "would you care to see our own archives, or let me run a special article on you. If you could come by my office tomorrow, say around eleven, we could have coffee, and talk and the like. I should love for all France, or at least Paris, to know how an American scholar views his country's war through the lens of the grand classics. If only we had done the same before Dien Bien Phu, or relinquished North Africa decades before we did! *Alors*! Please, don't say *Non.*"

"Well, I write every morning, but, I suppose I could forego that ritual, just once. *Une fois.* I accept."

"And you, Mademoiselle? You are invited, too."

"*Merci*, but no thanks. I'll just sleep in, or wander about *les Tuileries.*"

"Please be my guest," I volunteered. "We can wander together. I'd like to know more about Alabama and your own project, or dissertation, no doubt?"

"Watch him," warned Sullivan, with a trusting smile, this time. "You can never be sure about a Virginia Cavalier."

"Nonsense," interjected Mme. Gibert. "I'd invite myself to go with you, but I've several deadlines," she yawned sleepily.

"Why don't I meet you near the entrance to the gardens, say around ten a.m.?" Julene suggested.

"Fine."

"May I send a cab for you? Our own limousine?" Gibert asked the professor.

"No, I can take the metro."

"Then here is my card," said Gibert. "5, Rue de Forbage. The sixth arrondissement."

"Very well."

Mme. rose, smiled, and shook everyone's hand, in typical French style. She presented her perfumed cheek for me to kiss. It was very soft and tender. I brushed against it gently with my lips.

"We must meet again," she whispered.

"Yes. I agree."

It was hard not to look into her eyes, but she was deliberately glancing away, as if to ignore any freshness on my part, which she had intentionally awakened. I thought of Goethe's line:

I gazed into your eyes and lost my soul.

"I'll see you in the morning," I said to Julene. "Good night, to all."

2

Morning came noisily through the thin fog of the French capitol. In spite of the closed windows, I could hear the claxons' wails and the murmur of the traffic in the streets below. I rolled to my side, sat on the edge of the bed, then walked to the curtains. I opened them and the double windows and stared out across the city.

I was staying in a pension near the Garden of Luxembourg, about a thirty-minute walk from the metro stop where I promised Julene I would meet her later in the morning. An overcast sky added a somberness to the dull gray scene, appropriate to the slight headache that throbbed in my frontal lobes. I could see the numerous chimney pots on the tin roofs opposite the pension, as well as the iron grillwork and narrow balconies that protected the windows on the building opposite mine.

Two weeks ago, the major topic at the dinner tables on the second floor had been the bizarre murder of an elderly woman who lived on the third floor in a neighboring building beside ours. I couldn't help but listen with interest to the conversation of the two patrons who sat at the table next to mine.

"*Oui*. The killer must have gone mad, slipped out of his room, crept across the balconies to hers, entered through the windows, and slit her throat! *Alors*! Stabbed her body nineteen times. Nineteen!"

"Why did he do that? Could that happen here?"

"Ah! Who is to say! I don't know. Perhaps it was a foreigner."

"Do we have any here?"

"*Oui*! The American," he smiled, pointing his fork toward me. "The Belgian, three Japanese, and that quiet British girl."

"Ah, yes! But I hardly think of them as *les estrangers* any more."

In my case, I think that was because I frequently shared my bottle of wine with them.

"Ah, Monsieur, you are too kind," the shorter, black-haired man of the two would respond.

"Do they have any clues?" I asked.

"I don't think so. But yesterday a reporter from *Le Miroir Français* was there. I saw her from the balcony. Ohhh! was she *quelque chose*! Petite, feisty, glamorous! Ohhh la-la!"

"How do you know it was she?"

"I have seen her picture in the paper and in magazines. Ohhh, she is something!"

I wondered if he was referring to Mme. Gibert. "Do you know her name?"

"It's on the tip of my tongue, but I can't recall it at the moment," he grinned. "Is monsieur interested?"

"Who's to say?" I smiled.

After shaving, a quick shower, and dressing, I walked the two flights down to the second floor for the *petit déjeuner*. I thought of Sullivan and wished I had his book in front of me. His chapter on "The Chthonic World" had genuinely impressed me. It was about the caves and caverns and puzzling labyrinths that archeologists kept encountering on Crete. It had been preceded by a tedious chapter on recent archeological and anthropological research on the Cretean, Minoan, and Mycenaean sites. He argued that "such minutia is critical to any discussion of Homer's poetic worldview." His footnotes were rich in details, wherein he cataloged the numerous artifacts, designs, excavation levels, soil compositions, ash depth, implements and potshards. Such entries constituted the indispensable data requisite for bolstering his Introduction. But what Sullivan seemed most after were those recondite and audacious inferences and cryptic nuances that a scholar might venture without overt censure from his peers; those reasonable conjectures as to why these ancient peoples might have engaged in their supposed rites, or used the paraphernalia listed and tagged by the archeologists. Indeed, neither his Preface nor Introduction ever quite clarified his real purpose, but only hinted at "those dark and lost motivations that enabled them to endure and that permit us to probe our own subconscious." His goal was as psychological as it was noetic. Then followed a chapter on caves, grottoes, and labyrinths; the haunts of serpents and monstrous bulls; the symbolism of the womb, the vagina, the sepulcher; the place of birth and death, of fear and protection, of home and sanctuary, of hearth and nurture. I thought of all the times I had crept frightened to bed alone as a child, up the stairs in the loft of the farmhouse, though my mother and grandmother rocked in the parlor by the fireplace below. "We are never that far from our roots, from the eons of those primitive ancestors who preceded us," Sullivan had concluded. I had to agree and found comfort in that chapter.

After breakfast, I took the metro to the Tuileries station. Julene was already present, waiting near the top of the steps. She appeared to be admiring a sidewalk vendor's art work. She wore a pale yellow sleeveless dress of medium length. Her lithe arms and legs brought to mind the image of a gaunt mannequin, except her full breasts filled the bodice of the dress with erotic appeal. She smiled as I indulged my eyes. "You are so transparent," she laughed. "But I do like it, uuumm, but I do."

"Forgive me," I smiled, "but it's been a long cold winter, and lonely at that."

"I bet you've had opportunities," she replied. "I noticed you right off the bat last night. Who wouldn't?"

"I've had a few," I said. "I've not been interested until now. I was once in love with a beautiful girl, a woman of thirty-two, but all she wanted was sex. And once satisfied, she dropped me like a rock."

"The wounded lover! I'm glad I revive you. Carl treats me the same way."

She stepped in closer to me and took my hand. "Come. Let's take a walk. I'll tell you my story, if you'll tell me yours."

"I've nothing really to tell."

"I bet."

I pressed her hand in mine before releasing it. We wandered along the sandy aisles in the direction of the Louvre. The fog had lifted, and the sunlight bathed the plain trees in a whimsical green glow. Scores of pigeons cluttered the lanes. They strutted and cooed in front of us as we walked along.

"I was raped as a girl, as a child, you know. Many black girls are. Luckily, I never got pregnant. A white man on Carl's father's place raped me. He did it repeatedly and threatened to kill me if I told. Then one day, Carl happened to come by in an old Ford and heard me crying. I was standing by the door of the barn. The man had just stepped out and was brushing the straw off his shirt and overalls. Carl must have put two-and-two together. He got out of his car and ran toward the man. Carl caught him by the collar and threw him to the ground. 'You son-of-a-bitch!' he hollered at him. 'She's just a child. You get your freakin' ass off this land as fast as possible, or I'll kill you dead.' Carl was about twenty-two. He was big and strong and didn't wear glasses. He had just come home from Boston. His red hair was long and shiny with sweat. He kicked the man in the butt. The man got up and slapped the dust off his sleeves. 'You damned Sullivans ain't nothing but a pile of shit, nohow,' he said. He left. I never saw him again."

Sunlight peeped through the leaves overhead and filled the aisle with a luminous yellow-green tint. "How does your being cousins fit in to all this?" I asked.

"Oh, Lord. I knew I'd blow it. We're not cousins." She threw her head back and smiled. "Carl's my uncle. His brother was my father. The man's dead now, but I fell in love with Carl that day in the barnyard. He was my knight in shining armor. He'd come to check on my mother and me. Carl's own father was dying of alcoholism and emphysema, and Carl didn't have many friends, anyway. His father was schizophrenic and mistrusted everyone. Even his own doctor, Dr. Silverton. I once heard him tell Carl. 'Stay away from that nigger woman,' meaning my Mamma. 'She got your brother in trouble, and she'll do the same to you. The Sullivans have always cared for their black people, but we've suffered enough. If you mess with her, or that girl, I'll disown you down to your socks. Do you understand?' 'Yes sir,' Carl answered. 'By God, if I won't!' the old man threatened."

"Is the old man dead now?"

"Yes. Died six years ago. But he put it in a will. 'If my son ever marries a Negress woman, mulatto, or quadroon, he shall thereby forfeit all rights and privileges appertaining to this estate, its investments, lands, houses, buildings, and orchards, and the same shall be awarded to the State of Alabama.'"

She looked away, up through the tress and out across the lane and the big red geranium bushes that bordered the walkway. "I love him, and he loves me. But he knows what would happen if we marry. The law doesn't seem to mind our cohabitating, and Carl knows his father's will wouldn't stand up in court. But I know I can't marry him, because we couldn't have children. And I want him to have children, and I want children, too. I think every black woman wants children. Just something deep down inside our natures, like slaves longing for their children to be free and legal and become something they couldn't. It's been all so confusing lately. Carl doesn't even touch me any more, except to put his hands on my thighs, and he knows I'm crazy about him."

"I'm sorry I've looked at you so hungrily. I didn't mean to compromise your affection."

"Oh, Professor, you haven't and won't. Don't worry about that. I'm just a needy black girl, and I need you to be a friend, that's all." She clutched my hand in hers. "Maybe I'll change my mind if we stay here long. But I love *that* man."

I felt hopeful and sorrowful at the same time. Indeed, she was comely to look upon and obviously bright and wholesome. But I had done enough compromising in the past, especially with the woman I had told her about. I held firmly to her hand, as we approached the Louvre.

"Let's go to the Impressionist Museum. I'm not up to visit the Louvre," she said. She looked at me with a deep tiredness that had sunk to the bottom of her rich blackness and had washed away her earlier ebullient cheerfulness.

So we returned: down the sandy aisles, parallel to the Rue de Rivoli, and made our way to the museum. Once inside, we walked thoughtfully by each painting.

"How can anyone select a favorite?" Julene whispered.

"I tend toward Manet," I pointed to his *Blonde Woman With Bare Breasts*. "Look at her features, her eyes, her gentle face and nose, her breasts. Even the nipples are perfect. And see how the breasts are soft and fleshy and slightly upturned," I nodded toward the painting. "And look at the gold straw of her hat, and the way she tilts her head. She must have been one of Manet's mistresses. Look how pink and lifelike here skin is against that green background. He had to know her well. How he must have loved her arms and kisses!"

Julene looked at me with her dark brown eyes and smiled. She pulled on my hand and led me toward Pissarro's *Red Roofs*. "Those houses so remind me of old slave cabins on an Alabama plantation in the winter," she offered.

I stared at the chalky white buildings, their tall chimneys and red and purple roofs, and at the hill above the town. The bare trees in the foreground provided a demure screen, behind which the artist had enclosed his houses. A distinctive grandeur defined the work, without flamboyance or artificiality. As I peered closer, I could see where Pissarro had painted the hill's meadows different colors, some red, some green, some a pale citron hue, and others blue. There were even blue doors and shutters on the houses. I squeezed her hand, and we walked on.

"You know there are some black artists whose works are comparable to these."

"I'm embarrassed to admit it, but I can't name a single black artist."

"No harm," she laughed. "Most Whites can't. But if you ever come across any works by Thomas Benton, buy them if you can. His *July Hay* is brilliant. Black harvesters with graceful sickles are mowing a field of flaxen hay, bowed in the wind. There is a sweetness of breadth and color about it that only a black person can feel about our race and unending labor. The same is true of Charles Alston's *Deserted House*, with its despair of the old South in every brush stroke. Or John Wilson's *Elevated Street Car Scene*. It's a product of World War II. White women on their way home, or to work, are busy chatting in the background. They appear frivolous and distracted; but seated, and starring at you, is a Black man, on his way to his job. His eyes stare at you. They give you no quarter for compromise or distraction. You can only imagine his sufferings, the prejudice he has endured, but he looms amidst those women as a man of greater character than all the city's Whites, who have never had to suffer, or nurse their hungry children to bed at night."

"Julene! Listen! Segregation is over. Your life is still ahead of you: a bright and shining future, if you choose it. How old are you, anyway? Twenty-five? Twenty-six?"

"Twenty-eight! And here I am in Paris, in the city I love. With the man I love, but who can't make love the way I want. Or need him to. And I'm fighting it all the time."

"Pity does no one good, Julene. And self-pity is even worse. And black, self-pity must be the cruelest embodiment of all. If you want to be an artist, strike out on your own. I hate to say it, but the world is indifferent. It doesn't care one wit. It knows nothing of purpose. Nor does it fashion our dreams. We are simply on our own."

"I know that!" she winced. Tears suddenly welled up in her eyes. "You don't need to tell me that, friend or no friend. Even if it's true. And my blackness has nothing to do with that." She stopped and suddenly stared at me with her large soft eyes. "Have you ever had sex with a black girl?" she whispered. "With a real black woman? I mean 'real.' Hot, sweaty, panting, and all? Do you know what that's like? Have you ever felt her heart beating through her back or chest when lying up against her? Or listened to her breathe? Or understood her hunger and desire to be caressed and loved, treated like a lady, even if a whore? Black men understand that, even if they're worthless, or run away and behave like children. It's so damn hard to break free of our cocoon, our black and brown encasements that have nothing to do with our humanness. Do you understand that? Do you?"

I was still holding her hand. I pressed it gently in my own, then brought it up to my lips and kissed it. "No," I replied in a small voice. "But your color is part of your being, as much as mine is inseparable from me. You're fine, just as you are. You don't have to explain that."

She leaned against me and pressed a cheek against my face. A tear rolled down her own, lodged against my mouth, and trickled onto my tongue. It tasted hot and salty. One of the museum's guards coughed politely. With embarrassment, we smiled and hurried into an adjoining room. I felt saddened by Julene's anguish, by her helplessness, if not, somehow, partially to blame for it myself.

We ambled past numerous paintings, the art gems of the world. We passed Manets, Monets, and Pissarros, Renoirs, Degas, and Cezannes. Morisot's *In the Cornfield at Gennevilliers* caught my eye. Its pale golden wheat field seemed to soothe that forlorn feeling that had crept inside my breast. The lone figure in the blue shirt and straw hat, standing on the worn path, sounded an even deeper emotion, too subliminal to define. Yet it stirred a sense of holistic otherness, of being swept up imperceptibly into that larger world of unbroken green trees and white and gray houses with red rooftops that Morisot had created as a border. Here was an immersion into beingness itself that silenced any need for conscious explanations.

"I once had sex with a girl in a wheat field," I said in a whisper.

"Was it that beautiful woman you mentioned earlier?"

"No. She came later. It was with an Israeli girl, on a kibbutz, near Haifa. We had been working together in the kibbutz's citrus groves. We roomed in the same barracks. She and a roommate were at one end of the hall, and I and another guy roomed at the other end. After dinner one evening, we walked out into a nearby field. The stars were especially bright, and the night air was clear. It was in April, or maybe May. Her parents were from London, but had come to the kibbutz in the late forties to become part of the Jewish state. She was about seventeen and soon due to fulfill her military obligation. She wasn't religious, just an ethnic Jew, a true Israeli, a *sabra*, as she called herself. We lay down in the field together.

I had never had sex until then. We undressed each other amidst a flurry of kisses. We had dust all over ourselves when we finished. We laughed and ran back to the barracks and showered together. We met like that for a whole month, until she had to leave for the army. I left soon afterwards, myself. I never saw her again. Nor heard from her, nor wrote her. She had short, honey-colored hair, which, of course, was dyed."

"Carl and I had our first sex behind a smokehouse. He had come out of the big house to fetch a side of bacon. I guess I was fourteen. I ran along side of him. He was wearing overalls, a white shirt, and brogans. It was his last summer on the farm before returning to Harvard to defend his dissertation. I was barefooted, wearing a flour sack dress Mama had stitched for me. It was gray with pink flowers. We still had a mill in Alabama, not far from the farm. Its wheel is broken, now, and its wooden sluices split and spilling water, but it was quite a mill in its time. I'd been on the steps of the mill once when Carl looked up and saw my behind. I didn't have any pants on. He smiled and kept staring, until I moved. But that day at the smokehouse, I teased him: 'Where you headed, big man?' Then I ran ahead of him and got on the plank steps. God, he was tall, lean, good-looking. Sweat was coursing down his neck and soiling his white shirt. I barred his way to the door. 'Julene!' he said. 'You're too pretty to be acting sassy like this. You know I got hormones, just like my uncle had for your mama.' 'I ain't hiding nothin',' I replied. I put my hands on his arms and ran my fingers up to his shoulders. 'Dammit, girl. I got a notion to do it right here,' he smiled. I glanced toward the rear of the building. And, Lord, Clayton, we did it! I mean we did it, right there up against the back of that smokehouse. God, it's a wonder I didn't get pregnant. Mama had seen me and made me wash my pelvis with a douche of vinegar. I cried, it stung so much. 'You piece of trash!' she scolded. 'The Sullivans are gonna be the death of us.'" Julene's smile had now evaporated, replaced by a rueful scowl. She let out a long, slow breath. "After that, we used condoms." She turned and managed a smile that filled me with a rush of desire.

"We'd better slip out of here, if we're going to keep talking."

"Yeah. I guess so. But I want to see Manet's *Olympia*, first."

"I think we passed it. Come this way. It was in that other room."

We retraced our steps and found the painting.

"Yes, look at that!" she whispered. "Look at the maid. No one probably ever sees her. They're all gawking at the mistress, or the whore."

I stared at the prostitute in her inclined position, on the pale pink shawl and white bed linens. Her high heels seemed to mock any sense of respectability. Her hand over her private essence created a sensuousness all its own. Her breasts and legs shimmered with invitation! But the hardened and solemn stare of her eyes evoked an emptiness without joy. Then I looked toward the black maid. It was difficult to make her out against the equally black background. In her right arm, she cradles a large bouquet of colorful flowers. But the prostitute doesn't even notice them.

"Look at those eyes of the maid. You can see their whites. What she would give for a paramour to love her, to send her flowers, to have someone wait on her!"

"It is magnificent. Almost disturbing," I admitted. "There it all is. Life at a glance. Nothing lost. Her nudity. The uneasiness you are forced to feel, that you can't escape."

"Let's slip out of here for some lunch."

"OK! We're not that far from La Place de Vendôme. Let's find something there."

Near La Place de Vendôme we found a delightful café, squeezed between two elegant jewelry stores. We seated ourselves at a small table, reminiscent of those marble-topped tables in Degas's *In the Cafe*. The tiny restaurant radiated with light, dispelling any sense of depression one might bring into it. A large chandelier, suspended from the ceiling, brightened the entire café. Each table had been set with large white plates, dark green folded napkins, nickel-plated flatware, and tall stemmed wine glasses.

We ordered a salad, pâté of lamb, bread, and white wine.

"Here's to you, kid!" I smiled at Julene.

She raised her glass and clinked it against mine.

"Careful! Cheap glass shatters you know."

She laughed and rolled her large soft eyes. Her dark brown irises smiled back from their sea of aureoline white ocular spheres. Her nose was as splendidly chiseled and small as any of the painters' models we had viewed. Her dark chocolate lips, tinged with ruby, and her delicate and slightly rounded chin, bestowed an unparalleled air of grace upon her.

"I could fall in love with you. You know that, don't you?"

"Don't you have anything better to do? What do you do, anyway?" she smiled.

"Oh, I work some, write some, travel some." I glanced at her slender fingers. Just then she was toying with her wine glass. "I take long walks and reflect. It's been a great sabbatical."

"I guess so! Just what are you working on?"

"A new book. About Descartes, Pascal, Rousseau, and Kant. Paris invigorates me; helps me clear my mind of suppositions and allows me to think on my own. Plus, I'm interested in the existentialists, and being able to buy and read French editions of Marcel, Sartre, Camus, Merleau-Ponty, de Beauvoir, and others has been exciting."

"Sounds dreadfully morose," she arched her thin eyebrows. "'You are what you choose' and all that garbage supposes an inner freedom only a few of us have. Certainly blacks aren't that free. We're still possessed by demons of hurt and anger. That's why I like art. It's concrete, imaginative, *subtle*," she smiled, as she emphasized the last word. "It's fluid, emotional, and all that's good. Besides, it defies right or wrong, good or evil. It's just what it is, and what you see. And what you feel. It has a life of its own. And sometimes it grasps you, like the works we just saw, or haunts you, like Benton's *July Hay.* And it never leaves you in doubt, or with some 'overwhelming question' you can't answer, if I might quote T.S.," she chirped with smug playfulness. "It just leaves you with life, an instance of life. And that's what makes it so great."

"How triumphantly said! How delivered without *anxiety* or *despair*, if I might defer to a few heroes of my own."

"Oh, by all means do! Far be it from little ole me to know the whole truth. I'm just plantation trash, Honey. Or have you forgotten?"

"Don't be so snotty. No wonder Carl slammed you up against those boards and let you have it. Why do you need to be so feisty, anyway?"

"Why? 'Cause I've always had to fight for equality. Words are my only weapons, and art. I'm not as stupid as you think."

"I never said you were."

"I know," she glanced away, with a tiny hint of hurt and embarrassment.

"Besides, your facial expressions and vocal tones are as deadly as any words."

"It's all part of my nature, my race. We're basically still right-brained, emotional, imagistic, orrrrral," she smiled, devilishly.

"Um! I'd like to know more of that orrrral part," I grinned in return.

She shook her head from side to side. "You never give up. You're as bad as any white devil I've ever met. Is that all you think about, sex?

"Only when a beautiful woman summons up my molten, erotic, and horny magma, my libidinous depths."

She let out a prolonged, leisurely breath. "My, my. We really aren't good for each other. At least not yet." She looked at me warily, with a subtle blush about her eyes. I could detect it, in spite of her pale cafe-au-lait pigment.

"Tell me about yourself. Your real self. Beyond what you've already said."

"I can't do that right now," she averred. "The chemistry's too strong. Why don't you tell me about yourself?" she suggested in earnest. The light from the chandelier overhead sparkled in her glass. She raised it and finished off her wine."

"Let's get some coffee and I'll tell you—a little bit," I volunteered. I nodded for the waiter. "*Deux cafés noirs, s'il vous plait, Monsieur.*"

"*Bien sur,*" he replied. "As you wish," he said in English, as he began clearing our table.

Julene smiled and began anew. "Where are you from, anyway? And why did you become a Ph.D.? And why in philosophy? I could go on and on."

The waiter wiped the table dry and looked at me a little stunned, as if I hardly qualified in his mind as an academic.

"*C'est vrai,*" I said, trying not to smile. "It's the truth."

He managed a polite grimace and returned momentarily with two demitasse cups of steaming, black espresso.

"*Voila,*" he finally smiled, with a courteous bow toward Julene.

"He likes you," I said, after he departed.

"Come, on, tell me," she coaxed. "Where are you really from? I want to know."

"Rural Virginia. *C'est vrai.* I grew up on a tobacco farm, in the heart of the Blue Ridge Mountains, in the Knobs, as we called them. Probably not too unlike parts of your northern Alabama."

"Go on. I would have thought you were from Richmond, or Atlanta, or maybe up North."

"No, just the hills of Virginia. I never wanted to be anything more than a gentleman farmer, like your Carl, until I went to college and fell in love with Socrates, Aristotle, and Dostoevsky. Some mix, but that's what happened. I couldn't get enough literature. But I majored in philosophy and minored in literature. I also ran cross-country."

"Where was all that?"

"At a little school called Davidson, near Charlotte, North Carolina. It was an all-male school in those days, and took farm boys like me. But I loved every minute of it. My family wanted me to go to VPI, for that's where all my uncles had gone, or to VMI, where my great-grandfather, who fought with Jackson during that famous War of a century ago, had gone."

"O Lord! Sounds like Carl's family. Half of them died at Shiloh, the rest at Chickamauga and Atlanta. My own grandmother's mother was a slave and tended to the wounded after the Battle of Shiloh. She was Carl's grand-daddy's mama's slave, and half-white herself."

"Maybe we should take a walk. Say up the Rue de la Paix, and back to the Tuileries? If she was half-white, who was her father?"

"We don't know. She'd never say. But we don't think it was a Sullivan. She didn't look like any of them, and they never paid her any special attention. My mama's got a picture of her in her late 90s, along with her own mother. They're all buried at the Sullivan place, except my mama, who's still alive. Slaves and owners alike are buried in the same fenced-in area, overgrown now with bramble, apple trees, and a lone magnolia. Carl's father planted it for his mother, when he was a boy. My own father, Carl's brother, is buried next to his mother and father, and there's a space there for Carl and room for me—will or no will, and my mama, too."

I paid the waiter, and we wandered up the street, toward Napoleon's tall, commanding column. The bronze monument rose a dusty green in the noonday smog. Whirling traffic surrounded it, and bright sunlight glinted off the awnings of nearby shops. "They say that thing's made out of a thousand plus cannons, melted down. Look at the hero up there, cast like Trajan, or some Roman Caesar. The glory of war!"

"Maybe they didn't have body bags in those days. Just as Carl and I were boarding the plane in Tennessee, a flight returning from the west coast was filled with body bags. They hadn't even put them in coffins yet. I guess they were headed for Fort Campbell. Some glory.'

"I almost volunteered for the war. It was just before the Tet offensive. But the recruiter turned me down. 'You're past 31,' he said. 'We don't take 'em that old.' So I drove back to the university, where I've been ever since."

"I'm glad you're not over there," she took my arm. "I'm glad you're with me, whatever happens."

"What do you want to happen? Do you honestly think it can?"

We paused on the sidewalk, near a white-washed building, whose upper windows were all decorated with balconies of curled iron grill, Louis XVI gabled dormer windows, and a gently slanting roof.

"I am so torn, I don't know," she answered sadly. "How I love this city of culture, of art, and architecture! But I love my Alabama home and our Tennessee campus, equally. Their history here isn't ours, you know. Nor their triumphs, nor tragedies. My God, our own are immense and terrifying enough."

"Well said, dear girl. And with a philosophical import. But it is a place for dreams, for remembering what a civilization costs. Both to achieve and preserve, as well as to change. Monticello reminds me of that, whenever I go there. And so, too, the monuments along Richmond's boulevards. And, of course, the mountains of Virginia, and those vistas from the Appalachian Trail, where you see nothing but sylvan coves and forests of poplar and hemlock, as far as the eye can rove. Perhaps we're both dreamers, but a little too jaded to set our course on uncharted stars."

"I want to be a painter, even if only a dreadful one. I think I'll set up my easel tomorrow, in the faubourg where we're staying, and just paint the trees, grill work, buildings, shutters, and eaves.With a splash of pink and green and yellowish buff and black for people and cars!" There was a renewed excitement in her voice. She tugged on my arm with fresh enthusiasm, with an eager step in her walk. "What about you?"

"*I go where all things go, where go the leaf of the rose and the leaf of the laurel.* That's from a French poet, but I don't remember his name, or where I read it."

"It's too sad. You've got to do better than that. You've been reading too much existentialism."

"You're probably right," I smiled at her. "Please kiss me. I won't tell Carl, or anyone, for that matter."

She shook her head with a whimsical smile, put her hands up to my face, stood on her tiptoes, and kissed me hard on the mouth. "Ummmm," she moaned. "I've got to get back to my own man. I want to be there when Carl gets home and dig out his day with Gibert. I think I'll take the metro at the Opera," she pointed. "You've inspired me to paint again." There was a luminous glow about her face. "Oh, Lord! I almost forgot." She reached in her handbag and handed me a paperback book that was soiled and worn. It was a copy of Carl's *From the Minoans to Homer*. "He said for me to give it to you. We've got a few extra copies, so don't worry."

I accepted the book and turned thoughtfully through several of its brown-edged pages. "Please thank him. I'll start reading it again, tonight." I looked desperately into her dark eyes. I wanted her to know how smitten I was with her, how fortunate and lucky I felt, just being with her.

"I'd better go," she repeated. "What's your phone number?"

"I'll write it down." I took out our lunch receipt and scribbled down the pension's number. "The concierge answers all calls, but she'll call me to the phone if I'm there." I handed it to her. "What's yours?"

"I'd better keep that a secret," she looked away apprehensively. "Carl *does* get jealous. It would be better for me to call you."

"Julene! There's still more of Paris to see, and I hardly know you."

"Or I, you." She stared at my collar and straightened my tie. "I'll call you. That's a promise."

I put my arms around her waist. She slipped free, smiled, and disappeared down the street in the bright haze of the sun's orange glare.

3

After returning to the pension, I became restless. I emptied my jacket of its contents, flopped on the bed for a while, then paced in the semi-darkness of the room. I paused to look out the opened windows. A veil of fog hovered about the roofs and buildings in front of me. I leaned out over the narrow balcony and stared down at the street below. The drone of the traffic and the constant and magical pace of the city's life rose and throbbed unabated. It echoed off the rusting balconies along the street, down which I gazed in reflection. Afternoon shoppers and tourists walked briskly toward the street's corner, across from which stretched the Garden of Luxembourg. I picked up Sullivan's book, replaced my billfold and passport in my jacket's inside pockets, pulled it on, and descended the stairs for the park.

Near one corner of the garden, a statue dedicated to Baudelaire had become my private haunt for those inner dialogues with the self, for those quiet moments with the psychosphere, when one requires escape and self-examination. I took a seat on a concrete bench and opened Sullivan's book to his section on "The Myth of the Minotaur." I read the following:

> The story of the Minotaur is at once transparent and aretetical. Prior to investigating either of these poles, let us relish the myth anew. Having achieved acclaim by the time of his arrival in Athens, and having survived his father's wife's treacherous wiles, Theseus turned his attention to the dreadful calamity that annually numbed the city. At that time, the Athenians were compelled to send a tribute of seven maidens and seven youths to King Minos, ruler of Crete. Minos offered them as a sacrifice to the Minotaur: a grizzly monster with a man's shaggy head and the body of a bull. The Minotaur roamed a vast labyrinth, known for its numerous and terrifying passageways that snaked endlessly beneath the palace. Daedalus, himself, had constructed the maze. Once victims passed through its entrance, none returned or escaped. Theseus

> convinced his father, Aegeus, to let him go as one of the seven sacrificial youths that he might slay the Minotaur. With a father's anguish, Aegeus conceded. Theseus promised to change the ship's sail from black to white, upon his return, if the adventure produced success.
>
> Upon their arrival, the fourteen victims presented themselves to Minos. The king announced his satisfaction and set a date for the sacrifice. His daughter, Ariadne, however, became enamored of Theseus—the manliest of the youths—and he equally fell in love with her. The night before the ordeal, she managed to steal into his chamber and give him a magical sword and a spool of thread, the first with which to kill the monster, the second to retrace his steps to the entrance. Taking the lead as they entered, Theseus cornered the beast, slew it, and, with the help of the thread, saved the maidens and other youths. As Greek myths go, however, victory and prowess, valor and bravery, are inevitably accompanied by treachery and grief. On the return voyage to Athens, Theseus abandoned Ariadne on the Island of Naxos, and, forgetting to raise the white sail, arrived in port under the mournful black canvas. Upon seeing it, Aegeus fell on his sword and died.

I folded an edge of the page down and closed the book. Now would come Sullivan's reflections on the myth. In his Introduction, he had warned readers of a fondness for a methodology he intended to use ad nausea, if necessary, to ferret out the truth behind and between the lines of the stories. He never followed them in any particular order, but employed them with ingenuity and resourcefulness. Six motifs guided his approach. The first had to do with the *transparent,* or the historical kernel, to be identified. What was the story's "setting in life," or its *Sitz im Leben*? Could a date be determined on either archeological or historical grounds? A *cognitive*, or intellectual, thread formed a second concern. What does the story explain? What dimension of life does it elucidate? What intellectual enlightenment does it provide for understanding the self or the world? The *aretetical*, a third, had to do with value, excellence, or virtue. What insight into life's conduct does a myth possess? What virtues did it hallow for its ancient audience? What lingering aretetical values might it still convey? A fourth motif, he identified as *deontological. Deon* means "duty" in Greek. What were the duties to be gleaned from the myth? What further duties might human beings salvage from the story for today? Sullivan argued that a distinction between *aretetical* and *deontological* is important, since virtues are often highly winsome and admirable, but difficult to attain, whereas duties are essential to rights and concepts of justice. He proposed that this was as true of the classical period as of our own. At some point, a fifth motif involved *catharsis*. Sullivan acknowledged his debt to Aristotle for catharsis. Beholding how others have suffered and borne life's vicissitudes, as well as feeling a shared pity and dread with others, strengthens our own capacity to endure personal tragedies and private sorrows. This is especially so, since our own problems will go unsung and unheralded. To know that some are recorded and memorialized in dramatic epics provides a mantle for our own fleeting existence. They cloak our mortality with the solace of a universal immortality of the human spirit. Finally, but not always, Sullivan would sometimes address the *ontological* problem. By ontological, he meant something of the metaphysical. What does any myth or story tell us about the mystery of being? As in dreams and repressed fears, does the myth proffer a peek into the troubled subconscious, which, if we could probe and understand it, would bring us closer to the truth of our elusive humanness: that daunting mystery that still exists?

I was about to reopen the book, when a premonition of not being alone began to pulse from synapses to synapses, causing me to look up with a startle. Standing near the edge of the monument, the Viet Cong soldier, whom I had heard the previous evening, was staring at me. He wore a dull, silky green shirt, blue jeans, a Bolshevik cap, and sandals. A leather pouch, with long straps, teetered on his right shoulder. "*Bonjour*, may I join you?" he said in crisp French.

I knew what he wanted. For the past six months, a small legion of Vietnamese from the North had been in Paris, propagandizing any Americans they could.

"Why not?" I replied. "But it won't be any use, I fear."

"Please. Let us be at peace! At least, hear my side."

He slipped the pouch off his shoulder and produced several printed articles. I had seen them before, sometimes in restaurants where Americans gathered, or along the Seine near the waste bins, or on park benches.

He sat next to me and handed me three folded sheets. They were printed on both sides and contained the "history" of the recent conflict, its sufferings and illegality from the North's point of view, and the multitude of ills that wars of liberation and revolution spawn. The pages contained the story of Ho Chi Minh, his guerilla activity in support of the US during the Second World War, how Eisenhower had betrayed America's promise after the war by siding with the French, the burden of the Indo China era under French colonialism, and on and on. No mention of Viet Cong atrocities appeared.

"We are only seeking to liberate our country, to do what you did during your own Revolution." He studied me with his thin lips, his Asian brow only slightly furled. His dark eyes emanated the seriousness of his mission. "We want to unite our country and bring freedom and dignity to all Vietnamese. The Saigon regime is corrupt, and you know it. It's merely a puppet power in the hands of ruthless thugs, doing what your government bids because you want to be all powerful. Why can't you see that? Why can't you let us establish our own form of government, run by ourselves, even if it is a Communist one?" He seemed to relax. Having delivered the memorized essentials of his speech, he smiled widely and awaited my reply

"I guess that last point is why," I said, without blinking. "We're afraid of the Soviet Union, its Eastern Block countries, and Red China. Your system promotes insurgencies and wars of revolution, murder, and chaos wherever Communism goes. It forbids freedom of thought and expression. It enslaves poor classes and lowers the standard of living, rather than raising it. Like in Cuba and Central America and East Germany. Or Poland and Hungary."

A slight twinge of color darkened his high cheekbones. "We are not Cuba, or East Germany. We are Asians. Proud and with a long history and culture of our own. We fear China, ourselves." There was a touch of remorse in his voice, but no anger. Pride, yes, and perhaps a smidgen of desperation, but not anger. "Vietnamese have a right to determine their own destiny. We wish you no harm. I hate it that we have to kill your soldiers and they kill ours. Already I have lost my wife, my mother, two brothers, and a sister. My two children live with my father in a village north of Hue. They have known nothing but machine gun fire, grenades, mortar rounds, hunger, and, everywhere, death. You can at least understand that."

He tried to smile, putting the best face forward he could with respect to his country's war and his own miseries and personal anger, over which he continued to exercise enormous control.

"Do you do this every day?"

"Yes. My government is sacrificing dearly for me to be here. I want to be at home, with my children, and with my comrades at war. I bear you no animosity, nor enmity. You must surely know that."

"Nor I you. I long for this war to end, too. It's destroying us, as well."

"I'm due to go home in eight more weeks. I will rejoin my unit, and we will have to kill more Americans and some of our countrymen. Revolutions are never clean. Both sides suffer."

"I hope you survive. I hope your children will grow into adulthood, marry, have families, and die in their homes in peace."

He struggled to his feet, re-slung his pouch, and extended his hand. I realized he had a war wound of some kind by the way he favored one side. I rose with him, accepted his hand, and shook it firmly.

"*Salut, mon ami*," he smiled. "Perhaps we shall both live to see peace."

"Would that that might come to pass."

"You would like Viet Nam. Perhaps one day, you will come and visit it."

"That would be nice."

"Adieu!" he said, holding his head erect with dignity.

"*Au-voir*, to you, too," I bowed slightly, as I shook his hand a second time.

He walked slowly past the monument, the surrounding tall plants, and was gone.

After dinner, I retired to my room to resume reading Sullivan's chapter on the Minotaur. I had left the windows open; a light breeze stirred the long yellowed muslin curtains where I had pulled them aside. The room's warm air felt muggy, but it was comfortable enough to sit at the long cherry table and look toward the window. The glow of neon signs and the evening sheen of the deepening spring night filled the skyline with muted shadows that pulsated red, green, and purple.

What should I do the coming day? Perhaps translate more Pascal, or attempt some verses of Baudelaire. I had scarcely begun to ponder the possibilities, when a faint rap sounded at the door. Was it a knock or not? I heard it again, ever so timidly and softly.

"Yes? Is someone there?"

I went to the door and opened it. It was the British girl. Her hands were trembling and her face appeared pasty.

"I am so embarrassed, but I think someone's hiding in my room. I was sitting in the room, reading, when I heard a noise behind the drapes." The dark pupils of her eyes loomed wide open. Her lips had turned pale, almost dark blue.

"I'll come down right now," I said, with a smile.

"Number eighteen!" she referred to her room's number.

"Sure." I followed her to the end of the hall and slightly to the right, down another wing. "I didn't realize this floor was so long."

"And spooky," she added, "when the lights go out."

"Is it unlocked?"

"Yes."

I eased the door open and entered the room. The rush of air from the hallway caused the drapes to balloon outwards. No outline of anyone or anything appeared behind them.

"I'll check your armoire and under your bed."

The armoire was latched; no one was inside. I ran my hands between her hanging garments. "Sorry," I blushed.

"Oh, no! That's quite all right. I'll check under the bed."

While she bent down to complete her own inspection, I walked to the windows and pulled back the drapes, along with their frail dusty curtains. I leaned forward and stared out, first to the left and then to the right of her room's tiny balcony and down to a narrow street below. I realized that her room was on the same side of the hall as mine, but it looked down into an alleyway rather than into the busy rue that I was accustomed to viewing. "I'm not certain I would leave these unlocked." I hated to frighten her, but anyone could make his way up the building and enter this side of the rooms. Then, of course, the noise she heard might have been the breeze, or a puff of wind in the drapes. I looked again into the black pit of the alleyway. Only someone desperate or mad would attempt such an entry.

"I've never once been afraid, till now. Please sit down and have a glass of wine with me. I'm still very jittery."

"I guess we all are, since the murder across the street."

"Yes," she mumbled, attempting to smile.

In all the time that I had been at the pension, I had paid her but scant attention. She rarely showed for breakfast, and generally came in late at dinner. I couldn't help but return her smile. "I would love to sit down and have that glass of wine."

"Thank God! Incidentally, I'm Christine. Christine Cunningham. What's your name? What do you do?" she asked. "What brings you here?"

"Clayton Rogers Clarke. I'm a professor of humanities on sabbatical. An aficionado of French history, philosophy, and literature. What about yourself?"

From somewhere in the bottom of her armoire she produced a bottle of red wine and several glasses. She poured me half a glass and herself as much. We scooted the room's two fragile wooden chairs up to the table and sat down.

"I teach French in a little school northwest of London. I'm attending the *Institut Français*. I used to be a jeweler. Not really," she smiled. "But I clerked for this chap who trafficked in diamonds, gems, and silver. He made pendants, lockets, bracelets—you name it. My favorite gems were garnets and rubies. One morning, he discovered his shop's back door lock broken. The thieves had made off with everything. I was dating a somewhat brawlsome, rugged Welshman at the time. Clarence, the owner, accused me of tipping the guy off, and being an accomplice in the heist. I tell you, I had nothing to do with it, and I told him as much, too. The bobbies checked me out, but, of course, there was no evidence to charge me."

"What about your friend?"

"Tobby was just a rough pub boy. They searched his apartment, but found nothing. He dropped me like a stone after that and returned to the slag mines of Wales. He was ruddy, but I loved him."

She moved her chair a little closer to mine. I had left the windows open, and a cool draft ruffled the drapes and swayed the curtains. "Is that what you heard?"

"It was more like a stir, a muffled sweep of cloth against cloth. That's when I came to your room." She looked at me deeply with her twinkling black eyes. A full head of long brown hair flounced about as she turned her face toward me. I studied her fine aquiline nose, her high, arched eyebrows, her freckled pink cheeks and rich red lips and wondered why I had never noticed her before. Her sweater's rounded bulges of orange-sized breasts were equally noticeable. She smiled when she caught me looking at her. "I wish you would stay with me tonight," she said with crimson cheeks. "I know that's terribly forward and a bit hasty, but I'm afraid. Really, quite so!"

I leaned forward and kissed her. Her hands trembled as she touched my forearm. She pressed her soft, wet mouth against mine. I could feel her tongue. We each sipped our wine and kissed one another again. I studied her eyes. They were sparkling, yet demure.

"I need to go to my room for a few things," I said.

"I'll be waiting," she kissed me gently with her warm lips.

When I returned, she was clad in a silky, rose nightgown. I could see the curves of her breasts and the indentation that her naval created, along with the lines of her thighs.

She stepped toward me and began unbuttoning my shirt. I slipped off my trousers and underclothes. She removed her slippers and I my shoes, and we lay down on the bed together. I put my arms under hers and around her back and rolled against her. We kissed and fondled each other and changed positions while emitting a series of pleasurable moans. I had not loved a woman this way since the breakup with the "beautiful girl" I had mentioned to Julene. I wondered if intimacy with Julene would be as lusty or glowing as this.

Christine adjusted her legs and opened them fully. Her hands guided me along. The rush came amidst a powerful throe of audible groans of enjoyment.

"Oh, God! Don't let me go yet," she whispered. "Please don't leave for a while."

"I'm here for the night, if you want."

"Yes. Oh, yes." She kissed my ears and neck.

We lay there for a long time; then rolled out of bed to wash off and pour ourselves the remaining wine. We propped ourselves up on her long French pillows, lay naked under the sheet, and sipped the wine.

After a while, she began to talk. "My mother was killed during the Blitz. My father died of a seizure while working at the plant, near our cottage. An elderly aunt raised me and put me through school. What about you?"

"I was reared on a farm in Virginia, of proud Scots-Irish and English descendants. They were proud relics of ante-bellum aristocracy, including the Civil War. Only the land remained after that fiasco, and now much of it is mortgaged to banks. But I loved roving it as a kid, fishing its streams, and hunting quail in the fall."

"Sounds idyllic. You're a born romantic."

"That's what everyone says, though I teach logic and arcane subjects as epistemology and metaphysics."

"'Inane' might be a better word."

"Thanks a lot. Just for that, I'm coming after those breasts again."

I handed her my wine glass, while I rolled against her soft body and put my mouth over her right breast.

"Oh, God! I'm going to want to do it again, if you don't stop," she laughed.

She set the wine glasses down and we played with each other some more.

"What have I started?" she whispered. "I'll probably hate myself in the morning." She kissed my chest and stroked my loins.

"Why? Whatever evil lies in this?"

"No evil. Just pain. I'm not ready to have my heart broken again. You are beautiful, and your body is great. You're quite a chap, you know."

"That's the kindest thing any woman has said to me in months."

"You sweet man," she signed, as she placed her hands between my legs. "How I needed you tonight!"

I fondled her with my tongue and kissed her naval.

"Snuggle against me and hold me. Put your arm around my bosom and let's drift to sleep. I have to be at the *Institut* by seven."

I slipped out of bed, closed the windows and fastened the latch. I turned off the light and climbed in beside her. I lay my face against her long hair, nudged my nose against a warm ear, cupped her breasts in my hands, and listened to her breathing. Soon, she was asleep. The darkness of the room slipped within my own dream world; mists of white fog lifted me skyward. I was flying, soaring like a great bird, gliding across Paris, the Seine, Notre Dame, the *Ile de la cité*. From somewhere a black girl was calling. I was scampering through the wheat, near a split-rail fence. I was a child once more on the farm. I could see the hay, the ripening corn, the green tobacco plants, the dust from the horses harvesting the wheat, the trout stream in the bottom meadow, and the cattle on the pastured hills.

The next morning, we kissed, and I returned to my room. That evening she passed my table, smiled, and placed her hand momentarily on my shoulder. She walked to her seat without glancing back. I knew she needed time, just as I did. But the memory of our sensuous liaison fired my heart for more. I knew she needed me as much as I needed her. Perhaps time would bring us together again. I would have to wait and see.

4

Two weeks passed. Not once did I hear a single word from Julene or Carl, or anyone. Even Christine had disappeared. I filled my days with matutinal walks about the Garden of Luxembourg, or through it, if it were open, studied at the Bibliothèque Nationale, translated Pascal and some Baudelaire, and began drafting the first chapters of a new book. I intended to entitle it: *From Descartes to Kant: Exploring the Epistemology of Doubt.* A university press had already expressed interest in the project, which brought great relief. Consequently, I was able to write every morning on the book, without the anxiety of wondering who would publish it. In the afternoons, I would take long walks through the neighborhood, or take the metro to different arrondissements to revisit my favorite museums, or quartiers and parks.

It was now the third week of April. As I sat in my room, I found myself intrigued by Sullivan's exposition of the Minotaur story.

> Let us tackle the transparency of this myth, first. It has to be at a time prior to Greece's independence of the Minoan period. Tribute is still being paid to the Island of Crete. No unequivocal archeological evidence exists to support human sacrifice, but it might have occurred. The time frame appears to precede the Doric invasions, as well as the disappearance of fabled Atlantis. These "events" follow the massive volcanic eruptions that happened to the north of Crete and signaled, in turn, its own demise. Perhaps a date of 1500–1300 BC is not out of order. Troy is still on the horizon, but the displaced People of the Sea, who invade Egypt and the coast of Canaan, arrive at this time.
>
> Also to be noted is the secondary role assigned to the labyrinth and the Minotaur. From the rise of the Akkadians to the decline of the Babylonian Empire, a male-warrior society begins to undermine the role of the Goddess. Her symbols recede in significance and are replaced by more violent and virile icons. Among these are the fierce bull, tiered crowns that point to heaven to a dominant

Father Sky, to the epics that hail the victory of Marduk over Tiamat (maligned as a feminine chaotic force and goddess of water and the grave). Crete had heretofore been spared this diminution of the Goddess, as witnessed in the graceful depictions of both male and female acrobats, somersaulting over the backs of bulls, who serve the Mother Goddess. Now the bull has become a symbol of terror, of death to be appeased, a fearful icon of malevolence, brutality, and marauding power. Half-man, half-beast, he serves the gods of death. No longer does he grace the enchanting frescoes of Knossos as an aesthetic figure of a gentler age. The subtlety and charm of the Goddess's realm has been exchanged for a labyrinth of terror.

There is no need to berate the male world for this tragedy. Power had shifted from an agricultural and pastoral society to an expansionist and militaristic one. New migrations were sweeping across the Ancient Near East and the Aegean area. Plowshares and pruning hooks were being beaten into swords and spears; the arched bow and flaming arrow replaced the hoe.

What chords of response resonated in the hearts of those who heard this myth? How did they react, if at all? Perhaps women found value in the self-effacing actions of Ariadne, who willingly risked her life to assist the young Theseus. Her cunning and determination make her a candid exemplar for her gender, her abandonment, a warning to all women. Ambition must be tempered by loyalty. Jung finds a much more disturbing element. For the female, it lies in reconciling her inner anima with her true self. She must break free of her Mother'spower. The labyrinth, the womb, the menacing bull—all bespeak her need to become her own person, guided by her own forces as a woman. Theseus's role in the "rescue" continues to make her subservient to the male, but his abandonment of her is a mixed blessing. Her sexual impulse toward motherhood has now been freed from the "male mind" within herself. She will become Dionysius's consort. Her association with him blends her erotic needs with her creative unconscious. Ariadne will fulfill her anima as lover and mother.

A different universal theme commands the male attention. It becomes as deontological as aretetical. For the Greek world, the universal takes precedence over the individual. There are political duties (of the *polis*) that render ones private life subordinate. The State, or evolving clans of like-minded parties, demands an allegiance that puts the solitary life on hold. Courage, selflessness, magnanimity elbow the self to the side. One gains worth, only to the extent that one sacrifices ones personal will to the exigencies of

> ones city-state. Homer will make this a major point in contrasting Hector's valor with his brother Paris's effete disdain for battle.
>
> For the Greek mind, such fate exercises a paramount role; freedom of choice, a lesser one. Theseus is not really free to delegate the saving of the young Athenians to others. As his father's heir and champion of the hour, fortune places the burden on his shoulders. With his gifts of strength and daring, come obligations. In addition, great mortal achievements require a proportionate pain. It is the way of Greek wisdom. The gods have not granted glory without suffering, life without death. Again, for Jung, powerful psychological forces come into play. The male, too, acts to fulfill his animus. If he fails, he remains captive to his Mother's anima. His paralysis will become permanent. He, too, must break free of the Mother's power and assert himself as a man. That Aegeus kills himself is likewise a mixed blessing, since Theseus can now claim the throne in his own right. He has arrived as a man. The slaying of the bull also represents man's victory over his animality. He is more than just a beast. He is both subject and object. Unfortunately, Plato will carry this awareness too far, relegating mankind's sensual nature to the domain of perishable transformation, while locating his true nature in the realm of invisible idealism. Not until the Renaissance would this balance be restored.
>
> Those who heard these stories were able to share in the tragic nature of human existence. Acclamations must be earned; valor is never cheap; it defines the human essence, the human telos, or end. Its price is sorrow, its deeds worthy to be sung in ballads, or enacted on the stage or celebrated at the great festivals that mimic the tumultuous banquets of the gods, of the immortals, who, unlike mortals, never die. Examples for self-fulfillment abound for everyone.

I had just completed reading the section, when someone knocked at the door. "*Monsieur Clarke! Le telephone, s'il vous plait. Un Monsieur Sue-li-von* wishes to speak to you. *Vite*! I can't leave the receiver off the hook all day." It was the concierge.

"Great!" I blurted. I opened the door and stared into the sallow face of Mme. Angleterre. There she stood, her left arm somewhat deformed, she herself short and stocky in stature and clad in a faded black dress. As usual, she had applied too much rouge and mascara about her eyes and cheeks. Her stiff, wiry, dyed hair shimmered auburn in the hall's dim light. Streaks of gray lay visible about her hair's roots. Her candor and simplicity of heart, however, more than compensated for her less than bourgeois class. Often, she would bring me tea in the late afternoons if she knew I was working on my book. She wanted to know as much about *philosophie* as I would tell her. "I'm not an educated woman, you know, Monsieur, just a hardworking widow."

I followed her down to the second floor and picked up the receiver. "Hello! Is this Carl? This is Clayton here."

"Good! I have some intriguing news to run by you and desire your presence at dinner this evening. Can you meet Julene and me at the Golden Lotus near the Cathedral of St. Sulpice, about eight tonight? You'll be our guest."

"Of course! I'd love to. What's up?"

"That's a secret. We'll explain at dinner."

"Ok! I'll be there."

I replaced the receiver on its hook. Perhaps he and Julene were going on a jaunt and wanted to invite me to travel along. Or maybe he wanted to publish or edit a book jointly with me. That would be worth coveting.

Being a slave to routine, I resolved to pass my afternoon as originally planned before joining them for dinner. The sky had become metallic, heavy, and overcast, and a light drizzle descended with the fog. I pulled on my cap and slipped into a poncho and headed for the park. Traffic spit the misty mess into convoluted trails that swirled gray behind the vehicles. I dodged between a line of taxis and cars, then strode, head down through the Garden. A surprising number of pre-school children were still at play, and mothers, pushing carriages, seemed oblivious to the light rain. I stopped and bought a warm brown crepe, sprinkled white with powdered sugar, and continued toward my goal—the Pantheon, on the edge of the Latin Quarter and just to the east of the Garden. I walked around the little lake, void of children's sailboats, crossed the Boulevard Saint Michel, and approached the Pantheon by the Rue Soufflot. I had visited it many times but had never gone down to the crypt. I stopped in front of the building's massive portico of fluted columns and stared up at the pediment overhead. There Lady Liberty hands out laurels to France's great heroes and saints. In gold letters, the tribute reads: "To the Great Men, the Nation is Grateful."

On the steps sat a beggar, wrapped in beggar's rags. With the coming of Spring, squads of these miserable wretches had left their hibernacula, where they slept over the grates above the metro system, and huddled now on church steps, or crouched beside apartment entrances or wherever they could find refuge. I avoided them whenever I could, for to look on them was to experience a harrowing despair. An individual alone would soon exhaust his coins if pity were king. I stepped around the homeless person—a woman, I realized, and entered the great edifice and wandered toward the transept, under the dome. To my mind, there was nothing appealing about this grand stone structure, except perhaps its dome and the people it honored. I made my way toward the right crypt entrance and ambled down the steps into the long gray hall beneath the church. I passed Voltaire's vault and looked for Victor Hugo's and Rousseau's. These were the two giants of liberty and humanity as far as I was concerned. I paused before the tomb of each.

Rousseau's distinction between *amour de soi* and *amour propre* had always appealed to me. Man's "natural sentiment" versus society's "artificial sentiment" seemed to sum up both his genius and the folly of his era. The first, held Rousseau, leads to self-respect and, when coupled with reason and pity, produces virtue and humanity. The second, overlaid with social manners and customs, inspires greed and evil. If only Louis XVI had done his homework!

I left the crypt and wandered back out to the portico's steps. The old woman was still there. She was crying, with her hands raised in an imploring manner. I wanted to escape, to be left alone, to return to my room for tea and reflection, for more reading and, perhaps, writing. She was pointing to her mouth. Her hands were filthy and covered with the black grime of the streets. Her tears created dirty red streaks on her face. "Water! Water!" she begged. I was in the process of withdrawing from her, trying to step around her, when a woman next to me said: "She's calling to you."

With reluctance, I approached the woman and bent down. Her eyes stared into my own. They were filled with desperation and a mixture of disdain, if not overt anger, that I had sought to avoid her. "I was calling to you! I need water, something to drink, a little wine," she croaked with cracked lips. I bent forward and placed my right arm about the old woman's shoulders. "*Bien sur*, I will get thee something," I murmured. I hurried to a corner market along Saint Michel, grabbed a bottle of citron or lemonade from a kiosk, gave the startled vendor five francs, and walked quickly back to the church's steps. The old woman was gone. Her outer wrap was still there, but she was gone. Then I spotted her under the portico. Several people had gathered about her. At first, I thought she was dead. "*Ah, la pouvre ame*!" exclaimed a woman beside her. "They shouldn't let these people wander about like this." I pushed my way through the onlookers and knelt beside the woman. "Your water, Madame." She managed to sit up. I removed the bottle's cap and assisted her while she gulped a modicum of swallows. She began to aspirate. Her frail body shook with each cough. The spasms wouldn't stop. I could smell her body odor and horrible breath. I tried thumping her back with the palm of my hand. All was to no avail. The crowd of gawkers increased. "*Allez*, find a gendarme!" someone said angrily. "Yes, please!" I agreed. The woman's face turned ashen. A faint trembling vibrated along her body. Her eyes stared up at mine. They were swollen, watery, red. She was trying to say something. "Madame, we are sending for help." I heard a claxon's shrill horn somewhere down the street. A small car with two police officers arrived. It was beginning to rain. The taller of the two officers waved us away with his baton. They picked up the woman, carried her to their car, placed her in its backseat, and drove off. I set the bottle at the base of one of the columns and retrieved her abandoned wrap. Some other wretch would claim both soon enough. I pulled the front piece of the poncho over my brow and walked back slowly to the pension, in the rain.

Back in my room, I drew aside the curtains and opened the windows. A steady rain fell on the balcony and dripped onto the street below. It made a pleasant sound, like the patter of a stream over rocks. I drew up my chair to the table and began leafing through Pascal's *Pensées*. I wanted to quote and explicate his thoughts in my new book, but I wanted the translation to be my own. I heard a shuffling outside the door; then a knock.

"*Oui*?"

"*C'est moi*. It is only me," called Mme. Angleterre. "I have your tea."

I let her in and took the tray from her.

"I want to talk, sometime, when you're not too busy. It can wait," she smiled, seeing my books and writing tablets on the table.

"That'll be fine. Maybe tomorrow afternoon, *non*?"

"Oh, that would be nice. I'll bring tea for both of us."

"I'll look forward to it."

She left the room and I returned to my table. It could not be called a desk but was sufficiently utilitarian to serve as one. It had a drawer, an inlaid leather top, set within a cherry border, and measured about six-feet long.

My attention having been broken, I picked up a chapbook of Baudelaire's *Les Fleurs du Mal* and began reading. I sipped on my tea as I read. The Introduction reminded admirers that Baudelaire was the greatest French poet of the nineteenth century. Both modern and iconoclastic, he had burst upon the Paris scene as a "disgusting" representative of an age "that craved lust and all that is sordid." Born in 1821, he spent his days in "profligacy, debauchery, indulgence, and opium, living as a bohemian, pursuing a nocturnal life that led to bouts with drunkenness and venereal disease." His "half-caste lovers, mistresses and a bevy of society whores" supported him; still he died in poverty. It would remain for posterity to discover his genius. He had translated some of Poe's work, but it had not "influenced his own." The book contained Baudelaire's earlier Prefaces, which displayed his open contempt for the Parisian aesthetic tastes of the day. He described Paris as a "universal center for radiating stupidity." Her elegists were "virile scum." If beauty were to be found anywhere, it would have to be extracted from evil. The dullards of reason had suppressed rapture far too long.

It was the reference to the "half-caste lovers," however, that caught my eye. Were they as beautiful as Julene? I hoped so. He had dedicated one of his poems to his favorite traveling companion. I scribbled down its translation as I read it:

> My child, my sister,
> Imagine the pleasure
> Of life's journey together,
> Loving each other in scandalous leisure
> Embracing life's joys and forbidden treasures
> Free from fear, to the last dark measure.

Why was that appealing? I found it so. Reason demands discrimination, decision, and action. Rapture seizes upon the moment; it requires no dichotomy between the self and the other, the subject and objectivity. One is simply immersed in the course of being, in its ontological waves and rhythms. It is immediate, intense, emotional, subliminal, if not subconscious. As Julene had observed about art, it requires no explanations, nor judges between right and wrong. It is beingness in itself; beauty without evil; ecstasy soaring in flight above the tethers of reason.

I let out a slow, prolonged breath and picked up the *Pensées*. It was still raining outside; I finished the tea. My mind drifted. We were in Augusta, at a restaurant. Her short, black curly hair possessed all the qualities of a scruffy brillo pad. Her little nose seemed crazily too small for her lovely, rounded face and elongated eyes. A smile of perfect white teeth filled her mouth. Soft, gentle, strapless shoulders sloped away into the shadows and down her arms of pale peach. She slumped in her chair and smiled. Her black, V-neck dress revealed the faintest outline of small breasts. We were in love. Or was it infatuation? We were having an affair, behind her husband's back. He was the provost; we professors. We were teaching in a small state university, in a modest Georgia town. We had ordered dinner. It had begun to rain. We asked the waitress to box our dinners. We scooted out of our chairs and ran, laughing, across the parking lot to our room in the motel. Our clothes dripped with water. We undressed, dried each other off, and climbed into bed. Her lips met mine with a burning eagerness. We fondled and rolled in each other's arms. She climbed atop my torso and scooted down about my loins, her eyes fixed on me, smiling all the while. She rose and fell in slow motion, tilting her head downward; her dark eyes sparkled with fire; her tiny breasts bobbed back and forth across my mouth. "Gravity girl!" I teased her. "How I love you!" I was too enchanted with euphoria to think, or reason, or discriminate between subject and objectivity, good and evil, wisdom or folly. It rained and kept raining. We drove back, passed the campus, to our own places of lodging, in our respective and separate cars. I never knew what she told her husband.

I snapped out of my reverie, carried the tray down to Mme. Angleterre's cramped office, and knocked at the door. It was my turn to announce: "*C'est moi*!" There was no answer. I set the tray down and left a note on the pad on her door. *Remember, I won't be here for dinner this evening. M. Clarke*. The "monsieur" part was necessary, as even Mme. Angleterre observed those meticulous, formal, and antiquated rules of French propriety—that ritualized world of the *petit bourgeois et la Fonction Publique*. Civility has its virtue, though, I well knew, as I scrawled the note.

Just then, Mme. Dufavre, the pension's proprietress, came out of her suite near the dining hall.

"Professeur Clarke, what a coincidence!" She stared down at the tray. Displeasure darted from her eyes. Her tall, slender body, which she held stiffly erect, seemed to corroborate her opinion. "I've warned Angleterre. You know it's not permissible to take tea in your room. What if everyone insisted on *egalité*?"

"Please, Mme. The fault's entirely my own. She's not to blame. I have acquiesced in accepting it. That makes me culpable, too. I trust that that's all right?"

"Well, *non*! But you have been an enchanting guest, and an engaging gentleman. And have paid faithfully. You know, clientele have to be evicted from time to time. They can be quite demanding and cheap. This is a tight business, Monsieur."

"I'm very pleased to room here, and I've found all the guests congenial and *très agréable*." How I hated the insincerity of my own voice! But I wanted to defend the concierge as best I could. Plus, I did enjoy the two Frenchmen whose dinner table was next to mine. "You can be very proud of Mme. Angleterre, I think. She's dependable and a worthy servant. Wouldn't you say so?"

"*Mais oui*. Well, enough of that," she smiled. She looked at me, surprisingly, with something of interest. She brushed her dyed rusty-blonde hair to one side and then back across her neck. She was wearing a long burnt-red dress, black hose, and black low heels. Actually, she wasn't bad looking, but her chin seemed a little too large for her face. "Till a later time," she said, as she reentered her apartment.

What am I getting into now? I wondered.

I glanced at my watch. It would be nice seeing Julene again, as well as a pleasant challenge to converse with Sullivan. Why had Julene been so silent, and for so long a time? I would soon find out, I reasoned, as I reclimbed the stairs to my room.

5

By dinner time the rain had ceased, and a cool, silvery mist had settled over the park. The Garden was unlocked, which permitted me to cross an edge of it on my way to St. Sulpice. The gates were usually locked by dark, to discourage transients and street people from sleeping in it, as well as to deter crime. Occasional gendarmes walked their beat around its perimeter or along the major streets that bordered it. None was present that evening, however. I had worn a light tan jacket and walked hastily along the Garden's western aisles. I exited by the Rue de Vau, sauntered across several streets and down the sidewalks of two more, until I came to the restaurant.

Two large red yang dragons flanked the door. Their tongues of yellow fire and elongated ivory teeth greeted me with the sweet pungency of oriental chicken, shrimp, and pork. The redolence of starchy rice and buttered noodles scented the glowing evanescence.

Julene was in the doorway, smiling. "This way," she beckoned. She hugged me as I stepped inside. She looked stunning in her pink dress and pearl earrings.

"Where have you been? I can't tell you how much I've missed you."

"Shhhh! Hush yo' mouth, man. You know it's mutual. Carl is king tonight, and don't you forget that."

Her dark brown eyes searched mine playfully. A lusty quality lurked behind them. They glowed like coffee beans in tiny pools of rich cream. I slipped my arm around her waist and kissed her neck.

She slid free, her pink dress making a sound as she did. Suddenly, I noticed the large diamond that glittered on her left ring finger.

"Yesss!" she whispered. "Act surprised."

I swallowed the lump in my throat. It felt like an inflamed thorn, burning its way into my esophagus.

She led me to a table, spread with a red cloth and white dishes. Carl struggled to his feet and extended his hand.

"Congratulations!" I offered, as I nodded toward Julene's ring. "I assume you're the lucky gentleman."

"Philosophers should never assume anything," he smiled. He shook my hand and reseated himself.

I assisted Julene to her chair. Sullivan looked up somewhat chagrined, but unperturbed. "Sit down!" he half-ordered, half-commanded, in his gruff voice. "At least you know what I wanted to run by you." He smiled proudly toward Julene, leaned sideways, and kissed her cheek. "We plan to get married next week at the American Embassy. You're invited to attend."

"That's quite an honor. What brought all this on? I thought you were cousins, afraid to marry, plus prohibited by law."

"Now, now! Don't act impertinent. Julene told me she explained our relationship."

Julene blushed. "Go on, honey, and tell him the rest. He's dying to know," she eyed me in her luscious way.

"My attorney telegrammed us from Alabama. I had asked him earlier. 'You can do it in Paris, at the embassy, and it'll be legal,' he said. 'The law can't touch you when you return home.'"

"But what about children? Won't you be afraid?" I studied Julene's face for her reaction. A twinge of sadness fell across it. She dropped her glance and fidgeted with her napkin. "Forgive me if I'm still being *impertinent*."

"I welcome the concern," Sullivan replied. "Yes, we'll be uneasy. And who knows what we'll do." He turned toward Julene to observe her discomfort. He patted her hands.

"Love is strange" she added. "Taking you places you never thought you'd go." She glanced up, her face aglow with promise and relief. "It's been long in coming." She kissed him on the mouth.

"Now, now!" he said, with embarrassment. "We'll just have to take chances. What a hell of a character flaw!" he moaned, in reference to himself. "I've been mining the classics too long."

We ordered our food—a variety of shrimp and pork dishes, accompanied by vegetables, fried rice, and hot tea. The waitress brought us chop sticks, at our request.

"Look out!" warned Julene, as she flipped rice and slick peas on Carl and herself.

We laughed, ate, and sipped our tea. In between gulps, we lapsed into conversation.

"Just when is the event? And should I rent a tux?"

"Next week, on Thursday, at eleven a.m.," answered Julene.

"No tux!" added Sullivan. "But bring some champagne. The embassy will provide glasses. Or so they said."

"The Giberts will be there, too. We'll be lunching at an exquisite place on the Avenue de l'Opéra," said Julene.

"And the honeymoon?"

"Paris!" laughed Julene. "My goodness, *mon vieux*!"

Carl smiled at both of us. "No, not Paris. We'll be off to Greece, ancient Peloponnese, Troy, and Crete. Then, my sabbatical will draw to a close."

"I shall have to strain my brain for an appropriate gift."

"No gift!" pleaded Julene. "But I've got one for you." She reached beside her chair and produced a cardboard tube. "Go on, take it."

I accepted the "gift" and slid out its contents. It was a watercolor of the Roman ruins at Nimes.

"That's where we've been for the past few weeks," drawled Sullivan. "She's returned to her painting, thanks to you."

Julene seemed deeply self-conscious. "Don't you like it?"

"Yes! Of course! It's magnificent!" I held the un-scrolled watercolor in both hands. Julene had captured the circular grandeur of the old Roman amphitheatre, its pale salmon colored walls, arches, and gateways at sunset. It was done in pastels of beige and blue and coral. I smiled at her.

"Just wait till I get to Greece and Troy!"

"I will always treasure this," I said.

"There you go again!" growled Sullivan. "'Always,' like 'assume,' is too nefarious for a philosopher to use. But, the picture is charming."

"Incidentally, thanks for the copy of *From the Minoans to Homer*. I've enjoyed rereading it."

"You're quite welcome. I'd covet your assessment of the last chapters, as I'd like to explore some new ideas with you. My next book takes me into Plato and Aristotle, and I'm not pleased with the conclusions I deem forced to draw. Sweetheart," he turned toward Julene, "give him our phone number. Maybe we can meet," he directed his invitation to me, "and pursue some ideas."

"What's the new book about?"

"*Beyond Homer*. That's its title and subject. With the rise of philosophy comes the death of tragedy and the decline of myth. Oh, not that it ever died! My God, what is Christianity, if it isn't a myth? The continuation of the death and rebirth of Dionysus? And the resuscitation of the Mother Goddess, herself? Still, I want to pick your brain for some critical ideas."

"I'd be honored. Let me reread them, and I'll call."

Julene handed me their phone number.

"It'll have to wait till we return from Greece. It'll be an opportune way to complete my sabbatical," coughed Sullivan.

We talked some more. I reached for the tab before Sullivan could pay. "My gift!" I smiled. "It's the least I can do."

We shook hands at the door. "Next Thursday morning, at eleven!" He repeated.

"I'll be there," I gave Julene a huge hug. She kissed my neck. I could feel her warm body beneath her pink dress. Her earrings glittered in the soft red neon lights outside the entrance. I hated to let her go.

"Good night!" she whispered.

"And don't forget the champagne," Carl interjected. "No, no!" he suddenly blurted. "Tonight was enough. Just come as you are."

They went up the street toward the metro. I watched them slip into the rouge shadows of the night. It enfolded them in its wispy, ethereal gloom. "Come, sweet night, ere soon the pain return." I walked back in the settling mist, aglow in the soft lamp-lights that illuminated the Rue Guynemer, and headed toward the pension.

To my joyful surprise, Christine had returned. She was hauling a large piece of luggage down the hall.

"Well, *bonsoir*!" I greeted her. "I've been wondering where you were."

She turned her head and smiled. "Oh, God! I'm exhausted." Her hair was slightly plastered to her face and wet with mist. Her long, baggy black coat all but dragged on the carpet. "You look a little down yourself," she observed. "If it weren't so late, I'd share a drink with you at a café. I'm beat."

I caught up with her and clasped the bag in my hand. "Here, it won't hurt to walk with you."

"God, but I'm dead. What a story I've got for you."

"Tomorrow? How about telling me tomorrow? A date tomorrow night? Huh!"

"God, but you're a lovely chap! How about the day after tomorrow? Right now, I'm just beat. You can take me to a bar, and then. . . ."

"My room?" I smiled.

"No, maybe mine." She puckered her lips for me to kiss. Her eyelids drooped with sleep; her face was drained of emotion. It made me sleepy just to look at her.

I kissed her lips. She unlocked the door. I slid her luggage into the room. "Good night," I said; then I returned down the hall.

6

HEMINGWAY DUBBED PARIS "a moveable feast." For me, it was a wanderlust's dream. Sabbatical or no sabbatical, everyday the magical city—founded by no one less than Priam's son, offered up something new, totally avant-garde, or ancient and crumbling, or wondrous and shocking. Even if I never left my room, simply gawking out the windows at the chimney pots and tin roofs across the street, or listening to the drone and hum of the incessant traffic, or watching from my balcony the prostitutes ply their trade in the rue below, or translating French, or sipping tea—all of it was a philosopher's quest come true, a metaphysician's alchemy bubbling up, intoxicatingly delicious. I had arrived in Paris at that time in my life that psychologists might call "late youth," or "early middle years," when the wine in ones veins is still gurgling with passion and the desire to learn. I knew what I wanted. What the next steps up the long, tedious ladder of academia should be, even if I should stumble and fall, or never make it. Or so I thought I knew. Ambitious, yet cautious, single yet ready for marriage, I wanted to write that next book, or at least get it underway, before having to return to the States and the obligations of the classroom.

At the same time, a nagging uncertainty sported with my brain. What was the ultimate intendment of my goal? My impulses felt so dull. Rereading Sullivan's book, falling anew under its mythical sway, meeting the man in person himself, becoming bewitched by the charming spell of his incestuous bride-to-be, and forcing myself to read subjects that had lost their initial intrigue, created a burden that weighed heavier and heavier on my dubious pursuits. I knew I had to fight back, that I couldn't surrender my dream, or find refuge in the beckoning despair of self-pity. Perhaps that was why Christine had come into my life, I rationalized: to enable me to remain human, until I could regain my élan for the academic call. Besides, I knew I was on to something, just as Sullivan was, and I wanted with all my soul to discover what that "something" was. Sullivan seemed inseparable from it. Perhaps we would find it together. That following morning I turned to Pascal to translate and draft my chapter, devoted singularly to him. He writes:

> The principal illness of mankind is his restless curiosity of things he cannot know; and he is never in graver danger to his being than when he lapses into this useless and purposeless malady [*Pensée* 18].

In still another section, he adds:

> We always find obscure the thing we want to prove, and clear the method we employ in proving it; for when we propose to prove a thing, we are so filled with the notion that it is precisely obscure, and that, on the contrary, our approach is perfect, that we grasp it too easily [40].

Pascal knew there are limits to reason. "The heart has its reasons which reason can never fathom" [277]. He knew that the processes of rationalization can only carry us so far. In his quaint pre-Kantian way, he identified two methods of knowing, or of arriving at knowledge. One he called "the mathematical," the other "intuitive." The first involved the ability to conceptualize and to employ logical reasoning. The second was more immediate and belongs to the realm of sensory perception. Says Pascal, somewhat condescendingly, it requires only "good eyesight." Neither method by itself is sufficient. What Pascal really seems to have wanted was an immediate and unwavering knowledge of the truth that lies beyond the capacity of either method to establish. Without it, man tumbles headlong into an abyss of anxiety from which he is unable to extricate himself. It was his own analysis of a hellish *No Exit*, indigenous to the seventeenth century. In many of his *pensées*, Pascal examined that abyss, before attempting to resolve it. I found it exhilarating and challenging to wrestle with his dicta. But, then, that was what my quest was all about. For epistemology, or the science of questioning how we come to know, is the Holy Grail of philosophy, the quest of all quests. Oh, to know with certainty and to banish all doubt! But even philosophers recognize a pipe dream when they see it, though they smoke it every day. It is the aromatic breath of the gods: to know with certainty the truth or fate about anything!

> What is man when he reflects on himself? Let him consider his place against the totality of being. He is but an aberration in a sequestered corner of nature, his lodgment but a dungeon in the

> universe, from which he apprehends the earth, its kingdoms, cities, and himself. What is man in the Infinite? [72]

One can take only so much dazzling, or disruptive self-examination, even from Pascal. After translating a number of other relevant *thoughts*, I laid my pen aside and left the room. The rains from the previous day had enveloped the city in a soft fog. Cool air settled about the streets. The cafés and boutiques huddled under wet awnings. I had chosen no particular destination for my promenade, or better, my mindless wandering. But my mind was numbed by the dozen or so homeless people I noted, asleep in doorways along the side streets. To my horror, one was the old woman I had attempted to assist on the steps of the Pantheon. She appeared comatose, her body curled in fetal position against a doorframe. I paused and stared down at this human "aberration in her sequestered corner of nature" and remembered Jesus' famous maxim: "You will always have the poor with you and you can do for them what you will." I squatted beside her and placed a five franc note in her wrinkled right fist. I tucked it inside her clenched fingers. Hopefully, no one else would find it, or steal it from her.

Whatever I had intended to do evaporated as a goal, as I "considered my place against the totality of being." I wandered into a bon marché, stumbled upon a bargain department entirely by accident, and spotted rain gear on sale. I bought one and returned to the old woman. She was still asleep, the money still clenched in her fist. Perhaps it was out of sheer self-indulgence, or remorse for wrongs forgotten and lost, but I bent down and covered her shoulders with the coat. Feeling somewhat absolved and yet sad, I walked up to the Boulevard du Montparnasse and searched for a quiet café for lunch. I had lost my appetite but ordered a sandwich and beer, nonetheless. Afterwards, I hunched over a *café noir*. Slowly, I stirred in two lumps of hard sugar, until they dissolved into a brown froth of momentary anodyne.

Never one to waste even a glum day, I resolved to take the metro to the Louvre and revisit my favorite artworks. Upon arriving at the Louvre, I paid and mounted the stairs to gaze at the Winged Victory of Samothrace. With wings windblown and ready to take flight, the stone figurehead inspired my ascent as I drew ever closer to her pedestal. I stood before her in silence. After that, I sought out the rooms that displayed the Mona Lisa and Rembrandt's *Bathsheba*. I had included a description of the latter in my published dissertation: *The Ethics of Virtue*, and had never tired of viewing it, again and again. Bathsheba's comely simplicity, the contemplative look on her face, and the soft glow of lamp light about her hips and breasts, had a way of slipping into the deepest crevices of my humanity. Her nudity aroused neither lust nor inordinate desire. She was the complete opposite of Manet's *Olympia*. Before leaving the museum, I returned downstairs to gawk at the Venus de Milo: the Roman counterpart of the Greek goddess of love, Aphrodite. For me, her statue elicited the highest sense of grace and respect for love's mystery that a human masterpiece can create. I tried not to glance back as I departed her room. It was time to return to the pension for tea and Mme. Angleterre's visit.

I had no idea what the concierge deemed so urgent. She brought the tray, nicely arranged with two bone-white cups and saucers, a silver creamer and sugar bowl, with spoons and forks and napkins and two small shimmering peach tarts. "The British know how to do it better than we, but, *voila, Monsieur*. Just for you!" she gestured with a flourish of her hands, after setting the tray on my desk.

"Well, do take a seat and tell me what's up," I smiled.

"Ohh, a pension's secrets, Monsieur! The walls have eyes, you know, and ears. Don't be upset if I whisper."

"Whisper away," I grinned. "You've got my ears burning with curiosity, and my mouth salivating over these tarts."

"Ohhhh, you charming devil, if only I were younger and pretty, like the English mademoiselle. You like her, *non*?"

"*Oui*. She'll do in a rainstorm."

"Ahhh, *l'amour*, it isn't just for the young, you know? I was married myself," she boasted shyly. "But Robert was killed in the war; actually, during the Resistance. They shot him not far from here."

"I'm humbled to hear that."

"Humiliating was more like it. They lined him up with three others and gunned them down. Bang! Bang! Rat-tat-tat! Rat-tat-tat!" she motioned, as if spraying the room with a machine gun. "They left them on the sidewalk of the Rue D'Ulm for their families to take away. But, that's not why I'm here!" she frowned, regaining her composure. "It's to share a little scandal, *oui!*"

"I'm listening."

"*Alors*! It's Mme. Dufavre. She's hiding a man in her apartment, a lover, I do believe. He comes late at night and leaves before anyone can see him. I've watched him do it three times." She sipped her tea, while munching on the sticky tart. She wiped its glaze off her fingers and onto her apron, never once touching her fork or napkin.

"But how do you know he's her lover? Maybe he's just a friend, or relative?"

"Ohhh, Professeur! Come now, we're adults!" she said, raising her voice a tiny pitch. She completed eating her tart and, tilting her head back, drained the cup to the last drop of tea, then wiped the saucer with her napkin.

"My grandmother used to do that, only she drank her tea, or rather coffee, from a saucer. Perhaps that's an old French custom."

"I think there's more to Madame's lover than—," she paused, as if searching for the *mot juste*, "sensuality," she beamed.

"Oh!"

"Yes! Definitely! I think he's the thief who killed the old woman across the street."

"How do you know that, or that the motive was a theft?"

"The old woman was rich, they say. Kept her money in a pillow slip. The Madame knew her. She used to be a lodger here."

"Still, murder and theft would be hard to prove."

"I know, so I don't tell anyone but you." She leaned forward and stared curiously at me. "I'd keep an eye on her. She's a strange one, I tell you. Beware!"

Seeing I had finished my tart and tea, Mme. Angleterre gathered up the tray, with its empty dishes, and walked toward the door. I rose to open it for her.

"Remember. Watch your back."

"Yes! Thank you. I will."

After the concierge left, I returned to my desk to mull over her "secret." I hardly believed that Dufavre and her visitor were murderers or thieves. Why would Mme. Angleterre have even posed the possibility, unless she herself were implicated, or entertained an incredible, creative imagination, or thwarted desire for riches of her own? I could only assume the latter disjunctives, but, surely she wasn't involved! But that wouldn't be the first time a concierge was at fault. There were always whispers in the dining room about previous concierges, who had cheated Dufavre of clients' money. "They come to your room, pretend that Dufavre is ill, and that she has delegated them to collect the rent," the two companions to my right had explained. The short, black-haired one had shaken his head with great disapprobation. "*Terrible*! It was *terrible*!" he stated, with a dour look. "She made us pay again, twice! Called us '*Stupid*!' *Oui!*"

I didn't doubt it.

That evening, as I sat at table, I surveyed the room, wondering if any of the pensioners present might be involved. The Japanese rarely came down to eat. They cooked in their room. You could smell their food the moment you entered the stairwell. Dufavre frequently threatened to oust them, but they were still there. Other than the Belgian and Christine, the other guests were all Frenchmen, or widows, and elderly at that. One old gentleman always came down in coat and tie, smartly dressed, save for his unpolished shoes, and would line up a row of spices and hot sauces to douse on each course, save for his dessert. That was usually a pudding or tart. Once in a while I would see him in the park, reading newspapers, or playing *boules* with a small cadre of other old gentlemen.

The only younger pensioners were Christine, myself, the Japanese, and a French woman in her thirties, along with her teenage daughter. They sat at the far end of the *salle à manger*, near Christine. Both had dyed their hair red; wore short skirts, and squabbled quietly between themselves. Sometimes the mother would suddenly stand up, throw her napkin in her plate, and denounce her daughter for all to hear. My knowledge of her colloquial slang was limited, but I gathered she was accusing the girl of bringing boyfriends to their room when she wasn't there. Since they didn't room on my floor, I had no idea how true her accusations might be. The two guys to my right would turn their heads and listen with amused interest. "*Alors*! There you go, Gaston! No more bus rides across town. *Oui*?"

"Silence!" Gaston would blush. He was the taller of the two and younger as well.

The Belgian was an engineer and worked for an electrical company on the outskirts of Paris. He dressed conservatively—dark trousers and gray shirts, with black ties, and kept to himself. He never once spoke to me, but he would nod respectfully toward Christine and greet her with a smile. Maybe he was the one? To my knowledge, he roomed in the top floor, just under the attic, which was reserved for the dishwasher, server, and cook. It was unheated, and I always felt sorry for them. They wore the same clothes, or outfits, everyday, appeared clean, but, as in the case of the server, no amount of cologne could disguise or suppress their body odor. I never knew the cook's name, but the dishwasher was a tall, dark haired French girl, obviously poor, but pretty. The server was a shorter woman of medium height, jet black hair, her face always white from an over-application of facial powder, and her lips a bright red. Her name was Madame Cueillier. The dishwasher simply referred to herself as, "Charlene." She would have made a good match for Gaston. Surely none of these were suspects!

Upon returning to my floor, I walked down to Christine's room and knocked on her door. She had left the dining room earlier, glancing secretively at me.

"Hello!" she said, as she opened the door. "We still on for tomorrow?"

"Yes! You haven't changed your mind, have you?"

"Heavens, no! Remember, I have quite a story for you. But I want it to wait till tomorrow."

"Will I like it?"

"Maybe!" she cooed, with teasing eyes. "Tomorrow! After we've eaten dinner, I'll tell you. At the café-bar! Ok? Just come for me up here."

"Sure! There's a great little place on the Boulevard du Montparnasse, I've been wanting to try. We'll go there."

She opened the door enough for me to step in. "Kiss me," she said. "I need a kiss, till then."

I complied and returned to my room.

7

A delicate, translucent blue sky stretched across the morning horizon. I had awakened earlier than usual and had pulled back the curtains to peer out the windows. After so many gloomy and rainy days, it portended better weather. I glanced at my watch. It was 6:08, too early for breakfast down stairs. I shaved, showered and dressed and decided to catch a cup of coffee at the little news kiosk on the corner of the street just up from the pension. Its proprietor, a Greek, often managed a smile when he saw me coming. Usually, I didn't visit his stand until mid-morning. We would banter for a few minutes. Afterwards, he would steam up his machine and serve my coffee.

"Ah! My American friend, a bit early today! The sky is *très joli*, isn't it? You should be visiting my country. The smell of our coffee! The aroma of the beans! The odor of fresh baked loaves! Our cheeses and goat's milk—all fit for the gods! What will it be?"

By now he knew, so I stood there until he served up his Peloponnesian version of mud-thick coffee, which I drank without sugar or cream.

"Remember. Sip it. Don't gulp it."

I paid and bought a copy of *Le Miroir Français*. I had not read Gibert's paper's columns for over a month now. I preferred *Le Monde* and the international edition of *The Herald Tribune*. Even then, I read them less than twice or three times a week. My own work consumed inordinate mental energy. What little free time remained, left practically none for papers. Reflecting on each day's study, my findings, translations, writing, and walks claimed any residual vitality.

I sat on a bench near the metro entrance and turned to the editorial page. There was Gibert's column. "De Gaulle's Third Force and its Meaning for France." I knew that de Gaulle had abandoned the presidency less than a year ago and that Gaullism, as it was called, was fast fading as a polestar for a post-de Gaulle France. But as I skimmed the article, it was clear that

Gibert was still wed to the old General's vision of France as a *troisième pouvoir*, a third independent power, between the British and Americans, on the one hand, and the Soviet Union and its Eastern Block, on the other. He feared the thought that de Gaulle's successors would surrender that objective, and that France would reel back into political weakness. I looked for the major thread of his piece:

> We have lost our North African Empire, our prestige in Chad and in the Cameroon, our honor and pride at Dien Bien Phu. Who listens to us in London, Moscow, or Washington? Or takes us seriously even in Quebec? Or Cairo? Or Lebanon? Our voice has been silenced, our *langue* intermingled with the dialects of a hundred alien tongues. Our cultural achievements but monuments to a grandeur that is passing away. Who comes to our shores now, to our treasures of art and history, but the curious, the profligate, the philistine? That is not the France of the future, or with a future, but with a vestige of decay.
>
> Like it or not, France must interject herself again upon the Moulin Rouge of modernity. Fighting Cervantes' windmills in rusting armor no longer charms the world. We must command a say in the political affairs of the globe, in Eastern Europe, in the Middle East, Palestine, and the Far East, if we are to reclaim our place in history as a people worthy of her past. Yes, that may require a military force, prepared to protect and enhance French interests and culture, wherever either faces risk. Yes, it means continued opposition to NATO, when NATO excludes our interests.
>
> Yes, it means a courageous *Non* to American imperialism, when that imperialism imperils our own destiny and fate. De Gaulle sought to make us proud again. Yes, he made mistakes. He could be vain, pigheaded, and, yes, wrong. But in his heart of hearts, he was right. He was French. He was a nationalist, through and through. He tilted in the jousts of the greatest kings of the crown. Charlemagne, along with the Valois, the Bourbons, and Napoleon, would have understood his cause, embraced his zeal. No state is perfect; no king, emperor, or president is without fault. No nation of sovereign people has ever existed without revolutions, quarrels, and defeats. But how I despair to see our country become a stripped and silent mannequin in the shop windows of a decadent world, coming of age.

There was an advertisement at the bottom of the page for his forthcoming book; but no date of publication was mentioned. I turned to the arts and fashion section to see if Mme. Gibert had written anything. No, she hadn't. But the paper announced Mme. Monique Gibert's plans to conduct a guided tour of Fontainebleau, to include the chateau, its new furnishings, as well as a walk about the park. The date was the second Friday of May. One could reserve a seat on the tour bus by simply calling the number listed. The bus would leave from Sainte-Chapelle, promptly at eight that morning. I tore out the number, glanced through a few more articles, then dropped the paper in a nearby waste drum. I decided that I would sign up for this *événement*. Besides, Mme. Gibert had captivated my interest, and being in her presence again would be exciting and pleasurable. Her eyes had searched my own so invitingly, her glances at once flirtatious and monitorial, seductive and remonstrative. I would have to be prepared.Prepared or not for Mme. Gibert, I was unprepared for what erupted upon my return to the pension.

"Another robbery!" shrilled the French, red-haired woman, who had scolded her daughter the night before. "Will it be murder next?" she all but shouted in Madame Dufavre's face.

"Please, Madame, control yourself. I have called the police. They will be here soon."

I could have sworn I saw a man in the Madame's apartment. He had slunk behind the door the instant I looked his way. He had been slipping into his coat, as if to depart. I knew what Angleterre would conclude.

"My jewelry, Francine's, a watch, and my money—all, all are gone!"

"Ah, Professor Clarke, you are always so calm!" Dufavre addressed me, as if that mantra would bring solace to the woman.

"How does that help?" wailed the young French mother. "We shall have to move if it can't be found."

Dufavre looked away with grim intensity. Suddenly, Angleterre appeared with a torn pillow slip in her hands. "I found this on your balcony. It was caught on the inside window latch. Money and jewelry are still in it." She handed it to Dufavre, to verify her discovery.

"That's mine!" said the woman, snatching it from the proprietress's hand. "Thank God! What a hell of a place! What a way to start the day! At least, the bastard dropped it!" She immediately looked inside to see if anything was missing.

The man in Dufavre's apartment had still not come out. If he had been the thief, then how did he get off the balcony? Had he simply walked out through the woman's room? No! The pillow slip got caught in the window. He must have exited that way. We heard a siren in the street.

The gendarmes would soon be in the hall. I went back to the stairwell, climbed the steps to the fourth floor, and returned to my room. I would forego breakfast, study awhile, and take a walk. It was difficult, however, to concentrate on my work. Pascal was a thousand miles removed from my thoughts, as were Rousseau, Baudelaire, Descartes and Kant. Fighting distraction, I picked up a book of Rainer Rilke's poems and began reading. Like Baudelaire, Rilke had a way of inserting his consciousness into the objects of his lyrical observations. He brought a whole other way of lifting his subjects into the reader's awareness, and therefore of providing a shocking venue for an immediate self-consciousness and knowledge of the world. His way of knowing, his epistemological methodology, defied definition. Was it something I should use in my own book? It was more gestalt than logical, an all-at-once assault, a comprehension that revealed the truth, while concealing the miracle of how. Husserl attempted to "bracket the truth," but the phenomenological character of Rilke's approach inspired my interests. Nowhere was this more transparent than in his poem, "The Panther." After consulting my German dictionary for words like *allerkleinsten* and *angespannt*, I translated his work as follows:

The Panther

From ever gazing through the endless bars
his sight, now dazed, has lost its focal power;
before him looms a thousand tedious bars;
behind him, a caged-in world retires.

The soft gait of his strong and supple stride
turns on the circle of the tightest point;
like a ballet dancer poised at center stage,
his mighty will stares back, stupefied.

Sometimes his pupils' membranes blink
enough to let an image in;
it glides along his tense and quivering limbs
and dies unrecognized in his heart.

That kind of philosophy unnerved me. Yet it spoke the truth; it struck the limpid chords of my mind with somber reality. Yes! This is life. We know it in our head and in our soul. Life is dying in our hearts. Silent and stupefied, we gaze from our cage, like Rilke's panther, our wills petrified. Our outer frame remains, but our limbs do not respond. Heidegger would label this way of knowing *personal*. His famous definition of *Dasein*, or of being, hinged on the realization that the beingness of being is always personal, mine, my own, and that it equally includes the future, my future, and all its possibilities. The Panther had no future, because he had no possibilities of choice, no place to step, save in his endless path behind the iron bars.

Such knowing requires rigorous self-analysis and unflinching self-consciousness. From this epistemological basis, Heidegger would go on to characterize human life as a troika of stringent facts: that our *Dasein*, or our beingness, occurs at a particular time and place, within the context of a particular culture, language, and history. He called this its *facticity*, which we must own and cannot deny. Second is *existence*. It entails the recognition that we are accountable for our lives and what we make of them. To that extent, moods of *guilt* and *remorse* are not our enemies, but our friends. They represent choices that have run amuck but which can be rectified. Lastly, comes *fallenness*, or *forfeiture*. If we do not seize upon our existence, take accountability for its past and future, and acknowledge the facticity of our time and place—that we are here and not somewhere else—then we will fall into inauthenticity and forfeit our *Dasein*. "The Panther" was Rilke's symbol of fractured *Dasein*, long before Heidegger had taken up his pen.

It was all so clear on paper, in Heidegger's books and mind. But how could I tell that to Madame Angleterre, or Madame Cueillier, the waitress, or Charlene, the dishwasher, or even Odette Dufavre? "Listen, all of you. Cast off your forfeiture! Come down, dear waitress from the servants' floor; descend those steps, dishwasher girl; abandon that attic where you mold for a brighter world! And who will give you that brighter world? Why, of course, you and you alone! Yes! You, yourself. Who else did you think would give it to you?" Already their choices were compromised, their facticity defined by dishes and towels, by their failure to qualify for the *école normale supérieure*. Now they were faced with a thousand unyielding bars. Yet, Heidegger was right. At what point does the Panther's blink stop sinking in its heart, forcing its fangs to bear and its lips to snarl? I walked to the windows and looked out again. A topaz sky beckoned me to come into the streets, to find reprieve from the madness of learned tomes, and to experience existence through my own feelings and moods, my own sensory preceptors and psychosphere.

Bright sunshine filled the Garden of Luxembourg's aisles. Their flower beds and blossoming plants welcomed the radiant sun. A lemon hue bathed the refection pools and statues in languorous light. I wandered down past the central basin, where little boys skipped about the lake and watched their boats sail across the water. I found a bench in a quiet corner by the Medici Fountain. As I listened to its restful cascades, a chapel hymn from seminary days drifted through my mind:

There is a fountain filled with blood
Drawn from Emmanuel's veins;
And sinners, plunged beneath that flood,
Lose all their guilty stains.

I am seated with my Uncle Harry on his farmhouse porch. It is spring and the lone lilac bush in his front yard bows from the weight of clusters of scented purple blossoms. Honey bees fill the air with their hum. He rocks rhythmically to and fro. I have come to celebrate his eighty-third birthday. His tanned gnarled hands grip the rocker's arms, his faded bib-overalls are too large for him, and the crown of his sweat-darkened Stetson is stained deep red from so many years of handling. The air is cool, and he wears a dark, green, flannel-lined denim jacket.

"I'm glad you seen the light," he says. "We Clarkes was never meant to be religious. I told your Aunt Sally, you was making a huge mistake. Maybe we're spiritual when it comes to the land, but never religious. At least, you've gotten out. What triggered it?"

"The whole experience, Uncle Harry. The wasted afternoons of pastoral calls, when nobody was at home, or wanted you around. Plus the dogma. I had to make my peace with it.

I'd rather be a pagan, suckled in a creed outworn,
or hear ole Triton blow his wreathed horn,

to quote the bard,

than Sunday after Sunday preach a Jesus
I couldn't believe in any more."

"I figured you'd come around in time." He began rocking thoughtfully. "When I was young and still in the Navy, I messed around with a lot of whores. Maybe they wasn't whores, and maybe not that many, but enough. I stayed drunk most of the time. One night, when I was half-sober, half-lit, I slipped into bed with this young girl. She had the most beautiful long hair I had ever seen. She had dyed it blonde, and it fell full length around her shoulders, and about her breasts. She was slender, almost frail, and wanted to please me, since I'd paid her upfront. 'Let's do it doggie,' she said. She got on her knees and I got up against her back and placed my hands on her hips. Right there, under my palms, was two tattoos, linked by rose stems across her lumbars. On the right was the tattoo of an angel, with wings swooped back and bare feet as tan as the girl's body. On the left, under my other hand, was a cross, with the bowed head of the Christ hanging down. For months after that, I couldn't screw anymore. Then I met Sally and fell in love. After we married, I stopped drinking, went to church for a while, but felt more comfortable here, just rocking and daydreaming and sometimes talking to myself. But I've never forgotten that girl, or her tattoos. And I finally figured out what they mean. I've tried to live by them and offer it to you." He stopped rocking and looked at me. "*There's not a human life that ain't salvageable, if it wants to be*. That's what they mean. Remember that, and you'll treat people right. It'll be the only religion you need."

8

THAT EVENING, DURING DINNER, Christine smiled as she passed my table. She walked composedly to her own and sat with her back partially against the wall. That way we could glance at each other if we chose. A poster print of *Le Sacré-Coeur* hung on the wall behind her. Its majestic dome towered upward, filling the blue sky with its pale lemon crown. I must visit it again, I thought.

Just then, Pierre—the shorter of the two, whose table all but touched mine—came in and sat down with a peeved expression on his face. "A police inspector was here today and Madame Dufavre let him into my room. My room! And Gaston's! The very idea! That we were the thieves."

"You've heard about the excitement, then?"

"Ah, *Oui*! Gaston is so embarrassed that he's delayed coming down. But I told him the earlier the better."

"Agreed. Why have they singled out you two?"

"Who's to say! It's probably because we're just *petits fonctionnaires*, government workers at the lowest pay scale."

"What do you do, if I may ask?"

"I'm a postal clerk, in the Marais district. Gaston works for the city, delivering messages on a bicycle. Imagine, on a bicycle! At least city hall provides him with that. But we're not thieves!" he said, raising his voice, while still keeping it to a whisper.

"Well, if it isn't Gaston!" I nodded toward Pierre, as his roommate entered.

Gaston moved quickly and silently toward the table and hurriedly sat down. He scraped his chair, as he pulled it forward, causing some of the elderly guests to look our way.

"*Merde*!" moaned Gaston. "I've botched it!"

"No you haven't," I consoled him. "Just what happened, anyway?"

"Pierre, here, hadn't left for work yet, and I was on the bus, headed toward town. As soon as I got there, the police were waiting for me. It was *terrible*! Humiliating! Everyone was staring at me, as if I were some kind of criminal. Do I look like a criminal? *Non*. I am the victim!"

"Well, I see they at least let you go! *Non*!"

"Yes, but not until they grilled me with a score of questions: 'Have you ever been arrested before?' 'Why are you living at Dufavre's, when your work brings you here?' 'Are you hiding something under your coat?' 'Yes, a gun! You buffoon!'"

"You didn't say that?" Pierre grinned. "*Formidable*! '*Oui, j'ai un pistolet*!'"

"Of course not, you buffoon!"

"Hear, hear!" replied Pierre. "Who pays half the rent?"

"Listen, *mes bons amis*! Have a little wine." I twisted off the cork and poured each of them a small glass, before filling my own.

"*Salut! A votre santé*!" Pierre clinked his glass against mine.

Gaston hunched forward, with his elbows on the table, a bit dispirited, and waited for Mme. Cueillier to bring out the *potage*. "I hope it's not that left over cabbage," he wheezed, with a slight cough.

After dinner, I walked up the stairs and down the hall to Christine's room. She had left the dining hall earlier, with something of a childish pout in her face. What had I done or said? Maybe she was bipolar! You would have to be to study French at the *Institut*. "*You must always end your requests with, 'S'i'l vous plait!' How many times must I tell you that?*" "OK! I've got you!" I wanted to answer. But that was the Institute of 1958, when I first studied in Paris.

I knocked on her door. She immediately opened it.

"Whatever were you and those dunces talking about? I thought you'd never stop."

"Well, I have. Are we still on?" I smiled, as I stepped forward to kiss her lips.

"Oh, God!" she exclaimed. "Take me to that bistro, or bar, whatever it is!" She leaned her head back for me to embrace her and kiss her again. Her hot lips all but burned my own. "Ummm!'" she groaned. "Let's go."

We left the pension and headed toward the Boulevard du Montparnasse. On a little side street, near a quaint flower market that had just closed, we came upon Le Café D'Orion. "This is the place," I said. "I've been wanting to try it."

A slender woman of Gypsy descent escorted us to a quiet table, set for two. Her long braided pigtails hung black about her breasts. She wore a red scarf and a pleated, full-length yellow dress, with a wide black sash. A deep cleavage peeked out between her breasts. "For dinner?" she asked, with a lusty smile.

"Just drinks," I replied. "Do you serve cocktails?"

"Certainly, Monsieur, what will you have?"

"Christine, what would you like?"

"The strongest drink you serve?" she winked at the woman.

"Ahhh! I'll make it myself," she laughed. "It's an old Hungarian secret. You'll need a taxi to get home. What about Monsieur?"

"A dry martini, with lots of Vermouth and olives."

"I'll bring you some poppy-seed bread, a little cheese for the Mademoiselle, *Oui*?"

"Yes, that'll be fine."

The woman brushed her braids across the back of her neck and suddenly clapped her hands. Two musicians, with violins, came out from somewhere and began playing a Brahms folk dance. It was quick and lively, sad and melodic, all at the same time. It was the first in a medley of other Brahms folk tunes they played. I took Christine by the hand and kissed her right ear. One of the violinists came over to the table and began playing a soulful, Bohemian piece, just for Christine. He laid into the strings with his long bow and swept the hairs gently across the wires with artistic grace. I knew that would mean a huge tip, but I was hoping that Christine would soothe that empty pang I carried and still the restless flames that wavered within. I handed him a hundred franc bill, which he tucked miraculously in his coat pocket without missing a single sweep of his bow.

"What is that story you were going to tell me? Remember?"

"Oh, that! It hardly matters now." She rested her head on my shoulder and reached for my hand. "Will you love me tonight, like last time? I feel very, very needy."

"You know I will. I was afraid you'd never come back."

"I had to slip off to England. I had to know if Tobby still loved me. I went to his mother's home in Wales. "'He ain't livin' here no more, ma'am' she said. 'But you'll find 'im at this address,' she handed me a postcard of a pub. 'He rooms in an upstairs loft, with his drunken sweetie. Ahh, the humanity of it! The shame! I raised 'im better than that, you know!'

"I found the pub pictured on the postcard near a rail station. Bloody fools were drunk all over the place. But not Tobby. He was sitting at an oak table, drinking ale with a rather remarkably pretty woman. She was dressed in a dark green skirt and white blouse and had shimmering red hair. On her wedding finger, she sported the largest gaudy diamond I have ever seen. Tobby looked shocked when he saw me. He knew I suspected where that ring had come from. He rose awkwardly and addressed his fiancée with a shameful smirk. 'Dearest Elaine, there's an old friend I want you to meet.' Need I say more?"

"I'm sorry for your sake."

Just then, our Gypsy hostess returned. "For you, Monsieur, and for you, Mademoiselle," she smiled pleasantly, as she set our drinks in front of us.

"Let's drink the past away," I proposed, as I picked up my martini.

Christine eyed her cocktail suspiciously. It had come in a tall clear glass, garnished with mint and orange slices. The drink itself appeared a murky tawny color. "What's in this?" she asked, with playful misgivings.

"Ahhhh! No, no, no!" the woman wagged her finger at Christine. "I can't tell, but you'll crave another before you leave." She placed some muffins and cheese on the table, with a flat knife to spread the cheese. Turning with a smile, she motioned for the musicians to play again. They began playing "Yesterday." Quite content, the woman wiped her hands on her black sash and returned to the kitchen.

"God, this is good!" exclaimed Christine, "whatever it is. I think I'm going to get drunk."

"Please, don't get that drunk."

"Oh, I'll be sober enough when we get back." She laid her head on my shoulder again. "You've got to tell me more about yourself."

I repeated what I had told the Sullivans. "I hope to complete a major portion of a second book while here."

"How much longer will that be?" She looked at me with a kind of innocence that lovers experience before reality raises its ugly head. It was genuine, disarming, from the purest motives of her heart.

"I'll have to go back in July, or late August. What about you?"

"Early June, unless . . .," she smiled coyly, "something should happen to change all that."

"Like what?" I teased.

Just then, our hostess came back to our table. A good-natured smile glowed from ear to ear. "Ah, Monsieur, give me your hand? Let me see it," she demanded emphatically. She pulled a chair up beside mine, took my right hand, fondled it for a moment, then opened it. "Ah! Look at this magnificent life line! You'll live a hundred years, no doubt!" She continued to hold my hand and began examining it more closely. "But, this line here, see? It's not so good," she said, almost whispering. She shook her head with a pucker of her lips. "Whatever it is you're looking for, you'll never find." She looked into my face and stared directly at me. I couldn't determine if her pronouncement was a test or not. I waited for her to say more. Drawing in a deep breath, she exhaled it slowly. "It will find you," she stated. She twitched her dark eyebrows and let go of my hand.

She moved to Christine. "Cherie, let's out do him," she proposed. "Open your hand, dear."

Christine looked at the woman somewhat skeptically. She opened the palm of her left hand and held it out for the woman to study.

The woman's smile evaporated. A strange, dark glint possessed her face. It seemed too authentic to be fabricated. She closed Christine's hand instantly and held it for a while in her own.

"What's wrong? It's not that bad, is it?"

"Wrong and bad mean nothing," the woman replied, wriggling her nose, as if annoyed. "Sometimes it's better not to know the future. Even good Gypsies make mistakes. No, dearie, you're fine."

"Well, I wish I could share your optimism."

The woman removed her red scarf, revealing a tattoo of a black star where her hair-line and forehead met. "Tell me, are you lovers?" she asked suddenly.

I pressed Christine's right hand with my left and caressed it gently.

Christine turned and looked at me. "I guess you could say we're mutual . . . whatevers," she laughed. "Who knows?"

"Ooooh, both of you! What is love? Enjoy it while you can." She glanced up with a wave of her hand. "See all this!" she pointed around the room. "It was Joseph's dream. *Le Café D'Orion*! Like Orion, he never had a mother, or knew her. She died shortly after he was born. So, when he became a man, and we met here in Paris, he said, 'Evana! What is life without love? Will you marry me and help me build my dream, fulfill my star and yours?'" she pointed to her head. "Which was, of course, this café, named for the brooding Orion. He was a son of the gods, so they say, an orphan who never knew his mother." She shook her head with sad consolation. "I will tell you something more." Her face softened, as she placed her scarf back on her head. "It is from Goethe. You know, we had to study Goethe when I was a girl. It is from one of his poems. '*Happy alone is the soul who loves*.'" A melancholic anguish settled about her face. She winced, then smiled.

Patrons were beginning to file in. They were waiting to be seated. "*Alors*, I will have a waiter bring you more drinks. Orion is visible tonight, if it weren't for the city's lights." She scrunched her lips together, grimaced, and returned to her duties.

"Well, what do you make of that?" Christine stated.

"I don't know; I'll have to think about it."

"Well what about the robberies? Do you think the pension's safe?" Christine motioned for the server to replenish her drink. "God, but I'm thirsty! This is good!"

"I'm glad you're enjoying it. As for the pension, I think it's save. I think the robberies are the work of a novice. A seasoned thief wouldn't have panicked, or left his reward on a window latch. How he got on the balcony and back down is what intrigues me."

"You know, their room is on my side of the hall, just below mine. It spooks me that it wasn't the wind I heard."

"Maybe there's a passage from the street to the alleyway. Handholds he can climb."

"You will stay with me tonight?" A slight tremor quivered about her shoulders.

"You know the answer to that."

The waiter returned with a second tall drink for Christine, as well as another martini for me.

"*Merci, Monsieur*," I thanked him.

"What did you make of the Gypsy closing my hand so quickly, as if she saw something foreboding, too dreadful to report?"

"Theatrics, I think. It creates the very moods you described. And probably out of habit. Maybe she reads palms on the side."

"That Goethe piece she quoted, do you think it's true? That only lovers experience happiness? And those who don't love, never do?"

"I don't know. Goethe wasn't a romantic, but he certainly had a passion for women. He probably wrote it in his youth."

"I don't think I feel love in that way for anyone right now. Just a hunger to be held, to be caressed, to feel that rush that we experienced last time. That doesn't offend you, I hope."

"No. I was in love once, just as you were with Tobby. That was several years ago. Now there's just a numbness that won't go away."

"That's how I feel." She snuggled closer and put her hand on my thigh.

I ran my left hand along hers.

"Let's go back to the room," she said.

We finished our drinks and headed toward the pension.

"Do you think we could really see Orion, if we looked hard enough?" she laughed.

I glanced up into the night. A glowing sheen of red neon lights and sleepy yellow street lamps filled the darkness with a soft patina. "Maybe if we were outside Paris, we could see it, but not here."

Being in bed with her once more, and in her arms, brought that long delayed peace that accompanies sex. It welled up, from somewhere deep inside, and traveled along through the nerves and erotic channels of the body, then engulfed me in a semi-conscious paradise of euphoria. We soon fell asleep in each other's arms.

9

TWO DAYS BEFORE CARL and Julene's wedding, I descended the stairs to the second floor to telephone them, to see if there might be something I could bring. Simply showing up did not strike me as an acceptable option. First, I had to seek permission from Mme. Angleterre. She was smoking a cigarette in her tiny office, which was more like a booth. Suddenly, she noticed me and swept the fallen cigarette ashes off her lap. A pile of mail, bills, and magazines cluttered what little working space remained.

"Ah, Monsieur," she smiled, "forgive this mess. Oh, but it's bad!" she admitted with a grin.

"May I use the telephone? I need to call a friend. He's here in Paris. Nothing long distance."

"But of course!" she chortled, waving her hands and arms to disperse the stagnant blue smoke that had settled about her.

Many Frenchmen smoked her brand of cigarettes. They were probably the cheapest brand they could afford. They came in a silver paper box, with a blue lid.

"I'll wait outside," she said.

I stepped into the narrow space and dialed Carl's number. Julene answered the phone.

"*Allo! Oui. C'est Julene.*"

"Julene, it's Clay here. The big day's coming," I teased. "How's our Alabama girl?"

"Oh, Clayton! I'm so glad you called. You can't imagine what I'm feeling. Can we talk?"

"Sure. Where's Carl?"

"At the archives in the Bibliothèque. He won't be back till late."

"Where can we meet?"

"Why not your park, at the Garden, there? Or in a café nearby."

"There's one at the metro stop on Montparnasse. Why not meet at the stairs? I'll watch for you."

"Ok! When?"

"What about within the next thirty minutes or so?"

"I'll be there. Oh, but I've got to talk."

Watching Julene ascend the metro steps only confirmed my fascination for her. Her light coffee complexion and slender body, her shoulder-length black hair, and easy flowing polyester lime-colored dress, gave her a serene goddess-like countenance. She came up the stairs like a glorious spirit, rising from mystic realms below. Just observing her blurred the memory of that painful pit of unrequited love, in which I had been wallowing so long.

"You gorgeous woman!"

She slipped her arms about my waist and gave me a gentle hug. I could tell she had been crying. "Let's get me some tea, or lemonade, and talk."

"OK."

We seated ourselves under a green and white stripped umbrella at a nearby sidewalk café. Congested traffic crept by slowly; layers of gray pollutants fogged the air. I had learned to shut out such distractions, but the toxic fumes stung the back of my throat.

We ordered tea, croissants *au beurre et confiture*, and coffee for me.

"What's up?" I asked. "Second thoughts?"

"Perhaps. I was so in love with him and still am. But something's different now. Things have changed." She glanced up with a twinge of bewilderment in her eyes.

"Like what?"

"I wish I knew! Sullivan's Landing has been such a magnetic facet of my life, I can't imagine living elsewhere. But that's not a sufficient reason to marry, is it?"

"I suppose not. Incidentally, I like that name, 'Sullivan's Landing.' I assume that's what they call the estate?"

"Please, don't change the subject." She paused and glanced past my shoulder. "I intend to go on with the wedding. I love him too much to back out." Her hazel irises filled with tiny beads of tears. I leaned over and pressed her eyelids softly with the edge of my napkin. She clasped it with both hands and sobbed momentarily.

"Ah, Julene!"

"I want children, healthy little chil'ren," she wiped back her tears. "Just normal little fellows runnin' around. To call them 'Honey,' the way my mama and granny called me!"

"Perhaps a genetics counselor could determine your chances of having a normal child."

"Don't be a dreamer! Can we go to your pension for a while?" A despondent smile played about her mouth. She adjusted her dress, smoothing out a crinkle that had formed on her left thigh, where her right leg had lain against it.

"If we can sneak in! The concierge isn't supposed to let visitors past the second floor. But she rarely comes out to check on anyone climbing the stairs. I room on the fourth *étage*."

"I need to cuddle and be held. That's all. To lie with your arms around me and remain still, wrapped in my pathetic self. To meditate where no one can see me, but you."

"You're not pathetic. It's quite understandable, I'd say."

We left the café and walked the several blocks to the pension. I rang the buzzer, which unlocked the front door, and we quietly climbed the stairs. I held to her hand as she followed me. Whenever I looked back she smiled; an unhappy gravity seemed to fill her eyes. On the fifth landing we paused; then walked down to my room. We undressed in silence, but left our underpants on.

Her breasts were shapely and round and larger than I had imagined. I so wanted to kiss them and fondle her. She had to know what I was thinking, for a tender gleam sparkled in her eyes. She put her arms around me and kissed me. "You're not so hard to look at, yourself. Where did you get that body?"

"I ran cross-country in college and toyed around with fencing and volleyball."

"Oh, God! What am I doing? Just hold me Clayton. Cuddle me in your arms."

We climbed into bed. She lay with her back against my chest; I carefully reached over with my left arm and cupped her breasts in my hand. They were soft, yet firm. I laid my face against her neck. A delicate fragrance of perfume emanated from her hair. She lay motionless, her eyes wide open. "Don't look at me," she said. "Just hold me." I could feel her back and chest rise and fall as she breathed.

For a long while we lay there. I fell asleep. When I awoke, she was slipping back into her dress. She sat on the edge of the bed and stroked my face with her right hand. She never spoke a word. She wedged her feet into her low-heeled, white shoes, bent forward and kissed my cheek. "Don't stir. Please don't get up. Thank you for this moment. I'll never forget it."

For a full half hour after her departure, her perfume still scented the air. What would Christine think, if she had walked in?

I glanced at my watch. It was 2:30 p.m. I had spent the past four hours with Julene. We had bonded in a way that I had never imagined possible. I think I had fallen in love with her, but did I truly know what love was? Whatever it was, I didn't feel it for Christine, though I enjoyed our rapturous intimacy. I got out of bed, redressed, and began wandering the streets about the Garden. I had no planned direction or sense of purpose or goal in mind. I simply needed to walk, to ruminate, to put distance between Julene's and my exquisite slumber.

I took some side streets down to the Seine and walked out on the Pont Neuf. The swift currents below swirled in rolling motion. How many troubled souls had stared at these waters, as well? Why did contemplating its roiling action provide a healing balm? Somewhere in one of Jung's books, he had written: "it is better to go forward with the stream of time than to go backwards." It was one of those rare statements I had tucked away in my mental reservoir for onerous times. Now it floated up to mend me.

"You're not going to jump, are you?" asked a voice behind me.

I turned about. It was the Viet Cong propagandist, his pouch slung precariously over his left shoulder. He was smiling. He offered me his hand. I shook it and smiled in return. "Good day!" he chirped, as he resumed his walk, handing out leaflets to tourists and Frenchmen and anyone who would take them. After several minutes, he crossed the bridge and wandered out of sight.

I stared down at the river one more time. I recrossed the bridge for the long upgrade walk, past the Pantheon and past the park. On the way, however, I stopped, by a modest boutique and stared in its window. I still had no idea what to give Julene and Carl. Maybe I would buy some fresh flowers on the way to the wedding. That seemed like a good idea, so I crossed over to the park and returned to the pension.

Since dinner would not be served for a full hour, I slid out my book of Goethe's poems, which lay under my Pascal notes, and began searching for the poem the Gypsy had quoted. If it were in the collection, however, it was certainly eluding me. Finally I spotted it.

> Joyful, sorrowful, thoughtful, longing,
> suffering anguish with each breath,
> frolicking merrily to the heights of heaven
> to stumble sadly at the gates of death;
> happy alone is the soul that loves
> above all the rest.

Was that what the Gypsy was trying to say I would never find?

Prior to dinner, I walked down the hall to Christine's room. She was just coming out the door. "Well, shall we go down together?" she offered.

"Why not?"

"Don't look at me that way!" she smiled. "I've got a big exam tomorrow and a thesis due the next day."

"I've got plenty to do, too. I hope to complete my Pascal translations tonight and weave it all together by the end of next week. Plus, I'm attending a wedding Thursday. I wish I could bring you as a guest."

"Can't do it, ole boy! Remember, my thesis is due then."

"That's right."

"Ummm! You smell good. Been getting some coochie somewhere?"

"Not from any *mauvaises jeunesses*. I was by a boutique earlier."

"Wow! You must take me there some time."

As usual, we sat at our respective tables. Neither of us wished to attract any additional attention, other than what we had already aroused.

After dessert and a demitasse of coffee, I went back to my room to work on Pascal. If he had developed any overt program for coming to the truth, it had to be a psychological one founded on an ontological basis. I had determined that Pascal came to the truth from within. His passages in which he psychoanalyzed himself and humanity's failings constituted an inward approach. Descartes had followed a similar program. By looking within the self, or ones own being, or *ontos,* an enormous amount of information could be gleaned about the self and the world. With that as his own foundation, Pascal had dared to believe in a higher self that he could become, by committing his mind and heart to God. It was a "wager," as he called it. But he trivialized the wager by connecting it with gains that otherwise one might not have. Instead of making his leap toward truth based on his ontological discoveries, he wanted to associate them with rewards and punishments that awaited one in an afterlife. This sort of cheap epistemology undermined the very truths he had ascertained scientifically, or ontologically. Descartes before him had submitted everything to radical doubt, and only what could survive that doubt was worthy of belief. He had divided reality into two substances (thought and extension), which he conceived to be separate, when in reality thought is a mechanism of the brain, which is quite physical. Descartes and Pascal, each had offered a methodology within limits. But Pascal's sense of immediacy, of knowing directly the human condition, appealed to the very core of my existence.

> Man is but a reed, the most feeble thing in nature, but he is a thinking reed. The entire universe need not arm itself to crush him. A vapor, a drop of water suffices to kill him. But, if the universe were to crush him, man would still be more noble than that which killed him, because he knows that he dies and the advantage that the universe has over him; the universe knows nothing of this. . . .Thus, all of our dignity consists in thinking. By it we must elevate ourselves [347].

I was eager to draw my Pascal chapter to a close and move on to Rousseau.

10

On the way to the metro, I stopped by a flower shop to purchase a dozen white roses for Julene. I wasn't certain how soon after the wedding she and Carl planned to fly to Greece for their honeymoon. After all, they had been "honeymooning" for years. The trip to Greece would be more for Carl's benefit than Julene's. Julene could do with the flowers whatever she wished.

I came up from the metro at the Place de la Concorde, crossed two busy streets and made my way to the Embassy. A Marine in his bright blue, white, and red uniform stood sentinel at the gate. He smiled as I passed him with my roses, wrapped in crinkly tissue paper. I had pricked myself on a thorn, and a drop of red blood had stained the paper.

Finding the room posed no problem, as the Embassy had assigned a receptionist to direct guests. The girl appeared young, in her twenties, and wore a navy blue dress. Her blonde hair was clipped short, butchy, in fact, which detracted from her otherwise glowing femininity. Her eyes sparkled upon seeing the roses, and her mouth opened in a wide grin. "For me, no doubt?" she teased.

"No. But I'll bring you a dozen, if you wish."

She suppressed a smile and glanced, with obvious embarrassment, away. "No offense," I added, not wishing to implicate myself anymore than I had.

"Thanks, but I've got a great boyfriend. And that was a nice compliment. Just go through the doorway," she pointed. "You'll find the room on your right."

A small reception hall had been converted into a "wedding chapel" at the far end. I could see a white arch, showered with sprays of white and dainty yellow flowers. Julene was wearing a white, open-neck, sleeveless dress, with long gloves, white slippers, and a delicate raised veil that rested on her brow, allowing her shoulder-length black hair to complement her attire. Carl was dressed in a tuxedo and black bowtie.

To my delight, M. and Mme. Gibert were present. Monique wore a stunning strapless short garnet gown. A double strand of pearls decorated her throat. Her curly black hair, streaked with platinum threads, made her the equal of Julene in beauty. Her face lit up with a smile when she saw me.

Other guests were also in attendance. I had no idea who they were. I walked up to Julene and handed her the flowers. "They're gorgeous," she blushed, giving them to Mme. Gibert to hold for her. I shook Carl's hand and kissed Julene on the cheek. "Best wishes and congratulations."

"Aren't you a little bit premature," Carl muttered. "We've not tied the knot yet."

I ignored his comment and turned to shake Gibert's hand, then Monique's. "Enchanted, once again," I said.

"I'm so pleased you've signed on for the Fontainebleau tour," she replied. "Let's talk some after the wedding."

"Certainly. Thanks."

A baldheaded official looking gentleman, somewhere in his fifties, entered the room and approached the small party. "Good morning, everyone!" he greeted the group with robust cheerfulness. "Is everyone ready?"

"Yes!" came a chorus of replies.

He walked toward the arch, stood under it, and Julene and Carl faced him. I stood beside the Giberts. Carl took Julene's hands in his own.

To my surprise, the entire service lasted only seven minutes. The officiate's introduction was simple and brief. "We are assembled here, friends and guests, to join in matrimony Julene and Carl Sullivan. Marriage is a special relationship, uniting two separate hearts in one, forming a unique bond for life. It is to be held in honor by all. This wonderful couple, in particular, is worthy of all our hope and encouragement.

"Carl, do you take Julene to be your lawfully wedded wife, to have and to hold, in plenty and in want, in sickness and in health, in joy and in sorrow, from this time forward, as long as you both shall live?"

Carl looked at Julene. For a moment, a distant stare came over his face; suddenly his eyes softened, and he answered with profound tenderness, "I do!"

"Julene, do you take Carl to be your lawfully wedded husband, to have and to hold, in plenty and in want, in sickness and in health, in joy and in sorrow, from this time forward, as long as you both shall live?"

"Yes! Of course!" she blurted, to the pleasant laughter of the party.

"Are there tokens to be shared to solemnize this union?"

"Yes," said Carl. He handed the official two rings.

The officiate returned Julene's ring to Carl. "Repeat after me. 'With this ring, I thee wed and promise thee my love and faithfulness.'"

Carl repeated the words, and slipped the band on Julene's finger.

A similar exchange occurred between Julene and Carl. She had to force the ring over his thick finger. Once again, the guests laughed politely.

"By the authority granted to me by the State Department of the United States of America, I pronounce you husband and wife. Carl, you may kiss your bride."

Carl put his left arm around Julene's waist, drew her up against his chest, and kissed her affectionately on the mouth. She held to his neck with her right arm and kissed his lips in turn.

Everyone applauded. Monique handed Julene her white roses. The bride glanced toward me. Her lips parted slightly, as if there were so much she wanted to say. I smiled and, leaning forward, kissed her cheek.

"Ah, darling," cooed Mme. Gibert. "I wish you both all the happiness in the world. You are so young and beautiful, Julene. I should use you as a model on my page."

"A grand idea!" concurred Monsieur Gibert. "Yes, my little one, you are stunning." He, too, stepped forward to congratulate Carl and kiss Julene's cheek.

Other guests came forward to congratulate the couple. I stepped aside to watch.

"What are you doing tomorrow? or next Tuesday?" Mme. Gibert asked.

"Oh, nothing that can't wait."

"Have you seen the Chagall exhibit? It won't be open much longer."

"No, I haven't, though I've read about it."

"You must see it. It is absolutely extraordinary. Will you come as my guest?"

"I'd be honored. Which day would you prefer?"

"Let's say, Tuesday. Fridays are always so rushed."

"Where should I meet you?"

"Why not simply in front of the hall? You know how to find it, don't you?"

"Yes. I've actually walked by it several times, but never stopped to go in."

"Well, confirmed. Next Tuesday, say, at 2 p.m.? *D'accord*?"

"*Oui!* Tuesday, at two."

Following a modest reception of cakes and champagne at the hall, attended by both the guests and a smattering of smiling Embassy personnel, our party of five—Julene, Carl, the Giberts and myself, were escorted by limousine to a fashionable restaurant-café along the Ave. de l'Opéra. It's interior struck a patron immediately with its domed pink ceiling and pink and white paneled walls. Marble statutes of Greek and Roman figures adorned concave recesses. Their presence added a celestial grace to the already elegant semi-circular room. The tables were set with fine china, porcelan cups, crystal wine glasses, silver place settings, and napkins to match the pink and white table cloths that were so long and wide that they touched the floor.

A proud waiter seated us and politely attended to our every need. The Giberts had arranged for the luncheon, and, as soon as we took our seats, the parade of Parisian fare began. It opened with a delicate asparagus soup garnished with grated cheese and chives. Next, we were served a crisp salad of endive bathed in a melon dressing. The main entrée consisted of a filet of carp smothered in Serbian cream sauce and peppercorns, and *pomme de terre au gratin*. Cheeses and a dessert of creme brulé completed the meal, along with coffee.

While enjoying this marvelous repast, our conversation ran the gamut of interests.

"Will you be taking *une voyage de noces*?" Madame Gibert asked in French.

"Yes," Julene replied. "To Greece, Troy, and Crete."

"How exotic."

"How long will you be gone?" inquired the Monsieur. "I want to explore the possibility of the Professeur translating my forthcoming book into English."

"How embarrassing!" moaned his wife. "Always and ever thinking only of himself."

"Well, Carl is no shrinking violet, himself. He's probably hoping the Monsieur here will do the same for him," Julene intimated.

"Yes, I'm an inveterate philodox," Carl said gruffly. "You can't be modest or bashful in my field and succeed."

"Maybe that's why my poor *The Ethics of Virtue* never had a chance," I smiled. "Of course, it could also be that it was too hastily written and still reads like a dissertation," I volunteered.

"Ah, ethics!" Gibert uttered with jocular sarcasm. "I venture we French have abandoned such a noble quest for more pragmatic solutions. Today, honor, of necessity, is inseparable from a nation's aspirations."

"Please, darling, don't promote your views here. A toast to our nuptial friends! *Viva le mariage et la vie conjugale!*"

"Yes!" I repeated. I raised my wine glass with her. "To the conjugal life! And all its joys!"

"By the way," began Carl, "when is your book due?" he asked Gibert.

"Any time now. It's at the printers and should be out soon. If you're back in time, you'll have to attend a party I plan to throw to celebrate *Le Futur d'un Grandeur Passé*."

"I wouldn't want to miss it," Carl said, lowering his voice. "But as soon as we return, we'll need to pack up for the flight back to the States."

"Hopefully, not that fast," Julene corrected him. "There's two of us now, you know?"

"Sugar, I know. But, reality, my dear. Reality! The sabbatical's coming to a close. Plus, we've been gone seven months now from Sullivan's Landing. We have to go home."

"Yes. I miss it, too."

As our party broke up, Monique slipped a note in my hand. It was a reminder of our "date" for Tuesday. Her actual word was "*rendezvous*." She smiled as she gave it to me.

The limousine was still waiting for Carl and Julene. We walked out with them to the car. Julene was carrying the roses and sniffing their faint fragrance. Suddenly she turned and gave them to me. "Please, take them to whomever at your pension. I hate to see them die and wilt unseen." She gave me a tight hug and kissed my neck with her lips.

"*Au'voir*!" we waved, as she and Carl were driven away.

"Till a later time!" I greeted the Giberts, shaking their hands according to polite French etiquette. "Thank you for including me."

"Don't give it further thought. *Et Bonjour*!" Gibert waved, as I clutched the roses and began walking toward the nearest metro stop.

After the ride to the Montparnasse station, I carried my roses to a nearby bon marché and purchased six plastic, inexpensive rose tubes and returned to my room before the flowers could droop anymore. Within twenty minutes or so, I had arranged the roses in the tubes, two per fluted vase, and set one at Christine's door, then climbed the stairs to the servants' attic. I left one at the door of the poor nameless cook, one at Mme. Cueillier's door and, was about to set one at Charlene's door, when she suddenly opened it. She was clad only in her panties and a sagging brassiere. Her freckled legs bristled with unshaven body hair. Bushy black hairs poked out under her arm pits. "Oh, *bon Dieu*!" she put her hands across her chest. "I wondered who was on the hall! Oh, they're beautiful! For me?" she implored with her dark eyes.

"Yes. They were left over from a wedding, and I wanted to bring a vase for each of you."

"I don't know what to say. No one has ever brought me roses!" Tears came to her eyes. She accepted the vase, hardly noticing that in doing so, she exposed her breasts. They formed beautiful rounded bulges over her tattered brassiere. "Won't you come in?"

"I would love to," I said, "but I've got several more vases to deliver."

"Please, do come back. You are such a nice man."

I couldn't help but stare down at her body. Not that nice, I thought. Being involved with Christine, and nursing a secret crush on Monique, exacted all the psychic and erotic energy I had. I had to turn out more pages on my project, or I would never finish it.

She smiled expansively, adjusted her brassiere, and closed the door slowly.

I carried the remaining two vases to the second floor.

"Ohhh! What is our lover up to, now? Has he ditched his English girl for Mme. Dufavre?" Mme. Angleterre sang out upon seeing me. "You can't get past me without paying a toll." She hurried out of her tiny bureau to sniff the roses. "Ohh, so divine!"

I scrutinized the two vases and, selecting the fresher of the roses, handed those to her. "*Pour vous, Madame!*" I said, with a courtly bow. "They are yours."

"You charming devil. I accept them," she smiled with a cute curtsey. "Why don't you let me have the other two? The Madame," she nodded toward Dufavre's apartment, "will never miss them," she whispered.

"You are a sly one. Besides, it would only get you in trouble."

"*Oui*. But only if she found out." She bustled back to her office and set the flowers near an opened pack of cigarettes.

I entered the foyer to the dining room, crossed it, and knocked on Dufavre's door.

I could hear a movement of some kind in her room. She came to the door and barely cracked it open. "*Professeur*!" she said, somewhat startled. "I'm not really prepared to receive company." A red towel was wrapped about her hair. Dark strands, in the process of being transformed into blonde streaks, poked out from under it. She glanced nervously over her shoulder. "There is something I need to discuss with you, however," she confided.

"I wanted to bring you these fresh roses," I handed the vase to her. "They were left over from a wedding. The bride wanted to share them."

"How thoughtful!" She opened the door just wide enough to receive the vase and took the flowers in her large hands. "*Merci, Monsieur*!"

"Not at all!"

Just prior to dinner, Christine came by the room. She was clutching her vase in both hands. "How wonderful of you! How I needed a little cheering up! I passed that exam and will complete the thesis tonight. They are beautiful. They are from you?"

"Yes. Remember that wedding I told you about? The bride gave the roses back to me to distribute as I saw fit."

"'Distribute!' How many did she give you?"

"A dozen."

"And you only gave me two? And after all I've given you? What a thankless bore! No English chap would be so cheap!" She stared at the flowers, sniffed them, inhaled their fragrance, then asked: "What shameless wenches got the rest?"

"Dufavre, Angleterre, Cueillier, the dishwasher, and the cook."

"Not so stupid, ole boy, are you?" she retorted with a sheepish expression. "On those conditions, I'd rather say I'm lucky."

"You know you're number one, *uno*, anterior."

"'Anterior?' I've been called a lot of things, but never 'anterior!' I would say it's more like 'posterior' with you," she smiled.

"Tomorrow night? Anterior or posterior?"

"I've not had a better offer. Sounds keen to me."

"I'll check with you after dinner. There're some nice bistros off Montparnasse, *sans* Gypsies."

"Heavens! Don't remind me of that!" she uttered, looking at the palm of her left hand. "Well, I'm taking these down to my table. Are you coming soon?"

"Yes. I'll be down in a few minutes. I want to finish a sentence I'm translating from Pascal."

"Why not just stick with Shakespeare and his Sonnets? Or Elizabeth Barrett Browning? '*How do I love thee, let me count the ways.*'"

"I can do better than that, sweet English girl:

> Had we but world enough and time,
> This coyness, lady, were no crime.
> We would sit down, and think which way
> To walk, and pass our long love's day. . . .
> An hundred years should go to praise
> Thine eyes and on thy forehead gaze,
> Two hundred to adore each breast ,
> But thirty thousand to the rest.

"Me thinks thee, lad, art but a knave." Her lips parted in a lusty smile. "Until tomorrow." She leaned against my chest and kissed me. "Ummmm! 'Two hundred to adore each breast!' Is that all you think about?"

"All the time! I am the last American romantic."

"Thank God!"

Christine balanced the tube of roses in her right palm as she walked down the hall. I closed the door and returned to my desk. I found the sentence I wanted to complete:

> Acknowledge, then, proud man, what a paradox you are to yourself. Humble yourself, feeble reason; be silent, foolish nature; learn that man infinitely transcends himself. . . .[434].

After dinner, I took a brief walk about the Garden. Beds of tulips had bloomed. Their red, white, yellow, and blue bowls teetered sideways on their emerald stems and created a pageantry all their own. *Be silent foolish nature.* Why had Pascal taken such a scornful view of nature. He did not believe that one could reason ones way to the Eternal through nature. Nature only reduces man; it makes him sense his inadequacies, not his strengths. Over against the infinity of the universe, what was man? Nothing. Forced to acknowledge his miserable status, man was shocked to discover that, nonetheless, he was greater than the universe in which he lived, for without intellection, as Pascal reasoned, the universe still remained unaware of its infinity or man of his human misery. It was this *misery* for him that made man great, that gave him a *grandeur* that the universe could never know. And it was this *grandeur* that self-analysis had opened to man, which in turn became the epistemological basis for his seeking a way out. Nature could not provide this *via redemptio.* Only a heart hungry for the truth could find it, and then, not of itself.

As I walked along, I realized that therein lay the genius behind Sullivan's own studies. He was after far more than the mere history of the Minoans, or the ostensible facts behind the Homeric era and its gods. His quest for Being and its underlying structures not only motivated, but directed, his entire work. He had acknowledged as much in his Introduction, which fascinated me all the more. He was like a modern Pascal, coming from a different direction.

But I was too wed to Nature, to Mother Earth and Father Sky, to betray my trust in either. Growing up on the farm had made that impossible. Pascal was right, but only partly right. Sullivan was squarely on target to probe behind his Greek myths in the hope of discovering the dawn of our human awakening. But would his ties to the land moderate his approach? Perhaps that was what his new book, *Beyond Homer*, would resolve. But I knew his first book too well. He was too wed to Homer ever to go beyond him.

Before I realized it, I was standing by the hexagonal basin, alone. I say alone. A few stragglers passed now and then, but darkness was creeping into the park, claiming it for its own domain, spreading its long shadows in somnolent waves. A rouge dusk shimmered in the sky. Soon the park would be locked. It was time to leave, to go back to the pension, to read, and to sleep.

11

Dawn came with a clap of thunder. Sheets of rain pelted the windows. Horns blew as tires skidded along wet pavement. I pulled back the curtains and stared out. It would be a good day to stay in.

Following a breakfast of fresh baguettes, marmalade, and *café au lait,* I returned to my room to study. The gloomy ambience about my desk made it difficult to settle down. The single, overhead light bulb scarcely illuminated the room. A desk lamp cast its mellow beam of amber across my books and writing pads. It all combined to create a depressing mood. As the depression deepened and moved within, I donned my raincoat, pulled on my cap, turned off the lights, and fled the pension.

I took a narrow street that angled away from the boarding house and up toward the Rue D'Assan. The rain fell in cold streams, soaking my shoes. It ran down the sides of the buildings like seeping mountain springs. As I hunched my shoulders and tucked my face under my cap, I passed an open doorway between two buildings. I stopped and peered within. A dreary, tight passageway appeared to wiggle its way back between the two structures. The odor of rank, damp debris, and possibly dead rats, hovered about its walls. I checked the lock on the door. It was missing. I pushed the door fully open, wedged my way past the entrance, and began to explore the passageway. Drafts of cold air rose upward, but only sprinkles of rain now reached me. Beggars' rags and cardboard boxes posed occasional barriers, but soon I found myself in the narrow alley behind the pension's hidden side and beneath its dark windows. I looked up toward the top floors. Grilled, musty, and rusting balconies commenced on the third floor and continued to the attic. There were no windows on the second floor, and the two I counted on the ground floor had been bricked in long ago. The building was without a rear entrance. I couldn't detect a single door. I couldn't imagine how anyone might scale the wall, but an agile person might come down from the atelier, or somehow jump from balcony to balcony. Still, the balconies appeared to be too rusted to bear any weight. In the fine drizzle, a sparkling object caught my eye. I bent down and picked it up. It was a small gold ring, more of a trinket than a piece of jewelry. I slipped it in my pocket. Surely I would need to report what I had found to Dufavre.

Back out on the Rue D'Assan, I entered a small café for coffee. Its walls were as dark and dank as the passageway's. City workers in their heavy blue denims crowded the counter and, in between puffs on their cigarettes, drank wine. One man in a brown tee-shirt had deep red stains under his armpits. Was that from the wine? I would have to ask Angleterre.

The heaviest part of the storm had moved on, but rain still fell. It poured continually off the café's awning and splattered onto the sidewalk's paved stones. Then it gurgled loudly into the gutter. After a second cup, I resumed my walk. A steady, cold drizzle forced me to keep my head down, but the cooler air revived my tenacity. I passed an old woman and an old man, huddled together in a door way. Their hands were wet, gnarled, and wrinkled. I thought about the old woman I had tried to help and wondered where she was. Such poverty was not unknown to Pascal, but it lay outside his definition of "misery," which was of a different kind, a fundamental kind, that plagues humanity universally. But here was "misery," nonetheless, just as human and just as debilitating. I turned about and, with a heavy heart, made my way back to the pension. Rather than working any more on Pascal, I decided I would reread something in Sullivan's book. I flipped through the chapters and stared down at his segment on Athena.

> Who was Pallas Athena? What does her name mean? Was the city of Athens named for her, or was she named for the city? The answer to these questions, historically, may make no difference, but in every other way, they do. Nevertheless, an examination of the historical confronts us with ample intrigue.
>
> If we begin with the Near Eastern Canaanite god and goddess, *ba-al* and *Anath*, lord and mistress of the land, many mysteries fall into place and lend themselves to be resolved. Ba-al was the son of El and Asherah. He was also the god of thunder and lightning, like Zeus, and lord of the falling rain that inseminated the soil. Anath, his sister, was the passive earth in its capacity to receive her lover-brother's seed and thus impregnated by his semen provide grain. They were worshipped on many high places, amidst stands of the

cedars of Lebanon. The Israelites, themselves, succumbed to the spell of this powerful fertility cult, as witnessed in Psalm 29:

> *The voice of the Lord breaks the cedars. . . .*
> *The voice of the Lord flashes forth flames of fire [vss. 5, 7].*

This worldview, in its attempt to account for the phenomenon of the earth's fertility, was widely popular in various forms across the Near East and regions of the Hittite Empire that looked out across the Bosporus Straits. Might not this factor solve many problems? Take the name "Pallas." Might it not be a corruption of the Canaanite "ba-al?" And "Athena." Might her name not also be a Hellenic version of "Anath?" Athena is credited with being able to hurl thunderbolts as effectively as Zeus; she is also the mother of Greek horticulture and the creatrix of the olive tree. In her, Attic folklore combined both her brother ba-al and ancient Anath to serve their own needs. And where was this mother-father goddess worshipped? On the high place of the rocky citadel, Athens, named for the goddess, rather than the goddess named for the city. Or so I propose.

To this marvelous, proto-historical, metaphysical view, the brooding Greeks would add still another feature—the idea of "wisdom." Sprung from the head of Zeus, without the mediation of a mother's womb, Athena also represented "wisdom." She was the premier virgin queen of a wisdom that was both cunning and statesman-like, a gift essential to the transformation of a wandering band of pastoral raiders into the founders of a city state. She united for them their necessity for vigilance and strength—thus her depiction as a goddess with helmet, spear, and shield; as well as her gift of farming skills, represented by the olive branch, held in her hand. It is this gift of "wisdom" that in time would nudge the Greeks toward their love for *logos*, the word, speech, in song and legend, and eventually in the flowering of philosophy and its quest for principles and meaning.

I let his book collapse in my lap. I knew of no other scholar whose account of Pallas Athena was as penetrating or as tantalizing as Sullivan's. But where did all this acumen lead? How did it solve the riddle of Being? I could tell that the answer eluded Carl's grasp, as much as it had Descartes and Pascal's. Nevertheless, I was thrilled at the thought of Sullivan's analysis of what might have been true, and I found inspiration in his work. Ironically, however, it seemed to lead nowhere, as all his research merely adumbrated his love for Homer and his mythic era.Toward noon, I walked downstairs to search for Mme. Dufavre, if she were about. Her door was open, and the man I thought I had seen earlier was sitting in a spacious green armchair in her room. He noticed me and motioned for me to come in. “Please, Monsieur, *entrez-vous*; please do come in.”

Mme. Dufavre stood beside him. A worried expression filled her face; her large jaw seemed to droop, along with her shoulders. “Yes, *Professeur*, we need to talk to you.”

I entered her room, which was crowded with furnishings from different eras--from a Louis XVI gold and white table to an inverted pink plastic tub, on which she, or the stranger, had been standing apparently to change a light bulb. “Yes, you mentioned yesterday you had something to ask me.”

She closed the door. “I know you think this is highly irregular,” she motioned with her hand to the stranger, “but Monsieur Orgemont is my cousin. Daniel is a detective with our arrondissement’s préfecture. He has been investigating the murder across the street and thinks the murderer hides in the pension, but, where, we do not know.”

“Yes, Monsieur,” her cousin spoke up. He was of slender frame and gray eyes. He seemed swallowed in a dark tan suit that was entirely too large for him. I could have placed two fingers between his neck and shirt collar; his black shoes hadn’t seen polish in months. “If you see or hear anything unusual, please let us know.”

“Are you familiar with the alleyway that runs behind the pension?”

“*Bien oui*! I have searched it, but found nothing. How do you know about it?”

“I happened to stumble upon it this morning. I found this,” I showed him the ring.

A huge smile broke suddenly around the corners of his mouth. “I left that there, hoping the thief would come back. I’ve been watching the alleyway for several nights, but the rain drove me in this morning. May I have the ring back?”

“Certainly,” I said, handing it to him. “Do you have any leads?”

“*Oui*, but for your own safety, I think I need to keep them to myself. But you, Monsieur *Professeur*, you are not a suspect.”

“You will keep this to yourself,” Mme. Dufavre addressed me. “Mme. Angleterre must not know. She thinks Daniel, here, is my boyfriend. So much the better,” she said, without smiling.

“Very well. I’ll keep you apprised of anything unusual I hear or see.”

I shook hands with Monsieur Orgemont, and then with Dufavre. Her hand seemed exceptionally cold and limp. I wondered just how much of all this I should believe. Were they hiding something and using me to allay further anxiety?

Dufavre opened the door, and I left her apartment.

It was still raining. From my windows, I watched the raindrops run down the windowpanes. I read some in Rousseau. About twenty minutes later, I lay down to catch a nap. My eyelids grew heavy. My world became gray and still.

She is holding my hand and walking behind me. Darkness hovers about the trail, just where it bends through the dense forest. Hemlocks and poplars border the path. Suddenly, we approach a steep incline and struggle uphill. Deer scatter before us and disappear into the dark woods. Then I see their eyes, glowing bright as embers, swinging like lamps back and forth, low and near the ground. They are wolves, weaving in slow motion, coming closer and closer toward us. "Don't be afraid," I tell her. "They don't harm humans." She grips my hand; her eyes dart back and forth, as she cleaves to me. Her heart beats as loudly as my own. The two have become one. Yet her eyes are filled with trust. "They aren't supposed to come this close," my mind objects. I can see their black fur, paws, nose, teeth, and ears. Their weaving ring tightens about us. I cannot count their number; reserves with blazing green eyes slink back far into the woods. Suddenly, a young calf stumbles onto the trail below us. Where has it come from? Why now? The pack withdraws, their eerie howls echoing in the fading light. She runs her hands across my chest. My mouth searches for her lips. Her lips press against mine. She is gone. I stand alone, all alone, in the darkness, in the forest. A terrifying moan is rising from somewhere, from a depth too horrible to imagine or approach. I awake, covered with sweat, clinging to a pillowslip. My throat is dry and empty, as well as my heart.

That was not the first time I had experienced that dream, or nightmare. It was the first time, however, that wolves had appeared. I rose and went to the windows. Rain fell in a steady course, running slowly down the windowpanes. Reading Rousseau was the last thing I wanted to do. Rain or no rain, I pulled on my coat and descended the stairs for another walk.

The park was practically empty; water ran in trickling streams along the sandy aisles. Pigeons squatted miserably; a few cocked their heads as I passed, hoping up for a handout. A beggar, on a nearby bench, sat hunched under a soggy newspaper. "Please, Monsieur!" he held out his right hand. "Anything, please!" I searched my change purse and offered him three francs. They were shiny and new. He searched my face, as if pleading for more. I gave him another two, five francs in all. Enough to buy a cup of coffee and croissant, or a glass of wine and morsel of bread. Who was I to dictate which? "*Merci*," he choked back his self-pity and fear. I took the paths toward the St. Sulpice. Shiny puddles slopped under my shoes in the rain. I found a cozy café along the Boulevard Raspail, shook the rain off my dripping coat, found a seat, and sat down. For a long while I hunched over a *café noir*, before stirring in two lumps of sugar. Moments later, I began to drink it slowly: grounds, froth and all. I don't remember how long I sat there. I wondered how Julene was doing, to what purpose my studies would lead, and when I should return home. I loved this city. I could wander its streets forever, never settling a single resolve. What a commentary for a professor of philosophy! We were supposed to pursue the truth and criticize those who thought they had found it. But what was the truth? And didn't the method of our search determine the truth we found? If you look for it in religion, you will find it there, or the same with science, art, anthropology, culture, or myth. I wanted more, but I knew in my heart I would have to settle for something less. But I wanted that "less" to be worth my effort, to fulfill me as best it could. I ordered a beer and drank it, a second and all but finished it save for a few sips in the bottom of the glass. I struggled back into my coat, pulled my cap down over my brow, and returned to the pension.

During dinner, I watched Christine take her seat. I felt strangely aloof, my thoughts thousands of miles away. I don't recall saying anything to Pierre or Gaston, though I assume I did. Mme. Cueillier thanked me again for her flowers. She had snipped one and pinned it on the left strap of her white apron. "You are too kind," she smiled.

With the repast concluded, I went up to Christine's room and knocked on her door.

"Are you all right?" she asked me with a puzzled look in her face. "I spoke to you in the dining hall, and all you did was stare." She put her hand to my forehead. "Are you running a fever, ole boy? Are you *malade*?"

"No. I don't think so. I just feel strange. Melancholy. Sad. I can't quite shake it."

"Would you rather not go out?"

"Oh, no! I think it'd do me good. I might be worthless, but I need your company. Maybe we can talk."

"About more than sex? You really must be ill," she laughed. "But no fever," she removed her hand. "Where to?"

"Let's try something along the Boulevard Raspail, be daring and different."

"Like a noisy disco? or strip club?"

"You know better than that. Just a quiet place for wine and beer. Nothing more. Incidentally, how did your thesis go?"

"I had to read it to the class. They liked my accent. I wrote it about my father, instead of what we were supposed to. The instructor liked it, too. She could identify with the Blitz, my mother's death, my having to grow up with my father, and then my aunt."

"I feel better already. Let's go."

We barely made it to the Boulevard before we were caught in another cloudburst. Rain swept along the streets and past the buildings. It clattered like hail against the closed shutters and drenched our legs.

The little café we entered consisted mainly of a narrow hallway that had been converted into a bar, with tables for two in front of the stools and counter. A large mirror behind the bar had long lost its silver backing. Racks of wine and bottles of *apéritifs* cluttered the long shelf under the mirror. Smoke drifted in the air. The night chill settled about the table. I could see my breath. "Is it this cold in April in London?" I asked.

"Colder, old chap!" Christine answered. "It's perfect snuggling weather. But, first, why not unwind, and tell me about your *tristesse*. I'm a good listener, you know."

We ordered wine, and I began. "Some time ago, I fell in love with a beautiful young woman. Her husband was the provost of a small university where we taught. It was one hell of an affair! I loved her with a passion that wouldn't subside. I was confident we would marry. That she would be my wife for the rest of my life. How I wanted her! How I hated being separated from her! She was all I thought about, day and night. Whether lecturing or preparing lectures, she was constantly before my mind. I craved her presence, longed for her every moment, was mesmerized by her glance, her hair, her small but upturned breasts, her smile, her little nose, her graceful legs, and crooked toes. I thought it would never end, that she would love me all my life, that somehow we could make it work, that whatever happened, she'd be there. But somehow her husband found out. I knew it was inevitable. He gave her a choice. It was either him or me. Either way, I had to go. That night when she came by my apartment, she returned all the little love notes we had written, all the little pins and cards I had bought her, everything! 'Here,' was all she said. 'Don't blame it on me. You're the one who pushed it.'"

"That was all?"

"That was all. She turned and walked away. The provost cancelled my contract for the next term. I was out, on my own. But my dissertation had been published, and my resume was snapped up soon enough. Think of it? *The Ethics of Virtue*? That was the title of my book, and there I was, neither ethical nor virtuous."

"Nor was she. You can't assume the total blame, nor need to." Christine leaned across the tiny table and kissed my lips. Hers were wet and shimmering with wine. Her fingertips played with the corners of my mouth. "She's the loser, ole boy. Not you. She was stupid. You both were. You know that, don't you."

"Yes. But knowing it and forgetting it are two different things." I held her hands. How warm they felt! How self-giving and nonjudgmental! "You are a good listener, aren't you?"

"I told you so."

"I almost forgot. Guess what I discovered today? Actually, I had two discoveries."

"I'm all ears. What happened?"

"I discovered a narrow passageway that leads back to the alley under your window."

"You're putting me on!"

"Not at all! I was taking a walk this morning when I found it between two buildings, ours and the one next to us. I could look right up to your balcony and the one beneath yours, where that French woman and her daughter lives."

"You mean Gloria and Francine."

"Yes, if that's their names. But, better than that, a second revelation, ole girl! A real teaser."

"Well?"

"The mystery man in Dufavre's apartment is her cousin, an inspector with the Paris police. They motioned for me to come in and gave me an update on the murder and attempted robbery in Gloria's room."

"And?"

"He has suspects, but wouldn't divulge any names or anything more. You and I aren't supposed to know, but if you hear anything strange, or seen anything unusual, tell me, and I'll report it to Dufavre."

"I wonder who it could be? Do they think it's one of the boarders? Do they suspect me?"

"No! But they're not sure. It could be anyone, someone from outside, someone using the pension, hiding up in the attic, or who knows where?"

"You've got me creepy, now. I'll be afraid to open the curtains, or peer in my armoire, or unlock the door."

"You'll be fine. Whoever it is, they'll catch him in time."

A violent shiver shook her body. "You and your optimism. I think you're just setting me up for tonight," she smiled. "You think it's some kind of game."

"No, not at all. It's just got my curiosity up."

We drank several more glasses of wine. Finally we left for the pension. It rained on us all the way. We ran the last few blocks. We stripped down in her room, rubbed each other dry, and climbed into bed.

"Don't talk about love," she said. "Don't talk about anything. Just come here."

We wrapped our arms around each other, snuggled down into one another's soft embrace, and made love.

12

THAT WEEKEND, CHRISTINE WANTED me to visit Versailles with her and one of her friends: a classmate at the *Institut*. But I had been to Versailles many times, and as much as I was captivated by its grandeur, gardens, history, and art, six visits since my arrival in January seemed sufficient. I did, however, love its battle gallery and that powerful series of paintings depicting the rise of France: from the fierce Battle of Poitiers against the Moors, to Jean-Jacques David's colorful, colossal, and grandiose portrayal of Napoleon's coronation. How impish the Corsican looks in that painting! Yet, they appealed to every pore of my imagination.

Instead, that Sunday, I took the metro to le gare du Nord, and, thence, a bus to Senlis. I had toured Senlis in the late '50s and had fallen in love with its medieval towers and vast forest. Hemingway had referred to the latter in one of his novel's, either *The Sun Also Rises*, or perhaps, in his *Moveable Feast*. Whichever, I wanted to visit it again.

The ride took about an hour, past Paris's sprawling suburbs, and into the verdant countryside. A cold front had moved across northern France, clearing the sky of clouds and rain and bathing the meadows and orchards in brilliant sunshine. I could have been in America again, except for the beet fields and vineyards. The bus pulled into to the town's quaint station of rose-red bricks and terra-cotta roofing, and soon I was on my way into the heart of the medieval quarter.

It was hard to imagine that as far back as the third century, a Roman town of Gallo and Italian culture had existed here. Kings from Clovis to Louis XIV and from Charlemagne onward had passed through it, or hunted in its wild and bountiful woods. Joan of Arc, in her proud hour, had rested here. And Marshal Foch, as he rushed from Paris, had assembled his troops in its nearby fields to defend the honor of France. It was a quiet history book in the making, preserved in weathered walls and Roman ramparts, cobblestone streets and ancient masonry, with a cathedral that dated to 1153.

I walked along its narrow streets and ornate doorways, passed watch towers that still guarded the perimeter of the city. The trochal echo of wooden carts rumbled softly, as their vendors pushed them by. Toward the center of town, I stared up at the cathedral's spire. I strolled about its courtyards, visited its statues to Mary, and read the memorials to Jean d'Arc and Marshal Foch. I stepped inside, through its flamboyant portal, and sat down on a bench. Light streamed though its stained glass windows in long shafts of dusty yellow and solemn gray hues.

For lunch, I splurged at a rustic auberge—an old inn with rough stone walls and heavy pine or oak tables. I had a fillet of beef, sautéed in red wine, and garnished with a peppery sauce. A romaine salad and crepes of fromage and potatoes complemented the meal. I washed it down with a small bottle of *vin du Morac* and sopped up any remaining crumbs and gravy with a crusty wedge of bread. Later, after walking about in the forest, I enjoyed a glass of pilsner beer, which I drank at the bus station. When no one was looking, I lifted my glass in a silent toast to the saints of embattled Senlis, to its winding streets, and to its memories of *un age passé*. I wondered if Heloise and Abelard, or Anselm and Descartes, or Rousseau had ever wandered this way. Surely, Rousseau had!

Upon returning to the pension, I detected the faint scent of a pungent, cleansing agent lingering in the stairwell. Mme. Angleterre and Charlene were descending the steps above me. They were carrying pans and brooms, a bucket, dustpan, and sponges.

Charlene smiled when she saw me. "My favorite Monsieur!" she waved, with a sponge in her hand.

"Ahhoooff!" expelled Angleterre, with a disgusted nod of her head. "*Cochons. Riens des cochons!*" she muttered. "Those Japanese! They were living like pigs, like swine. But, pooof! They're gone!"

"What happened?"

"Ah! Their papa discovered they weren't studying. So, he yanked them home. They left this morning. Gone. *Tant pis*! *Tant mieux*! So much the better. Grease! It was everywhere! And this!" she waved a bottle that reeked of musk and foul odors. "Whale sperm!" she gagged! "Ahhh! *Merde alors*!"

"Such a lucky day!" I smiled. "What a nice tip!"

She grimaced and stuck out her tongue. Charlene glowed with a coy embarrassment, as they passed me on the stairs.

For dinner, Dufavre served a clear consommé, garnished with thin vegetable strips. Her main entrée was grilled veal, basted in a sweet and sour mustard spread, then salad and a raspberry yogurt for dessert. I felt surfeited after the fine luncheon in Senlis, and, now, a second sumptuous fete.

Christine had not returned, so I retired to my room and read several Baudelaire and Rilke poems. Both poets knew how to plunge their artistic epées into the dreamer's soul.

Baudelaire's "Le Voyage" went straight for the jugular.

> For the child, in love with maps and engravings,
> The universe is equal to his vast appetite.
> Ah! How grand is the world in the clarity of lamps!
> How small it appears in the eyes of memory!
>
> In the morning we depart, our mind full of fire,
> The heart overflowing with spite and desire,
> Following the rhythm of the swelling wave,
> With delusions of infinity on a finite sea.

I remembered Sullivan's request for repartee, upon completing his honeymoon. I would have to reread his chapters on Homer's *The Iliad* and *The Odyssey*; otherwise, my comments would be useless for wherever his thoughts might take us. But Baudelaire's poem had rendered my rested mind restless again. Why does our conscious brain, I wondered, so often seek a meaning beyond the fulfillment of the moment? Rilke and Baudelaire were right to put our existence to the question. But what I really needed was simply to experience the sights and sounds of daily life, freed from the necessity of overlaying them with the anguish of being. Oh, for an epistemology, for a way of finding the truth, that could set the human condition free, even with its "delusions of infinity on a finite sea!"

13

THAT MONDAY, I WAS quite surprised to receive an airmail letter postmarked from Athens. I knew it had to be from Julene or Carl. I opened the thin blue sheet with the blade of my pocket knife and unfolded the *aerogram* carefully. It was dated Friday, the day of their arrival in Greece. It was from Julene.

> *Dearest Clay: What a flight! We were grounded twice before getting here. One of the engines died as we approached the airport. Fire trucks met us on the runway! Lord! What a close one! Customs was even worse. They searched every tiny bag I had. Some dissident group had threatened to blow up one of the government buildings because of the prime minister's stance on Communism. As if I could care. Then the ride to our hotel! The cab driver took us for suckers, and drove us all over Athens. We wound up at Piraeus. "Sorry!" he grinned. "My mistake." Carl refused to pay him more than he thought the original ride should be. The driver threatened to call the police. The man reeked of cheap wine and garlic. His unbuttoned shirt was slick with grease. Carl said something to him in Greek. Suddenly the man grew ashen. He let loose with a string of obscenities. Carl has gotten fat, as we know, but, Lord, was I proud of him! He stepped up to the driver, doubled up his fist, and pulled on the man's ear. "Take this!" he shoved the money in his face. "And to hell with you! Call your police, and I'll accuse you of molesting my wife!" At that, Mr. Greaso turned even paler. He swore again, pushed Carl's hand away from his face, and accepted the money. Ohhhh, Honey! I wish you had been here! But that's not the worst. Carl couldn't function, after that. You know what I mean? It's our wedding night, or the one after it. He's depressed again. Tomorrow, we visit more sites: the Acropolis, museums, and, of course, the national library. Then, it's off for Turkey and Crete. I know I made the right decision, but will I always be unhappy? I've bought some paints and chalk and will bring you back some sketches. Love, Julene*

I placed her letter in the back of one of my folders, the one in which I was storing Pascal notes. There was no way to write her, or them, since I didn't have their itinerary. I stared down at my translation of Baudelaire's "Le Voyage." "Will I always be unhappy?" How could such an ebullient person, so gregarious and affable, become so dolorous in so few days! What did their future hold? What crime had they committed? Save a crime against nature? *Thou shalt not fall in love with thy niece, nor with thine uncle, nor any bearer of thy genetic code!* Had not sisters and brothers married before: in Hawaii, Spain, in Canaanite myths, and Neanderthal caves? Had not cousins married cousins of cousins' cousins, all over the world? Yes, but nature says *No, Jamais, Nein, Lo, Oux, Lookout, Mé.* Maybe the immortal lecherous gods of Greece and Rome could sport their nights away, but not their mortal playthings: those earthbound *anthropoi* who must die. It was time to read Rousseau.

By early-afternoon, I had pored over the Genevan's thought all I could endure for one day. I resolved to visit a part of Paris I rarely toured. Where would that be? The Marais, I decided: that quaint sector on the Right Bank, with its squalid streets of old, where from earliest times the Parisian code had exiled its prostitutes to live. André Malraux had attempted to restore it, but parts of the Marais were still seedy and dirty. I got off at the St. Paul metro station, but had scarcely enough time to visit the Place des Vosges. What in the world had I been thinking? It would take numerous jaunts to cover even half the *quartier*. I entered the ancient square through one of its many shaded arcades and sat on a bench under gracefully cropped plain trees, and admired the Royal Palace. Henri IV had begun the structure in 1605 and completed it about 1612. The houses that encircled the square were as elegant as any I had seen. They stood two stories tall, with alternate white stone and pink brick facades, constructed over ground-level arcades. Steep sheets of gray slate covered the roofs. Dormer windows looked out proudly onto the square below. The houses surrounded the entire square. Some of France's more venerable citizens had lived here—including Cardinal Richelieu, Hugo, and the artists Gautier and Daudet. After resting on the bench for half an hour or so, I walked up a nearby street and discovered a charming pastry shop, with enchanting wood carvings over its doors. I treated myself to an orange tea and chocolate tart. It was close to six o'clock when I returned to the pension.

New guests had moved into the room that the Japanese had vacated. I met them at dinner.

"We are from Poland," the husband said. "This is my wife, Anna. I'm Jacob Wetzel. As you can see, we are Jewish," the little man smiled.

"He always says that," his wife responded, "as if he were apologizing. We've been Jewish too long to have to do that. You must be an American?"

"Yes. It's not hard to tell, is it?"

"Your hair, the way you cut it, and big feet! It's hard to hide those," she said, her eyes flashing with spry humor.

They were an adorable couple, if one might use that word. He was squat, pudgy, short-limbed, with a red birthmark under his right ear. He wore glasses and gestured a great deal with his hands as he talked. Anna had dark eyes, gray hair, a long nose, but a beautiful smile. She was wearing a dark green dress, with a dainty silver six-pointed star on her lapel. Her husband wore a blue shirt, navy tie, a tweed-striped coat and dark trousers.

"How long do you plan to stay?" I asked.

"We have some family near Orléans. We plan to join them in a week or so," Anna explained.

"We were in Israel," Jacob said, "but it was too harsh for us, too new, too young. I missed Europe, my music—I'm a musician—and its culture. We lived in Warsaw and survived those horrible days." A faint scar was visible about his Adam's apple.

"He is too humble," Anna smiled. "'Musician?' He's a composer, but no one in Israel cared for his style. So, we come home, back to Europe. We can't go to Poland, so we come here. It's very good, I think."

"I think so."

"We're not really welcome anywhere," he uttered, with a droll frown. "Paris is no Mecca for Jews. But, where else can we go, anyway? Germany? Russia?"

"Now, stop that, Jakkob! Stop that, right now! We'll be fine. We still have many years ahead, a sister in London, and family in Orléans. That is enough!" The woman looked at me, as if she were still on trial, and I the prosecutor, jury, and judge.

I smiled, sought out my table, and sat down. From Medieval times, Jews had been persecuted in Paris. Hopefully, these wonderful souls would find respite now.

Christine came in and suddenly sat at my table. There were tears in her eyes. "I received a wire this morning. Tobby has been hurt in an accident. Rather seriously, it seems. It's from his mother. He wants to see me. Tommyrot and dammit all! Will you come by later?"

"Of course!" I reached across the table to clasp her hands, but she had already gotten up. She had left the dining room to go upstairs.

My hunger plummeted after that. I sipped on my soup—a potato potage—ran my fork under several morsels of pork, and munched on the salad. I drank a glass of wine and nibbled at a few flakes of cheese.

"Mme. Cueillier," I whispered, as she brought out dessert. "Will you fix a little tray of something for Mademoiselle Cunningham? A close friend of hers has been injured, and she didn't feel like eating."

"Oh, Professeur! *Mais oui*. I'll prepare it myself!"

I carried the tray to Christine's room. She let me in. "You shouldn't have done that," she simpered in a teary voice. "Come in."

I sat on the edge of her bed while she tasted the soup, swallowed a few spoonfuls, and drank some water.

"I don't think I'm going to go," Christine began. "He had his chance. I loved him. He betrayed me. I know his mother won't understand. But it's that clear in my mind." All this she said, without affect or emotion. "What do you think? Am I wrong?"

"No."

"Would you go back for Miss Beautiful? For Miss Little Tits?"

"Did I say they were little?"

"I don't remember." A rueful smile slipped across the edge of her mouth. "You like mine, don't you?"

"I'm glad you're feeling better. What a nice recovery!"

"Only because of you." She came over to the bed and sat beside me. "You're not such a bad oaf, you know. English girls like a bit of a rogue in a man. A bit of a roving lust in his eyes. We get it from our royal families. They're about as saintly as dogs in heat."

"Oh, my goodness! My Lady Cunningham! I didn't realize how classy you are. My apologies, mum!"

"Let's fuck!" She kissed my lips and pushed me back on the bed.

After our maddening frolic, I returned to my room, sat at my desk, and stared at the walls. I had never noticed how dark, tea yellow, grimy, and soiled they looked. After a while, I concluded that maybe the darkness was in me. *The Ethics of Virtue*! What a joke! And tomorrow, I'd be going off with Monique! At some point I had to recover whatever it was I had lost with Leeta. Yes, Leeta. I had suppressed her name for the past five years. I had incarcerated it in the loneliest cells of the heart's asylum, buried it in the deepest layers of subconsciousness and unconsciousness possible. I had condemned her to exile. But to what avail! Always, she came back. Always the Sphinx, always the Phoebe, rising from the cold ashes of desire. What was the riddle I would have to unravel to cause her to disappear? I knew the answer lay solely in me.

I went to the curtains, drew them aside, opened the windows, and looked out across the roof tops, toward Montparnasse. The street life of Paris rose audibly in muffled sounds, amid its lamp lights of evening's dreams and lovers' quarrels. Should I awaken Christine?

"Get up, sweet girl!" I knocked on her door. "Let's go for a walk."

"Shhhhh!" someone uttered in a neighboring room.

Christine came to the door. She was naked, except for her panties.

"Please come with me," I whispered. "I think I'm in love with you."

She brushed back her hair. An incredulous look seized her face. "Not so loud!" she nodded toward the room across the hall. "I'm too sleepy. Go back to bed! You're just hallucinating! 'In love!' What a time to tell me!"

I stood there, admiring her breasts and feeling like a fool. "Ok! If that's what you want."

She put her right hand around my neck, pulled me gently into her room, and kissed me. "Go back to bed!" she repeated. "I'll still be here tomorrow."

Yes, I thought. And I'll be traipsing around with Mme. Fashion and wondering what to do.

I returned to my room and went to bed.

14

I AWOKE, SHIVERING AND cold. I had pulled all but one of the blankets about my neck; my pink, bare feet protruded beyond the top sheet and stuck up, exposed. Light was streaming wildly into the room. The windows were wide open and the curtains still drawn back! I stared at my watch. It was past 7:30. I had never slept that late before.

After dressing, I strolled up the street to my Greek compatriot's kiosk. A black armband was pinned to his left upper arm.

"A death?" I nodded toward his arm.

"A memorial," he replied, sadly. "Two years ago to the day, I lost my beloved wife. 'May her memory be eternal!'" he quoted from the Orthodox Tresagion.

"Yes. Eternal is the memory of God." I had always found the theology of the Greek Orthodox Church beyond credulity, save for its credo of death. That somehow the eternal God of the universe should never forget a single soul he had created or loved seemed divinely appropriate. What happier an afterlife could one want? What greater fulfillment than always to be in the heart of God? But who could believe that, except a grieving heart?

"We came here from Greece together thirty years ago. From our little village near the sea, south of Athens itself. Ah, my learned man, my *anthropos sophos*, what more can be said? Yes, may her memory be eternal! But, ah!" he clapped his hands. "Look at the sky! It's actually blue! Imagine, a blue sky in Paris. The usual? *Oui*?"

"Yes, I guess so. And this baklava? How stale is it?"

"Ohhhhfffff! *Mon homme*! How can you say this thing? It is as fresh as my mother's milk. May her memory be eternal!" A huge smile parted his dark purple lips from ear to ear. "Just for you, two pieces." He handed me the sticky, honey-soaked wedges on a paper napkin, along with my coffee. He started to say something more.

"I know. Don't gulp it down. Just sip it."

"Ah, you have it! You make me joyful, even on this sad day."

I was humbled that he could laugh, buoyed by a faith and a memory that filled his heart with happiness.

I spent the remainder of the morning studying Rousseau, piecing together threads of his thought that reoccurred in his major works. Like Pascal and Descartes before him, Rousseau, too, had taken an ontological approach, but with an appreciation for "nature," as he defined it. That made his views quite different and considerably, if not irrefragably, more positive than anything Descartes or Pascal had imagined. His approach had made him far more optimistic and hopeful than Pascal, and much, much less dogmatic and rationalistic than Descartes. It forged him into someone wholesome, human, likeable; a child of Nature in its finest sense; someone approaching that human essence that Sullivan himself was seeking to recover before the Greeks had morphologized it into a myth.

By two o'clock, I was waiting outside the entrance to the Chagall exhibition center. I think I actually expected Mme. Gibert to be on time. I should have anticipated some delay, but it was 3:15 before she arrived.

"Oh, I am sorry! Just everything happens when you least expect it," she threw off her tardy appearance with a fetching smile. Rouge eye-shadow, with faint blushes of blue feathering tapering off in Egyptian style, gave her smooth skin a hieroglyphic quality. She had streaked her short red hair, which was beginning to curl again, with gold threads to complement her eye-shadow. She wore a tight black sweater, a long gold necklace, black petal pushers, and gold slippers. "You like it!" her face glowed. She turned about for me to admire her neck and back, along with her firm buttocks. She glanced over her shoulder with a look that would have seduced Diogenes. "It's the new look. Very *vache*!"

I couldn't help but smile, as *vache* was the latest hip slang for "cool," "chic," "in style," etc. It meant "cow," or "cow-like." How it got started was beyond me. "*Très enchantant*!" I mumbled. "Very seductive! Is that the new rave?"

"Always!" she swung back, her dark eyes playing games with my own. "Well! This exhibit 's on me. I have complimentary tickets," she held them up for me to see. "Of course, I'm expected to write a flattering review. *Bien sur*! But, I'm after more as well."

"How's that?"

"Fashion! Chagall's in vogue. His colors, fantasies, caps, frocks. That beret I had on when we met the Sullivans—remember?—is more Russian than French. Are you ready? Shall we go?"

"Yes. How nice of you to invite me."

"You intrigue me. You have, shall we say, a certain boyish magnetism about you. You know that, don't you? An innocence that needs to be matched by, say, a woman's maturity and guile."

"I'm not that innocent. And I doubt any magnetism. And, unfortunately, I understand guile all too well. Besides, professors of philosophy are not noted for their charm."

"You don't know France. Abélard, anyone? Moliere? Voltaire? Sartre? Camus? You think only their ideas inspire us? Come now! Their lives. Their *mistresses*," she drew out the word with a vexing smile. "Their mystique! That's what makes them interesting. *Non*? Yes! And you have it, I think, a little. But, we need to develop it more. *Oui*?"

I couldn't determine if she were serious or only mocking me. I shook my head, somewhat chagrinned. "You are very lovely, and you know it."

"You mustn't be so overt, so obvious. You must act more indifferent. That is what makes us French. It is part of our Gallic inheritance." She explained all this while we were walking into the exhibition hall, expressing herself with her hands and pursed lips as much as her words.

"Where to start?" she shrugged her shoulders.

"It appears the line begins there," I nodded to my right.

"Ahhhh, so it does! But stay with me. The directors know me; we can see whatever we want."

I politely followed her as she broke in line, time after time. She had a leather notebook and made many entries before the artist's more famous paintings. At several points, I simply left her and wandered about on my own. I had never seen any of Chagall's works, except in art books, and knew less than a modicum about him. Here they were, in all their magnificence! Paintings taller than I am, close enough to have touched! I stood spellbound before *Le Violoniste*, the fiddler, with his yellow and orange violin, dressed in his white/tweed coat and black boots, a solitary, isolated figure, playing against a landscape of snowy twilight. His face was green, trancelike.

A Jewish man beside me pointed to the painting. "You know about the fiddler? What he represents?"

"No. Joy, sorrow?"

"Maybe!" he shrugged his shoulders. "He stands for Judaism, our births, weddings, and funerals. Both merriment and despair are in his bow. Can't you feel it? Can't you hear it? It's all right there."

I walked on to other paintings. *The Jew in Green, The Blue House, The Promenade, the Equestrienne, I and the Village*. So many of Chagall's figures and people, houses and churches were painted upside down, or floating in the air, as in the case of the girl in *The Promenade*. Translucent shades of blue, green, red, pink, black and white dominated his canvases. His was a world of folklore and symbolism, religious legends, Moses, David, hallucinatory visions of life, of suffering and sacrifice, laughter and exile, represented no doubt in the figure of the wandering beggar, with the bag on his back.

"That is God!" someone said. It was the man who had explained the fiddler. "We Jews are nothing but beggars. The beggars of God. How else could God function in the world, save as a beggar?"

"There you are!" Monique called. I watched her petite form, as she hurried to my side. "Fantastic! *Merveilleux. Non*!"

"Yes, quite so!"

She seemed less self-assured, less haughty, less openly vain. We stayed together after that, and, after another half hour, left the hall.

"Would you care for a drink?"

"Yes," she answered quickly, with a smile. "I feel I have just been to another world. What about you?" she asked in a soft voice.

"*D'accord*. I too."

We spotted a bar, down a crowed street, and stepped quietly inside. She lit up a cigarette, inhaled, and let out the smoke in a long slow stream. A pensive aloofness cast somber shadows about her eyes. I drank a cognac; she white wine.

"How will you write that up?"

She looked at me without smiling. "I will write about the mirror effect, the colors, the tones, the anguish and vitality of his art and its lingering realism. How I will relate that to the fashion world is another matter."

I reached across the table for her hand. She accepted mine and squeezed it gently. "I must be off now," she announced. "Will I see you on Friday? On the Fontainebleau tour?"

"Yes. I wouldn't miss it for anything."

She leaned in close to me. I raised her fingers to my lips and kissed them.

"You are learning," she whispered. "I like that, very much." Her eyes radiated an intimacy I had not expected.

"On Friday," I said, as we rose to leave.

I had scarcely entered the pension's stairwell when I heard a woman scream. It reminded me of the exasperated howls my grandmother made when chasing a mouse, or swatting at barn swallows that had gotten into the kitchen. The woman was fussing and tossing things in between her shrill "Ahhs!" and "Ohffffs!" Someone was attempting to calm her. I stopped on the third landing and peered down the hallway. The noise was coming from the room that the Jewish couple occupied.

"Anna! Anna! Please, Anna! We will be all right!" Monsieur Wetzel was trying to reassure her. "You don't have to be so loud."

"No, I will say what I want!" she snapped with agitation. "The *mamzers*! *Mamzers*!" She began jabbering in Yiddish, or Polish, which went totally over my head.

"May I be of help!" I offered.

"Oh, Monsieur! Yes, yes!" she wrung her hands.

Monsieur Wetzel looked utterly bested, confused, alarmed. "They have taken her jewelry, her star, and our money! Ten thousand francs! We should never have carried that much. It's all my fault!"

I entered the room to console them. "Have you called the police or reported the loss to Madame Dufavre? She will know what to do."

"No. Not yet! It was in a large old handbag with gold embroidering. It was my mother's," Madame Wetzel's voice broke with grief.

"Are your windows unlocked or unlatched? Did you leave them open?"

"I haven't looked," she moaned.

I walked to the windows and pulled back the curtain. The latch on the left panel had been broken; pieces of it lay on the floor. I peered out the window. Below in the dark was the dank alleyway, at its narrowest point. Drafts of cold air ruffled the curtains. I realized their room was to the right of Gloria's and Francine's. I leaned out and looked up toward the skyline, toward the attic above. How were they getting in? How were they getting out? I was no detective, but enough was enough. I climbed out on the balcony, on its tight concrete ledge, to examine the rusted grillwork. I held to the window frame and glanced about. Yes, it was possible to lower oneself on a rope, or step from balcony to balcony if one were nimble and strong enough. But to climb up? I looked for evidence of rope marks on the iron grill, but found none. Just then, I glanced down. Light was streaming from the window below. Someone had opened it. I drew back against the building beside the couple's windows. I could smell rank cigarette smoke. I heard a man's cough. A pinpoint of fire briefly illumined the night, then drifted into the alleyway. It was the man's cigarette butt. Who roomed there?

"Don't say anything yet to Madame Dufavre," I whispered, upon re-entering the room. "I have an idea. Please give me a few minutes or so, and I'll be back."

The couple appeared dazed, but willing to wait.

I hurried down the hall and stairwell to the room below theirs. I could see a thin line of light under the door. I knocked. My hand trembled slightly.

I could hear someone closing the windows and coming toward the door. They turned its lock and switched off their light.

"Open this door!" I ordered, "Or I will break it in!"

The light came back on. I could hear the key turning to unlock the door.

"Please, I am alone and old." The door swung open.

There stood the old gentleman who always ate in his coat and tie, and who so meticulously lined up his spices and sauces.

"Please, Monsieur! What is it? How dare you!"

When he recognized me, his mouth fell open, and his chin quivered.

"*Bon Dieu*! Monsieur! I am so sorry. I apologize. I thought someone else roomed here. Please forgive me. *Pardonnez moi*!"

"Oh, you had me frightened," the old man said. "I was preparing to go down for dinner. What has gone wrong?"

"Another robbery, sir! In the room above yours. I thought perhaps the thief had come up from your room. I am truly embarrassed, truly!"

The old man's hands trembled, along with his chin.

"You'd better lock your windows, sir. One never knows."

"Yes," he mumbled. "Good idea. But what do I have other than these old ties!" he pointed toward his armoire. He smiled good-naturedly and shuffled back inside to latch his windows.

I all but bounded downstairs to report the incident.

"Ahh! How remorseless! How unrelenting! When will it stop?" Madame Dufavre nervously pulled on her hands. "I must tell Daniel. He's not here tonight. But he's narrowed the suspects down to two."

"What can you tell me? Your guests need to know something, at least to calm them down."

She looked at me sternly, her jaw jutting forward with determination. "You must tell no one. Daniel has learned that one of our renters is a former mountain climber; another a petty thief. One rooms in the building where the old lady was killed, the other off that half-flight of stairs under the attic." She paused and studied my face for reaction. "I'll call the police right now. Please tell Monsieur and Madame Wetzel that they'll be safe, that dinner is served. I'll place a bottle of wine on their table. And don't go near the attic, or nosing around. Daniel's seeking a search warrant, and we want to surprise them. "

After dinner, I sought out Mme. Angleterre, but she wasn't in her office, and I was hesitant to go up to the attic. I would have to wait to ask her about the room.

"Well, aren't we playing preoccupied!" Christine confronted me in the hallway.

"Ah, woman! Let's go somewhere for a real drink."

"You're on!" she smiled. "You're a strange one, you know. For all your charming blarney, you're a mystery. But, I like it," she kissed me. "Let's go."

We walked up the street, past the Montparnasse station, and down the boulevard to the café where the Sullivans, Giberts, and I had met that first night. The posh restaurant was filled with customers, but a few vacant tables remained under its spacious green awning. We took seats and ordered drinks. Christine wanted a dark rum beverage, rimmed with crushed mint, sugar, and ice; I settled for a bottle of sparkling champagne, which I knew would numb me, if I drank it all.

"You know there's been another robbery?"

"Yes, the new couple told me. It has to be someone inside to have acted that quickly."

"Possibly. Or at least they eat there. I've narrowed it down to Gaston and the Belgian."

"Why them?"

"They're both pretty fit and could be coming in from the balconies when no one's around."

"What about your Angleterre? She has keys to all the rooms and knows who's in and out, day and night."

"I think she's too meek. Plus savvy enough to realize that she'd be the first suspect, and, if caught, what a dead-end life she'd have."

"Let's change the subject." Christine held her drink close to her lips and sipped it thoughtfully. "I'll be finishing my studies in another two weeks. Then, it's back to England." She looked at me with a forlorn uncertainty. "You wouldn't be interested in a jaunt about Normandy, would you? Before I leave?"

"That's possible."

"You don't sound very enthusiastic," her eyes stared into mine with disappointment.

"I've been there before, back in the late '50s. I was traveling by myself. It was all so lonely. I became despondent and had to leave. I took a bus back to Paris, packed up, and returned home."

"Loneliness sucks, doesn't it?"

"Yes. Solitude I can take, even for long bouts of time. But loneliness is something else."

"You think we could make it together? You said you were in love with me. Remember?" She rested her glass on the edge of the table and stretched her fingertips toward mine. She took my hand and caressed it.

"I'm sure comfortable enough. I love your body and talking like this."

"I like it, too. I think you're still hung up on that wench you talk about. What has she ever done for you, other than rot your soul. Can't you give her up?"

"I think I have. The hurt lasted so long. Now, there's only the memory. I threw away what pictures I had of her. She still comes to me in dreams, but I can't see her face anymore. It's like my subconscious psyche is trying to protect me by blotting out her face, her smile, her eyes. But her presence is still there, aloof now, at a distance, as if still watching me."

"You've just described me and how I feel about Tobby."

"Have you heard anymore? Has he survived the accident?"

"I don't know. His mother'll wire again, if things go bottom. Like a fool, I'd go back to him if he wanted me. But wanting him to want me has lost its appeal anymore. May I have a sip of your champagne? I don't think I can manage two of these rum drinks," she laughed.

I poured her a half-glass of the sparkling pale liquid.

"Whoa! There'll not be any for you."

"I've had ample. Here's to you, girl!" I toasted her, as we touched glasses.

"Well, would you care to go? To Normandy, if it's possible?"

"I don't see why not, but can I wait till the last minute? I promised my friends, the Sullivans, I'd be here whey they return from Greece. They'll be heading back to the States after that, and I hate to miss them. I'm hoping that he and I might co-edit a book together."

Her disappointment could not be suppressed or obviated. Shadows formed about her eyes; they filled with tears; the corners of her mouth grew dry. She raised her right hand to her mouth and pressed her lips with her index finger, then wiped her eyes with the palms of her hands. "We may never have a chance like this again. Your witch doesn't want you, Clayton. My Tobby could care less about me. If we don't go, we'll always wonder. I can't believe I'm being so forward, but, dammit, I'm right here. And so are you."

I felt horrid, stupid, inane, my response insipid and cruel. Was I not behaving just as Leeta had behaved? Was I somehow transferring her rejection of me onto this wonderful, intelligent woman? Where would I meet anyone as candid, out-going, and caring as Christine? Julene was taken; her fate or destiny beyond my power to nullify or change. Monique had her *mari*, her husband, Jacques-Maria, a man whose *grande vision de la France* and of himself would no doubt wing its flight of dreams to a successful *fini*. Christine was right. Leeta would never want me back. She had probably already forgotten our adulterous affair, with all its ardent, aphrodisiac, and tender episodes. Plus I knew it was time to let her go, to stop blaming her for something that was my own fault.

I reached for Christine's hands. They were warm and soft. "You're right. Absolutely right. Even if I miss the Sullivans, I can contact them back in the States. Yes, I'll go. Just let me know when."

Tears glowed in her eyes. "You won't regret it. I'll be the best *pussy-cat* you've ever had."

We celebrated with a second bottle of champagne, paid, kissed, laughed, and fondled our way back to the boarding house. About a block away, I noticed a picture of a insatiably beautiful woman in a disco's window. There was an announcement about her below her photograph. "Look at that!" I blurted. "What a blonde!"

Christine laughed and pulled me closer to the window. "Hello, read it again, ole boy!" she tugged on my hand. "Or let me read it to you. '*Les plus beaux transvestites du monde!*'"

"Oh, no!" I laughed with her. "*Bon Dieu*, but she, *he* looks good!"

We made it back to the pension.

"Shhhhh!" she giggled as we staggered up the stairs.

At our landing, she put her arms around me, kissed me, and said: "Look here, I can't do it tonight, or for the next two weeks, unless we use something we've not done, or I'll get pregnant."

"I was wondering about that. I've had too much to drink anyway." I walked to her room with her. "Better take a good look inside," I advised.

We did. Nothing appeared molested or out of place.

"Good night!" we mumbled to each other as our lips met and mouths opened, hungering for that quintessential rapture we'd have to delay.

15

LEVIATHAN CREATURES LUMBER IN clumped herds, crushing the undergrowth with their enormous feet. Plumes of red dust rise in the gray sky. The armada of pachyderms stretches across a horizon of parched land and truncated green acacia trees, as far as the eye can see. Black vultures hunch in the tree tops' dead limbs. Stalking between the herds' legs, lupine forms weave back and forth, their green eyes glowing in the clouds of red dust. What have wolves to do with these behemoths of jungle and plain? A creek bed through a dry wadi, bounded by steep sandstone cliffs, opens before me. I enter to follow. "No one who takes this road has ever returned," a voice in the dusk whispers. The largest animal in the pack lopes directly toward me, bears its fangs, lunges, but collapses at my feet. Its dark red fur is soft, thick, even black in places. I seize it by the neck; its fiery eyes hold me in their gaze. Suddenly, it rolls on its back; my hands are buried in its dense fur; it whines like a dog. A light breaks through the darkness; the menagerie of elephants and wolves, crashing and trumpeting, howling and racing in the night, fades into a monochromatic blur. I awaken. Someone is knocking at the door. "Monsieur, Monsieur! Get up, quickly." I recognize Madame Angleterre's voice.

I slipped on my trousers and a shirt and opened the door. "What is it?"

"Gaston is dead! He hung himself in his room last night! It is *terrible, terrible*, Monsieur!"

I ran my fingers through my hair and followed her down the hall. Then we clambered up the steps to the fifth floor, to that half-hallway that Dufavre had mentioned. Madame Dufavre, her cousin, two gendarmes, and Pierre were crowded in the room. So this was where they rented! Pierre sat by a narrow window, in shock.

"He had just returned from his breakfast, when he discoveredthis . . . ," Madame Dufavre pointed to Gaston's grotesque body. It was hanging from a rope of ties that were knotted together inside the armoire and thrust over the shower stall's pipes. His head lay tilted, all but separated from his neck. He had attached a note to his clothes. It was pinned to his lapel: *Innocent! Innocent! Pas culpable!* it read. The sour odor of death had already begun to befoul the room.

"Monsieur, see if you can calm him," Dufavre said. She took my hand and led me to Pierre. For some reason, her grip felt unexpectedly strong, her fingers rough and chapped, but perhaps that was due to my own state of half-consciousness.

The gendarmes had successfully cut through the knot of ties and were lowering Gaston's body.

I put my hand on Pierre's shoulder. He buried his face on my shirt sleeve and wept.

"It is all my fault," said Daniel. "When we searched his room last night, he became disoriented and paranoid. But, of course, we found nothing!" he groaned, raising his hands in helpless supplication. "It is the sad part of my work. We can only go on reasonable suppositions. He did have a record, Monsieur. But only a petty one."

"You did your best," I consoled him. "Gaston was just upset more than anyone realized."

"It was his sense of *honneur,* his *estime* and *dignité*," sobbed Pierre. "We were very, very close. He was like a *frère*, my brother." He pulled out a dirty handkerchief and blew his nose. "It's my fault, too. I should have been here last night; instead, I spent it with my mother at St. Denis. She's old and not doing well."

The gendarmes wrapped Gaston in their capes and carried his stiff body out the door and onto the stairwell. "We will have to take him to the morgue, first," explained Daniel. "Where is his home, Pierre? Do you know?"

"No. I think, perhaps, in Bordeaux. He never mentioned his parents or home."

Pierre's eyes were red with tears. "What am I going to do? I can't pay for his funeral, nor maybe even stay here," he looked toward Mme. Dufavre.

"Well, we will not worry about that for the moment," she replied.

"You will need to come with us to the préfecture, to make a report," Daniel explained to Pierre. "Then, you can go."

"This could mean my job, if I am late. Can't you call the post office for me?"

"Certainly," Daniel answered. "Please, no one is blaming you. Try not to be so distraught." He looked up at me. "Monsieur, *Professeur*, you are *très distingué*. Your words of reassurance are most welcome. Please help my cousin's renters to understand."

"I'll do my best."

Mme. Angleterre had remained in the hallway. I stepped out and stood beside her while the procession made its way awkwardly down the stairs.

"Maybe she will get an elevator, now," Angleterre mumbled. "You never know when these things are going to happen."

I wasted several hours trying to get back into Rousseau. I had been reading his section on the Savoyard Priest's credo, and had taken several folders of notes, as well as drawn some conclusions of my own. But my mind resisted the tedium of having to outline my findings and sketch or draft a defensible chapter. Gaston's death overrode such idle reflections.

Sullivan would be returning in two weeks or so, and I hadn't reread his last chapters on either *The Iliad* or *The Odyssey*, nor perused his segments on the gods. Being, thus distracted, might help my cognitive abilities to recover sufficiently to launch into Rousseau again.

His opening lines suggested the direction he had elected to follow.

> As with Pallas Athena, I think one might advance a similar thesis. Herodotus claims that Homer and Hesiod gave the Greeks their gods, or at least put a face on them, but I beg to disagree. Aristotle's analysis comes closer to the truth, in which he surmises that Homer chose Achilles' *anger* as the epic's central theme. It is this anger, or *ménis* in Greek, from which we derive our own word "maniac," and which means for Homer "vengefulness," or "implacable anger," that provides the clue. Later, the Greeks would replace *ménis* with the word *orgé*—which has enriched our own language with words like "orgasm" and "orgy." Why this anger? Why this rage, this frenzy, that borders on the maniacal and theorgiastic? And from whence these Olympian gods, who suddenly appear with such dominant personalities, resulting in quarrels and humanlike bickering among themselves? What is the source of these quarrels and jealousies that characterize these dazzling immortals who now emerge on the stage of Greek history? I propose that, once again, it is the Near Eastern religio-politico "wisdom" of the Mesopotamians and of

their more barbaric kinsmen, the Canaanites, who are the forerunners of the Olympians. Faces and names had already been assigned to the forces of nature and the conundrums of human destiny as early as the Sumerian creation story, *The Enuma Elish*, its successor, *The Gilgamesh Epic*, and the period's laudatory hymns to Ishtar: mother goddess and prototype of Aphrodite and Athena. The Greeks, somewhere in the late Bronze Age, as they settled along the coastal plains of Iona, Hellenized these older, more established, Near Eastern deities, and molded them to serve their own needs. Factor in also the Indo-European invasions, that threatened the Fertile Crescent from Eastern Europe to the Ganges River, and you have all the cross-cultural elements necessary to create new and dynamic civilizations, ready for expansion, change, conquest, and synthesis. Still, it is Homer's *anger* that proves the most resourceful ingredient. Why this *ménis,* this *orgé*? Why this rage? Was it not because these earlier gods of agriculture and empire, of nomadic wanderings and village settlements, could no longer answer the basic questions of life?—those more human and mortal, mundane and personal issues? What is life's purpose? What is its worth? *The Gilgamesh Epic* cannot resolve this question. After the death of Enkidu—the counterpart to Achilles' Patroclus, slain by Hector—Gilgamesh mopes in mournful despair, knowing that once man goes down to the shadowy pit of his death, there is nothing but darkness to mantle a mortality, which he knows must have the final word. Against this helplessness, the soul of Hellas's rising stars take issue, to create a human reason for existence, that blends the incontrovertible powers of heaven with the insatiable longings of mortal men. If one cannot have immortality, what can one have? The gods represent those inexplicable powers that limit human beings. Chance, fortune, abilities are different for each person. The gods and goddesses, with their whimsical interferences and double-edged gifts, account for these limited and confining boundaries. The rest is up to mankind, to achieve what notable deeds and memorable words one can summons from ones existence. Then one may go down to ones grave in the peace of knowing that one did ones best by accepting mortality with grace and courage, while leaving a string of noble accomplishments for bards to sing, as long as humanity endures. Homer's *Iliad* knows that anger is not the solution. But anger when funneled into the quest for being can lead to wisdom, valor, and meaning, but not without loss, pain, and suffering, and conflicting choices between vengeance and mercy, triumph and tragedy, victory and defeat. All these are in *The Iliad.* Thus, it stands as a watershed when Western mankind was risking the transition from reason the void, to reason the enemy, and from reason the enemy to reason the friend, to paraphrase the philosopher Alfred North Whitehead.

I turned the pages to locate his *ontological* motif.

It is to the depth psychologists that we must yield to discern its ontological importance. From the very beginning, mankind's history consists in a struggle between his sense of inferiority and his feelings of arrogance, as Achilles and Agamemnon so aptly model. This audacity cannot help but eventuate in suffering and death. It is a state of the unconscious in conflict with consciousness. The gods represent the symbolic wholeness of the psyche. They constitute the larger and all-inclusive self-identify that the personal ego lacks. The Homeric myths encourage the hero to develop his own individual ego-consciousness; to become aware of his own strengths and weaknesses; to equip himself for the untrammeled tasks of life ahead. Once he claims these powers for himself, then the myths about gods and goddesses have fulfilled their purpose. Until that moment arrives, one is in a constant state of *mater natura,* a victim of unconscious drives, the *horror vacui*. Throughout this pilgrimage, we will never comprehend everything fully, nor perceive anything completely. We simply come to a finite boundary, beyond which our knowledge cannot pass. This enigma is without boundaries; its mystery is unlimited; it can only be fathomed by our ciphers and symbols that speak of a knowing beyond certainty. Our psyche is part of this order, as bound to heaven and earth as the Greeks were to Zeus and Artemis, Apollo and Dionysus, or reason yoked to an uncontrollable frenzy. Somewhere beyond and unknown, within yet hidden, lie the forces that preceded the Beingness of our own being, before anima and animus, id and superego quarreled and renounced each other, and now seek reconciliation. Homer's gods are an echo of that time, of that transmigration of human consciousness. They represent that fragmentation from all that had passed before to what suddenly loomed ahead, from gods worshipped as unpredictable casual forces to latent powers within the human mental sphere of self-expression and self-determination. Yes, gods are created in the image of man; yet man creates himself in the image of "gods" that draw him secretly and strangely toward a self-fulfillment, whose telos lies beyond his understanding or capacity to fathom. He longs to be reunited with his past and searches for it and himself in his future. How far back must we go to know the truth about the self, about being? And how much of that must we absorb, excise, and grow beyond, to have a future?

> Homer offered his answer to the Greeks: a valiant life in speech and deeds, in spite of time's mortality. For what we say, and how we say it, and the deeds we do, and how we do them, creates an immortality, equal to that of the gods.

Sullivan's world made perfect sense on paper. Such an explosive and creative time! Had any epoch since matched it in terms of its imaginative universe of Olympian giants, heroes and villains, nymphs and maidens? To trace its origins would lead only to cults, animism, migrations, the Ice Age, the numbing evolution of Cro-Magnon Man, the decline of the Neanderthals, the rise of Homo erectus, and the plains of Africa. Carl's book triggered a restlessness, stirred a powerful agitation, that would not be silenced by so frail a human art as reason.

I laid the book down, scooted my chair back, and paced the room. Remaining within its walls was simply not possible.

The fresh air of the park, a blue, adamantine sky, and bright sun soon dissipated the morose state into which I had fallen. With reinvigorated strides, I set off for the Boulevard Saint Michel and the glorious Seine. Within twenty minutes, I was staring again into the swirling vortices of the river. How pleasantly its waters tumbled through that antique channel that had marked the northern borders of the Roman's tiny garrison. They had nestled it on this narrow island that became the capital of Napoleon's Empire and Charles de Gaulle's *Cinquième République*. I crossed the bridge and walked on down to Notre Dame, entered its central portal, and ambled the length of its stained-glass nave. Near the transept, and its statue of Mary, I took a seat and stared up at that magnificent North window of magenta, mauve, green and blue glass that silences the mind's endless syllogisms and nurses the heart's wounds with the light of its wondrous glow. I sat there for a long time before the Virgin's statue and watched the votive candles flicker reddish orange in the semi-darkness under the vaulted ceiling overhead. *My God, my God, why hast thou forsaken me*? a dying Jesus had prayed from his cross. Would he have found comfort here?

I was about to leave, when a petite and slender figure, covered from head to mid-waist in a long black shawl, made her way suddenly to the statue. She lit a candle, placed it before the Virgin, genuflected, crossed herself, then placed something against the flickering taper, turned, and walked slowly back up the aisle. She paused near me, as if she wanted me to notice her, but I could not see her face. She appeared to be young, frightened, unsteady. I could see her sandals as she passed. She appeared to be wearing jeans. She hurried toward the narthex, her head bowed beneath her black shawl.

Out of curiosity, I advanced toward the candles, looked up into that ivory face of Mary's, and scanned the votive flames. Something sparkled near the base of one of the narrow tapers. It was the silver, six-pointed star of Mme. Wetzel! I glanced over my shoulder toward the narthex. The woman was gone. I retrieved the pin, crossed myself—though I am not Catholic—and looked into that serene surface on the statue's face. I knew exactly what I had to do.

Back at the pension, I presented the pin to Anna Wetzel.

"Oh, my goodness! Where did you find it? How wonderful! It's not even bent! Look, Jakkob! It's my pin!"

"Pure luck! It's not a good sign at all!" the old man moaned. "Not at all!" he flailed his arms, while rolling his eyes toward me. "The thief will only come back for it again."

"Oh, you pessimist!" Anna waved him off. "The *bon professeur* knows better than that, *n'est-ce pas*, Monsieur?"

"True."

"Where did you find it? I must know. Please, tell me."

"I found it at the base of a candle in front of the Virgin's statue in the cathedral of Notre Dame. That's the truth."

"There must be more," she implored.

"Yes, but I'm not certain what to make of it. A lone woman left it, after kneeling for prayer. I couldn't get a good look at her." I was hesitant to say that she was young, or petite, or wore jeans, for my mind had already raced ahead to suspect the one, or two persons, that neither Dufavre, Christine, Angleterre, nor I had considered—Gloria and Francine! Still I couldn't imagine either of them agile enough to scale the building or balance themselves on its rusting, tight balconies.

"Guilt! *Die Schuld*!" Jacob added somewhat bitterly in German.

"No! Be grateful, you old man!" Anna scolded him. "It's a happy day. We can earn the money back, but not this pin."

"How did you acquire it?" I asked.

"A gift! My grandfather, Herman Schweisberg, gave it to me when I was a girl of fourteen. It was just after the outbreak of the First World War. He and his companions had volunteered to fight on the Russian Front. He knew he might not come back. 'Anna, beloved,' he said. 'Wear this proudly, wherever you go, whatever happens, dear child. May the angels of Paradise watch over you.' And, of course, they have," she smiled, as a large tear trickled down her powdered face and caught on a gray hair on her chin.

"Well, keep it hidden for a while," pleaded her squat, worried husband. "At least, until we are safely away from here."

"That's a good idea," I advised, not wanting Francine or Gloria to know of its whereabouts, until I had had an opportunity to snoop around, or even confront Francine.

Feeling somewhat relieved and more self-assured, I returned to Rousseau that afternoon, and to his notion of the "natural man," or "the nature of man." It was this "natural man" of his, or this supposed "man of nature," that I suspected was the epistemological starting point for all that he deduced about man himself, his societies, and future. But of course this "natural man" of his was itself a creation of Rousseau's own imagination, a product of his inner selfhood, or projection of an idealized self, free from the effete machinations of the elitist society of his time. In this regard, he represented an extension of the Cartesian school that had begun by meditating upon the self, as well as sharing something of Pascal's own affinity with a fallen and finite self, imprisoned within a corrupt and fallen world. My new book's direction was clear in my mind. All I had to do was complete my chapter on Rousseau, and I would be ready for Kant. The more I thought of it, the more I liked the title: *Explorations on the Epistemology of Doubt: From Descartes to Kant*. If only I knew how to tie that in with Sullivan's world, I felt I'd be capable of writing that book of books that Heidegger himself had longed to write. I would know the secret of Being, and what could be believed and what couldn't. Talk about pride! I was fascinated with my research.

Just before dinner, I walked up to the Boulevard du Montparnasse in search of a pharmacy. I found the toiletries, plus a certain commodity I needed, purchased the items, and returned to the pension.

During the evening meal, I noted that Gaston's place setting at his and Pierre's table was missing. Pierre had not come in, either.

"*Bonsoir*, Monsieur Clarke," Mme. Cueillier smiled. As usual, her face was pink with entirely too much powder, her lips a bright red, and her hair dyed a coarse black. "It's so sad, all of it, isn't it?" she nodded toward Gaston's empty chair. "Perhaps Monsieur Roget will dine with us later."

"Yes, let's hope so."

She served the potage, filled my water glass full, and returned to kitchen to wait on the other guests.

Madame and Monsieur Wetzel smiled from their table. Anna pointed to her lapel, which was void of any pin, and arched her eyebrows. It was just in time. The two French women, whose first names were all I knew—Gloria and Francine—took their seats to the right of the Wetzels and away from me. Francine was wearing sandals, but not jeans. A long hippie dress covered most of her legs, save her ankles. Her mother looked haggard and bored. She had pinned her red hair up into a mass of wild curls. Her blouse of pink silk was noticeably open, displaying a sensuous mound of curvaceous breasts. I knew she worked as a hat-check girl somewhere, but wasn't certain where. "He is not to come tonight," I heard her say to Francine. "Never again. We will leave here, if he does." Francine kept her head down and averted her mother's eyes, as well as anyone else's. "Mama, not so loud!" she pleaded. "I won't," she whispered, but still loud enough for all to hear.

The Belgian, whom I had not seen for several evenings, entered with a newspaper under his arm. He glanced toward the Wetzels, Francine and her mother, and, noticing Pierre's empty place, looked first at me, then about the room, before sitting at his table. When Christine came in, he rose, spoke to her, reseated himself, and opened his paper. The old gentleman, who was so fond of lining up his condiments, could be heard slurping his soup. Other guests arrived, as Mme. Cueillier made her rounds. Christine glanced my way, smiled, and casually pointed her spoon toward the ceiling. She whispered a silent "upstairs tonight" with her lips. I nodded my approval.

At long last, Pierre arrived, his curly hair disheveled and bunched about his neck, his shirt soiled about his collar, his tie missing, and his usually smiling face, puffy and grim. He sat opposite me at his table and released a sigh. A breathless hopelessness sent a quiver down his sagging chest and torso. "Quite an ordeal! It's been quite an ordeal," he said. "His body will be carried by rail to his home tomorrow."

"In Bordeaux?"

"No. Soissons. The police located a brother in Soissons. He's an invalid, so couldn't come to collect his remains. A veteran of *La Guerre*." Pierre rubbed his face with his hands.

"How about a little wine?" I held my bottle over his empty wine glass. "It's a good strong red wine. You'll like it."

"*Oui, Monsieur*. Pour away!"

"*In vino est veritas*!" I smiled. "*Non*?"

"You are too kind. Yes." He held his glass up and touched it against mine. "*Chao! Salut, salut*!"

Francine had leaned forward to observe us. A frightened look filled her face. Her mother glanced our way and smiled. Could the one know something the other didn't? Or was the mother simply remarkably callous? Or were they innocent, and Francine just curious, or afraid that what had happened to Gaston might happen to her? She turned toward the Belgian, whose back was toward everyone else. Then she stared down at her plate and stirred the potage with her spoon. "Eat up," said her mother. "I've got to be at work soon, and you need to study."

"Yes, Mama," the girl replied in a child's voice.

Following the meal, I returned to my room. I wanted a few moments of reflection, before walking down to Christine's. I had scarcely taken a seat by my desk, when someone knocked at the door. It was a very timid rap. I knew it wasn't Christine's, as hers was usually quiet, but solid.

"Yes. Come in!"

The door opened, and there stood Francine. "May I come in?"

"Heavens, yes!" I rose and waited for her to enter.

She closed the door and smiled nervously. "I need to talk. Will you listen?"

"Of course. Please sit down." I pulled up the room's only extra chair and placed it near my own. "Please. Take a seat."

Francine expelled a deep breath and sat down.

"Monsieur. I have to talk to someone. I'm scared."

"I'll not tell anyone. Your secret will be safe."

"It's worse than that." She stared into my face. It was a pretty face, of dark complexion, fine nose and mouth, black eyebrows, and shining green eyes. Her dyed red hair seemed entirely inappropriate for such a lovely young face.

"I followed you this morning, you know. You never saw me. I wanted to talk to you on the bridge, but hesitated. I followed you into the cathedral and watched you sit down. I was confident you would recognize me, but you didn't. I thought, maybe, if I wedged the pin against the wax and genuflected, you'd notice. I paused at the narthex and saw you get up. I watched you retrieve the pin. Then I ran out. I knew you'd return it to Mme. Wetzel. I was afraid to."

"Why? Where did you find it ? Or how did you get it?"

"A certain Monsieur gave it to me. He said he'd found it in his hallway. He asked me not to wear it for several weeks." She glanced at her lap, where her hands were tightly clasped and almost white. "He's a very nice man."

"May I ask who?"

"I can't tell you."

"Why did he give you the pin? If I may ask."

She looked toward the curtains, then toward the bed. A knowing smile glowed momentarily about her face, filling her eyes with a tender sparkle. "I rendered him a favor. You know, sex!"

I took a deep breath. "How old are you, Francine?"

"Fourteen. My mother and I came here when I was eleven. We're from Algeria. *Pieds noirs*, as folk say. My father's father was a colonialist. My father was killed in 1958, during one of the uprisings. We moved to Marseilles first, then to Paris. We've been in Dufavre's pension since 1968. If you haven't guessed it by now, my mother's a stripper. She takes clients in a back room. It's a wonder she hasn't invited you to come and see her."

"I didn't know all that, but I won't tell anyone."

"It's no secret. Dufavre, Angleterre, the old man, and several others know. It's a way of life. That's all."

"Is this man, the one who gave you the pin, involved in the thefts, possibly? Has he said anything about them? It's gotten serious, you know, with Gaston's death and the murder across the street."

"That's why I followed you. I don't know. My Mama was afraid Dufavre would think we're involved. That's why she staged our 'theft,' and hung the pillowslip on the latch. She made me do it. After what happened to the Jewish couple, she was so glad she had."

"Perhaps you should mention this to Dufavre. She needs to know that Mme. Wetzel's pin was found in this man's hallway. Does he room here?"

"No, not here! He rooms across the street."

"Is he the Belgian? I won't tell anyone how I found out."

"I promised I wouldn't tell. He gives me money when we have sex. We do it when Mama's at work. It's the only money I have."

"But a woman was murdered across the street, and Gaston has hanged himself in despair. Who might be next?"

"I gave my word. He's a good man. And strong, too. Gentle, and he's always careful. And fun. He climbs up the building and slips in my window. He used to be a mountain climber. He showed me how he does it."

"How is that?"

She turned sideways in the chair and pretended to produce a rope. "Like this. He throws this light weight nylon cord, tied to an aluminum hook, up to my balcony. Then he pulls himself up. He has great muscles." Her face beamed with embarrassed but culpable satisfaction. "We have great sex."

"Aren't you afraid you'll get pregnant?"

"No. We're very careful."

"Francine. This is no brothel, or fun house. Someone else could get killed. If the Belgian isn't the thief, perhaps he knows who. Do I have your permission to talk to him?"

"Please, don't! I gave him my word. Plus, I need the money. Besides, you said you'd keep it secret. Remember?"

"Yes. But there are such things as overriding duties. If that means anything."

Francine wet her lips with her tongue. "You appear muscular yourself. I would like to have sex with you." She ran the fingers of her left hand along my right arm, while she stared down at her lap. "I wouldn't tell anyone, nor would I ask for money." Her eyes looked directly into my own.

Francine! I thought. Yes, I could and probably would. But with a fourteen-year-old girl?

I clasped her hands as warmly as I knew how. "Sweet child, I'm seeing Christine, as you probably suspect. I can't let her down just now. But, what a flattering offer! Thanks, just the same. I'll keep your secret, and hope our mysterious thief won't strike again."

Francine gave me a huge hug. I could feel her petite body trembling and her small warm breasts against my arm. She kissed me on the neck.

"Thank you, Monsieur Clarke. I knew I could trust you."

"Well, hello! It's taken you long enough. Where have you been?" teased Christine.

"Oh, I had a tiny emergency. Nothing special." I reached in my pocket and showed her the package I had purchased.

"Ah, really! A fine ripper, ole boy!" she smiled.

"Would you like to go out for a drink, or be boring and stay here?"

"Boring, my can! Let's cuddle! Kiss me and tell me how gorgeous I am. Then, you know what to do, and how to do it." A wonderful aura of sensual delight shone about her. She unfastened my shirt and turned for me to pull up her blouse; she canted her face sideways and we kissed. Cupping her breasts in my hands aroused every sensation. They were so soft, full, delectably supple, yet firm in my hands, and so superbly shaped, with exquisitely formed nipples.

She laughed as I fondled them and pressed my mouth over them.

We backed up to the bed, practically fell in it, and made love. For a long, long time, we just lay there. How good it felt to hold her body in my arms.

She rustled about, rolled over and kissed me. "You're not thinking about that woman, are you?"

"No. I was just relishing you."

Christine nuzzled her face against my chest. "Don't say anything," she whispered. "I'm not ready for you to go, yet."

I pressed her against my body and lay on my back. She rolled her right leg over my torso. After about a half-hour, we got up, washed off, and I returned to my room.

I was sleepy, but not ready for bed; tired, but mentally awake; rested, but restless within. After pacing the room for a while, I sat at my desk and turned to one of Rilke's poems.

Solemn Hour

Who just now weeps anywhere in the world,
without cause weeps in the world,
weeps over me.

Who just now laughs anywhere in the world,
without cause laughs in the world,
laughs at me.

Who just now goes anywhere in the world,
without cause goes in the world,
goes to me.

Who just now dies anywhere in the world,
without cause dies in the world,
beholds me.

16

On the eve of the Fontainebleau tour, I walked up the street to my favorite Greek-Parisian's kiosk for a demitasse of his infamous coffee. He had removed his armband, but a dark cast of sorrow lingered about his eyes.

"Good morning, my fellow world citizen! How are you!"

A toothy grin dispelled any spirit of disconsolation and awakened his eyes to the new day. "Ah, Professor! You know, we've never exchanged names. I'm Demetrius Santanos," he shook my hand.

"And I'm Clayton Rogers Clarke. The Odysseus of Montparnasse and its *jardin* to the world."

"Oh! How I love your spirit! It is so Greek, you know! So flamboyant and macho! It's like shouting for the world to hear: '*Listen, I am here. I am somebody! I laugh, I drink, I dance.*' You do dance? Yes! '*I eat, I think, I wander, I love!*' You do that, too, don't you?"

"Yes. I do all those things. But tell me, where's the best place to dance around here?"

"The *disco jazz de New Orléans.* It's near your pension," he pointed toward the Boulevard de Gaspail, not far from *Le Jardin.* You must go!" he smiled. "And take some *belle fille* with you. I know some, if you need one, yes?"

"I'm ahead of you on that one," I replied. "How about one of those mild coffees of yours, the kind that would bring hot tears even to Zeus."

"Ah, may the holy patriarch of Athens himself forgive you. The gods would love my brew, its aroma, its. . . ."

"Grounds!" I interrupted, with a smile. "With milk! And a pastry, but not that baklava. It's too sweet."

"What I don't do for you!" he leaned forward and pinched my cheek. "Just for you. The best!"

We laughed and carried on some more. I bought a paper—*Le Miroir Français,* downed the last sips of café, and headed for the Boulevard de Gaspail. I clutched the newspaper under my right arm and walked briskly toward the jazz disco, wherever that was. I located it on a dirty, debris-littered side street, opposite the park. I had passed it many times but had never so much as glanced at its marquee. An actual jazz band from New Orleans was its featured group, running through June. Performances commenced at 8:00 p.m. nightly, with American style drinks served until 3:00 a.m. The poster in the window displayed a photograph of a seated, large black man, wearing a straw hat, pink shirt, and red suspenders, holding a saxophone in his lap, with a cigar wedged between his orange-brown teeth. No cover charges nor tickets required.

Before returning to my room, I wandered over to the park, sat down in a quiet section on a damp bench, and began reading the paper. I searched for Gibert's column. His article was entitled: "Not Always Civil."

> Yes, it is true, we French are not always as civil as our codes of honor summon us to be. Tourists are forever flabbergasted at our Gallic indifference to their needs, or still better, our refusal to parley with them, except in French. How dare we not speak their language, or even respond to their Franglais, or Pigeon English, or Italian, or, yes, German! Didn't we endure the latter's guttural and garbled "acks" and "unds" far too long? Is it not enough to have to count the bullet holes in the gray facades along our major boulevards to know that we have every right to say "*Non! Non! Non*!" to such barbarisms! Is it not our "*Non*!" that defines us as much as our "*Oui! Mais oui! et Bien surs?*"
>
> In his *Being and Nothingness*, Sartre reminds us of our obligation to say *Non*, particularly when that may be the only thing we are allowed to say. We said it during the *Résistance* against the Nazis and our own fascist collaborators—even at the constant risk of death. De Gaulle helped us say it again against the Allies and the Soviets, who would paralyze our revival as a great nation with a continual destiny to work toward liberty, egality, and fraternity.
>
> A new era awaits the wakening of a resurgent sense of national pride. I am not talking about being foolish, boorish, obscurantist, indifferent, conceited, defeated, or isolationist. Our past is too grand for us to settle for a second-place national psyche, as if Jean d'Arc, Phillippe Auguste, St. Louis, Francois Premier, Louis XIV, etc., etc., never existed. We are the nation of Geneviève, the Capets, Valois, Napoleons; home to Moliere, Dumas, Balsac, Hugo,

> Malraux, and Maurois; the city on a floating isle of breathless chapels, cathedrals, and palaces. Our monuments remain the envy of the world. Our mission is still that of serving as the one beacon of civilization and art, culture and imagination, for a decadent world, inebriated on its foul dregs of grim and ghastly wars, détentes, and imperialist deceptions. It is time to forge ahead, to claim our destiny afresh, undeterred by the rabble noises and miscalculations of sycophants, East and West.
>
> Vive la France! Vive Paris!

I took a deep breath, smiled, and turned to the "life and fashion" section to be certain that the tour was still on. Yes, there it was. Monique's unique tour of Fontainebleau would leave at 8:00 a.m., as scheduled. The bus would await guests, as planned, and leave promptly by 8:15. All seats had been reserved. "Please be on time for a most enjoyable excursion," Mme. Gibert promised. I expelled another long sigh and returned to the pension for study and lunch.

After lunch, I gathered up my writing materials of note pads, pens, and a pocket dictionary, and set off for the National Library, or Bibliotheque Nationale. My University at home, along with the assistance of the State Department and the American Embassy in Paris had acquired the different passes I needed to study at the archives. Certain sections were off limits, mainly those of Francis I's first collection of manuscripts, which he authorized the humanist William Bude to purchase and assemble in the king's name. But the library's holdings on Descartes, Pascal, and Rousseau were accessible, though the rarer manuscripts and first editions could only be viewed. Most of what I needed could be purchased in sound scholarly editions in surrounding bookstores about the University of Paris. It was mind-boggling for me to keep realizing that I was studying in the environs of a university system that was founded by Philippe Auguste, in the 1200s.

Still, once a month or so, I made my pilgrimage to the library's rare rooms, checked out the in-house-for-loan-only books I wanted to peruse, read the more relevant chapters, and took what notes my bent deemed desirable. Then, I would stroll quietly along some of the aisles and into the vaulted and paneled reading rooms, pull a book from the shelves, and read a little Balzac, Zola, or whomever.

I felt very pleased with my research and was confident that I would complete most of my book before I had to return home. There were several secondary resources I discovered that would be useful. I purchased them on my way back in a narrow drafty bookstore in the Latin Quarter. Its shelves were brown with crusty-edged and buff-colored paperbacks that ranged in subject from history to language, science to philosophy, and art to literature. I paid about eighteen francs per book.

It was a relief to mount the stairs to my hallway, wash, and descend for dinner. Other guests were seated, as I was late, and, spotting Christine, I walked over to her table.

"I found a great place to dance, if you're interested."

"No kidding! Tonight?" She had drawn her long hair back and looked more Italian or German than British.

"Yes! Tonight!"

"Ok," she beamed without hesitation.

"I'll come to your room around eight. *Ça va*?"

"Yes. That's fine. I'll be ready," she said.

The *disco jazz de New Orleans* throbbed with excitement. You could feel the music's vibrations as far out as the sidewalk and hear its clarinets, horns, and saxophones pulsating with turbid and soulful sounds. The fast, squeaking rhythms created a steamy mood—haunting, joyous, and sensuous. We located a table and seated ourselves. A young, black, African girl waited on us.

"Yes. What you like?" she asked in English. Her large teeth flashed nacreous in the darkness of the disco; her black curly hair was cut short, almost severe. Her dark eyes bespoke a racial blend more Arabic, or North African, than Sudanese or Cameroon. The whites of her eyes glowed milky pale against the velvet night of the room. "We have Bloody Maries, Gin and tonics, Hurricanes, all the American drinks! So many to remember," she laughed good-naturedly. "Just tell me. I write your order down."

"Oh, I'll try your bloody Bloody Mary," Christine said, with an air of defiance.

"I'll take a mint julep, with lots of julep."

"What is this thing, 'julep?' How to spell it?"

"'J-u-l-e-p.'" I enunciated each letter slowly, then winked at Christine. "It's the bourbon, Cherie. Your barman should have them in his refrigerator."

The girl looked at me, nonplused, smiled and walked off.

"What's this? Why be such a smartass?" Christine asked. "I know! I was sort of curt myself. It's been a long day."

"More *rudesse* at the school?"

"Well, it was a bit of a cock-up today. Mother Superior didn't like my pronunciation of *feindre*, no matter how mellifluously I tried to trill the 'r.' 'Up your *r*,' I wanted to say. Yes, up y'r bloody 'r.' Your bloody French 'r.'"

"Well, that is quite a word to *fall* down on."

"Oh! How nasty! I hate puns! You Americans love them. 'Fall down!'" she groaned with a smiling negative nod of her head.

"Here come our drinks. I'll drink to your 'r' if you'll drink to mine."

"Yes. And here's to you before you can say it:

Drink to me only with thine r
And I'll forever be thine.

"That's not quite how it goes, but I love it anyway."

"I beat you on that one," she said.

We touched our glasses together and each took a long sip. I leaned across the narrow table and kissed her lips. I could taste the Tabasco sauce and feel the zing of the light vodka.

The band was just then playing a medley of old New Orleans jazz tunes. The young crowd of noisy Parisians had cleared several tables and were dancing to the lurching, shuffling clarinet notes and saxophone swoons.

"Come on," I grabbled Christine's hand. "Let's just swing to the music."

"Ohh!" she screamed. "God, this is madness. Just cocky madness." Her face glowed with pleasure and sheer physical, carnal joy.

We danced a quick step, to the sway of the trumpet and mellow tones of the deep sax, punctuated by the high notes of the clarinets. Sweat popped out on both of us, and I had to loosen my tie. Christine kicked off her shoes and I spun her around and brought her back into my arms. We must have danced like that, nonstop, for twenty minutes. Exhausted, I wrapped my arms about her shoulders and we collapsed in our chairs. To my amazement, the Parisian crowd of young couples began applauding and chanting, "*Encore! Encore! Sauvage*!" I waved them off, and Christine and I ordered a fresh round of drinks.

"I haven't had mint juleps in years," I confessed. "I think I'm going to get drunk."

"Oh, now, what's to be said for getting potted, ole boy! But, keep sober. I want you in bed!" she declared quite definitively. Her eyes shimmered with happiness in the multicolored green, pink, and yellow lights that swirled overhead.

"Then you've got to get me out of here. Damn, but I feel dizzy already."

"Now, now! We're only steps away from our soiled sheets. Incidentally, when was the last time they changed your sheets?"

"Three weeks ago, I think. I turned them last week. Mine aren't too bad."

"God! Here we are in Paris. In France! And they still don't change their sheets but once a month! Really, isn't that something?"

"No. You're the something. I could fall in love with you, you know."

"Now, now! Remember, we're not to talk of love. I don't want that ghostly past of yours coming back to haunt a lovely night. You have forgotten her, haven't you?"

"Yes. She's just a ghost of the past. You're very lovely, you know. Let's go."

The second julep had contained too much bourbon, and I could smell and taste it on my breath. But we made it up to Christine's room, undressed, and tumbled in bed. It was all I could do to make love. As I kissed Christine one last time, I suddenly remembered the Fontainebleau tour! "Oh, God, I've got to get in my own bed!" I moaned. "I'm supposed to go to Fontainebleau tomorrow. Can you believe that?"

"Don't ruin our night," Christine protested in a slumberous trance. "Ummm!" she held on to me. "Don't go."

"I have to," I kissed her. I slid her arms off of mine, slipped out of bed, gathered up my clothes, and tiptoed down the hall.

17

THE COLD MORNING AIR choked my throat, thanks to the slate-blue clouds of pollutants and noxious traffic fumes that swirled about the street in front of the Palais de Justice. Buses idled loudly along with fleets of taxis awaiting clients in the commercial parking zone. I could see the needle-like spire of Sainte-Chapelle when I turned to look over my shoulder. Just then, I wished I were inside the reliquary's walls. I would have, except it didn't open until 9:00 a.m. I had visited it in February and again in March and could still see its spindly tall windows of cobalt and deep blue that sent waves of delicate light shimmering across the chapel's muted glow to the muffled murmurs of traffic outside.

The bus for Fontainebleau was just pulling up. I could see Monique seated behind the driver. She saw me and waved. A long line had formed where the bus was about to pull in. Suddenly, the French men and women, scheduled for the tour rushed about its doors, leaving the others stunned as they waited in the broken line. Welcome to France! I thought. I remembered how angry I had become the first time I had experienced such rudeness, but I had simply come to expect it in Europe—except in Germany, where such boorish public behavior was never tolerated.

Monique had stepped down into the bus's open doorway and waved for attention. "I must read your names, as you registered. They will not be in alphabetical order, but only as you called in." I was toward the back of the crowd but could see her full, petite, five-feet or less stature. She was wearing a black beret, a silvery, mother-of-pearl blouse, and black tights. Her hair was still growing out, but nestled under her beret in a coffered web of lustrous platinum curls. "Monsieur Clarke. You are number one! The first on our list."

A bemused smile broke across my lips. I doubted that at all. But I wriggled my way through the annoyed sightseers and grinned broadly as I approached her. "Thanks," I whispered.

"No. It's the truth," she beamed. "I want you to sit by me, right behind the driver."

"*Bien sur*! *Merci*!"

As I took my seat, I watched her leaf through her list. Tiny pearl earrings adorned her earlobes. Occasionally, she would look back and smile, in the midst of reading off the names. It took about twenty-five minutes to collect everyone, get them seated, and the bus underway.

"Welcome aboard *Le Miroir Français*' unique tours. We will be featuring others later in May and June, to Chartres and I'm not certain where else. But good morning, ladies and gentlemen. We'll be taking the auto route to the northeast, and then to Fontainebleau. We should arrive in about an hour or so, with any luck." She stated all this with a charming professionalism, while toying with the microphone in her hands. She glanced toward me to see if I had noticed. She was quite the enchantress!

"Once we get out of the city, I will present a little review of the chateau, its history, architecture and art, so you can know what to expect once we arrive. But for now, enjoy your trip. *Bon voyage*!"

"Well, it is so nice that you came," she said, as she sat beside me. "You are comfortable? Yes?" Her gray, steely eyes penetrated to the core of my libido.

"Monique, I would not have missed this for anything."

"I'm so glad you've come. These tours get so boring after a while. I have to invent things to say and do. Once we get there, the chateau people take over, and I just herd the group gently along." She glanced at my tie, my collar, and took a deep breath. "What sort of cologne are you wearing? I like it?"

"Oh, something I brought from home. Old Spice, but it can be quite ragged if I don't shower."

"You Americans and your showers! We are still too medieval. Too primitive, I fear, and hooked on our *eau de colognes* and inimitable perfumes to change. Incidentally, my name is '*Mon*-nique.' You pronounce it '*Mo*-nique.' As if you were saying '*mo-ron*.' You need to stress the '*Monnnn*' part," she emphasized, deliberately shaping her lips and mouth in a devilishly sensual form.

"'*Mon*-nique!'" I repeated after her. "Is that better?"

"Much better."

The bus lumbered and lurched slowly through heavy traffic, ever wending its way toward the Northeast.

"Have you heard anything from the Sullivans?" she asked.

"Yes. I received an aerogram from Julene. It was posted from Athens, and they were on their way to Troy, or Istanbul, I think."

"A marvelous couple! Don't you agree? She *noire*, and he *blanc*. Returning to an America that, I assess, is still racist and prejudiced, *non*?"

"Unfortunately, yes! But we're struggling with it. I think we'll make it one day, God help us!"

"God has nothing to do with it, you know! Not that I'm trying to be their advocate. We have increasing numbers of blacks coming into France from our former colonies. Many are hopeful and ambitious but are still shunned by most French. As Jacques-Maria says, 'We're paying for the cost of an empire, and who knows where it will take us?'"

"I gather he doesn't want that empire to end, or at least not its influence."

"True, the latter, but *la France* is no longer *la France* we once were. It is a sad era for us French. But, enough of that! I don't like it. Tell me about yourself. I've got to get back on this microphone soon."

"Nothing to tell. Just your typical professor on sabbatical, an admirer of French culture, art, history, and philosophy. And Paris. It all comes crashing to an end in August."

"That's a pity. But I don't believe you. You're a man with a mission. I can see it in your eyes, in the way you hold back your true feelings, in the way you looked at Julene and even me. There's something about you I'd love to know. I can't quite put my finger on it. But it's like you're searching for something you've lost. Something you can never have again. *Oui*? Tell me I'm right. Isn't that so?"

"You're as wise as Minerva. Maybe, maybe not. But I think any philosopher of my generation feels as I do. Camus said it best. We live in a time without consolation. We can never have that again. I just don't accept his notion of absurdity, or that we have to conclude that Sisyphus is happy. That rolling his stone up the mountain every day, again and again, is an act of courageous virtue."

"Shoosh! That's for you and Jacques to discuss. Besides, I don't think it has to do with philosophy, but something more down to earth and human. Right?"

"Perhaps."

"You poor man. All I wanted was an amorous sigh, a *coup de caress*. Maybe a little hug, or wink, or peck on the cheek. Not your existentialism, even if it's French! Well, time for my speech," she chirped. "Ladies and gentlemen," she began. She rose to her feet and looked back at me, somewhat disappointed, yet all the more determined to pursue the attraction we felt. She balanced herself against the armrest of the seat and reached for my shoulder with her right hand. She held the microphone in her left. I could feel the pressure of her finger tips. I reached up and touched her hand. She did not remove her own, but kept it there. Her fingers were warm, soft, alive, both with excitement and uncertainty. She gripped my fingers in turn.

"We are off to see France's oldest hunting lodge—though it hardly looks like one today. If you're a hunter, we'll have to leave you in the forest." There was a polite titter of laughter. Monique glanced down at me and smiled. "In 1169, the exiled English priest, Thomas à Beckett consecrated a chapel, which of course has since vanished, but not in the fashion in which he was dispatched." More laughter. "But we must take our imaginations back to the sixteenth century, at the time of the grand Renaissance, for our present chateau to make sense. It was our Francois I, that flamboyant monarch and contemporary of England's Henry VIII, who acquired Italian architects to build his new hunting lodge. Of course, speaking of Henry VIII, whereas he executed his infertile or displeasing wives, our more enlightened Francois simply took on mistresses." Another ripple of light laughter drifted to the rear of the bus. "You are going to see many ceilings and panels and frescos painted by Francois' legions of artisans. Wars have been kind to spare them all. Though Allied troops in World War I ate all the fish in the great *Etang des Carpes,* and our gracious occupiers of World War II seined the basin for any finned denizens that had escaped our allies' fine appetites." Once again, Monique glanced down and smiled. "King Louis XIV added many gardens, but it is our Napoleon, however, who transformed Fontainebleau into the chateau it is today. Napoleon turned it into his Versailles, commissioned new gardens, even held Pope Pius VII a prisoner in its confines in 1812, and, of course, made his famous farewell speech to his soldiers from the horseshoe staircase in the *Cour des Adieux.* So much history, so much grandeur, something of the soul of France still breathes in its courtyards, salons, and forest! I know you will enjoy the tour."

An enthusiastic outburst of applause embraced her speech, especially in reference to her penultimate line. The tourists were principally French, from the middle and lower classes, and only a few on board were foreigners. I had taken tours like this before, and had always come away softened by the patriotism and genuine admiration of their past that the French possessed beneath their Gallic exteriors of blank or haughty stares.

Monique released a long sigh and sat down. "How did I do?"

"You know how you did! You won their hearts and stole their souls."

"Jacques would have been proud."

"Yes. I've gathered from his articles that he's quite devoted to your country's past and its potential future."

"Yes. Whatever that is. But he's too much of a dreamer, with political ambitions as well. And he can be cruel and abusive when he doesn't get his way," she added in a soft whisper, as she pressed my hand with her fingers.

"I'm sorry to hear that," I replied.

Once we arrived, she assembled us into a semi-herdless shoving cluster of tourists and led us toward the ticket booth. I really had no interest whatsoever in making the tour or seeing the rooms and ornate galleries or hallways. Still, I complied and stationed myself as close to Monique as discretion would allow. The rooms on the first floor did appeal to me, as they contained Napoleon's apartments. I saw what every tourist must see: a lock of his hair, his imperial sash and handsome uniform, his prized medal—the *Légion de Honneur*—and other paraphernalia connected with his reign. I found Henri IV's old library fascinating, but it had been converted into a long hallway of displayed masterpieces. The elegant ballroom highlighted the tour's final moments, with its paneled walls and gleaming hardwood floors and delicate atmosphere—so human and livable, so unlike the ornate Hall of Mirrors at Versailles.

The tour included free time for browsing in the chateau's shops, cafeteria, courtyards, and forest.

"I'd better lunch with the guests," said Monique. Her eyes sparkled, as she studied my own. Her petite face and nose glowed with a hint of the risqué and forbidden. "Why not meet me at the fountain of Ulysses around one o'clock. We could stroll a path or two in the forest before reboarding the bus."

"Good. When do we have to leave?"

"At three. We meet where we disembarked."

"*D'accord*. At three."

She gave my hand a tiny squeeze and scrunched her lips up in a comical kiss. "Till later," she whispered.

I found my way to the staircase, where Napoleon had made his farewell speech before his exile to the Island of Elba. His life seemed like a dark chapter in an otherwise mesmeric tome of French history. With all its battles, killings, razing of towns across Germany and Russia, it had done more to awaken the hunger for freedom and liberty than to gain lasting glory. From Goethe to Schiller to Hegel, it had fueled their own cries for *Freiheit*, and, as in the case of Hegel, for *Recht*, or Law, which only a duly constituted state could impose. All of which then inspired the violent uprisings of the 1840s. But here was the staircase, winding and elegant, paying tribute to France's *grand homme*, who had at least saved her from the butchers' blades and guillotine of the Reign of Terror. I supposed he compared in some way to Grant, who saved the Union while the South continued to wallow in its defeat. I wondered how Julene and Carl were doing.

The statute of Ulysses was not as impressive as I had imagined it would be; but then I had been reading Sullivan's commentaries so long that only Apollo himself could have sculptured the perfect stone; and that only with the help of Athena, who had protected Odysseus throughout his voyage home. Perhaps Julene and Carl were at that very moment enjoying a voyage of their own, if not across to Crete, to one of the lesser islands in that jewel-studded sea of brilliant blues and white-crested waves. I had seen the Aegean myself in 1960. The lucky couple!

"Why are you staring like that?"

I looked down into Monique's eyes, her open mouth. Her breasts were slightly visible; they filled her silky, mother-of-pearl blouse to the swelling point. "Who knows!" I replied. "Just day-dreaming."

"It's that look I told you about. It's so transparent. My instincts tell me it has to do with a woman. Not philosophy. Right?"

"What if you are that woman?"

"Uhhh! You have to have more *élan*, *class*, or as you say in English, 'subtlety.' I like being kept in doubt, always wondering, not quite certain. *Oui*?"

"But what if you're no longer in doubt and don't need to wonder?"

"Ah, ha!" she threw her head back. Her teeth glistened in the sun light. "Come on. We don't have but an hour or so, you know. Let's stroll about."

On our way to the chateau's woods, we admired the flower beds of yellow and blue pansies and red geraniums that bordered the gray graveled walkways and ancient boxwoods. Sandy paths led off a major tree-lined aisle of stately hardwoods, trees of Lebanon, and red-barked pines.

Slender green vines crept up and filled the crowns of the taller trees. Ferns grew profusely in the soft damp undergrowth. Their light and dainty serrated leaves bowed quietly toward the earth.

"Have you ever noticed how humble ferns look?" I asked.

"Humble? They look pretty firm to me, and lacy, like a lady's fan or feather for a hat. You haven't said much. I haven't hurt your feelings, have I? You know, with all my palaver about being coy and subtle?" There was a softness to her voice, an empathy that raised her question above the merely curious.

She suddenly turned and put her arms around my waist. "How discreet can you be? Must I have to put into words what I feel?"

She placed her arms around my shoulders and stretched her body to meet my lips. I could feel her breasts against my chest as her toes sank in the soft sand of the path. "Kiss me," she whispered, as our lips met. They were wet and hot, soft and voluptuous. "Ummm," she moaned. "I have always wanted to be kissed by a tall, handsome man. At least you're tall," she smiled. "Ummmmm. Don't let go, you handsome *man*," she said the last word in English.

"I have wanted to kiss you since the night you joined us at the table." I held her tighter against my chest, lifted her off the ground in my arms, and continued to kiss her. Her cap fell off. I released her and picked it up. I brushed it off and cocked it sexually on her head. "Why do I always fall in love with married women?" I panted with my heart in my throat.

"I knew I was right. It was a woman, wasn't it?"

"Yes. A beautiful, sinewy, luscious woman, but married, all-too-married, I fear. I was stupid. And now I'm being stupid again. Forgive me for violating your appeal for class."

"Don't ever forgive a woman like me. I wanted your lips, too. Jacques, I love, but he is so preoccupied, so sure of himself. So mean when he wants to. He has struck me with the back of his hand from time to time. I've been neglected, you know," she said, as she pouted her lips pretentiously and screwed up her mouth for me to kiss again.

"I'm sorry to hear he's abusive." I embraced her once more.

"Jacques will be gone, you know, for several weeks." She glanced at me, as if to test my reaction.

"*Good!*"

"Yes. To Lyons and Marseille. To market his book, when it's finally published."

"Do you plan to accompany him?"

"No." She pressed the fingers of my right hand in hers, brought them to her lips, and kissed them. "I will be right here, in Paris."

"When does his book come out?"

"In another two weeks or so. We plan to host a party at our house to celebrate. You will come, if I invite you? I plan to invite the Sullivans, too, if they're back."

"Yes. I'll come. I'd be honored."

"And circumspect, *oui*?"

"Yes. You won't have to worry."

"But I think I will. I like to worry about a man like you. You are . . . different, *je pense, n'est-ce pas?*"

"Not really. Just myself. Whatever pretensions I once held, I hope I've given up by now."

"Don't be so sad, my *grand gaillard*. The history of France is a catalog of secret affairs, of unfulfilled desires of lovers, from Abelard and Heloise, to Sartre and his poor Simone. Sometimes they go public, but most are kept hidden and imprisoned in hearts. I've had a misadventure or two myself."

"I can't say I blame you."

She stopped in the path and stretched up her petite body for another hug.

I complied, wrapping my arms, as if in a dream, about her waist, with my hands on her buttocks.

"Will you visit me when Jacques's away? There are places we can go, in privacy."

I thought of Christine, Julene, and, yes, Leeta. And that book I was supposed to be writing.

"Will you? I'll be so alone."

"I will." I looked into her eyes:

> *Who dies just now anywhere in the world,*
> *without cause dies in the world,*
> *beholds me.*

"Yes, *Mon-nique*! I'll come."

Just before we left the park, I saw a tiny green lizard, peeking out at us from under a shingle of decaying oak leaves. Slowly his pigment turned from green to a rusty brown. "Look, Aphrodite, in one of her many disguises," I pointed it out to Monique.

"Yes," she smiled. "Do you know the poetry of Max Jacob? He died in 1944. He was a friend of Picasso's and something of a mystic. He loved composing intricate and imagistic lines. He could mask the simplest feelings in a haze of soul-searching words. Like this:

In the silent forest, night has not yet fallen,
nor the storm of sadness assaulted the leaves.
In the silent forest, from which the Dryads have fled,
the Dryads will not return.

18

WHILE READING ROUSSEAU'S HYPOTHETICAL theory of his "man in nature," a soft knock rapped on the door. It was still mid-morning, Saturday, and my thoughts were vacillating between Monique and Julene. I went to the door. It was Francine. The Belgian was with her. He was slightly taller than I had estimated, and younger as well. His black hair had been freshly showered, and he had combed it back, slick. A set of slate blue eyes examined me. I scrutinized him in return. He had shaved, but his putty-colored facial flesh bristled black with stubble. A pointed chin and thin lips gave him the appearance of a discrete man of the streets. His silky blue shirt was partly unbuttoned, and a mass of back hair covered his chest.

"May we come in?" he asked.

"Of course. Please sit on the bed; I haven't but two chairs."

Francine appeared distressed. Her youthful smile, eyes, and lips masked whatever anxiety she bore. The two sat on the bed and held hands.

"Francine has told me what she told you. Believe me, I'm not the thief or the murderer. I found that star in my hallway, midway to my room. I don't know who rents there. He doesn't eat in the dining room, and I've only caught glimpses of him. He's heavily bearded, smells worse than a Frenchman, and often comes in late with a woman. I can hear them carousing and sometimes cursing through the walls, though he rents two rooms down from me. I've never told this to anyone else."

"Perhaps you should say something to Dufavre. Her cousin's an inspector with the préfecture, and they've been trying to resolve this for some time."

"I don't trust Dufavre, and I'll tell you why." He smiled awkwardly and looked at Francine. "I think she's bisexual, or maybe transsexual, though I'm no prude or judge of that. But, you know that transvestite disco up the street, where they post those erotic photos of *beaux gens*? I went in there one night, and she was there, admiring these guys to no end. I was terrified she'd recognize me, so I left immediately. But the sad part is that Francine's mother sometimes works there as a stripper and hat-check girl, while working at another place."

"It's the money. Mama hasn't any skills to do anything else," Francine added. She looked up at the Belgian with a mixture of sorrow and admiration.

"I want to marry Francine. I'm thirty-one, but I can't until she turns sixteen. I plan to rent an apartment closer to my work and take her with me. That's provided her mother agrees."

"Would you be willing to help us?" asked Francine. "Mama respects you, because you're tall, quiet, good-looking, and, obviously, somebody important. We're just 'Algerian castaways,' Mama says."

"You arrange the meeting, and I'll sit with you. Why not meet in the Garden."

"I'll see," fretted Francine. "Are you willing, Claude?"

I could see him squeeze her hand for reassurance. He placed his right hand on her left thigh. She was wearing a skimpy skirt and sandals; her uncombed hair fell in long strands across her shoulders and black, low-cut blouse. He nodded, yes. "If we have to, I'll take you back to Belgium. I doubt if your mother would really care."

Francine's small face turned white with splotches of pink under her eyes; tears suddenly welled up in her eyelids and streamed down her cheeks. "Don't tell Mama," she began, "but I'm pregnant." She put her hands to her face and wept.

Claude looked away.

I reached out for Francine's hands and smothered them with my own. "Francine, take Claude with you to see a doctor. Try to remain strong. You're not the first couple to be in love under duress, nor will you be the last."

Francine snuffled back her tears. Claude kissed her wet lips and nose.

"Thank you for letting us come in. We'll see about that meeting," said Claude.

I rose, as they did, and walked to the door with them. "Till a later hour," I said.

Claude shook my hand. Francine raised herself on her tiptoes and gave me a hug.

"What is the room number of your bearded friend?"

"He's not my friend, remember. Fourth *étage*, Room 5."

Toward late morning, I descended the stairs to Dufavre's apartment. She and her cousin were having tea. "Please come in," she said. "Daniel and I have made an unfortunate discovery."

"Yes? And I, too."

"Please, sit anywhere."

I sat in an musty leather armchair. Its back and armrests were brittle and cracked yellow with age.

Daniel sat forward. His countenance had taken on an ashen hue. He wore a brown housecoat, dark slacks, and slippers. "The other night we were having drinks at a nearby disco, a sort of off-limits place," his face turned red with embarrassment, "when we saw Mme. Bretagne, that is, Gloria, laughing and fondling a very bearded and uncouth man. Odette recognized him as one of her boarders in the annex across the street. His name is Leon Coubert. His fists were full of franc notes. He was handing the Mme. a necklace, with a large garnet pendant, set amidst sparkling diamonds. Odette's certain that it belongs to the lady who was murdered last month. I have since had the national police check his record. He's unemployed but worked for several circuses as a high wire daredevil. At some point, he became a lush and dropped out, or was fired. We plan to raid his room tonight. And, I regret, Mme. Bretagne's as well. We'll search hers during dinner. While she and her daughter are down here. You will keep this to yourself."

"Of course."

Dufavre wet her lips with her tea-stained tongue and glanced uncertainly toward me. "You said you'd made a discovery, too. Yes?"

"You've confirmed what I've learned. Are the Wetzel's still here?"

"*Non!* They left last night. If Coubert's the thief, perhaps we'll recover some of their loss. But, who's to say?" she looked way somberly.

"I may want you to help us," Daniel directed his statement with awkward hesitancy to me. "Bretagne will not know we've searched her room. About ten p.m., we'd like you to go to Coubert's and tell him he's received an important phone call, and that Mme. Dufavre is holding the receiver for him. The police and I will we waiting at the bottom of the stairwell when he comes down. We're afraid if we go to his room, he'll try to escape from one balcony to another. They say he's very agile, very quick. We'll also have some people posted in the street."

"I'll do what I can. I hear he rooms on the fourth floor, in room five."

"Yes. That's correct. We'll be at the foot of the stairwell when you go up at ten."

Just after lunch, Mme. Angleterre brought me the mail. It contained a statement from my bank in Virginia, indicating that I had fewer funds than I thought. I had also received a letter from my dean and two post cards from the Sullivans: one from Julene, the other from Carl. They were postmarked from Istanbul, sent airmail, with colorful green and brown postage stamps in the upper right hand corners. Carl's displayed a photograph of Schliemann's citadel at Troy; Julene's pictured the rugged, majestic Mount Ida. Wrote Carl:

> *Arrived here tired; somewhat depressed. Ilium is a mound of excavated stones, loose dirt, trenches, not much to go by. One has to stick with Homer, but all worth seeing. If only our guide hadn't been such a malaka. Carl*

Julene's was in total contrast:

> *The air is cold and dry, the sun fiercely hot. I've drafted a few sketches of villages, vineyards, goat herds. Can hardly wait to get back and put them into paint. Excited. It is so beautiful here. Love, Julene*

I had read all this while poor Angleterre was still standing in the doorway.

"*Alors*, Madame! I apologize. Thank you for bringing these up. How have you been? I've hardly paid attention to anyone around here, save myself."

"It's been a busy week, hasn't it? I hear things and see things I'm not supposed to know. May I step in for a moment?"

"Please do."

She glanced over her shoulder, first to the right, then to the left, entered and closed the door. Her dyed red hair hung in her face; bright lipstick was smeared across her upper lip. "Bad news! I've got to leave tonight." She stared down at her hands, which were trembling.

"Are you in trouble?"

"No, and yes. While changing sheets across the annex, I saw a photograph of Mme. Bretagne on this man's dresser. She was—shall we say—naked, in a very compromising position. This man who rooms there is a Monsieur Coubert, a filthy nobody, a disgusting animal. They were drunk. In the picture, money was spread across the bed, along with purses, wallets, and jewelry. Just then Çoubert came in. He saw me staring at the picture. 'You have seen nothing! Get out of here, or I'll kill you,' he threatened. 'Get out!' he shouted. '*Allez, allez*!'"

"Don't leave for a while," I urged. "I hear and see things I'm not supposed to know either. There may be some—how do you say it in French?—*feu d'artifice* later on."

"Fireworks! Yes!" she smiled. "I'll wait and see. Thank you, Monsieur. Will you have tea this afternoon?"

"I'm not sure. I haven't checked on Mlle. Cunningham since Thursday."

"You haven't heard, *non*?"

"*Non*, what?"

"She has a visitor from London," a sinister smirk filled her face. "Oh, la la! Big, strong handsome man, on a cane. She calls him 'Tobby.' 'Oh, Tobby!' she cried, when she met him downstairs. I was the one who told her he was here. He gave me a nice tip. Very, very handsome. Didn't she tell you?"

"I'm pleased for her," I mumbled. I thought he was on death's bed!

"Maybe you'll meet him at dinner. *Tant pis!*" she grinned. "How do you say it in English? '*All ees fair een loove an' war*'? *N'est -ce pas*?"

"I might need more than tea," I smiled. "But, yes. Bring it up, about four."

Any thought of working on Rousseau evaporated. Once Angleterre left the room, a part of me remained in shock, yet a deeper and lonelier part seemed reposed. I could have fallen in love with Christine, but, in truth, Monique and Julene fascinated me more. I had all but forgotten Leeta. But what did I think was going to develop? Both were married, just like Leeta! What sort of a personality disorder did I have? Why did I nurse such impractical fantasies? Again and again? My throat grew tight. My spirit sank. Down, down, down it sank.

Who weeps just now anywhere in the world....
weeps for me.

I would walk it off. Yes, walk it off. There was no city like Paris for just walking it off. I left the room, hurried out of the building, and crossed the street to the Garden. I had no idea where to go, what to do, just walk. Walk and walk, I told myself.

Workers were setting out new flowers in the garden's beds. Some were geraniums, others were tall pink and blue spiraled flowers whose names I didn't know. Bushes were being trimmed, fresh soil raked about the plants, and everywhere ubiquitous pigeons cooed and strutted. A glorious yellow sun filled the park with its languid rays; a delicate sky of pale blue looked down from above, from its infinite celestial dome of Olympus. Walk, I told myself. Walk, walk, walk. And so I walked, all the way across the park, and down the Boulevard de Saint Michel, and across the river to Notre Dame, to Charlemagne's colossal statue, and into the church, and back out, and up the river to the Pont Neuf, where Philippe le Bel—the *Vert Gallant*—had the Knights Templar burned at the stake, purely out of spite. Self-pity and spite. Nietzsche had warned about self-pity and spite. But can we ever be warned enough? *Arrived here tired; somewhat depressed.* Yes, I was tired and depressed. All of Paris seemed tired and depressed. The great river looked tired and depressed. It sloshed against the piers, tired and depressed. It was time to walk back. Time for a philosopher's tea. I had to smile.

Just before entering the park, I passed a small bookstore. Perhaps they had a copy of Max Jacob's poems. To my surprise, they had four volumes of his works. I purchased one entitled: *Le Laboratoire Central 1921.* At least it would provide something to read, distinctly different from Rousseau, Baudelaire, and Pascal.

I arrived at the pension just at four. Mme. Angleterre was knocking on my door as I came up the stairs. She carried her tray in both hands.

"*Ah, bon*! I was afraid you were asleep," she stated. "Or that maybe you had hanged yourself," she smiled with droll satisfaction.

"A lot of comfort you are!"

"Monsieur, we must all forget these petite love affairs we have, that, that amount to what? Wounded hearts? They will heal. Take it from a *vieille Parisienne. Oui?*"

"You are too kind. If only I were younger!"

"And I Brigette Bardot! This tray is heavy. Help me."

After she left, I walked to my windows, drew back the curtains, and stared out across the street at the annex. The fourth floor was one storey lower than my own, and the fifth room appeared to face the street. Its window was dark and its iron balcony chipped and rusted. As I thought about it, I realized I had rarely seen a light at that window or its curtains drawn back, or windows open. The balconies to either side held flower boxes, and the balcony directly under it appeared crushed, or bent. Its window was bricked in. I could only imagine what the occupant of Room 5 must look like. Based on Angleterre's repugnance and Claude and Daniel's descriptions of the man, he was either large, ugly, bearded, and brutish, or agile, quick, fierce, and robust? Perhaps he was all eight. I supposed I would soon find out.

I returned to my desk, sat down, and sipped on the tea. It had become tepid, and Angleterre had forgotten to bring any lemon. I drank it anyway.

Slowly I began leafing through Jacob's book, in search of the poem Monique had quoted. I was about to give up, when I discovered its title: *Dans le foret silencieuse.* His work reminded me of Rilke's, until I got to the last lines:

> *In the silent forest, where the Dryads shall never return, there are three black horses. These are the three horses of the Magi kings, and the Magi kings are no longer on their horses nor anywhere, and these horses are speaking like men.*

I thought of Chagall and his upside-down houses, and people, and farm animals. His paintings and Jacob's poem made Kafka intelligible. The latter's tortured stories of the Law, the Gatekeeper, the Trial, the Castle, the Wall of China, and now these three horses, all black, talking like men—made perfect sense. The twentieth century had dumped all its writers, all its true poets, all its more creative painters, upside-down. All their values had been turned on end. The whole world had been turned on end. And no one had yet realized it, save these poets, and composers, and artists, and philosophers like Nietzsche, Sartre, and Camus, and novelists like Hemingway in *A Farewell to Arms*, or Remarque's *All Quiet on the Western Front.* Sullivan's world, too, had been turned upside-down, and his search for that Being behind being was his own quest for a Grail, turned right side-up. I was eager for Carl to return, so we could pursue his thought and see where it would lead.

At dinner, Christine entered with Tobby. He was a rugged, ruddy-faced man of six feet, or slightly less, with square shoulders, a muscular and full torso, and thick head of black curly hair. I judged him to be in his early forties. He seemed a little embarrassed and out of place but smiled expansively as they approached my table.

"Clayton, this is my Tobby," Christine introduced him. An aura of sheer joy shone in her face.

"Pleased t' me you, lad. The name's Tobias Thomas." His entire manner was one of a sincere Brit, just a little thrown off under the circumstances.

Christine flashed a secretive glance toward me, edged with an uneasiness, lest I divulge too much.

I smiled as I shook Tobby's hand. "The name's Clayton Clarke. The pleasure is mine," I said.

Christine seemed relieved as they walked to her table.

Claude had come in with Francine, and the two sat at her place. "Mama's not feeling well," I heard her explain to Mme. Cueillier. "She's gone to the *pharmacie* for some paregoric, or something."

Pierre sat dejected at his table.

"Have some wine, Pierre," I offered, tilting the bottle toward his glass.

"Thanks, but no," he covered his glass with his palm. "I don't feel up to it, but *merci beaucoup*."

I wanted to cheer him up, but it was obvious that he needed to sit there in solitude. Cheerfulness would have to await another time.

Around seven-thirty, I bid the pension guests adieu and retired to my room.

I thought about wandering up toward Montparnasse, to kill a little time. But I needed solitude, too. I was with Leeta again, at Hilton Head, on the beach. The May sun's rays fell bright and molten on the water, and the ocean's gentle breakers tumbled white and lazily ashore. She stood silhouetted in the streaming light. Her tight teal bathing suit smothered her small breasts, pressing them against her chest and outlining her slender body. Her tanned and beautiful thighs were spread apart, as the surf washed past her waist and down around her calves and ankles. She laughed as she stumbled toward me. We embraced, smiled, and kissed. We had collected two plastic sandwich bags of sand-dollars. Some were still alive, and the minuscule hairs on their sandy and gritty bottoms were quietly oscillating, as if swimming in a vacuum. We picked them out and released them in the shallow waves. Leeta's curly hair, small lips, mouth, and nose aroused every nerve in my loins. I kissed her again, as we waded ashore, dried each other off, and ran up the beach toward the hotel. Together we stood under the steaming shower, caressing each other, soaping each other up, groping, laughing, kissing, before wrapping ourselves in the hotel's warm fluffy towels and racing toward the bed. "Let's be decadent," she whispered, as she flopped her lithe body across my chest, her legs astraddle my face, and buried her own in my groin. "Oh, God, Leeta! Oh, God, woman! Promise you will never leave me." Nor did I think she would. Where was she now? With whom? Was she still married or single? Why did I ever say "Yes" to her that first time? Why are some women so irresistible? And why are men such fools? Would I ever forget her? Was I forever condemned to bear that albatross about my neck?

At 9:45 I pulled on a light jacket, locked my door, and headed for the annex. I had never been in the building before. Neither Daniel, nor any police were there; nonetheless, I resolved to go in. It was an older structure than the pension's, one storey shorter, and constructed of building stones and red bricks, covered with peeling mortar. I rang the outside buzzer, entered the hallway, and groped for the light switch. A steep set of stone stairs led in a circular pattern up the dark stairwell. I had to reset the timer again on the third landing. I approached Room 5 on the fourth *étage*, which is actually the fifth floor of a French building, and knocked on Coubert's door. I could hear nothing. The hall's light went out and I had to find the switch again and reset it.

Just as I approached his room a second time, I heard a scuffling sound inside. Two persons were talking, just above a whisper. One was a man's voice, the other a woman's. It was Gloria's! I rapped loudly. "Monsieur Coubert! You have an urgent phone call at the pension. Mme. Dufavre is holding the receiver."

The shuffling quit and the room grew silent.

I knocked again. "There's a phone call for you. Dufavre says it's very important."

I could hear his window open and someone climb out, on to the ledge. A flurry of more whispering aroused my worst fears. I rapped again, loudly and boldly.

Instantly, the door flung open. A bearded man with wine-red lips and piercing eyes grabbed me and threw me against the hall's wall. The lights went out. He was trying to choke me. I turned my face to the right, brought my left hand up under his chin, placed my right leg behind his, and slammed him to the floor. I had learned this trick long ago in a gymnastic class. It always worked, and I could hear his head hit the floor, hard and with a solid thump. I looked in the room. The windows were wide open and a stiff breeze rippled the curtains. I rushed over and peered out. Gloria was rappelling off the balcony on a thin silvery rope. Her shoe had come off on the ledge below, and her foot appeared to be caught in the grill. She was dangling and couldn't descend farther.

Just then I felt a crushing pain in my back. Coubert had wrapped his arms about my body and was forcing me toward the window. I struggled to turn around, but couldn't. His face and sour breath were inches from my mouth. He was panting heavily. We both teetered on the balcony's edge, when his weight suddenly fell away. He had slipped over the grillwork, but was holding fast to my ankle through the grill's iron bars. As he pulled himself up, I felt my body being dragged toward the dark abyss of the night. We would both be hurtling down within seconds. A powerful force clasped my jacket. Arms locked under my chest. I looked around. It was Daniel and Claude. They were hauling me back from the window.

"Hang on, Monsieur," gasped Claude. "We're right here."

I glanced toward Coubert. A wild look filled his face; his eyes glittered in the pale light that radiated cold and yellow from his room. "*Merde*!" he cursed. His grip loosened, and back he fell, down, down, into the night. I could hear Gloria scream, as his body thudded against the cobblestones. I looked down. Police crowded about his crumpled torso.

"Madame Bretagne! Hold still." It was Claude. "I'm going to come for you. Don't move."

He hurried toward his room, then moments later, began lowering himself from his window on that aluminum hook and nylon cord that Francine had described. He descended to the ledge below his own, pulled on the cord to test its strength, to see whether the hook would hold, lowered himself a little more; then he swung out to Gloria. As he passed her I heard him say, "Just grab me on the way back." She had managed to pull her foot free from the balcony, which had broken loose and was dangling above the street. As he swung by, she lunged for him, clasped her arms about his waist, and rode back to the other balcony. A woman in the room had opened her window. A gendarme assisted them to safety. Several minutes later, an ambulance arrived. I could hear its loud klaxon before it turned the corner and stopped by Coubert's body. Gloria's hair was disheveled, her face streaked with tears, her hands bleeding from rope burns. Her fingernails were broken at the quick. She had lost both shoes.

Dufavre, Angleterre, and Francine had come out into the street. Francine was crying. She ran to her mother, but Gloria turned away. Two officers helped her climb into the back of a police van. "Don't look at me like that. You're on your own!" she snapped at Francine. A grim, quiet sadness flashed in her eyes as she took her seat in the dark van. Claude put his arm about Francine's shoulders and let her weep against his chest. Across the street, I could see Christine and Tobby standing in the shadows. We all watched as the van pulled away.

"Madame Angleterre, will you have a drink with me?" I proposed.

"Oh, Monsieur! How can I refuse? There's a fine cheap bar, just down the street. I'm not dressed for anything better."

"You look fine." I took her by the arm, and we strolled toward the bar on the Rue d'Assan, where I had watched it rain and watch the water run off into the gutters. The gutters were clogged with filth, and trash blew in the street. A large rat ran out from the alleyway and scurried across the coble stones to sniff where Coubert's body had lain.

Angleterre observed it with me. A frown of disapprobation formed about her mouth. She shook her head from side to side. "We are lucky to see such a fine part of Paris."

I didn't say anything, but I liked her realism. Rilke could have written a poem to celebrate her sarcasm, or Jacob a line of prose peppered with irony. I expelled a heart-sore sigh of my own.

19

THE WOLF HAD BEEN stalking for some time. The night storm had littered the campsite with white pine limbs. A pewter sky masked the dome of the coming dawn. Our fire had sputtered out, drenched by the torrents of rain that had swept through the camp. Ours was the only tent in the levinless shadows of the forest. Leeta was gathering branches; they crumbled in her hands as she picked them up. They were black with mold and dampness, too decayed for building a fire.

Dark woods surrounded us on all sides. Rivulets of ground debris and rotting leaves had formed straggled ridges of litter where the rain had washed them across the soggy earth. As I ventured from the site in search of dryer firewood, the wolf raised its head and crept closer, its fur a mass of matted black hair. Its paws were black, and its nails, a nickel color. Its green eyes followed my every move. From somewhere, the noise of other campers broke through the struggling morning sky. I looked for the wolf. At the sound of the campers' voices, it disappeared. My heart sank. I had grown used to it. It was my omen, my mascot of nocturnal dreams and recurring sojourns; my angel of the Jabbok Brook, where Jacob wrestled with the stranger. I wanted my lupine portent to return.

As I awoke that Monday in May, I was surprised at how cold the room felt. Once again, I had left my windows open. A clear sky of tantalizing blue bathed the district of Montparnasse with a crisp luster and freshness all its own. As I stared across the rooftops, my soul revolted against the thought of having to pursue more Rousseau. My mind, however, vetoed such a feeling and argued, to the contrary, that I must. Mind versus heart. Reason versus soul. Would the two ever experience reunification? Rousseau had sought to achieve it in his theory of "man in a natural state." Reality versus fiction. Percepts versus concepts. "Percepts without concepts are blind, and concepts without percepts are empty," Kant had written. I would simply have to sit down and complete my chapter on Rousseau. Paris or no Paris. And without Christine!

She and Tobby had already left for her tour of Normandy, Honfleur, Deauville, Bayeux, and le Mont St. Michel. They were probably on their way at that very moment, or having breakfast in some pension, just outside Honfleur, or Caen.

Before departing, Tobby and I had visited *Les Invalides*. We had to hail a cab between metro stops, because of his limp, but, with Christine attending her last week of classes, it gave me something to do and created a positive way of helping me to let her go.

"Ya know, you're quite a decent type," he said, clipping the ends of his words. "Takin' the time to waste on a limper, the likes o' me. Ye Yanks are all alike. 'Least ya educated kine. I'm no philosopher m'self, but I got m' own philosophy. 'Keep fit, a'mit you're mistakes when you're wrong.' Ya know I g've back the diamonds they say I stole, I did. 'An' pursue the woman ya love.' I couldn't let her slip away, ya know. Not Christine. God knows, I've mad' m' mistakes. But I'm reformin' now, an' pledgin' m'self to her."

At least he hadn't lost the woman he loved. *Clarke*! that silent voice reprimanded within; *don't*. It was my mentor Nietzsche, that subconscious *daemon*, as Socrates used to call it, that warned him what not to do when he needed to hear that voice the most.

"Ya know, I served in the British forces, back when we had an empire," he grinned. "In Jordan, Egypt, and Iraq. I was young, and Gawd, the things I did! 'Don't ever let 'em see ya sweat,' my sergeant used to say. We wasn't supposed to let 'em think we weren't their masters, ya know. We made a lot of mistakes."

Our visit to Napoleon's tomb was marred by an ugly incident while we were in line to buy postcards. The woman who managed the little stand outside the precincts was being typically nasty to two men ahead of us. They were German, possibly veterans of World War II. Their French had deteriorated, and they were trying to purchase a box of film. "*Ich mochte gern kaufen disen Film, Madame*," one of the men pointed to the box for the lady. She snubbed him with a rueful huffiness and, raising her hand, waved him aside. "*On ne parle que le français ici*," she muttered rudely. However many postcards I had intended to purchase, l no longer wanted them. "Let's move on," I said to Tobby. "Agreed!" he said, with his teeth clamped tightly in his rugged jaw. His eyes stared at her in baffled surprise. I thought of Gibert's column. Yes. But this time the Gallic essayist was wrong.

Rousseau's volumes laid open before me. I had taken unstinted notes form *Emile, Discourse on the Arts and Sciences, What is the Origin of the Inequality Among Men,* and *The Social Contract.* Few philosophers, or historians of philosophy, had devoted significant attention to Rousseau's epistemology, or theory of how we come to know what we know, but all the strands were there. Descartes had begun by questioning and doubting what mankind was supposed to know. Equally—somewhat like Descartes—once Rousseau began the process, he too met no obstacles in affirming his own existence or God's. He had simply deduced from the rules of reason what appeared to him as the higher and nobler truths of the mind, and, with optimism, resolved to launch his theories on those "self-evident . . . propositions that I could not sincerely refuse to believe." Above all, he resisted remaining in a state of doubt, for fear of the eroding consequences that skepticism would have on the foundations of society. "I meditated on the sad fate of mortals adrift on that sea of human opinion." He did not relish floundering from doubt to doubt, or uncertainty to uncertainty. Believing in the basic goodness of mankind, he concluded its corruption was due to the profligate and selfish interests of the arts and the sciences, fueled by greed and flattery. He struggled to know what "man in a state of nature" might have believed and how he might have acted. Yes, he would have elevated his particular needs over the universal demands of others, but, upon reflection, as mankind grew in "wisdom and stature," the man of nature would foresee the value of a general will over his personal ego's desires. Thus, the social compact was born, and the role of a legislature between the individual and society came into being. Sadly, "man is born free, and is everywhere in chains," Rousseau observed, but this did not have to be his fate. Having confirmed his own existence as a feeling and thinking entity, he acknowledged with Pascal, that when he looked outside himself, it was with a "kind of shudder," as one "cast into this vast universe, lost in the immense numbers of entities" without knowing what they were. But when he reflected further on this dichotomy, he discovered that he was "incontestably in the foremost rank" and able "to comprehend the meaning of order, beauty, and virtue." He could contemplate the universe and raise himself toward "the hand that governed it." All this gave him a "feeling of gratitude and exaltation toward the Creator," which in turn was not something philosophers had taught him, but which was "dictated to me by nature herself." Here, I felt, was that bond with Being that Carl himself was after and which the Greeks had lost once they abandoned their Olympian gods and distaff consorts and stumbled headstrong down the road of reason, shorn from its Dionysian passions.

All this constituted that ontological approach I could not reject. There are truths that come to us in the agony of searching the self, which, while no science can validate, nonetheless we cannot deny; among them that we exist, that we belong to an order and beauty and mystery that transcends us, that our feelings of finitude and grandeur are not without warrant, and that this inner truth takes precedence over every skeptical system that would reduce us to nonbeing. And the fact that mankind has worshipped it as a Thou, and not as an It, cannot obviate its significance, whatsoever, but discloses the deepest secret of human existence: that our very substance is a conscious element of the universe's throbbing pulse. We have come from it and shall return to it. Now with "gratitude and exaltation," we may die in peace. "*There isn't a human life that isn't salvageable, if it wants to be.*" That is what the "state of nature" taught Rousseau, whose voice he could not silence.

As I jotted down these ideas, I was pleased that I had stayed in the room and forced myself to draft more lines. By midmorning, I was ready for my break and sought out Demetrius's kiosk, near the Montparnasse metro stop.

"Ah, *Professeur*! My brew hasn't killed you yet!" he greeted me. "You must know quality when you taste it?"

"Listen, I need to know the meaning of a Greek word a colleague sent me."

"Yes!"

"*Malaka*! What does it mean?"

"Oh, *bigre*! Here all along I thought you had class! '*Malaka*?' It means 'fool,' 'idiot,' 'nit-wit,' 'scoundrel,' '*jerk*,' as you say in English. Only, it's worse than that." He pretended to stroke his private area, while making a ludicrous face. "Disgusting! Was he calling you one?"

"No. He's visiting in the Greek Isles and Turkey, and that's what he either called or thought of his guide."

"Ah, ya, ya! A *malaka* himself!"

"Not hardly! He's a Ph.D. from Harvard."

"I wouldn't know."

He served my coffee and a sweet, gooey roll. "Try this one," he smiled. I paid and bought a paper, as well.

I walked to the Garden, found and empty bench, and sat down. The war news in the paper was bad. More and more troops were being killed every day. The VC were everywhere. A photo of a bleeding child in a rusty wheelbarrow, being pushed down a street, was most disturbing; let alone the bandaged heads and eyes of wounded GIs. An article about Nixon praised his and Kissinger's efforts to "find peace with honor." The two were pictured, drinking tea with several Asian diplomats.

Three months earlier, a neighbor in my hometown in Virginia had written me about her son, Rowland's, death. Rowland and I had grown up on the farm together. He was two years younger than I. He had graduated from VPI, had been a member of the cadet corps, and was serving his second tour of duty in Vietnam. Originally assigned to ordnance, he had been promoted to Captain and made director of the homebound dead. His job was to check the body bags, see that they were tagged probably, write letters to the parents, wives, or children, and ship the bodies home by plane. One day he didn't report for duty. His room in his barracks was empty. A week later they found his remains, zipped in a body bag. He had zipped himself inside, before blowing his brains out with a pistol. The bag was properly tagged and found lying in a corner of a hangar.

Rowland and I loved to play cowboys and Indians. We had seen a Saturday movie, featuring Randolph Scott as Buffalo Bill, and some red man as Yellow Hand. The two, according to legend, had met in a creek bed, knives in hand, and had fought a duel to the finish. Of course, Randolph Scott won. Rowland and I would take turns being Yellow Hand and Buffalo Bill. Barefoot and in our frayed blue overalls, we would square off with only a shallow ford between us and race toward each other. Poor Yellow Hand never won. Exhausted, blue from cold, shivering and wet, we'd run to his house, where his mother would serve us a hot fluffy biscuit, steaming with butter and strawberry jelly. And a tall Pepsi to wash it down. I had written her back:

> *I am so infinitely sorry. My heart breaks with yours. I have always cherished your warmth and kindness. I promise I will look for Yellow Hand when I, too, cross the brook. Love, Clayton.*

Later, she sent me a picture of his grave.

Passing time became a labor of love: an art. Once a scholar has his or her hand on a book, a clearer vision of its theme and task emerges. An hour here and an hour there seems to put one squarely on the mark, and less time is spent in ancillary reading. So it was.

A second aerogram from Julene had arrived. It was postmarked Salamis, Cyprus:

> *Oh, so beautiful here! Knossos is lovely. The avenues of olive and cypress trees! The green of the verdure and gold of the hills! I cannot believe how stunning the palace ruins are. The pink figures of undulating birds and dancers, the stained pillars of fading red hues, the steps leading into the so-called labyrinth, and the marvelous murals of acrobats tumbling over the horns of bulls! Never have I witnessed such agility and grace, painted on walls. Our hotel is plain, simple, but clean, the food too spicy, the bread too hard. Carl's spirits have revived. Reviewing the mound, chambers, and halls have enlivened his step again. His confidence in his own findings has soared anew. It is so good to see him cheerful, smiling and prowling around like a man (ha!). You would love it here. So much to talk about when we return. That should be soon. Carl plans to leave for the States in late June or early July. Will you call the Giberts for me. Please tell them our plans. We do hope to see them again. Their number is: 28-32-04. Love, Carl and Julene.*

I stared at the Giberts' number. In all likelihood, both would be at work. But, at least, I had Monique's number. Did I dare call? It was still early. I paced the room, descended the stairs to Angleterre's office, and asked to call. She handed me the phone. I dialed the number, listened to it ring, and waited for an answer. Fortunately, or unfortunately, no one picked up the receiver.

What to do? Thinking of Monique brought to mind that exquisite tour of the Chagall exhibit and the Russian's magnificent paintings. The newspapers had announced that the exhibit would close at the end of the week. I took the metro to the hall and re-wandered its length. To my joy, only a handful of visitors had chosen to do the same. Time abounded for standing before each work, or sitting on the benches in the aisles, to admire the haunting scenes of Jewish culture that had compelled Chagall to paint his hometown of Vitebsk. Time and again, I wandered about, stood engaged, absorbed, enthralled before his canvases, meditating on their finer details, constantly dazed and benumbed by what I saw.

La Maison Bleue especially possessed enthralling qualities. It looked like a polished manifesto, celebrating Russia's rustic past, with its more baroque and warm present. An ancient log house, swathed in purplish blue, rests on a precipice. It overlooks a steep ravine across which rises the bucolic town of Vitebsk with its old monastery of onion towers dominating the hill. Sheep appear to be grazing below the blue house that rests on teetering pillars of red brick. A brown path disappears down the hill, then reappears as a diminished line, leading to the banks of a river. The town's buildings tilt in hues of pale brick and muted gray. Fields of green and pea yellow border the town's walls. Faint crosses are traceable on each of the monastery's towers, which in turn are reflected in the river below. Nature is as much a part of this painting as are the dwellings and distant windows and the blue log-cabin's missing panes. The cabin's door is open, but it is too dark to see inside. Should one enter, or take the steep path down the hill? Does one go with the past or the present? Isn't all going into the present a going from the perspective of the past? Rhythm, balance, equilibrium, distance, confront the viewer on all sides. To stand frozen in time before this picture allowed my own restless psyche to find anchorage again.

The Promenade was just as powerful. The youthful Chagall had painted himself, holding his beloved Bella's right hand. She floats in the air, in her purple dress and purple shoes. Chagall holds a dove in his right hand. His enlarged white shirt collar laps over his black tuxedo's lapels. An enormous smile of beet red lips cuts across his brownish-gray face. Cubic houses of green and black form the background. Slightly off center, the curving pink dome of a church catches the eye. Figures, town, and fields are set against the horizon of a milk-smooth sky. A bright red, yellow-flowered picnic cloth, spread with a glass and decanter of wine, lies near the artist's feet. A tree's blue leaflets adds a mystical touch. Optimism, exuberance, and charm seize the viewer. Love unites this couple, yet each is an independent person of his or her own. I had not expected to receive instruction, some sort of aretetical lesson on the human condition. But it was all there in *La Promenade*.

Upon returning to the pension, I was shocked, as well as elated, to discover Monique sitting in the dining room, having tea with Mme. Angleterre. It was almost six. Dinner was less than an hour away.

"A reporter friend is here, Monsieur," beamed Angleterre, "to interview you, she says."

Monique's eyes subtlety sized up Angleterre's suspicious airs, while simultaneously signaling relief at my arrival. A cryptic and enigmatic smile slipped across her face. She had cut her hair again and dyed it black with silver strands. The style exposed her short neck and gave her profile a slightly crisp hieroglyphic look. She wore a medium-length tan skirt, dark brown cashmere sweater, and matching lipstick. Long silver earrings dangled above her shoulders. "Ah, *bon*! I was afraid you'd never come," she extended her hand. Her face mirrored a contradictory blend of seriousness and mischief, risk and loneliness. Her hand felt cool and her grip uncertain.

"Thank you, Mme. Angleterre," I glanced toward the concierge.

"Well, I shall be off," she said, searching my face hesitantly. "*Adieu, Madame*!" she addressed Monique before leaving the room.

"Can we go somewhere more private?" Monique asked.

"There are lots of quiet places nearby. Plus my room," I suggested, softly.

Monique pursed her lips and glanced about. "Can we have drinks somewhere, and possibly dinner?"

"Of course. I'll tell the kitchen not to expect me tonight. They like to know in advance."

After conducting such courtesies, I led her across the street, by way of the Garden, and toward the oriental restaurant, near St. Sulpice. We were seated at a lovely table, covered with a bright red linen cloth, set for dinner. We ordered drinks. Monique started to light up a cigarette, then snuffed it out, and crumbled it in an ashtray.

"Why don't you smoke?" she asked. "I get nervous when I don't."

"Please, go ahead. I don't mind."

"No. I'll wait," she smiled. "Where were you this afternoon?" she suddenly asked.

"Believe it nor not, I went back to see the Chagall exhibit. Such haunting paintings!"

She let out a nervous sigh. Her fingers were trembling. Her cocktail sloshed audibly in her glass.

"Can we go to your room? Jacques's out of town for the night. Can we sneak there without being seen?"

"Yes. Around seven, dinner is served, and most guests are seated by then. We'll not meet anyone in the hallways."

"*Bon Dieu*, but I'm hot!" she fanned herself with a napkin. A tender smile broke suddenly across her mouth. "Is anyone looking?"

I glanced about. "No."

"Kiss me. Lean over here, and kiss me."

I stretched my upper body across the table and stared into her eyes. They reminded me of Leeta's. My mouth moved slowly toward Monique's glistening lips. She placed her right arm about my neck and drew me toward her open mouth. Our lips touched; then pressed hard against each other's. A rush of near sub-conscious bliss blotted out the room's interior and flickering lanterns along the wall. My groin grew tight. I did not want to break the spell.

We completed our drinks and walked back toward the park.

"What time is it now?" she asked.

"A little past seven."

We were holding hands. Dusk was on the verge of extinguishing the sky's eternal light under a cape of gloaming twilight. Phoebus Apollo would soon be stabling his tired steeds once more at Mt. Olympus's underground gates, having made his long night journey back from West to East.

We climbed the stairwell, all but tiptoed to my room, and, once inside, undressed. I pulled up her sweater; she turned for me to unfasten her brassiere. Her breasts were firm and ample, her nipples erect and round. She slipped off my trousers and underwear. She put her arms around my neck and straddled my waist with her legs. I pressed her against my body and carried her to the bed. Not since Leeta had I burned with such passion. Not since Leeta had I held a woman whose own passion blazed so hot with the flame of desire. We kissed, caressed, and rolled in each other's arms. Finally, around ten, we straggled out of bed. We sponged each other off, redressed, and slipped out of the pension.

"I'd better go home."

"Aren't you hungry?"

"No."

Outside, the night air felt cool and clammy; the glow of Paris shimmered over the housetops and buildings. Its neon hues of rose, green, and mellow saffron bathed the district in surreal magic. Over the quiet locked Garden of Luxembourg, a star or two was actually shining.

I hailed a taxi for her, hugged Monique one last time, before shutting the door and watching the cab drive off.

20

SINCE JULENE'S RECENT AEROGRAM had been postmarked less than a week earlier, I knew the couple would soon be returning to Paris. Thus, I reread those last chapters of Carl's I had promised I would. Perhaps I hadn't promised him, but I knew I needed to review them, at least cursorily. Otherwise, the proposed discussions he wanted to have would prove fruitless.

I turned to his long, multi-sectioned chapter on Zeus, and began reading:

> Note the epithets ascribed to Zeus: "first among the gods," "greatest and most glorious," "wise in counsel," "Father Zeus," "Father of men and gods." These are but a few of the most used to laud Zeus. They portray him as pre-eminent, almighty, inscrutable, omniscient, glorious, and wise. As he warns Hera, "There is nothing you can do. . . . You may take it that my will [shall be] done." He is the deity of "absolute power," "supreme in might." If these ascriptions attest to Zeus's general pre-eminence, Homer employs an additional three to substantiate his royal and undisputed lineage: "son of Cronus," "son of the sickle-wielding Cronus," "almighty son of Cronus." Let readers remember that Zeus already represents a third generation of progenitors. The first two were corrupt, inept, or unworthy of the highest supremacy. Cronus emasculated his own father: Uranus. Zeus overthrew his divine parents, Cronus and Rhea, and cast them with their monstrous allies, the Titans, into the abyss of hell. Already we stand on the brink of a cosmic fall, similar to Marduk's conquest of Chaos and the entangling threads of Tiamat—myths that surface again in the scriptures of the Old and New Testaments!
>
> Like his prototypes of the Ancient Near East, Zeus is associated not only with the stratospheric realms of heaven, but also with its atmospheric bands of lightning and thunder. Listen to these mighty phrases that say it all! Zeus "who drives the storm

cloud," "who darkens the clouds," "who delights in thunder," "who marshals the clouds," "lord of the lightning flash," "light thundering Olympian," and "far thundering Zeus."

Alas, however, if Zeus is almighty, he cannot be said to be all good. Menelaus calls him "spiteful." Achilles' mother persuades Zeus to torment the Greeks, simply in revenge for Agamemnon's arrogant behavior toward her son. Hera and Athene unite against him to obstruct his will in every way they can. Both goddesses resent, berate, and despise him to his face, though they cringe in fear of his vengeance. Along with Aphrodite, these three powerful and meddlesome goddesses are able to intervene in human affairs, though always with Zeus' knowledge and passive concurrence.

Homer's epic is far from maligning the powers of a Mother Goddess. Hera, Athena, and Aphrodite all express concern for justice and fairness, as seen from the human side. Yes, Aphrodite quite naturally interferes on behalf of Paris, to whom she granted Helen, since he favored her as the most beautiful of the three. In turn, Hera and Athene equally champion the house of Atreus, the home of Menelaus, whose wife the gods bestowed on Paris. More than jealous antipathies are at play here. In the opening chapters of *The Iliad*, sacrifices of bulls and grain are offered to Zeus and Apollo. The gods accept these offerings, but Zeus, in particular, refuses to grant his suppliants' prayers. From the sky down, mankind becomes shorn of justice. Appeasing the gods no longer works. Sacrificing to Father Sky and Mother Earth increasingly ends in frustration, sorrow, confusion, silence, or conflict.

The grand ancient synthesis, inherited from Near Eastern cults and the rites of the Indo-Europeans, had begun to falter and fail. Who is in charge of heaven and earth? Who is in charge of life? Who directs the ways of men, their mortal passage, determines events, and human fate? If the gods alone enjoy immortality, what is the purpose of human life? For Homeric men, it is glory in battle and eloquence in counsel, the one personified by Achilles, the other by Odysseus: "equal in wisdom to Zeus." For women it lies in the stability they bring to their loyalty to husband, hearth, and kin. They suffer as much, if not more, than men, and probably always have, long before Cro-Magnon Man poked in smoke his charcoal lines on damp cave ceilings, in his reach for the godlike stars.

Homer writes in a time of transition. *The Iliad* and *The Odyssey* depict this transition. They witness to it in the twilight of its baronial gods, as mankind moved from hunter/gatherer to settler/landowner; as bands of small tribes created walled, city-states. I detect no willful, conscious, or overt attempt to suppress the

> Mother Goddess in favor of the Sky God, Zeus. Greece was moving toward the time when Protagoras would surmise that "man is the measure of all things, of the things that are that they are, and of the things that are not, that they are not." But that is the subject for another book, another study, that takes us far beyond Homer.

As May brightened the boulevards of Paris with banks and beds of brilliant geraniums, yellow, red, white and blue pansies, and the lofty plain trees' buds metamorphosed into full green leaves, a cold snap settled across the suburbs and parks, and cool winds blew restlessly down the cobblestone streets. More of the city's homeless poor crowded into recessed doorways, huddled over the metro's grates, or hunched head down, backs to the wind wherever park benches provided exposure to the sun.

I was strolling toward the Pont Neuf, when I passed a man weeping in the shadows of a cinema. The woman in the ticket booth was explaining to an elderly well-dressed lady in line, her predicament.

"It isn't fair to us. No, it's not right. We have to stand here all day, selling tickets, watching this parade of misery beg for seats inside. Sometimes they pilfer enough coins from somewhere to purchase one. Then they sleep in the back corners, or crawl under the seats to stretch out. You can smell them, too. Sometimes we find them in the morning, still sleeping in the aisles. We have to force them up, slap them, sometimes. It's hurts to have to be so cruel. But it's not our fault. Most of them stay drunk, anyway. Their families should care for them. Not us hard-working classes. My income is practically zero. It just isn't right. I can't sit here and eat, even nibble on a crust or crumb, without one of them trying to make me feel guilty. *Coupable*! Me! As if it were my fault that they're poor, sickly, and wretched. Doesn't the city have a home for them somewhere? Why must we bear their burden? Isn't life hard enough for all? Forgive all this chatter, but look at that old sot right there. Yes, the one sobbing because I wouldn't share the last bite of this rotten apple with him," she pointed to the core next to her. "Off with you!" she raised her voice behind her glassed-in window. "Shooo! Get on!"

The man looked up at me. His red nose dripped with tears; mucus glistened on his upper lip. His eyes appeared swollen, his cheeks feverish. His hands were black with grime and filth.

"Go on!" the woman continued. "Get on!"

I bent forward and offered him my hand. "Sir, there's a grocery back up the street. Please take these coins and buy an apple or orange or whatever. Please!" I handed him a fistful of change—seven or eight francs worth.

He accepted the money, but hid his face from me while the woman continued her tirade.

"Look at you!" she addressed me. "You're not helping him one bit. Some rich American, no doubt. You're the ones to blame. You think you own everything, anywhere, wherever." She shrugged her shoulders and, with a callous smirk, handed the woman her ticket.

The well-dressed lady looked horrified. A distraught expression filled her face with sudden pity. She tore up the ticket, shook her head with disbelief, and came to my side. "This is all so horrible, all so horrible!" she said. "You're not to blame." She handed the man a five-franc note and walked on down the street.

The woman in the ticket booth made a face at me, an ugly face, and pulled her shade down. I could see her peering out at me as I walked away.

On my return to the pension, I walked back through the Latin Quarter and stopped by the bookstore where I had purchased the Jacob poems. Its dark aisles and tall dusty shelves had become a haven. Reading the titles and names of great authors and books, slipping them off the shelves and running my fingers across their dust jackets and covers, inspired a sense of transcending time, of touching the very hem of the mystery of being, whatever that was or is. All the main works of the French philosophers, poets, and writers were represented. Most of the books were cheap, but readable reprints, bound in soft brown frayed paper covers. The pages were still uncut, and one had to read such books with a penknife, slicing up through the rough pages' folds, and across the top before turning the page. Purchase was necessary before this luxury was possible. Still, one could browse the shelves, read the table of contents in the backs of books, and wonder what secrets lay inside. Hard jackets were very expensive; however, moderately priced editions bound in glossy yellow covers, were affordable. I had accumulated a trunk of these, which I knew I would have to ship back to the States by boat. Airfare would simply cost more than the tomes were worth. In addition to Pascal's works, Descartes,' Rousseau's, and a few volumes by the luminaries Hugo, Zola, Balzac, Dumas, and Malraux, I had purchased picture books of the various provinces, rivers, chateaux, and mountains, along with posters of some of my favorite Impressionists' works, plus a volume containing photographs and color plates of the more famous holdings in the Louvre. I had equally sprinkled in books of French history and a few popular books on Paris. How I would use all this in my classrooms remained unclear, but when would I likely return to Paris on another sabbatical? Or what better way to pass winter evenings in the Valley of Virginia than snuggled up beside a fireplace with one of these books?

I longed for Leeta. I wanted Monique. I wanted Julene. I was weary of loneliness, of tramping across Paris, of walking up and down its stately boulevards, shaded avenues, and past its spectacular fountains, parks, statues, and archways. Sipping coffee and aperitifs at outside cafés, eating lunches alone in gay or seedy parts of the city, and forever wandering past churches, restaurants, discos, tobacco shops, boulangeries, fruit stands, and chickens and pigs hanging dressed for purchase in open-air stalls, had created a vacuum inside. Nothing could fill it; no anodyne soothe it. I wanted to return home, but still have access to Paris. I wanted to be back in the classroom, lecturing about Plato, Aristotle, Seneca, Augustine, Pseudo-Dionysus, Anselm, Abelard, etc, etc. I wanted to see the faces of my students again, listen to their laughter, marvel at their questions, especially the ones I couldn't answer and to which I was forced to say, "I don't know." Those were the questions that led to further questions, doubts, insights, and discussion. That's when the students came alive and returned to the sources with renewed interest of their own.

I left the bookstore and wandered up toward the great Pantheon, its dome towering in the cold bright sunlight over the edge of the Quarter. A crowd was scuffling in the street. A fight had broken out. Two men were mocking a third. One shoved him, and the second knocked him down. As he sprang up, both struck him again. It was the young hippie I had seen at the rally in a camouflage shirt! "Oh, yeah! Prove it! It's the truth, and you f...in' well know it!" he shouted at the two.

Although I hadn't agreed with his political agenda or cocky, anti-American propaganda, I admired his spunk and his refusal to run from the encounter. A Frenchman, smaller than he, wearing a black beret, with a tattoo of an Asian girl on the back of his hand, was shoving him along. "Beat it, you bastard! I was there and know." The second man appeared to be a Dutch youth in his late twenties, with a blond beard, wire-rimmed glasses, and a hairy blond chest. He was wearing an old French Legionnaire's hat. The hippie's right cheek, near his eye, was purple with a bruise, and the boy's lower lip was bleeding.

"Come on," I said to the youth. "Let's go somewhere and have a beer, and tell me about yourself."

"Coward!" the Dutchman smirked. "He's a coward. Get him out of here."

"I don't see him running," I said.

"Why you *son-of-a bitch*!" the man said in English. "Are you calling me a coward?"

"Suit yourself," I replied.

The small Frenchman stepped back, his face aglow with a smile. "Hit him," he coaxed the Dutchman.

I stepped immediately in front of the young Dutchman and quietly doubled up my right fist. I had no desire to hit the man or be hit in return.

The Dutch youth shook his head. "Proud, stupid American!"

Just then a gendarme on a motorcycle appeared. He dismounted, blew his whistle, and began shouldering a path through the crowd. The two opposers melted away, leaving me and the kid in the street. The gendarme observed the boy's face. "Do you wish to file a report? What has happened here?"

"Nothing that a little water and iodine can't heal, officer," I volunteered.

"I'll be all right," the boy said. "I had it coming," he patted his lip with his fingers. He tried to smile, but the pain in his face was transparent.

The gendarme raised his white gloved arm, blew his whistle, and motioned for the crowd to disperse. "*Aller, aller*. It's always something!" he said. "*Bonjour*," he smiled, as he returned to his motorcycle.

"Thanks," the boy said to me. "I couldn't have taken much more."

"Why are you doing it, then? It's a very volatile subject, even for the French."

"I don't know. Our whole damn country's going to hell."

"You're not running from the draft, are you? Did your number come up?"

"Yeah! Dammit! Yeah!"

He rubbed his jaw, nursed his lip in his palm, and, searching the crowd as if looking for someone beyond it, focused his attention on a young, frightened girl. "I gotta split," he said. "Thanks, man."

As I backed away, the girl hurried to his side, and the two, arm in arm, hastened down a narrow street. It was lined with shops of faded, rotting awnings. "Rooms-for-rent" signs could be see in the windows of the buildings' upstairs' apartments.

Later that night I felt numb from the day's events. What I would have given for Christine! Her arms! Her body! Her lips!

I stared down at my desk and at a Baudelaire poem I'd been reading to myself.

> The deafening street around me howls.
> Tall, slender, in deep mourning and majestic sorrow,
> A woman glides by, one hand fatuously
> Lifting and balancing her scalloped hem,
>
> With regal agility and the help of her leg.
> I? I am drinking, bend like an eccentric, while
> In her eye, a pallid sky, where the hurricane whirls,
> The sorrow that fascinates and the pleasure that kills.
>
> A flash of lightning, then night! You fleeting beauty
> Whose penetrating glance, brings me back to sudden rebirth,
> Will I see you no more, except in eternity?
>
> Somewhere else, far from here, too late, never perhaps!
> I know not where you're going, nor you I.
> O you whom I might have loved, O you who know it.

It had been a long day. If only the Sullivans were back!

21

WHILE I WAS PERUSING sections of Immanuel Kant's *Critique of Pure Reason*, Angleterre knocked at the door. I could always tell her knock from others' as it had a distinct rap and richness of its own. No timidity about her, except when she was frightened. Then all boldness and temerity drained away.

"Yes! Come in!" I glanced at my watch. It was 4:30 p.m. Time for tea, I supposed.

"You have a visitor," she smiled, as she opened the door. "Madame, please enter."

To my surprise, it was Julene.

I leapt up from my desk and embraced her. "How wonderful to see you!"

There were tears in her eyes. Her honey-brown skinned looked lovely. She was clad in a summery dress of green silk, but wore a black jacket, due to the lingering cool spell.

"Mama's had a stroke. She's in a hospital in Huntsville and not expected to live. I can't go home just yet. But maybe I should? I don't know what to do."

Angleterre looked over her shoulder, smiled painfully, and shut the door.

"Aren't there others to care for her?"

"No. Mama never married. Daddy was the only man she knew. Mama was writing her 'memoirs,' as she calls them, or having someone write them for her, just before Carl and I wed. Mama doesn't know we're married, and probably wouldn't approve."

"I bet she would! Don't all moms want what's best for their children, even when they disagree?"

"Don't make it sound so simple. I don't know what to do."

"Well, sit down and tell me about Greece, or your honeymoon, or whatever. You can't be everywhere at the same time. I'm sure your mother would understand."

I pulled up a chair for Julene and sat facing her.

She reached out her hands to take mine, held them for a moment, then entwined her fingers together and placed them in her lap.

"It was wonderful, but so tiring, expensive, nerve-wracking. Sometimes it got scary. Everything you'd expect."

"Why scary?"

"Occasionally, Carl would get moody, or ugly with a guide, or with a cab driver, or a hotel clerk. I'd never seen him that way before. It was like he hadn't found what he'd expected. And it was somehow my fault. He never said as much, but he made me feel that way. Lord, how I wish I knew! I'm just an Alabama nobody from old aristocracy, but I've never done anything to hurt him, save love him." She dabbed her eyes with a wadded up handkerchief she had been clasping in her left hand. She smiled. Her beautiful mouth of white teeth and rich lips sent sensations of pleasure down to the depths of my ever-libidinous soul.

"What did you bring me, gorgeous woman? You make me wish I were Carl," I said, hoping to change the subject.

"Clayton, please don't talk like that. I'm a married woman. Not some Cajun whore." She pressed my hands again, then let go. "But you can kiss me anytime you want," she rolled her eyes in a devilish fashion. "I think it's all right to love two men, as long as one of them doesn't know."

"I tried that with a married woman. Remember that beautiful one? The one I told you about? It didn't go so good." I should have added Monique, but how could I mention her? "How did your painting go?"

"Great! I've brought you back several charcoals. A black and white of the Parthenon and one sketched in pink. It's supposed to be of the columns at Knossos, but I got them too round. They're rolled in a tube. I'll bring them to the Gibert's for you."

"Gibert's! I haven't heard. Is it a dinner party?"

"No, no! It's her party for Jacques-Maria's book. It's finally out. She said, specifically, for me to bring you. You'll get an invitation, she said."

"We'll see," I released a long sigh. "How's Carl doing since your return? Is he feeling better?"

"He's asleep, the last I saw him. We didn't get in until way late. He called the Giberts from the airport. Jacques was out of town, but Mme. Gibert had the newspaper's chauffeur drive us home."

I glanced toward the bed. "Remember?" I nodded.

"You're bad! And I mean, *bad*!" her mouth opened with a luscious smile. "What if I leave my clothes on?"

I rose and took her by the hand.

"Don't let me go to sleep," she warned. "Just hold me." She reached up and kissed me.

I lay down on the bed and scooted over to make room for her. She took off her jacket and shoes, and lay down beside me. I put my arm around her, with my lips near her neck. Slowly, she drifted asleep. Finally, around 5:30 I awakened her.

"Time to get up, Alabama! Your limousine awaits you."

She rolled over, kissed me, and slipped on her shoes and jacket. I walked out to the street with her. We hailed a cab. She hugged me before leaving. I wondered where she and Carl rented? I guessed I would never know.

I had scarcely re-entered the pension, when Mme. Dufavre waved for me to come to the concierge's office. "A Madame Gibert for you!" she handed me the phone. "Just hang it back up when you're finished." I took the receiver as she walked away.

"*Allo! Oui! C'est toi, j'espere?*" I ventured.

"Yes, you know who it is! Are we free to talk?"

"Yes, I'm by myself. What's up?"

"The Sullivans are back, and I want you to join them and a group of others at our house to celebrate Jacques's book. It came out the day before yesterday. At last." Her voice was warm, soft, conversational, not rushed, but nonetheless exciting.

"I'm honored to accept. When's the occasion?"

"This weekend, Saturday, about four o'clock. I plan a quartet to entertain us, then some heavy hors d'oeuvres, and champagne. You can come, I hope?" Her voice had mellowed, and its sensuous inquisitiveness returned. "I've missed you," she added.

"And I, you. Are you alone tonight?"

"Yes. I was afraid you'd never ask. Can I come there? I'm still afraid for you to come here. Plus, I'm hungry. Can we meet at that oriental café?"

"I know a better place. A little Hungarian, or Bohemian restaurant, called *Café D'Orion*. Very quiet and very quaint."

"Perfect. I want to look my best."

"No. Just come as you are. Just take the metro, or get in a cab, and come as you are."

"Then, what about seven, or seven-thirty?"

"Seven-thirty would be fine. Why not meet me at the exit to the Montparnasse metro stop? The restaurant's not far from there."

"Chao!" I could hear her release a deep breath. "You *grand gaillard*, I can hardly wait."

As Monique came up the metro steps, she glanced about, uneasy lest someone should recognize her. She wore a thin pink veil pulled about her head and cheeks, and a light-weight tan trench coat wrapped and buckled about her petite body. Black strands of hair poked out from around her scarf or veil; her eyes sparked as they met mine. She was wearing those high-heeled pearl-studded slippers I had seen her in at the café the first night I met her. I couldn't help but smile. I reached for her hand and kissed her cheek.

"Ah, Mme. Incognito, *ça va bien*? I think even God would recognize you in that outfit."

"Thank heavens you're not God!" she kissed me back. "I feel so, so cheap!" she said, as she averted my gaze. "Where is this place?"

I took her arm and held her tightly against my side. "Just a block or two away. You'll like it, I think."

"As long as I'm with you," she smiled.

I looked down into her face, into her grey, penetrating eyes, and at her little nose and mouth, and the strands of hair plastered to her brow, and her red glistening lips. What I felt, I held back. I wanted her to experience that sense of doubt, élan, class, and uncertainty she professed she preferred. I felt it, too, like a synapse that triggers a spark of anagnorisis, of recognition, along the neural paths of the brain.

She clutched my arm all the more tightly. As we walked along, I asked: "Just where do you live? How will I know how to find your place?"

"Oh, stupid me! Here," she handed me a wadded up slip of paper. It contained her address. "It's in the seventeenth arrondissement, just off the Avenue des Ternes."

Within several blocks, we were at the café.

"*Ah, Monsieur! Et Madame*!" the Gypsy proprietress greeted us. Her eyes searched Monique, aflame with surprise yet satisfaction, but with a hint of inquisitiveness. She rolled them roguishly toward me. "And the Monsieur, how have you been? We have missed you. Yes!"

"It's been awhile," I conceded. "I believe your name is Evana, *Non*? Madame Evana! *Oui*?"

"Such a good memory," she smiled. "'Madame Evana!' Even I like it."

Without snapping her fingers, the two musicians appeared if by cue and began playing softly and passionately their romantic repertoire, all the while smiling as they played.

"I should have warned you," I confessed to Monique, trying to suppress a bemused blush.

"Oh, God!" she whispered. "You're worse than I thought."

For dinner we splurged. After a potage of onion and radish soup smothered in light pepper and served with dark bread, we dined on baked pecan-encrusted duck breasts, wrapped in cabbage leaves and sautéed in a lemon and butter sauce and garnished with peas and new potatoes. A white goat fromage, apricots, and a delicate white Romanian wine completed the meal.

During the dinner, the lead violinist approached the table twice. Each time, Monique politely waved him off. A vast disappointment filled his face, along with a glimmer of hope that I'd not forget him. My smile reassured him. In any case, he and his fellow musician played, with enthusiasm and ardent deftness, a medley of Hungarian melodies of Bohemian folk-life and sorrow.

While I nursed a last sip of wine, Madame Evana returned to our table. She pulled up a seat, smiled, and took my hand. "Monsieur, it takes many readings to get it right," she stated, teasingly. "What have we tonight? Ah! That same wonderful life-line, but," she raised her eyebrows, "something different. Yes! See? Love! *Amour*! It is in your palm and eyes. No?"

"Read mine!" said Monique. "Please, I've never had mine read before."

"Why, of course, Madame. Let me see your hand? Do you have a preference?"

"The right one," she extended her small hand to the woman. "And don't tell me you see money, or fame. They're too boring. I want life. Happiness. Joy!" she glanced warmly at me.

"Oh! Maybe the Madame should be reading my palm? *Non*?"

"No! Tell me what you see, the good and the bad," Monique pursed her lips.

The woman took Monique's hand, held it gently, and peered into her palm. "Ah! So much! A life so full! Only one thing missing!" she glanced at her. Her dark eyebrows arched, then bristled and formed a series of wrinkled folds across her brow. She quietly smacked her lips. "The good and the bad?" she repeated. "*D'accord*! The good! You will know love. It is in your eyes, and in your heart and in your hand. The bad? Who can see that far into the psyche, into the future, into the caveats and machinations of love? Not even I, my dear. Not even I." She patted her hand and kissed Monique on the cheek.

Following dinner, we wasted no time returning to the pension. We ran like lovers in a carefree dream. Afterwards, we lay in bed for a long while, simply holding hands and exchanging kisses. I had opened a bottle of effervescent champagne, and, in between kisses, we sipped from its mouth.

"When does Jacques return?" I asked.

"Tomorrow. He's somewhere in the Northeast, around Rouen, Amiens, and Lille. But, please, don't ask about him." She rolled against me, slid her legs across my body, and held my arms back. Slowly she lowered her face, her mouth, her lips, to touch mine. As our lips met, I could feel her heart, beating deep inside my chest. I craned my neck to kiss her breasts and nipples.

Toward midnight, we walked to the window together. I had drawn the curtains back earlier. In the darkness of the room, both naked and holding hands, we stared out across the buildings and the narrow street below. The glow of the Montparnasse district glistened in a haze of gray, pink, and citron yellow, to dissipate in the night sky overhead.

I kissed her one last time, then we dressed. I accompanied her down the stairs, out into the street, and watched her depart in a cab. I thought of Goethe's closing lines to his poem *Reisezehrung*, or "Provisions for the Journey":

> *What I need is above all to have,*
> *And to take with me, that alone which is indispensable—love!*

22

THE LITTLE CAFÉ OPPOSITE the square and down a side street across the Seine from Notre Dame had filled with customers. It would soon be too crowded for any privacy let alone a late lunch. Carl had not arrived, and as patient as I deigned myself to be, I was afraid I would become petulant and restless by the time he did. I had ordered a beer, half a crusty baguette, and a small serving of liver pâté. As I spread the last pasty knife full across the bread, he showed up.

"Sorry!" he mumbled. "Hard to get going today."

I rose to shake his hand; then reseated myself. Luckily, the waiter was standing nearby, probably hoping I would leave, but his face lit up when he espied Carl.

"Monsieur," the waiter addressed him. "Are you ready to order? And you, sir, would you care for another beer?"

"Yes," I replied. "The same, please."

"A ham sandwich, and whatever he's drinking," Carl nodded toward my glass.

The waiter picked up my empty glass and moved on.

Carl let out a heavy sigh. His face looked sun burnt and hands tanned. White splotches formed circles under his eyes. His red beard appeared tattered, a bit gray, and his receding hair line was pocked with pink freckles. "I don't tan well," he muttered, noticing my inadvertent stare.

"It must have been a very pleasant trip. I made it to Athens, once, but never to Ilium, Rhodes, Crete, or Cyprus."

The big man hunched his shoulders forward, removed his glasses, and rubbed his face with his hands. His eyes were blood-shot. Tiny veins on his nose had turned red. Was this the man that Julene had fallen in love with as a child? Surely not. I suspect he then weighed fifty pounds less, moved like a panther in the dark, and thrilled her with his powerful arms, warm smile, and gentle touch.

"I need to return to the States. I've done my stay here. Whatever whilom aims and schedule I previously set, I've discharged," he said with a grim, self-righteous smile. "I've been no mouse of the scroll! What about you?"

"I couldn't be more pleased. One chapter to go, then it'll be off for me, too. Back to the Valley of Virginia, to the Shenandoah. But, I will miss all this. I love it here. No Rome, nor Greece, nor London town can replace Paris for me."

"Ever the wasting poet, the Romantic," Carl huffed. "What do you teach, anyway?"

"The usual courses in philosophy: epistemology, metaphysics, logic, the history of Western Philosophy, a course on existentialism, etc. I love it. No one could ask for a better life."

"What about this ministry stuff? Why did you give that up, if I may ask?"

"I wish you hadn't. After seminary and one year in the pulpit, I knew it wasn't right for me. I couldn't say the creed with conviction anymore. Bultmann had made that impossible, if not Schweitzer. The more I thought about it, the more I realized that the only Jesus who ever *lived* was the *historical* one, whoever he was, and that the only Christ who *lives* is the *incarnated* one in a person's heart. That pretty much empties the creed; it emptied me as well. What I'm doing now is precisely what I should be doing. I have no regrets."

"I doubt that," he frowned. "We all have regrets."

Just then, the waiter brought his sandwich, beverage, and my second beer.

"How is your own work coming?" Carl asked.

"I still need to read a lot more Rousseau, though I think I know what I'm doing."

"Well, here's what I want to know. And listen to that! I'm deferring to a philosopher! I'm a classicist! A philologist! We pride ourselves on knowing it all."

"You're in good company. Go on."

"Well, all this work on a post-Homeric world has left me depressed. Researching and writing *Beyond Homer* has done more to undo me than energize me. Once the great playwrights had exhausted the Homeric themes, found them void of soul and justice, and the sophists, Socrates, and Plato had followed them, along with the maniacal cult of Dionysus—with all its intoxicating charm and hope—and Plato hypothesized that immortality was possible, when it was clear that even Homer dispensed with such a ruse; when all that I tell you had occurred, it was a tragic step backward, not forward. And all Christianity has done is to transfer the entire myth of Dionysus and Plato's disdain for the flesh onto your historical Jesus and to continue the default of Being, down to our own time. There it is!" he threw up his hands. "And these new studies that harp about the Mother Goddess miss the entire point." He shook his head. "*Do I dare to eat a peach?*" His bearded mouth widened into a toothy grin.

"Why let it disturb you? Isn't the truth supposed to set us free? Why not wring it for all it's worth? Why not hail the Homeric truth as a positive message? That we've never progressed beyond Homer? That Plato ruined it all!" I said all this with a feigned smile. "The only tragedy is," I lowered my voice, "there has to be more. There has to be! I know there has to be. Though I don't know what it is."

He looked at me somewhat shocked, as if I had failed to grasp the point. "There's nothing positive about it. No truths to claim, let alone acclaim. There is nothing more *that has to be.* His was a dying world, in transition. '*Panta rex*,' as Heraclitus put it. Nothing is permanent. Our ambiguity will never end. I'll publish the book, but my mind's already forged ahead to its sequel."

"Which is?"

"You'll find out in time." Carl had dropped a few pink and greasy morsels of ham on his tie and lap. He noticed them and brushed them off. Crumbs had stuck in his beard, and his whiskers twinkled with droplets of beer. He smiled. He tucked his chin against his chest. I thought he was going to burp, but he didn't.

"You've been helpful," was all he said.

For the next few days, I moped about Paris. I took the train to Versailles, visited it once again, rode the metro over to l'Etoile, drifted down *Les Champs Elysées*, and walked up those endless flights of steep steps to the Basilica of the Sacred Heart. Nothing, however, could appease or silence my restless agitation. What were the springs that fed it? Why wouldn't my disquietude abate? Why couldn't it accept comfort? Why couldn't I settle down and return to my work?

I resolved to tour the Louvre, one last time. None of its great artworks, however, rallied my listless emotions or excited my languorous thoughts. Finally, I took the metro to the Bois de Boulogne and began walking its paths. I found a large elm entwined with ivy and encircled with late-spring flowers, and cast myself down under its seraphic boughs. I thought of Monique. I thought of Leeta, of Goethe's one thing alone that is *indispensable*.

It is Spring break. Leeta's husband? Who knows where he is? Somewhere in San Francisco, a colleague said. We have slipped out of town, to the mountains of North Carolina. We lug our camping gear down a treacherous muddy path to set up tent beside a stream. Its white water leaps over the jagged rocks in the middle of the current; alders and dog hobble hover over its banks. Their branches twitch where the limbs dip into the rapids.

A carpet of lush grass struggles to grow through the black rocks along a narrow bottom. We pick our way back into the woods and set up tent on a mantle of pine litter and soft brown leaves. Cool drafts of air slip down the mountain slopes. We break out fleece jackets; I build a fire. Its crackling flames soon warm our hands. I assemble my fly rod, feed the line through the eyelets, test the tippet's strength, tie on a gold hare's ear nymph, and wade out past the alders. The fly touches the water; I wiggle the line; down it sinks and out it stretches. Leeta's face lights up with surprise. She stumbles into the water with my net. Together we land three trout before the cold current forces us back to the fire. We have brought butter, lemons, salt, pepper (plus some cans of meat, just in case). The sweet aroma of sizzling butter and frying trout fills our nostrils with hunger and pleasure; our mouths salivate. Dusk settles around us; darkness follows. The glowing embers sparkle red, as yellow flames lick the night. I see her outline in the firelight. Her face, her nose, her eyes, her curly hair, the soft impression of her tiny breasts against her gray fleece. I build the fire higher; the dryer wood, mingled with the green, pops and crackles, the green limbs hiss and sing.

> *Come to me, Leeta. Come to me. Come to me, darling!*
> *Only one thing is indispensable!*

Something has rolled against my leg.

"Monsieur, may I have my ball?" squeaks a tiny voice.

I sit up. I find myself starring into the bright green eyes of a lovely child, a little girl. Sunlight fills her face; long blonde curls fall about the shoulders of her flouncey canary-bright smock. She squints as she stoops for her ball, then runs to her mother.

23

THE HIGH, BLACK, WROUGHT-IRON gates to the Gibert's home stood wide open. Tendrils of dark English ivy crept over the gateway's red block walls. A shaded, dank, cobblestone driveway curved in a graceful crescent between the gateposts and the *maison*'s elegant entrance. Its architecture reminded me of the facades, brickwork, and slate roofs of the houses about the Place des Vosges. Citroëns, Mercedes, Renaults, and other automobiles lined the sequestered street of the elite faubourg. All the neighboring houses along the street possessed the air of affluence and aristocracy.

A line of people waited at the door to be ushered into the hallway. I joined them and awaited my turn. A young woman with a pen and pad checked people's names as they stepped forth. "Monsieur Clarke!" I announced, enunciating the "k" with a hard sound.

"*Mais, oui*!" the girl replied. "*Professeur Clarke, je croie, n'est pas*?"

"Yes. That's correct. Thank you."

She checked off my name as I entered. The hall was packed mostly with Frenchmen, smoking those rank, pungent cigarettes of theirs. The rooms to either side, however, bulged with couples: with men and women dressed in formal wear, or sporting casual sweaters and jeans, mainly black, their hair cut short, their shoes unpolished. Everyone seemed to be talking, but no one listening. A servant carrying a tray of champagne squeezed ever-so gingerly through the guests. "Et Monsieur, will you have one?"

"Yes," I thanked him. He smiled, quite pleased to be serving at so grand a gala. He was wearing a tuxedo, a starched, white, jewel-studded shirt with huge gold cufflinks. A string quartet was playing Debussy's "Prelude to a Fawn" in an adjoining anteroom. I spotted Julene and Carl, and wriggled my way inside. Carl was seated in a high-back, wide-armed chair that was covered in a dark brown fabric; Julene stood beside him, appearing as fresh and youthful as ever. She was wearing a low-neck, cream-colored, silky dress and matching high-heels. The two were engaged in affable chatter with a tall, refined, Frenchman, whose red scarf-like cravat created a handsome backdrop for his navy blue waist coat and tan trousers. His highly polished shoes gleamed in the room's light.

Carl's pink face lit up when he saw me. He struggled to his feet. "Monsieur Thiers, permit me to introduce a friend and fellow philosopher, Professeur Clarke."

"I'm honored to make your acquaintance," I said, extending my hand.

"No, no! The honor is mine. The name is Henri Thiers. I've read your book—*The Ethics of Virtue*, and would love very much to see it published in French, along with Professeur Sullivan's here. I'm a publisher, and, of course, I'd like to see some of our offerings translated and published in English. Perhaps, Monsieur might be available for such? *Oui*?"

"That might be possible," I smiled. "What did you have in mind?"

"A political history by one of our new writers. Perhaps you've heard of his new book? *Le Futur d'un Grandeur Passé*?" he beamed.

I smiled. "That would be a challenge and a joy. It's not my field, but I'd try."

"Yes. We're presenting it tonight," he pointed toward a sheet-covered stack of books. "Copies for everyone. But not until Madame says so," he nodded toward an archway that opened into a brightly lit dining room.

I peered past his shoulder and gazed about the room. I could see Monique. A beautiful white orchid was pinned to her shimmering dress. She stood surrounded by guests, along with staff members of their newspaper, no doubt. She wore a long, dark green gown, with a tiara of gleaming pearls in her hair. Behind her stretched an oak table laden with hors d'oeuvres, all under a twinkling chandelier of crystal pendants.

"Lovely, isn't she?" remarked Thiers.

Just then Monique saw us, smiled, and beckoned for us to join her in the dining room.

Julene took Carl's arm and glanced with disarming cheerfulness toward me. She had yet to say a word.

"*Et Madame Sue-li-von, comment ça va,* my dear?" I smiled. "You've been awfully quiet."

"It's not my night, Honey!" she rolled her eyes. "It's Monique's and Jacques's. No?"

"This damn culture's gotten to her," grumbled Carl, smiling at his lovely bride. "She won't be worth a damn, at this rate."

Julene craned her neck back to stare at me. "Well, come on, translator! We mustn't get in front of you."

"Like hell," Carl said. "It's not over till the philologist sings, or *signs*, in this case."

I smiled and followed them into the room.

"Ah, there you are!" called Jacques. He had come in from the hallway to stand with Monique. He had opened his hand with a flourish and was gesturing toward Carl and me. "*Voila!* There are our renowned authors, both published! Behold, they've come from a distant and barbaric land, like the Magi of old, in pilgrimage for our wisdom and truth."

The crowd of guests stared at us; then laughed.

"And now, the Madame!" Gibert announced, bowing with a bold, yet Gallic reserve, toward Monique.

Her face fluttered with pride and excitement. "Ladies and gentleman! Welcome to our home and to this marvelous occasion. Jacques has a little surprise for you later on, but first, please find seats in the parlor," she motioned across the hallway. "Our friends from the National Conservatory of Music are about to present an evening of delightful pieces: a performance, I'm certain you'll love. We're setting up more chairs in the hall."

The room and hallway burst into chatter. Slowly, the guests made their way into the parlor, its walls aglow with a variety of rich paintings. Lavish drapes flanked the tall French windows. The musicians had already taken their new position, doing so while the Giberts had been talking.

"Let's just take seats here," I suggested. "Out in the hallway, we'll be less crowded and noticeable."

Carl, Julene and I sat near the room where the quartet had originally been playing. We each accepted one more glass of champagne. It was a translucent, bubbly vintage, fruity, yet light, with a delicate bouquet.

The guests had begun to settle down, filling at first the parlor, then the chairs in the hallway. The musicians were just inside the doorway, between the hall and the parlor.

"How is your mother?" I asked Julene. "Any better?"

"We don't know. Shhhh! " she whispered. "We can talk later."

For the next hour and twenty minutes, the quartet played a wide range of selections including pieces by Ravel, Dukas, Saint-Saëns, the Beatles, the theme song from Dr. Zhivago, and music from the Broadway score "The Westside Story." A well-deserved, loud, enthusiastic applause capped the performance. Someone shouted, "*Encore*!" to which the quartet responded with "*Sur le pont d'Avignon*" and "*Ma petite est comme l'eau*." Everyone joined in singing the two popular folksongs.

As the musicians cleared away their instruments, the guests encircled the dining room table to sample the numerous dishes of pâtés, cheeses, meats, clams, crepes, fruits, breads, and lemon, orange, strawberry, and chocolate tarts. Twenty or more uncorked bottles of the finest wines awaited thirsty pallets. I thought of poor Pierre. How he and Gaston would have feted with self-conscious jollity! I noticed that the publisher had disappeared. Then I heard someone clear his throat. It was Monsieur Thiers. He had stationed himself in the anteroom, in front of the stack of sheet-draped books.

"*Messieurs et Mesdames*!" he began. "Ladies and gentlemen!" he repeated. "Let's not forget why we're here!" There was a ripple of laughter amidst the loquacious din. Folks began quieting down as heads turned slowly in the Monsieur's direction.

"Thank you. Thank you, all." He stretched his neck upwards and rocked on the toes of his shoes. "Of course, this has been in the planning for sometime. Not since de Gaulle's resignation has any government official come forward with a workable vision for the future of France. *La France* has simply lurched ahead, like a slumbering giant, without a goal or polestar during this interim. But, *mes amis*—my precious friends—our own Jacques-Maria has seized the national baton with imagination and vigor, and like a modern Saint Louis, offers us a path toward our unique destiny."

There was a warm smattering of genuine applause. Pleased smiles radiated on many faces.

"Monsieur Gibert, please come forward. Yes, right here."

There was more applause. Gibert promptly stepped to Thiers's side and stared pleasantly at the guests.

"I wish to present the first copy of *Le Future d'un Grandeur Passé* to the author himself. Monsieur, your copy," Thiers withdrew the sheet and handed Jacques a handsome, glossy, hardbound book, in a striking dust jacket, picturing a sun-lit Arc of Triumph, with the tricolors of the French flag—blue, white, and red—unfurled and flapping in a stiff breeze. "We thank you, Monsieur; all France is in your debt."

"Yes, yes!" a grateful roar went up.

Gibert's face reddened with deep embarrassment. It was genuine and sincere. Monique slipped forward, leaned her head back, looked up admiringly at him, and kissed his neck. "I get the first copy!" she corrected the publisher, as she slid the book out of Jacques's hands. She turned toward her quests with a dignified, but droll, smile. Her eyes caught mine. She blushed, cocked her head coquettishly, and returned the book to her husband.

As the crowd milled about the stack to receive copies of their own, as well as to congratulate the author, Monique stole quietly over to me. I was sipping champagne and munching on a lemon tart. I bent forward and kissed her neck, just below her ear. "Congratulations to you, too," I said.

Her eyes brightened, savoring both my message and kiss. While she held me in her gaze, she slipped a folded wedge of paper between my wet fingers and the stem of the champagne glass. She looked with a disinterested passion into my face; her lips formed a silent perceptible kiss. She smiled, turned, and rejoined Jacques.

Julene, who had just then come over, followed her with her eyes. "What's this all about?" she asked tersely. "Honey, you're gonna get in trouble, if I read those eyes right."

I took Julene's arm. "Woman, but you're beautiful! Has Carl ever told you that?"

"Man, oh man! You are one slippery devil," her mouth opened wide, drowning me in her ever-so trenchant and disarming smile.

I bent forward and kissed her neck. "Your mother? What's happened?"

"We don't know. Whoever's been caring for her hasn't called or answered our wires. I think she's probably had a stroke and can't communicate. We may just pack up and go home. Like, next week. I don't know."

"You were going to bring me several charcoals. Remember!"

"Oh, Lord! I totally forgot."

"Alas, my dear, it's time for us to go," sighed Carl. He held a copy of Jacques's book in his left hand. He opened it to the title page. I could see Jacques's autograph, but couldn't read it.

"What a veil of lines and scribbles!" I said. "I guess I'd better get mine."

Julene touched my left arm with her long and lean fingers. Tenderness and uncertainty glowed from her eyes. "I may just mail you those charcoals in a tube. OK?"

"Do we have your address?" asked Carl.

"I don't know, but I'll write it down for you."

Julene looked about and handed me a napkin. I took out a pen and jotted down the pension's address.

"Will you be leaving for the States, soon?" I asked Carl.

"Probably so. I've done about all the research I want to do here. The book's ready to go. I mainly needed a quiet place, free of distractions, phone calls, and students, to complete it. What about you?"

"I'm not sure. More Rousseau, like I said the other day. Maybe some Montaigne. His skepticism warrants inclusion, though that's about all."

"Perhaps we can get together one last time," he huffed, dabbing his forehead with a handkerchief. Tiny beads of perspiration had popped out all along his hairline. His face appeared splotchy and swollen.

"At that restaurant where we met the Giberts," added Julene.

"That would be nice," I replied.

I shook Carl's hand; Julene placed her right arm around my waist and hugged me. I looked down at her mouth, her lips, and her eyes. She smiled. The two turned, thanked the Giberts, and, threading their way through the guests, left the house.

"I must be off, myself," I said to Jacques. "Congratulations. I shall look forward to reading every word."

"Let me know what you think. Henri has told me that he might ask you to translate the book. He has connections with one of your publishing houses in the States. Balfour House, I believe. *Non*?"

"Yes. It publishes only the best."

He smiled, autographed a copy, and presented it to me. "*Voila*!" he announced triumphantly. He shook my hand and returned to signing books for his colleagues and other guests. I looked about for Monique. I had stuffed her note in my coat pocket. I saw her by the door.

"Madame!" I said, as I approached. I wasn't sure what else to say.

"Jacques is going to be gone next week, for three days," she whispered. "Read the note when you can, and I'll be in touch." She puckered up her lips and studied my mouth and eyes.

I bent forward and kissed her neck. "Good night, Madame!" I stated quite audibly. "A most charming evening. And such a lovely home!"

She looked straight at me, her lips sealed, and turned her face to bid "good evening" to others in line behind me.

I stepped out into the night. A cold breeze stirred the ivy along the wall. I walked down the quiet, cobblestone street, past several Renaults and Deux Chevaux, and out into the limpid lamplight of yet another street. I could hear the roar of traffic about the Arc of Triumph, still several blocks away, and see the glow of its lights in the night sky. I leaned back. Directly overhead, the black dome of heaven arched across the night. It twinkled with a band of myriad stars. The Greek word *myrias* means "countless, numberless, indefinite." The Myrmidons were a Thessalonian tribe, who followed their king, Achilles, to Troy, and blindly fought at his side. Their loyalty was unsurpassed. How strange that I was suddenly troubled by that thought, by all the associations connected with it, or that it even came to mind!

24

EARLY THE NEXT WEEK, Christine and Tobby departed for London. She gave me a huge hug before they left for the *gare du nord.* Two days earlier, they had returned from their tour of Normandy, and we had spoken briefly, but she was excited and eager to get on with her life. How could I blame her! Even Tobby was radiant and full of resolve to turn his own life about. As the time approached for the final farewell, I walked with them to the front of the pension.

"Ay," he chirped, "I've a long road. I know it. But, it kin be done!"

We shook hands.

"Good bye!" Christine said. "You were a swell chap, you know!"

I held her against my chest when she stepped up to hug me. I could feel her heart beating and her breath against my neck.

Tobby threw their bags in the trunk of the taxi. They waved as the cab pulled away.

So much for:

Drink to me only with thine eyes,
And I will pledge with mine.

When Madame Angleterre brought my tea that afternoon, she asked if she might chat a moment. She handed me the tray.

"Of course. You're my only *fille maintenant*," I said. "You're the only one!"

She shook her head with perturbed sadness. "No, no! Monsieur! I've got eyes, my friend. They see everything. That newspaper madame! *Professeur*, it's none of my business, but she's no good," she shook her finger at me. "*Non, non*! I'm telling you the truth. Only trouble lies ahead for you. Mark my words. Trouble! *Rien que piene et souci.* Nothing but grief and sorrow."

"I know you're right. But, I can't say no. I can't stop it. I need her."

"Shooosh! Like a whore needs sores! No! Get a prostitute! One out here in the streets! Or sleep with Charlene. She's dying to have sex with you. Haven't you figured that out? *Bigre*! How stupid, Monsieur. Forgive me, but how stupid! For all your studiousness, you are such an *idiot*!"

Angleterre was still standing in the doorway. I was holding the tray.

"Won't you come in?"

"No!" she said in a cheery voice. "I've accomplished my mission. *Bon appétit*!"

She smiled victoriously and returned down the hall.

I wanted to say that it wasn't just sex; that it wasn't something a prostitute could resolve, heal, or absolve, even if she were beautiful, or clean, or had the patience or insight of a psychiatrist along with the most tantalizing hands in the world, or lips, or erotic thighs. It was far more inveterate than that; something profoundly disquieting, weighed down, and fractured; a sense of abandonment, of having betrayed myself and others; of having been betrayed; of a moral despair at the very center of being. Something that was always present, like the wolves in the dreams and the memories of Leeta that wouldn't go away. It was everything, or anything, or nothing in particular. It was just there. Whatever it was, it was always there. It was there in the room, in the doorway, as I stared down the hall after her.

Poor Angleterre. She had no way of knowing that in less than three hours I'd be at Monique's. I had already informed Mme. Dufavre that I wouldn't be present for dinner.

"Oh! Another night out?" she queried. "You know, I don't give refunds."

"None expected," I replied.

"Well, if you're seeing that marvelous couple—that professor and his wife—please give them my regards."

"I most certainly will. I know they'll appreciate your interest."

"Yes. A most extraordinary couple." She had applied too much makeup to her forehead. I could see flakes of reddish powder caked in her wrinkles above her eyebrows. "Well, a pleasant evening, Monsieur. It's nice to have the Coubert incidence behind us, isn't it?"

"Yes, it is. Incidentally, how's Francine? I haven't seen her lately, or Claude."

She gave me a hard look. "I told them to leave. I'll not have this place a brothel, or under the surveillance of the law. My business is down enough," she stated, with a tone of invective in her voice. "Good afternoon, Monsieur!" She closed her door.

While I drank my tea, I thumbed through several chapters of Gibert's book. I had opened it numerous times, glanced at the illustrations, grafts, and maps, and read the leading paragraphs of five or six chapters. My heart wasn't quite into it, or ready to plunge into the maelstrom of Gibert's *histoire de la condition française*. His Introduction, however, was quite contemporary and swept the reader into graceful phrases of sardonic realism:

> *La France*? What is France? What is modern France? When does it begin? Just how far back must we go? To the Ice Age? To those remarkable and soulful paintings on the cave ceilings of Lascaux in the grotto of Montignac? Or to the Neolithic Era and the valley of the Rhône, or along the river banks of the Aude in Languedoc? Yes, we could go back that far, to lands yet to be conquered by the marauding Franks, but Frankish, nonetheless! To understand ourselves best, however, we must commence with the sunset years of the Sun King's reign, for that is the watershed whose fountains feed the springs of today's France and in whose twilight the grandeur of the nation took root. Versailles and its gardens define the glory of France at the very moment that that glory was passing. It would not rise anew, until Napoleon Bonaparte's Grand Army seized its banner and carried France's *savor de vivre* to new frontiers and the cold hearths of Moscow. Then we can drop back to the Paleolithic Period and those descendants of Cro-Magnon Man, whose artistic brushes left a legacy to flower again with the coming of Caesar and Roman Gall, Romanesque art, the Renaissance, and the Impressionists of yestermorn. The DNA of those Ice-Age clans and fur-wrapped wanderers of wind and rain still pulsates in our national cells and defines our Gallic temper.

What a joy it would be to translate his book, if Thiers's deal with Balfour House should go through! I read a few more pages, showered, changed clothes, and prepared for the rendezvous with Monique.

Thin layers of fog had formed as I walked along her street. Surrounding houses hovered in the evening gloom. They rose spectral in the lamplight's glow. Heavy wisps of fog had settled about her gates. I swung the right section open, attempting to close it quietly, but its weathered hinges creaked as the wrought-iron segments scraped against each other. Just then the front porch light came on. The door opened, and I could see Monique's silhouette against the hallway's maize incandescence.

I hurried across the cobblestone drive and mounted the steps. She was wearing a sheer silk bedroom gown of light taupe. She had allowed her dark hair to grow out and had drawn it back behind her ears. She was barefoot, with only a minimal touch of silver lipstick to set the night, with no eye-shadow whatsoever to brighten or highlight the soft tissue under her eyes. In truth, she needed no such products to enhance her face; she was naturally beautiful, a goddess of comeliness and desire in her own right.

"You would make Aphrodite jealous, and even Hera and Athena envious," I said, as I wrapped my arms around her shoulders and kissed her lips. Her breasts felt warm and firm against my chest.

She opened her lips for me to kiss again. Our tongues touched and explored each other's mouth. Her eyes drenched mine with a haunting spell, pleased and gratified that I had come. She closed the door.

"Won't you have something to drink? Are you hungry?"

"Later," I whispered.

She led me to the end of the hallway, up a cantilevered staircase to the first floor, past ornate tapestries, and into a large homey bedroom. Dark green drapes with swooping valances and gold sashes on bronze knobs guarded the windows. A tall cherry armoire, mahogany dresser, leather armchair, and a Louis XVI table and stool provided an attending array of furniture in front and to one side of a spacious bed. The latter was covered with a white downy quilt and long rolled pillows. A carpet of deep blue created a sense of wading through a dream, or looking down through a hole in the sky, on a silent infinity beneath ones feet.

I stood in the middle of the room, not certain what to do. The thought of making love to her on her and Jacques' own bed, on their nuptial dais of cloud-like pillows and linens, disturbed what frayed conscience I had left. I knew what Socrates and Nietzsche would have advised. But I began undressing, anyway. Monique quietly approached me, smiled, and assisted. I slipped her gown over her shoulders and dropped it next to my clothes. We climbed onto the high bed, our hearts and thoughts captive to but one desire, one yearning, one desideratum of concupiscence and *amour*.

We had spread the evening out against the sky.

To love at leisure,
To love and to die,

. . . as Baudelaire had dared to describe it. A time of cupidity, shining through tears.

Afterwards we lay in bed and talked.

"Why did you come here?" she asked.

"I thought you wanted me to."

"What made you think that?" she laughed. "Didn't you want to come, too?"

"What do you think? That I'm made of steel, or something?"

"So it's only the flesh, the exterior and nothing more?"

"Please! It's you; all of you, the entire you, flesh and *esprit*. The *fantôme* you."

"The *fantôme moi*! I like that. Sincerely, I do." She slid out of bed, off the high mattress, and performed a droll curtsey.

I rolled toward to the edge of the bed and fumbled for her breasts. "Come back!" I urged. "The bird is on the wing!"

She laughed and climbed on top of me. "I like it this way. Just call me Lilith!" she rocked back and forth teasingly. "The *fantôme moi*! Oh, Monsieur, how you please me!" She buried her face against my neck, under my throat, kissed it, then kissed my mouth with her hot lugubrious lips. She continued to rock back and forth with panting breath and panting motion. I rode the wave to its crest. As it crashed, we rolled over, and I kissed her again.

"I'm famished! Aren't you hungry?"

"No. But I'll watch you eat," I replied.

"So gallant! So reserved! You're becoming a Frenchman, you know."

"Not with the name of Clayton, I fear. Clayton Rogers Clarke, farm boy from Virginia, from the Knobs, where wolves and bears once roamed and elk herds grazed. Nothing French about that."

"Not so fast. The French were there on the other side! Remember? But Roget might do! *Claude-Roget DuClarc*! But I love what you said about the farm boy, where wolves and bears once roamed and Indians must have lived. Tell me more. You know we French love our fictitious *sauvage noble*. Your Franklin and Jefferson stole our hearts with their tales of backwoods lore and frontier America. Jacques adores it as well. I want to know more."

Jacques! Yes, Jacques! Monique was so irresistibly enchanting; so like Leeta, but different. But it was Jacques and would always be Jacques, I realized. You spirited, facetious, seductive, acerbic, and charming woman! I wanted to say. "Let's get that bite to eat, and I'll tell you."

We dressed and descended to the kitchen. I opened a bottle of champagne while Monique made a sandwich of leftover ham and Swiss cheese. She piled it on a large croissant, stuffed with Romaine lettuce and spread with creamery butter. She cut it in half and placed the larger portion on a plate for me. I found some glasses and poured the champagne. We sat by a table covered with a blue oilcloth, with onions and garlic, fresh spices and herbs arranged in a wooden bowl.

"You should really go first," I said. "I don't even know where you're from. Or how you met Jacques, or came upon your career, or anything, to tell the truth."

"Evasion! Nothing but tactical evasion!" she laughed, in between bites of her croissant and a gulp of champagne. "No. I'm not from here. My home is in the region of Toulouse, south of the *Midi Central* and its great river systems and cliffs of vineyards and cellars. My grandparents were wine makers before the War. My father expected to inherit it all—the vines, the presses, the bottling shops, the storage *caves*—everything. But the war changed all that. He was killed in '42, in a munitions blast north of Rheims. My mother disappeared during the Vichy reign. To this day, I don't know where she is, or what happened to her. My grandfather died in 1956 and my grandmother in 1957. I came to Paris to study at the Sorbonne. I failed my exams, but by then I had met Jacques—Jacques-Maria Gibert, heir to nothing but brilliance and hard work and self-determination, as well as temper, jealousy, and self-destruction. He taught in a lycée for several years before we married, then he became a journalist, and the rest you know."

"Do you have any children? Or didn't you want any?"

"My, but you're personal! Yes, we wanted children. We even picked out their names. But after three miscarriages, *alors*, that was enough! Shall we open another bottle? One is not going to be enough."

I opened a second bottle of champagne.

"Now, it's your turn," she said. "Who is this man I'm sleeping with? And you will have to spend the night, you know." She glanced at the clock on the wall. "The metro's already stopped running, and the cab drivers here are as gossipy as crones and old harridans."

"I don't mind spending the night. I'd like that," I said, "very much."

"Well, for now you're my hostage, and I want to know the truth about this country farm boy, namely, you."

"I was reared on a tobacco farm in Virginia, near a little town called Abingdon. Daniel Boone first founded it in the 1750s, when he was exploring passages through the mountains of Appalachia. He stayed in a cave, after driving out a pack of wolves. He had to hack his way through tangles of rhododendron and laurel, but to the west on his path lay the Cumberland and its gentle gap through the mountains. Later, a Scotsman, by the name of Ian Campbell, assembled a militia of rugged mountain men in a meadow near Boone's cave. From there he led them across the Blue Ridge to defeat another Scotsman at the Battle of King's Mountain. My family's descended from that man, Ian Campbell. In time the Campbells married into a clan of Rogers and later Clarkes. True civilization didn't come to Abingdon, or our farm, until the Civil War. But most of the land was lost during the Confederacy. In fact, it wasn't until twenty years ago, that my grandmother's farm finally got electricity. Until then, she burned kerosene lamps, carried water from a spring, bought ice in town to store in an icebox, and prepared all her meals on a cook stove. I used to spend the summers with her, until I went off to college. My father's farm was nearby, and we all worked like peasants to scrape a living from the land. Now, both my parents are dead and are buried high on a hill, overlooking my grandmother's farm and the distant Blue Ridge Mountains. There's really nothing else to tell."

Monique reached for my hands. "What a lovely history! What a family it must have been! What a sorrow that only its memory remains! I assume all is gone, no?"

"All but my grandmother's farm. An older brother bought it from the bank after my grandmother's death. The poor thing had mortgaged everything she had, including the barns and dry-rotting harnesses, to stave off disaster. It took my brother fourteen years to pay off the mortgage."

I raised my glass to Monique. Through the bubbly champagne, her face appeared an apple-jelly color with wavy-like crystals of sucrose in a clear glass jar. I wondered what sort of a farm wife she might have made!

As we climbed in bed to fall asleep, she lay on her right side and scrunched her back against my stomach. Her legs and flanks felt warm, her body comforting to hold, her chestnut hair in the shadows of the room so fair to bury my nose against, her neck so delicately perfumed, her left hand so soft to touch with my own! No, it wasn't just sex. It was infinitely more. It was a euphoria of quintessential fulfillment, as sacred as the Holy Grail, as salubrious as Adam awakening that first morning to discover Eve, nestled in his arms, in Paradise.

"At dawn I will have to leave," I whispered, as I kissed her goodnight.

25

On the eve of the Sullivans' departure, we met at the chic café where we had first become acquainted. Two whole months had passed, yet it seemed like only yesterday. As fate would have it, a cold rain fell hard on the outside awning and forced us to seek sanctuary inside. The green velvet wall covering and dark paneling mirrored the gloomy weather without. It also betrayed our melancholia within. We had begun with afternoon apéritifs before ordering wine. I had requested the café's finest *vin du patron*. It was a robust light purple wine with just a slight fruity edge that went deliciously with the dark orange cheese our waiter recommended.

"And so its back to the States," I said, somewhat sadly.

"Yes. It's time. I'm ready," huffed Carl. "Paris will always be Paris, whatever they do to it. And Julene," he turned and kissed her cheek, "and I will always be able to come back."

Julene smiled dolefully, but her eyes and mouth were cast downward in a grim stare.

"Come, sweet bride, you'll feel much better once we're home. We'll come back, I promise you."

Julene wore a plain, long gray dress and black slippers. Both were wet from the rain. She had pinned a silk ruby flower in her black curly hair. But her face refused to be comforted; it was as if she had dressed for mourning.

"Julene, you forgot my charcoals, again. Or were you afraid to bring them," I nodded toward the heavy downpour.

"Oh, no!" she uttered. "They're still in the tube I meant to mail you."

"And that's in our footlocker," Carl grunted.

"I'll have to mail it to you in Virginia."

"I don't have anything to write on, or I'd give you my address."

"Here," said Carl. "Write on this."

It was their flight-tickets' holder. I scribbled down my address and returned the folder to Carl.

He stared at it momentarily, before reaching into his coat pocket and slipping out his wallet. He handed me one of his academic business cards. It contained his address, his university phone number, as well as a different number.

"What's that one?"

"That's our Alabama number. We spend most of our weekends there."

"At Sullivan's Landing?"

"Yes. How did you know?"

"I picked it up somewhere, " I looked at Julene. A worried cast played about the corners of her mouth. "Maybe it was at the Gibert's." Her restrained smile returned.

"Speaking of him, have you read his book?" mulled Carl.

"I've started it several times and like what I've read. What about you?"

Sullivan shook his head in the negative. "Not yet. His style lacks appeal for me. Well, we'll have to keep each other posted. I trust your epistemology book will make you famous," he grinned.

"I know your *Beyond Homer* will be a best-seller. I'll want an autographed copy, you know."

"You'll have to visit us in Alabama," said Julene. "I'll write you myself, as soon as I find out about Mama. We still haven't heard a word."

Carl had struggled to his feet. He seemed almost lame. He had to balance himself by leaning on Julene's left shoulder. I wondered if he were diabetic and didn't know it, or was a candidate for poor heart circulation. "Shall I call a cab?" I offered.

"No. Hell, no!" he blurted. "I'll feel better once I get more exercise."

"But you didn't bring an umbrella," I protested, as I glanced at Julene and the glimmer of desperation that had materialized in her eyes.

"We've got these," Carl motioned, turning to retrieve two raincoats he had draped over a chair behind him. "We'll survive."

He held open the smaller of the two for Julene. I watched as she slipped her slender arms into it. It had a hood and was still damp. He squirmed about fitfully as he stuffed his arms and portly frame into his own. He extended his hand. I shook it and tired to smile, but I fear my mouth had metamorphosed into a frown.

Julene put her arms around me. Her eyes said it all. They were wet, puffy; a tear had trickled down her left cheek. I held her tight and kissed her cheek. I paid the bill and left the waiter a small *pourboire* and watched them walk out into the rain. They ran several yards and hailed a cab. I waved to them from under the awning, but it was raining too hard for them to see me. I pulled my own collar up and walked, with brisk steps, down the street, across several more, and jogged the last few yards toward the pension. Water dripped off my coat, trousers, and shoes. I thought I would never make it to my room. The flight up the stairs endured for what seemed an eternity. I dropped my clothes beside the bed, crawled in, and listened to the rain against the windowpanes. I glanced at my watch. It was 3:30 p.m.

The familiar 4:30 knock at the door aroused me from a fitful slumber.

It would be Angleterre with her tray of tea. I quickly dressed and went to the door. "Good news!" she chimed. "More patrons have checked in. Two groups! One from South Africa; the other from East Germany. They'll fill the dining room and Madame's coffers, and maybe, just maybe, there'll be a tiny pittance left for the rest of us. *Non*?"

"I wouldn't know. Does she usually give you a bonus when that happens?"

"Sometimes, yes! Here, take this tray. It's march, march, march, now!" she smiled good-naturedly. "*Allez, allez, allez*! Go, go, go!"

I carried the tray to my desk and set it down. It was still raining, but not beating against the windowpanes as before. I drew back the curtains, unlatched the right window, and opened it slightly. A damp breeze rushed into the room. I stood in its cool path and let it re-invigorate my rueful lassitude. I rubbed my face with my hands, then sat at the desk. Angleterre had brought a dainty dish of sliced bright lemons, three sugar cubes, and the usual steaming pot of hot tea. Dark green tea leaves trickled out the spout as I poured an amber stream into the small cup she had brought. Two dry butter wafers lay beside the slices of lemon. I placed a ten franc note under the dish. I hadn't tipped her in several days, and that would more than compensate.

Outside in the hallway, I could hear guests moving in. Christine's was the only room, to my knowledge, vacant on my floor, but below, and over in the annex, I knew a number of rooms were available. From what I could discern, the guests (a man and a woman) were speaking

Afrikaans. Having met South Africans in America at several international conferences, I knew they'd speak English as well. I didn't envy them their apartheid state, but the Afrikaners I had met had all been sterling people, aristocratic and urbane, yet victims of a time-warp, like the one that still gripped the South. As for the East Germans, they would constitute a new experience.

As dinner drew near, I descended the stairs to the second floor. Mme. Angleterre was explaining the seating arrangements to a dark-haired couple. "You will be sitting there," she pointed, "opposite the Sacré-Coeur poster. See?"

"*Ya! Je le vois*," a man of ashen completion, medium-height, dressed in a gray, woolen tweed coat, replied in a slightly amplified German accent. "*Ya! Sehr gut! N'est pas*?" Upon seeing me, he smiled and addressed me in English. "An American! Yes?"

"Yes," I offered the man my hand. "And you, Madame," I nodded toward his wife. "Welcome to the *Conrad Hilton Pension* of Montparnasse."

"Your humor!" the man chortled. "It is *gut*. You can't imagine how drab life has been these past years. You're not a spy, are you?" he suddenly smiled, placing his hand to one side of his mouth as he lowered his voice.

His wife seemed a little fearful and Angleterre a little annoyed that we were speaking English and not French.

"*Monsieur et Madame, je pense que vous aimerez ce pension ici beaucoup, voyant qu"il est près de tous*," I said, not wanting to exclude either Angleterre or the man's wife. "All of Paris is just meters away, its parks, bistros, museums, everything! You'll love it."

"Thank you, so much," his wife said. She was short, stocky, her black hair cropped neck-length, a rather nondescript person, without makeup, lipstick, or jewelry. A genuine smile broke through the wrinkles about her mouth and lips. I noticed that her hose were brown and thick, and that her flat shoes were square at the toe. She wore a navy blue suit jacket and a matching skirt that was entirely too tight on her. She reminded me of pictures of my grandmother taken in the early '40s, when gabardine was still in style.

"We're from the *Sowjetzone*, near old Potsdam, if you know where that is. Incidentally, my name is Franz Schuldermann," the German said.

"I'm Clayton Rogers Clarke, a professor on sabbatical."

"Ah, you should be studying in Berlin, or Weimar. Too bad we couldn't have lived in the '20s, when life along the *Unter den Linden* was in its heyday! Now bullet holes riddle the grand old buildings where once elegant restaurants fed the elite of the world. But I am here for cultural reasons. And Communism is on the rise, even here in Paris. It's a new day. It's a shame our two worlds are at odds. Don't you agree?"

"I'm not a politician, I fear. Just a dreamer."

"Oh, come now!" his wife beamed. "It is a shame for ideology to separate people. I'm confident we'll have a marvelous time."

"*Ah, bon*!" interjected Angleterre. "Everyone loves Paris. Even the French!"

"Isn't that true!" concurred Herr Schuldermann, as he escorted his wife to their table.

"I don't like Krauts," Pierre whispered, as I took my seat. "Look at them! Communists. Here to woo us poor proletariat into embracing their classless rhetoric. I don't trust them. It's hard enough being a Frenchman. Do you trust them?"

"No. I don't trust the Communists either, but the couple there seems to be decent. Let's give them a chance. Have some wine," I uncorked my bottle and began filling his glass.

"*Bien, merci*! It's been a long day. And I'm still wet from the rain," he lifted his jacket's arms for me to see. "This is the only coat I have. Can you believe that? I work all week, and this is the best I can afford." His eyes glanced about the dining room, his tiny table, the dim lights overhead, and then me. "What is America like? Is everyone rich there? Or are they just as wretched and miserable as we poor Frenchmen?"

"My good Pierre. There's not an avenue in America the equal to what Paris can boast. Not a wine worth drinking as delicate as yours, nor a history as triumphal or engaging. You live in a sumptuous world of luxuriant boulevards, architecture, culture, art, and history, unparalleled elsewhere. A *grandeur passé* as well as *présent*. Yes, you might make more money in America, in New York, Atlanta, or Denver, but you'd never have Paris again, even in the rain or the cold, or when you're feeling triste and downhearted. No. I'd think twice about leaving France, or my home, or Paris, if I were you."

"That's easy for you to say," he replied, somewhat irritably. "Being poor is no panacea, sleeping in a smelly room on filthy sheets not exactly a luxury, and having to eat the repetitious meals Dufavre serves up here as *cuisine* soon loses its *enchantement*, its delightful spell, I assure you."

"Well said," I mumbled. "I didn't mean to be patronizing." I poured him a second glass of wine. I shook out the last few drops into my own glass. "What should I try next?" I asked, as I held the empty bottle up. "A red or white wine? Or something in between?"

"Anything dry, or full-bodied, or sweet, or sparkling. I love it all," he grinned. "You've been wonderful to share with me."

"No one should drink alone, *n'est -ce pas*?"

"No. I wish you hadn't said that. But it's OK. I understand," he whispered, with measured despair. "You miss that English girl, and I miss Gaston. Isn't that so?"

"You're a better man than I, Pierre. I'll go with something sparkling next time."

A group of Afrikaners came in and took seats at the long table, past the Schuldermanns, and next to the table where Christine used to sit. I had expected the men to be wearing rugged outdoors clothing, felt Afrikaner Stetsons, with garish bands and wide brims, but this was not the case. They dressed in business coat and ties, with casual slacks and casual shoes. Their wives' dresses were long, monochromatic blues, dark golden and rusty-reds, and the women themselves wore either short or shoulder-length hair of brown or blonde, and a hint of lipstick. Small earrings of gold, silver and diamond complemented their outfits. They spoke to the German couple in German, French to Madame Cueillier, and a mixture of Afrikaans and English among themselves. As I surveyed the room, I felt both strange and proud to be the only American. Since my arrival, my identity had never been in doubt due either to my size thirteen shoes or my accent. Whichever it was no longer bothered me, and the old gentleman, who so meticulously arranged his sauces and pepper jars, had even begun to speak to me in the hall, outside the dining room.

"Good evening, sir," he would say. Or "Good day," or "Good morning," depending on the respective hour. "To be young again!" he would smile. Or, "You haven't threatened me, lately," he would grin.

"You must forgive me," I would have to rejoin. "I was trying to catch that thief."

"*Ah, bon*! The Devil got him instead! *Non*?"

"I'm afraid so."

In fact, while wandering the *Jardin* one morning, I caught sight of the old fellow, seated on a bench, basking in the rays of the sun. "*Bonjour*!" I said. "May I sit with you?"

"Please do," he turned with a smile.

Large bruises were visible on his twisted hands. His face and skin had turned sallow with age. He caught me noticing his condition and chuckled to himself. "The same will happen to you, young man. If we're lucky, we all grow old." He held his hands up. "I'll be seventy-four next month. And these hands have seen a lot of life."

"What profession did you hold before you retired? You strike me as being more than a worker, or *petit fonctionnaire*."

He nodded his head in concurrence. "Yes. I was a banker, a financier. I was sent off to Düsseldorf, *fur Arbeit* during the War. That's when I mangled my hands. But, after the Allies' victory, I came home and resumed my post with the Exchequer National Bank. *Alors*! but only as an assistant. And low pay."

"Were you ever married?"

"Ah, you are so personal! But, yes, I was. Chrystelle was her name. She waited for me to come home. For weeks she showed up every day at the *Gare de l'Est*. Lists of who might be on the trains were posted, but they were always wrong. One simply had to show up, wrestle through the throngs of mothers, widows, and wives, hoping ones husband would be on board. And there she was! I was half the size I am now. My coat draped like a death pall on my shoulders. My face was bearded, my hands raw and cold, yet she recognized me. She ran down the platform toward me. She was carrying a loaf of bread and a bottle of water. Tears flooded my eyes and cascaded down my face. "René, my René!" she called. I fell into her arms; together we knelt on the quay and wept." He looked at his hands. "How I miss her, Monsieur! How I miss my Chrystelle!" Tears had formed in the old man's eyes and his hands were trembling. "When you stop to reflect on it, there's nothing golden about the Golden Years. There's nothing good about growing old. Look at my hands!" he held them up again. "They're useless now. I used to paint some and play the piano, but not any more."

The sun was very warm; the breeze was cool. He squinted as he looked into the sun's bright rays.

"What is the one thing now you look forward to the most each day?" I asked.

He turned and looked at me squarely in the face. His countenance fell, but his eyes took on a resolute shade. His jaw tightened; he slowly sat up, more erect than he had been. "Death!" he answered. "Death!"

The weather that week was impossible to gage. One day it would rain, the next it would be cold; then the sun would burst through the clouds, and it would become insufferably muggy. The weather reminded me of the Valley of Virginia, the mountains around Roanoke and Lexington, especially in the Spring.

One morning, quite late, Mme. Angleterre knocked on the door. "A phone call, Monsieur. A Monsieur Thiers wishes to speak to you. Shall I tell him you're coming?"

"Yes," I said, as I yanked the door open. "Please, go ahead."

I was in socks, but no sandals or shoes, and hurriedly slipped on a pair of the former.

"Yes," I said, when I got to the phone. Angleterre had quietly turned away as she handed me the receiver. She pretended to tiptoe down the hall, but I knew she would listen.

"Yes, Professeur! I've received a telegram from Balfour House. They're quite interested in a translation of Jacques's book. They'll let me pick the translator. Are you willing to do it? The pay will be good, well, minimal, but think what it will mean to us!"

"I'd be honored. I've read part of the Introduction and am very pleased with his style and substance."

"Good. Jacques and I would like to meet with you to discuss the details. Balfour House will send us a copy of the contract, as soon as we reach an agreement of our own. When can you meet?"

"Any time. Just pick a date."

"Ah, let's say next week, Tuesday, at the Café Atlantis, off the Rue de la Paix. *D'accord*?"

"*Oui!* What time?"

"One o'clock! *Bien*?"

"Fine. I'll be there."

"Good. *Au'voir, Monsieur*!"

"Yes. Till then."

I handed the receiver back to Angleterre. An inquisitive grin spread across her face, from ear to ear.

"Now, now, Monsieur," she said. "I'm not telling anyone. Not Angleterre. Who is this Thiers, anyway?"

"The leader of the Paris Mafia, I think. I'll share some of the cut with you."

"Oh, Monsieur. Don't mock me. Is his wife after you, too?"

"Angleterre, you are the worst! No, he's a publisher and he's asked me to translate a book, into English."

"Book! Books! That's all you do! Write books. Read books and pile them on your desk! And once your life's gone, what then? Of what value your precious books? Everywhere books? Look at me. I'm an old woman! Or soon will be. I've lived too long. *N'est pas?* But I've *lived,* yes, *lived!* I married, once loved a man—a good man—lost children during the war, half starved, fled the Gestapo, survived on the meagerest of rations, endured the harshest humiliations, groveled to stay alive. And you! Monsieur! You! You write books. What are books, anyway? You need to find a woman, marry, love someone with your heart, and not just your, your...., yes, your *flesh*. You need to discover life—life as it really is—Monsieur, and not as you wish it were. Even an old fool like me knows that!" She threw up her hands and collapsed in her chair in her tiny office. "Forgive me, Monsieur. I speak out of turn. I've no right to judge you. Yes, your books are important. They are the language of memory, of love, the poetry of history. I know that. Forgive me. Yes, Monsieur. But I think I'm right, though I'm just a babbling fool."

I bent forward and kissed her cheek. "One must never deprecate the truth, *la vérité*. You're no fool. You're my voice of Nietzsche, reviving me, saving me from a recidivism I can't shake. You should be writing books, not me."

"No, no! Get back to your desk. I'm just jealous of those other women. Maybe some day you'll find the truth. Who knows! Flesh or no flesh!"

I returned to my room and began reading Montaigne with renewed vigor. I would have to squeeze him in between my Introduction and Descartes, but what Angleterre had said stuck in my brain like a hot arrow.

My "library," such as it was, contained only excerpts from Montaigne's *Essays*. I knew I would have to return to my favorite bookstore, as well as the *Bibliothèque Nationale* to determine what I'd need. I was in the process of debating whether to stay at the pension for lunch, or walk down to the Latin Quarter, when I heard someone outside the door. They had dropped something and were trying to pick it up. It sounded like the "clunk" of a bottle. A sigh of desperation escaped the person's lips. I opened the door.

"Monique!" I whispered in surprise.

"Shhhhhh!" she placed her right index finger to her lips as she signaled for me to hush. "No one has seen me so far," she whispered. She was clutching a paper bag and her purse. A big smile creased her lips. I could see the dull, lead-covered cap of a wine bottle that poked out of the top of the bag. "Let me in."

"Of course. *Vite!* Quickly! Get in."

She set her purse and bag on the desk, while I closed the door. Longing, desire, uncertainty, incrimination, passion—all burned in her face and in her eyes. The flames of cupidity leapt from her own heart to mine. She put her hands to my face, held my cheeks with her tender palms, and, standing on her tiptoes, kissed me. Her mouth and lips bathed me with lusty fire. I wrapped my arms about her waist and crushed her against my chest. Flesh or no flesh, I craved her with all my being. Her presence dissipated my gravest doubts about who I was or what I wanted or what I needed. It was she! "Monique! Monique!" I whispered, as if chanting some magical mantra or mystical rune.

Silently, we undressed, our eyes never once disengaging from one another's eyes, body, lips, or mouth. We embraced again, ran our hands along each other's loins, and breasts, and ribs, and limbs, then lay down on the bed and entangled ourselves in the curative balm and aphrodisiacal wonders of love. Whatever Homer's gods had denied man, the therapy of love, with its restorative powers and mending cures, was more than ample compensation for however brief the mortal coil. If only its intensity could persevere throughout a marriage and into the waning twilight of old age! I didn't want to think about it ending. My only thought was then and there, her arms, her breast, her body's warmth, her vulva's rise and fall, her lips, her mouth, her face, her hair.

Glücklich allein
ist die Seele, die liebt.

"Happy alone is the soul that loves." If only Homer could have known Goethe! Would he have assigned Hector a different fate, or even Achilles? I thought about what Angleterre had said.

"I have to go now," Monique kissed me. "The bottle of wine is for you. I've got to return to work."

"I thought you had come for the day."

"No. I'm covering a story at the Palais du Luxembourg in less than an hour. But I couldn't come this close to you and not stop."

"I'm falling in love with you. Don't you realize that?"

"I know; I feel it, too. But this will pass, I fear. And you'll be gone. Back to your frontier America!"

I started to object, to say that surely there was something we could do.

"Shhhhh!" she placed her fingers over my lips. She kissed my neck and chest, as if to reassure me. "Please bring me a wash cloth. I've got to go. You do love me, don't you?"

Her eyes melted whatever resistance my heart and mind felt. A feeling of abandonment stuck in my throat. I tried to swallow it, but the feeling would not abate.

"You know I do."

I brought her the cloth and helped her redress.

Researching Montaigne's skepticism generated both a positive and a negative reaction. He had preceded Descartes by a generation, his own dates being 1533–1592, while the latter's were 1596–1650. In turn, just as Descartes was motivated by his predecessor's doubt and relativism, so Montaigne's own bent was fueled by a resurgence of the Italian Renaissance's interest in the classics, namely the works of Pyrrho and Sextus Empiricus.

Owing either to good sense or pure luck, I had brought a folder of a number of my lectures on philosophical figures whom I knew I'd have to incorporate in my project. I pulled out my folder on "Classical Skepticism" and reread some of its highlights. I had noted that Pyrrho of Elis (360–270 B.C.), founder of Skepticism, had accompanied Alexander to India. He had been influenced by the atomic theory of Democritus, the relativism of the Sophists, and Epicurus's fixation on tranquility. All this I had lectured on to my students—from 1) Democritus's notion of uncaused atoms free-falling in a vacuum, which gave rise to a vast universe of change and devolution, where everything returned to an infinity from whence it had come; to 2) the views of the Sophists, including Protagoras's notion that "Man is the measure of all things"; Gorgias's conclusions that reality in itself can never be grasped, therefore all knowledge is uncertain, if not beyond "knowing"; to 3) Thrasymachus's political realism that "might makes right," seeing there are no absolute criteria for right and wrong, or good and evil. Thus, when Epicurus came to Athens and founded his Garden, his major pursuit was for a tranquility of spirit, that, given the conditions of human brevity and the limits of reason, might result in a freedom from the fear of death and the discomforts of mindless pleasure.

So, too, Montaigne found refuge among these classical academics and relativists. With them, he doubted that our sense perceptions, or reason alone, can discover the underlying nature of anything, or posit enduring truths about life or the beyond. The more he explored the inner world of the self, the less he was confident that his own reasoning abilities could ever somehow stumble on the absolute truth, or goodness, or Being of beings. Thus, like Sextus Empiricus of the Roman Empire, he advocated clinging to the nobler traditions of ones era, or, in his case, to the ancient traditions of the Church and its faith in God and its teachings. This was the only way he knew to escape the bottomless pit of skepticism, or relativism and its corresponding abyss of despair. It is said that he carved Empiricus's sayings into the beams of his house and added one of his own: "*Que sais-je*?" "What do I know?" There was a modernist for you! A great doubter who knew how little we ever really come to know before Death steals up the steps and snatches us from the bed of the living.

All that, I concluded, would make a proper introduction to René Descartes, whose methodology or quest for "indubitable truths" sought to go beyond skepticism. I was glad for Angleterre's sarcasm and her tongue-in-cheek reprimand. But where it would lead still drowned me in incertitude, in coils of misgivings and pessimism that no amount of reading dispelled. O Monique, I would trade it all for you! How I wanted her in my arms again!

26

THE MEETING AT THE Café Atlantis left me feeling depressed. As the translator of Gibert's book, I would make less than two percent of the Balfour House's net profits. Thiers's company would earn twenty percent on gross sales, fifteen going to Jacques.

"*C'est bon! N'est-ce pas*?" quipped Thiers, adjusting his fashionable handkerchief in his lapel pocket. "No one really gets rich in France off books," he assured me. "It's the engagements and invitations to speak, the surge in notoriety, and endorsements that count."

Jacques glanced away when I turned to him for reassurance. There was a subtlety about his demeanor, almost a warning that suggested Theirs's offer was less than genuine.

"I can't do it for that," I replied. "I think I'd need at least fifteen percent of the net."

"Ossshh! Mere percentages! Besides, I'm eager to publish your own book in French. Remember?"

"*Oui*. And how much royalty do you pay?"

"Monsieur! Professeur! I am suprised! *Etonné*! Truly. You can't mean this? Think of the opportunity I am providing you!"

"True, but the university press that published my *Ethics of Virtue* will determine your profit, not I. And they will be the ones who say yes or no to you when you approach them. *N'est -ce pas*?"

"You are being stubborn! Tell him, Jacques. We can always find someone else."

"Tell this Balfour House to give him ten percent of their gross! I want to be known in America, to be read there," Gibert said with sudden agitation. "Who knows Jacques-Maria Gibert in America? *Personne*? No one? Of course, not! Think about this! Or of your own *libraire. Non*?"

"True. *C'est vrai*! I'll approach them for more," Thiers offered, glancing somewhat sheepishly at me. He released a long sigh; then finished off his glass of wine. His mask of conviviality slipped slowly away. "We'll meet again? *Non*?" he said grimly.

"I'll be waiting. Please let me know."

Just before we broke off, Jacques turned. "Incidentally, please accept my invitation to dine with Monique and me tomorrow evening. At our home. About seven? Yes? You can come?"

"*Indeed, honored!* May I bring some flowers or wine?"

"No, no! Flowers would be too, too suggestive!" his face turned red, almost purple. A bit of a smirk formed about his lips. "We don't do that in France. But, Monique will understand the gesture. I will explain," he calmed down a bit. "As for wine! I have a *cave* in the cellar laden with the finest wines our country produces. I will show you myself. And a surprise, too," he smiled with a challenge, if not a hint of revenge. "You are athletic, aren't you?" he queried with triumph.

"I ran cross-country years ago."

"We will see," he smiled. "Seven! *N'est-ce pas*?"

"I'll be there."

Before taking the subway to the Gibert's, I spent the afternoon perusing sections of both Jacques's and Sullivan's books. Gibert certainly knew how to seize a reader's imagination, as well as capture his eyes and ears:

> Can you not see it now? The splendid, convex dome of the Basilica of the Sacred Heart, its pale yellow cap white in the noonday sun? Or see the smoky frail contours of that stupendous mesh of painted pig iron we know as the Eiffel Tower? The brilliant, stunning, and heart-breaking Arch of Triumph, solemnizing our history of conquest and defeat, victory and sacrifice? Or the Ile de la Cité, with its ancient gothic towers, magnificent gilded gates, royal palaces, chapels, and cathedral, drowned in the hum of a whirling traffic that never sleeps, lulled by the pulse of the flowing Seine, blue and crimson and sulfur under the spell of a regal sky? That we have not lost, nor ever need to lose. Proud Parisians, our *jour de gloire* is here to stay, but our nation's mission is to marshal and summon the best from each of us. I invite you to journey with me as we review our past and ponder our future together. *Que nous commencions*!

Sullivan's style was gripping, and his substance all the more so:

> Let us not forget that Zeus transcended jingoistic bounds. Remember what Plato says in *The Laws*? Offenses committed against foreigners attracted Zeus's attention and aroused his anger. Like Yahweh of old, vengeance was his. He would repay! Plato calls him the "God of Strangers," " their guardian spirit," the "protector of foreigners," the "keeper of boundaries." As Plato surmises: "Which category of men should we call the most blessed by heaven? Those who live the supremely just life, or the most pleasurable? The gods can't choose the latter, without contradicting themselves as the highest beings." But my point here is that such a characterization does not belong to Homer, but lies beyond Homer. Homer's Zeus is still the paragon of a Father Sky. It is men who make rules and fashion constitutions, who legislate laws and define customs. Being itself espouses no such restrictions or moral bonds. That is why Nietzsche's balance of the Apollonian and the Dionysian is closer to Being than Plato's ever was. The equilibrium between wisdom and exuberance has forever haunted mankind, ancient and modern.

The street lamps had yet to come on as I strolled in the warm, pre-twilight, pink glow toward the Giberts' rue. The street's ivy-draped walls and my hosts' heavy iron gates exuded an air of sequestered nostalgia. A fine, grainy golden dust hovered about the place, adding its spell of magic to the evening. I was in love with Monique. And Jacques knew it. What else did he know? I wondered, as I rang their bell.

"*Ah, le bon Monsieur fait comme ça*!" he chortled as he opened the door. "I am just about to have an apéritif. Will you join me?" He was dressed in a light-weight, gray, turtle neck sweater, blue jeans, and sandals. He had slicked his black hair back severely behind his ears; I could see the comb marks in his hair. In spite of his casual appearance, however, he generated a feisty flamboyance, if not a surly demeanor. I should have taken this as a warning, but my eyes were searching for Monique, much to my own embarrassment.

"*Vous cherchez* the lady of the house? *Non*?" Jacques smiled. "Yes, Monsieur, she is here. Come, darling, our guest has arrived."

I followed Jacques into the drawing room, where Thiers had unveiled Gibert's book and made his speech of that evening past. Monique was wearing a white apron that dangled loosely about her neck and down the front of her own sweater and jeans. She had fluffed her auburn hair into a mass of shining curls accented by sparkling diamond earrings. She had brushed her eyebrows, too, and her lipstick glowed silver in the room's light. I stepped forward to greet her; she turned her neck for me to kiss. Her perfume's delicate scent performed its charm, as well she knew it might. She smiled and returned to the kitchen. "It'll be a moment more. Please, relax with Jacques," she called over her shoulder, as she passed through the dining room.

"Let's sit in the main parlor," he gestured toward the *salle de séjour*, where the quartet had set up at the party. "I'm having gin and a hint of vermouth, with a twist of lime. What would you like?"

"Scotch? Or the same as you."

"What about a sip of malt from Edinburgh? One of our reporters from England brought it to us this past winter."

"That'll be fine."

While Monique scurried about in the kitchen, we sat in the parlor and sipped our drinks. I noticed Jacques's hands. They were trembling slightly. He set his glass down and flexed his fingers. Tiny beads of perspiration glistened along the furrows of his forehead.

"Are you feeling feverish?" I asked. "It has been warm today, hasn't it?"

"Yes, it has. No, I'm feeling fine. Just agitated, I think. Sales are slower than I thought they'd be. It's a good book I wrote. Don't you think so, if I may put you on the spot?"

"Very much. I like your bold style, your audacity and vision. What are the critics saying?"

"That it's too grand, even self-aggrandizing, if not *gauche*, say some. Imagine that! Clumsy and thrown together, like 'the work of an amateur,' *Le Monde* charges. *Bigre*! Few appreciate the truth today." He wiped at the beads of perspiration on his brow and emptied his glass of gin and vermouth. "Ahhh! What would we do without alcohol?"

"The potage is ready!" called Monique. "Please, quickly, come while it's hot. I'm serving the rest *à l'amérique*. Everything at once, after the soup!"

We moved to the table. Monique took a seat to my right, stationing herself near the kitchen, while Jacques sat at the opposite end. I sat between them. The potage was a mixture of sweet onions, cabbage, and leeks, flavored with chicken broth.

The main dish consisted of rabbit, simmered in a brown gravy, served with carrots, peas, and white stalks of crisp celery. Salad and cakes of camembert accompanied the meal. A large basket of fresh bread and plate of real creamery butter were passed up and down the table throughout the repast. Two uncorked bottles of white wine slaked our thirst.

"Tell us something about yourself," Jacques suggested. "You know enough about us. We're simply French, in love with life, the haughty bane of the rest of the world," he grinned, "the keepers of the gates of culture. *Non*? Isn't that so?"

"You know I hate to admit that," I replied. "How can you come to Paris and ever think of leaving it, or returning to your own country again?"

"Surely you get home sick," demurred Monique, her eyes burning with soft passion. "What is here for you, anyway? Don't you want to go home? Isn't there someone there who wants you? Or needs you?" She wet her lips and tried to smile.

"Too personal!" Jacques remarked. "We are getting too personal. Everyone loves France. Its history beckons all. Some come and stay for the rest of their lives. Isn't that so?"

I glanced at Monique. If I could have had her, yes, I should have wanted to have stayed for the rest of my life. But how much longer could our affair last? And didn't Jacques suspect it already? Wasn't he leading up to it? Politely, at least? Frustrated, but polite about it, nonetheless?

Monique's eyes met my own. Yes, she would have liked that, too. She was still willing to risk it. I could see it. And so could Gibert. I was appalled at the thought, yet helpless to suppress it.

"When do you return?" he asked, almost with demand. "We shall miss you, I'm sure."

"By August, I suspect. Within six or seven weeks, I fear."

"And have you heard from the Sullivans? We've heard nothing. Marvelous man, he is. And his Cherie! Such a darling! Why are you so prejudiced back home? Don't Americans like blacks?"

"Of course we do. We're part of each other. It's just that we've let the past keep us separate. Who could say 'No' to Julene?"

"This is depressing," sighed Monique. "I want to visit America. Your college someday. Your South. I don't want our friendship to end. Won't you need to come back if you translate Jacques's book? *Oui*?"

"Yes, I'm sure. Even if Balfour won't pay for it. Yes," I stared at Gibert.

"Eh! Enough! I want to show you my wine *cave*, and that little surprise I promised. Remember? You are game for a little contest, aren't you?"

"He's being vain!" interrupted Monique. "He likes to show off his cellar, then his closet of foils and *epées*. He will cut you if he can," she stared at her husband with visible disapproval.

"Come now, my dearest! You make me sound *fou, sauvage*, uncouth. I am certain Monsieur Rogers can hold his own. *N'est-ce pas*?" his mouth parted with grim delight.

"I might know enough to survive," I smiled him off.

"Then it's done! Let's go!" he pushed back his chair. "Follow me."

Monique looked horrified. She rose to block the way. "Jacques-Maria, this is not funny. You are being *bête*!"

"Ah, my dear! And just who has been *bête*?" he stared at her with an exultant smile.

"Don't worry," I mumbled to Monique. "I apologize if I have somehow offended you."

"Apologize!" glared Gibert. "This is man-to-man. I will show you what a real Frenchman can do."

He led me to his basement, past his wine racks, and into a large room that appeared empty at first. Then I saw the foils in cases against a wall, several mats, fencing masks, vests, and gloves, all hanging from pegs about the room.

"Select a foil and suit up," he said. He took one of the foils from its case, whipped it about like a switch and suited up.

I put on the longest vest I could find, pulled on a large mesh mask, and selected a limber foil. I noticed that the foil's blunt tip had been filed slightly, just enough to give it a sharp point. He had done the same to all the other foils. I had not fenced since my junior year in college. I had barely qualified for the team and had lost as many matches as I had won. I watched Gibert carefully out of the corner of my eye. By God, if this is what he wanted, then so be it!

"*En garde*!" he shouted, as we touched blades. Then he stepped back and lunged immediately for me. I had anticipated his move and deflected his thrust with a parry I had been taught by our fencing coach.

"Ah, ha! What have we here!" he chuckled, as he swished his blade about. He resumed his stance, but more cautiously this time. He approached and lunged.

For several quick seconds, our foils slammed off each other, as we parried and thrust. Suddenly, he lunged again. His foil slid along mine and found its mark in the soft tissue of my left shoulder. The blade's tip had penetrated the padded vest. A tiny spot of red blood spurted out over the gray padding.

He stepped back, obviously pleased. "Ah, *mon vieux*! Just a little touch, old chap. *Non*? Shall we try again?" Once more he crouched in his stance, cut a slow circle in the air with his foil, and advanced.

He had tilted his foil to the right as he faced me. He was so confident. If I could lunge fast enough, I could touch him. What did I have to lose? In a flash, I went straight for his forearm, the closest target to me.

"Ah!" he groaned. "*Merde! Touché*. You have touched me." He swung his foil about and sprang for my chest. His blade bent up and back as it hit the padding, making a thud and twang as it glinted in the dim light of the room. "You are supposed to say '*Touché*!' when I score like that," he instructed me breathlessly. "You have cut my arm. See! It is bleeding now."

The right sleeve of his gray sweater had turned moist. Blood trickled a bright red down his wrist and into his glove. "I know how to go for the throat," he said. "I want you to stay away from Monique! Do you understand? I don't know what you two have been up to, but she likes to flirt. I have eyes throughout this city!"

We continued with more fencing. It was obvious that he didn't want to stop. He made several serious attempts to strike my throat, slashing the air with his foil when he missed. Up, down, sideways, our foils bent and rang off each other. The game was coming back to me, and I felt I could become his match in time.

"You are faster than I thought," he groaned, as he struck my face mask with a glancing pass. "You have not answered me. I must presume your innocence, but my honor is at stake. You understand? Yes?"

"*Oui*. You have made it quite clear."

"*Bon*!" he announced, as he stopped and removed his mask. A smile actually appeared on his face. "I like a good match! A challenge! Let us wash before we go upstairs. I have a first aid kit in the box, there," he indicated with a nod. "You will say nothing to Monique. We must let this pass. I need you, and you need me. I want my work translated. At least by someone I know."

"I understand. If Balfour agrees, I'll do you a damn good job. *Supérieur*!

We hung up the foils, vest pads, masks. and gloves. The dried blood on his wrist had turned brown.

"It is nothing! Here is *la trousse de premiers secours*." He opened the first-aid kit and handed me a sterile swab encased in a small package, along with a bandage. "Here. Let me take a look at your shoulder." The tone of his voice had surprisingly modified, becoming even soft and sincere.

I had worn a white shirt and yellow-and-black-striped tie. A small spot of red blood had stained the shoulder of my shirt and had faded out into a pink circle. I loosened my tie and peered at the wound. Jacques craned his neck to have a look as well.

"*C'est rien*," he said. "It's nothing to worry about."

I unbuttoned my shirt and bathed the cut, then applied the band-aid.

Jacques winced a little as he rolled up his own sleeve. The foil had torn a long, thin, but shallow groove into his fleshy forearm. He cleaned it with several swabs and held out his arm while I placed the widest band-aid in the kit across the deepest wound. He rolled down his sleeve. I put on my jacket, and we walked back upstairs.

"You are worse than little boys!" Monique scolded us. "Well, who cut whom? And don't tell me it was a draw," she glared at Jacques; then at me.

I was trying to suppress my smile, but she noticed it anyway. A sigh of relief rose from her throat and a twinkle of surprise appeared in her eyes.

"Well, I guess it could have been worse! I have made an apple tart, and we still have some good champagne left over from the party. Do I have any takers?"

"Yes, dear! I love you, with all my passion and cavalier's heart," Jacques bowed slightly, kissing her hand.

Her face lit up with a radiant merriment and a feigned blush. "You never stop!" she laughed. "He used to do that when we were dating," she smiled with faltering gravitas. "Alas! Men! *Les hommes! Toujours gallants; toujours enfants*. They never change."

"Nor ever learn!" Jacques retorted with a rakish grin. He looked deeply into her eyes. Suddenly, an icy hardness replaced his playful jest; his gaze turned into a stare.

Monique wanted to glance toward me. I could feel it, see it in her eyes, in her partly opened lips, sense it in her movements and in the subtle shift and cant of her shoulders. She knew Jacques was waiting for just such a glance, a flicker of her eyelashes. Her cheeks turned ashen, then a bright red. A frown formed along her mouth; it distorted her beautiful and fulsome lips and marred them with grim determination. They bristled as much with worry as with anger and disappointment. "One day you will go too far," she warned him.

Gibert seemed embarrassed. He uncorked the bottle. The three of us nibbled at Monique's tart and sipped champagne in silence.

"*Alors*! I need to go. Your meal, dessert, and everything has been superb. Truly marvelous," I thanked Monique.

I rose to my feet. Jacques pushed his chair back and offered me his hand. It felt cool and limp. "I shall be pleased when all this waiting is over and we hear definitively from Thiers. *Non*?" A strained smile returned to his lips.

"Yes. I agree," I shook his hand warmly. "I apologize if I've inconvenienced you. You have been gracious to receive me."

"The honor is ours," said Monique, as she studied her husband's face and then mine.

As I walked toward the door, it was Monique who accompanied me down the hallway. Jacques was still standing at the table, bent forward, staring silently at his glass.

"You must forgive him," Monique whispered. "He is very jealous and equally vain."

"With reason. I have hurt him. It was wrong."

"Shhhhh!" she placed the fingers of her right hand across my lips. "Love is never wrong. *L'amour a toujours raison.* Kiss me now, until later. Leave him to me."

Our lips touched as if on fire, as my heart sank into Aphrodite's warm and waiting web. But the pang in my heart would not subside. I walked in the dark toward the metro. What was I to do? I loved Monique. Perhaps even more than I had loved Leeta. Yet I had loved her; truly I had.

27

THE DARKENED HALLWAY OPENS onto an exposed metal stairwell. I am standing on an iron grate between two buildings. I cannot determine what floor, or how many stories up I am. Bitter drafts of wind whip against my trousers. Beyond the rickety stairwell, far out across a snow covered field, a lone wolf pauses to look up. It sniffs the air and stares in my direction. Can it see me? How can it not? Brown tufts of grass poke through the crusty snow's mantle. Snow continues to fall. The wolf slowly makes its way across the field. It keeps stopping and raising its head and looking in my direction. Swirls of downy flakes obscure the shadowy lupine. Has it lost its way or fallen behind the pack, or is it searching for me? Yes! Could I be the object of its search? I hold tightly to a flimsy banister as I step toward the edge of the metal grate. The wolf stops. Its ears perk up. The wind is blowing snow in its face. I am shivering, and clutch the throat of my coat as I wave. Fear has all but paralyzed me. Why? I have missed the wolf's presence. How can it harm me here? Why am I afraid? The wolf detects my movements, crouches in the snow, springs up, and bounds out of sight. My head is swirling with the snow. I am falling. Down, down, down I fall. I grab for the banister, for anything that will hold me. Anything. I brace myself to break the fall. My wrist hurts, but the snow is soft and still descending. I look up. I am on the floor. I have pulled my white quilt off the bed and have landed on my wrist. My shoulder burns with pain. I have knocked the band-aid off, as well. Such is morning. Sun light streams in soft lazy rays through the curtains. The new day had dawned.

I struggled to my feet, gathered up the quilt and other bedding, tossed it back on the mattress. It was time to shave, shower, and dress, and go down for *le petit-déjeuner*.

"Are you all right, Monsieur?" asked Pierre. "You seem, different. *Non*?"

"I'm fine," I mumbled. "Too much champagne last night, I fear. How about yourself? We haven't talked much, have we, since Gaston's death."

"*Non*. It's like a dream. A very sad one, Monsieur. I think after this year I'll move somewhere else."

"Like America?"

"No, no. You're right about Paris and how miserable I'd be outside France. *Oui*? But there are other places to live in this city, and I am due a promotion soon. There's a little village south of here, called DuValliémont. I have been promised a position there. Maybe as postmaster," he beamed. "Really! *C'est vrai*."

"And well deserved, *mon cher*, I've no doubt."

"Well, I must be off. *A toute à l'heure*."

"Until this evening. Yes!"

After breakfast, I felt too glum to plunge into Kant or Rousseau, or even Rilke, Goethe, or Sullivan's Homer. I needed air, the morning breezes of reality, even if redolent of Parisian traffic and toxic fumes: the blue pollutants of crowded buses and speeding cabs. My heart raced to the beat of the throbbing taxis that idled in line, as they merged slowly into the morning's rush hour along the Rue de Vaugirard and the distant St. Michel. At the corner of Montparnasse, I made my way toward Demetrius' kiosk.

"And where have you been, good man?" he asked cheerily. "You see the pigeon there?" he pointed. "I was about to ask him: 'Have you seen our professor? *Non*?' When, just then, the pigeon turned up his tail, looked down the street, and, behold, here you are!"

"Thanks a lot! And just how do you say, 'Asshole!' in Greek?'

Demetirus laughed and served me a cup of his black, steaming, Montparnasse coffee.

"It is good, yes?"

"Yes," I smiled.

"Some day you will come to Greece. You will admire her skies of cobalt and lapis lazuli, flung like the lazy robes of the goddesses across her white hills. You will see her ancient cliffs of gray chalk and white granite, and groves upon groves of lemon and citrus trees, and feel the sting of the sea. Ah! And you will wonder, Monsieur, my dear Professor, what poor ole Demetrius of Piraeus, the king of this kiosk café, is doing here! No! I think so," he shook his head with a tired longing for his native land. "I love this place, but I'm still just a stranger here," he motioned theatrically with an upraised hand. "But enough of this—this pining away. It is lovely, isn't it? Look at the sky, the leaves on the trees, this magnificent plane tree! They are so big, so large, their veins swollen with new green growth. Our life here is short, my friend. Like my dear wife's, may her memory be eternal! God never forgets us. No? Don't you think so? Sometimes, that's my only hope. *The eternal memory of God*."

I had not expected so passionate a theological review, at least, not for the cost of a single cup of coffee. I assumed that the grieving process for his wife was far from over. "Yes," I somehow managed to reply. "It's back to work now, for me, too."

Settling down to organize my fractured thoughts required a long moment of reflection. I tried to think of nothing and just let my thoughts bubble up. While waiting for the philosophical spirits to sing their siren songs, I turned to Gibert's first chapter. A section entitled, "Napoleon's Maxims" caught my eye. Wrote Gibert:

> Hints for a guide for our arduous task may be gleaned from Napoleon's famed "Military Maxims." Using even the most paltry imagination, we can summon them to serve us today. Maxim 78: "Read and reread the campaigns of Alexander, Hannibal, Caesar, Turenne, Eugène and Frederick. Model yourself upon them." Maxim 66: "In war the chief alone understands the importance of certain things; and he alone by his will and superior knowledge can conquer and overcome all difficulties." Maxim 77: "Keeping one's forces united, being vulnerable at no point, moving rapidly on important points—these are the principles which assure victory, and, with fear brought by the reputation of arms, maintains the fidelity of allies and the obedience of conquered peoples."
>
> We cannot reclaim our past grandeur aside from a bold, united effort to define anew France's purpose and goal in a modern, postwar Europe. We must not allow any nation, other than our own, to determine our foreign or domestic policies. We alone must create them, dare to imagine what they might be. Nor can we abide continued foreign influences to erode our rich heritage of unique architecture, eloquent and flowing language, long history of luminous art, music, poetry, and customs, nor challenge our hard-won and rightly acclaimed stature as the world's acknowledged producer of civilization's finest wines, most elegant and tasty dishes, or our status as fabled capitol of fashion and design.
>
> But all that requires an underpinning of *sagesse*, of statesmanship that envisions France's appropriate and attainable place among

> the powers of the globe. Thus, we cannot forego rebuilding a strong independent defense, neglect world alliances, or turn a deaf ear to our former "conquered" colonies. That is why de Gaulle's concept of a "third force"—*une troisieme puissance*—was and remains vital. That de Gaulle himself appointed André Malraux as his Minister of Culture reinforces all that I am simply trying to offer to a generation that sadly favors foreign fashion and disco rhythms, peace at any cost, and political withdrawal from the fevered struggles and wars of the world, as an acceptable panacea. We must say, "*Non*!" to such delirious thinking, if it can be classified in any way as *pensée* at all!

I shook my head and smiled; nevertheless, I had to acknowledge Jacques's fervor and dream for a new and proud France. He wanted it to take its place once again upon the stage of world history. Indeed, it would be exciting to translate his work, for, beneath his charming rhetoric and Gallic bombast, ran an underlying search for mankind's meaning, for what it means to be human, holistic, and optimally fulfilled, not only as an individual but as a society. I resolved that Sullivan was after the same thing, and I, too, but each from a different perspective. Perhaps the perspectives didn't matter, so long as we somehow reconnected with our deeper selves that seemed so harborless, so aimlessly adrift and battered by life's relentless setbacks. How I wanted to be part of a new era of discovery, of offering mankind more than just endurable despair! But of what value would my own ramblings on an epistemology of doubt be? As for Sullivan, if he had any character flaw at all, it was his disparaging demeanor and absence of any uplifting joy, together with his slump into intellectual resignation, which reminded me that I hadn't heard anything from him or Julene. Surely some form of correspondence was long overdue. And there was Monique! I loved her. Even the fool in my heart knew that. But how could I give her up? I treasured every second with her. And what about Jacques? I could still see the peeved *bonhomme*, crouched and waving his foil cautiously about, slicing the air in slow circles, eyeing me behind his mask. Yes, *honneur* for both of us was at stake!

Just before lunch, I descended the stairs to walk in the park. Shafts of mellow sunlight filled its aisles with a lethargic glow. Supine shadows beckoned passersby into the indolent shade beneath the plane trees' great boughs. I selected a bench in the sun and sat down.

A rustling in the branches of a flowering bush behind me caught my attention. A guttural voice was attempting to address me. I turned to see who it was.

"Ho! Ho! Tweekkkk! Mmmmmmm! Rrrruuuutt!"

It was a large pigeon. It had been eating some peanuts that someone had cast behind the bench.

"Well, don't look so shocked!" it said. The pigeon craned its neck, puffed out its whitish-gray chest, plucked and fluffed its feathers with its beak, and strutted out into the aisle. "You were at Demetrius's earlier. *Non*? I would know you anywhere."

I rubbed my eyes. Rogers, keep calm! It's only a bird.

"And just who are you?" I demanded, in an equally Gallic tone.

"You should know. You pass me all the time, or sit idly staring into space, while I circumvent your bench or scurry in front of your legs, waiting and hoping for a handout, however meager it might be. But do you ever notice me? Do you ever address me, 'Ah, my fine feathered friend, *comment ça va? Ça va bien? Oui!*' Or, '*Salut, mon cher! A tu faim*? Are you hungry? *Alors! Voici pour toi. Bonjour! Bonsoir*!' No. You never think of me. Only of yourself, no doubt, and whatever it is you do, or think you do. What a fine scholar on sabbatical you are! And do you think your *largesse* toward the poor fares any better? Your piddling two francs here and your stingy five francs there? Oh, my! What hypocrisy! Huh? *N'est-ce pas*?" The pigeon cocked its head to one side and waited for my reply.

I thought for a while, then addressed it with equitable, trenchant sarcasm. "You and your typical arrogance are the bane of every major city. Your slimy green guano stains everything, from bronze to marble, from granite to grass. Lovers may welcome you, and children and the widowed tolerate your presence, but you are a royal nuisance, and you know it. Besides, the few *sou* I give to the homeless, I give because I want to, not because I have to. And would that I could do more! Yes! 'I was hungry, and you gave me to eat.' I don't expect you to understand."

"Whoa, Monsieur big foot! Don't quote your pious scriptures to me! 'Not a sparrow shall fall, but that your Father shall take notice.' And again, 'Behold the birds of the air: they neither spin nor gather into barns, yet your heavenly Father feeds them.' *Non*? Am I not right? Of course!" the pigeon cooed with typical Parisian smugness.

"What do you know about love? Or about lovers? Tell me, Mister Pigeon, how constant are you? Is your twittering crowd not as foul as mankind?"

"*Foul*! Indeed! Yes, we are *fowl*! And proud to be fowl! And what do we know of monogamy? I have been faithful to every mate I have ever had. Don't cast your spiteful aspersions on me! Every day is a struggle here. My kind suffer as much as yours. Life makes no distinction that I can see."

"Well, offer me some advice, since you are manifestly such a learned advocate of justice and fairness. Is it all right to love another man's wife, to gather your rosebuds while you may, before the bloom and the flower of youth fade? What do you say, O winged, wise messenger of Minerva?"

"Don't mock me! I warn you. You know the answer to that already," he replied mournfully. "Don't you?" A sadness seemed to fill his sagging craw. He looked up, his beady, black eyes still imploring me for a handout. After all, a pigeon is only a pigeon, as the Gullah of Charleston say.

I searched my pockets for a crumb, for a morsel of bread or cookie or of anything. A tiny flake of chocolate fell out and slipped between the crevices of crushed gravel beside the bench.

"It's a hard life, I tell you," said the pigeon. "Manna is hard to come by these days. We have to compete with the beggars, you know. We are all brought low, eventually, they say. Please, Monsieur, next time, be a little more generous. *Oui*?"

I rubbed my face a second time. When I glanced down at my feet, the pigeon was gone. Clayton, you'd better check your shoulders for bird doo, or maybe your brain. Great Scot! A pigeon! A talking pigeon, at that! The insides of my pockets were still dangling out. I felt like a creep! At least, my fly wasn't open. "You'd better get back to Kant or Homer," that hidden voice of Nietzsche's whispered. "And, for God's sake, don't mention this to Angleterre! Maybe you've been eating too much fruit. You know, it never helped me, either," Nietzsche's voice sighed. "To this day, they still talk about me in Sila Marias, in the Italian Alps, where I used to summer. Alas! We philosophers have always been the laughing stock of the sycophants of slave morality. 'We are always too soon,' says Zarathustra. Such is our fate. *Auf Wiedersehen, miner lieber Mann*. All that is noble will prevail. Chao! Remember me, when you read Goethe."

Back in my room, I stared at Kant's *Critique of Pure Reason*. I knew what I wanted to argue, or what needed to be said, to advance my thesis. For Immanuel Kant, our most important concepts are not the product of intuition, as he called it, but of reason. In Kant's scheme of things, there are two principal means by which we come to the knowledge of anything: sense experience and reason. The former (*Sinnlichkeit*) has to do with perceptions of phenomena, or perceptions of things as they appear to us. We can never really know noumena (or things as they are in themselves), but only things as they appear to us. Moreover, the things that appear to us come to us in space and time. They are inseparable from our temporal-spatial experiences. According to Kant, we can't help but impose on these experiences certain inner categorical structures of the mind, such as quality and quantity, cause and effect, and the notion that things are either possible or impossible. In other words, our knowledge of objects comes to us through the lens of the mind's own operations. This latter source of knowledge Kant called reason, or thought (*Vernunft*). Human knowledge is limited, but beyond noumena, we still have knowledge of certain ideas that we are driven to posit from our scrappy visions of objects. Kant referred to these as "*transcendental ideals*," namely, the *self*, the *cosmos*, and *God*. When we enter the self, we encounter no enduring ego, but only an immediate field of changing perceptions, memories, longings, feelings, judgments, etc. And these are constantly occurring and fading away. Whence, then, the concept of a self, of a singular ego, as an enduring reality? We are driven to posit it, in order to unify the numerous immediate perceptions and continuous stream of consciousness that we experience. The same holds true for the ideas of cosmos and God. No one has seen the cosmos, per se, but we are driven to postulate it as a reality, in order to do justice to the countless bits and pieces we know exist. As for God, God, too, becomes a postulate of human reason, as the being that is the sole and sufficient cause of all else.

All of which had led me to the conclusion that the realm of certainty is wide open but limited. It is rich in variety and concurrences, ripe with possibilities for choices, actions, achievements, and ideals—whether in art, politics, science, or religion. And dreams, too, but, above all, it results in consequences that are commensurably real and often harrowing. Sullivan's quest, as I understood it, was for a self-understanding that preceded the emergence of philosophy, that preceded that dichotomy between exuberance and reason, on which Socrates and Plato would build their castles of wisdom, dedicated to the life of the mind at the expense of our sensual natures. Demythologizing Homer meant for Sullivan the way to true wholeness, but his flagging spirit signaled that something was still awry. Sullivan wanted to compromise the life of the mind in favor of some vitalistic *esprit de nature* that was free of philosophical conjecture and flights of speculation. To that extent, he was a child of modern positivism: that the value of any opinion is determined by its method of verification. When applied to the classics, it simply swept away the very foundations that Carl most needed to explore in order to establish his thesis. What would his *Beyond Homer* really offer? When would I hear from him? And how was Julene? Why were they so silent? Had something happened to her mother? Was Julene pregnant? Had she told me that, or was I only imagining it? Alas! It was time for lunch. I would have to come back to my work later.

Following *le déjeuner,* I re-climbed the stairs, opened the door and collapsed on my bed. I wanted to take a nap, but my restless ego would have none of it. "Up, up!" it urged. "An idle mind is the Devil's workshop. After all, you are a scholar!"

Rolling over, I struggled to my feet and flipped through several pages of a collection of Goethe's verses.

Nature and Art

Nature and art: as soon as they have fled each other
They long for unity again.
Even in me, their savage struggle has disappeared
Yet both are dear to me.

Only an honest effort will do!
But that requires numerous precious hours
Devoted to Art, with all our flesh and soul (*Geist und Fleiss*)
Before Nature may flow freely in our hearts anew.

That's the way it is with culture, too.
In vain will unfettered spirits strive
To reach the heights of pure perfection.
Whoever, likewise, aspires to greatness, must pull himself together.

Only in limitation is mastery revealed,
For law alone sets us free.

I wished Sullivan were there. Here again was that Grecian balance between the Dionysian and the Apollonian, exuberance and reason. Was not the reunification of the two every philosopher's aspiration? Oh, well! At least I was stumbling closer toward the truth, or so I felt. The things we doubt the most we can never know, but they underlie our lives and pulsate in our very being, like Kant's transcendental ideals. We don't have to prove them to know they exist; they are a priori as guiding lights, as postulates that regulate our pathway, like glowing sumptuary signposts. We can heed them or not, but life will go on. Between the two polestars of Homer's *ménin* and Plato's *sophia,* between our anxious frenzy and moments of reason, life progresses, struggles to transcend its sorrows and sufferings, reaches within and beyond itself for sustaining succor, and, if it attains its nobler possibilities, reaches out to assist others. If reading Descartes, Pascal, Rousseau, and Kant had taught me anything, they had taught me that. An epistemology of doubt sweeps away all else as dross and pretension, but it leaves the heart with a yawning pit in its wake. Can we accept reality for what it is, with all its self-limitations, and be content to live it with joy? I was ready to conclude my work. But how unfulfilled I felt! Oh, Monique! What I would give if you were mine! Julene, Julene! Ebony star, throbbing in the heart of myriad palpitating celestial lights! I am always too soon! Or perhaps too late! Was that your fate, too, dear Nietzsche?

I had scarcely gathered these vagabond thoughts under the wings of reflection, when I heard Angleterre at the door. I could always tell it was she; a certain click of her shoes' flat heels, swish of her corset or slip, and quickness to her step, surreptitiously announced her arrival. I opened the door before she could knock.

"Ohh!" she burst into shock. "My word! What a coincidence! There's someone downstairs to see you. I wouldn't let them come up."

"My secret lover? *Oui*?"

"Heavens! I hope not! It's the Belgian. He wouldn't tell me why he's here. He wants you to come down, if you will."

"I'll be right there."

As Angleterre retraced her steps down the hall, I grabbed up my wallet, slipped on my sports coat, and ran a comb through my hair. After locking the door, I joined Claude on the second floor. He was clasping a leather cap in both hands. Deep furrows of worry played about his lips. They had worn grooves into his forehead. His appearance was one notch above sloven: uncombed black hair, gray, unshaven face, with shirt and trousers wrinkled, the latter baggy at the knees.

His face brightened momentarily as I approached. "Thank heavens you are here! Can we go somewhere and talk?" he said nervously, glancing toward Angleterre with no small embarrassment.

"Of course. There's a small café-bar, just around the corner."

"*Bon*! I'll follow."

We walked up the Rue d'Assan to the narrow slit of a bar where Angleterre and I had sought refuge following Gloria's arrest. We sat at a small round table in a cramped corner and ordered *café noir*.

"Francine has disappeared," Claude blurted, in a garbled, breathless voice. "I've been looking for her all morning."

"What happened, if I may be so bold?"

"We had a quarrel. She wanted to visit her mother. She's in jail, you know. I encouraged her not to. She began to cry. She accused me of 'raping' her. Of all things! I assure you, it was mutual! She did it for money, at first. Then out of love. I don't know what to do, or where to search. I'm afraid of going to the police."

"You could always seek out Daniel—Dufavre's cousin, or whatever. If she visited her mother, he would know. Or if she's run off, " I added hesitantly, "not knowing where to go or what to do, surely he'd be able to find out, or stumble onto a few leads. Don't you think so?"

"Maybe you're right," he sighed. Marks of anxiety cast shadows across his face. "I've not told my own parents. No one knows I'm living with her, save you and the people at Dufavre's. Oh, me! I have always been in control, but this is too much. She was very upset when she left, whenever that was. I woke up about five a.m. and discovered she was gone. The bed was still warm. I thought she had slipped out to the WC. When I awoke again at six, I knew better. I've been all over the city, down in the metro, and elsewhere, wherever I thought she might go. I've been afraid to look in the Seine. You don't think she'd do that, do you? She was awfully upset."

"Have you checked Notre Dame? I was meditating there one day when she slipped in and knelt before the Virgin. She might have gone there."

"No. But to stay there all morning? I don't think so. She's hardly pious! Good heavens! She wouldn't have gone off to a convent! Surely, not!"

"That would be preferable to the Seine," I replied. "I have the feeling she'll come home. She's young, sick, frightened, alone, in spite of having your love. And the thought of having a baby, and no mother of her own to express joy or come to help her, and the two of you not even married, all that is pretty weighty. Terrifying, no?"

"True! Oh Christ, what a fool I've been! I must marry her. *Non*?"

"If she's not back by tonight, call me. If she is, call me anyway. I'll not be able to rest, until you do." I tried to smile. What if she had hurt herself? Had taken her own life? I exhaled a long slow breath of my own.

He caught my hands in his. There were tears in his eyes. "You would make a great priest, professor! Do you know that? *Père Clarke*!" He raised my hands to his lips and kissed them.

"Please! No. I am all but an atheist. Go to the cathedral, kneel with her, if she's there. Comfort, respect, and love her. It is her hands you should kiss. Not mine."

"I will. I'm heading there right now." He rose, looked back at me and smiled. Tears glistened in his eyes. Bright droplets gleamed in his stubbly beard. "*Au revoir*!"

I paid the bill and walked back toward my room. What if she weren't there? What if she were dead? What if she had gone to the jail, and her mother had rebuffed her again? Anything was possible. But I had the strongest premonition that Claude was going to find her, just where I thought she'd be.

What a relief that night when he called, just before dinner, to confirm precisely what I had presaged! I looked at myself in the mirror. Was it just luck, or something more? Something that only the gods fathom, but keep secret among their own? I moved toward my desk, placed my face in my hands, and wept. Moments later, I splashed cold water about my eyes and descended the stairwell for the evening repast. I suddenly remembered that I hadn't fulfilled my promise to Pierre. Sparkling wine, it was? A fine wine shop, opposite the Garden of Luxembourg, was less than a half-block away. I hurried along the street, purchased a bottle of St. Montanard, at a cost of fifty-five francs—which was *assez cher* for me, and returned to the dining room, just as Pierre arrived. Mme. Cueillier was still serving the potage. She smiled as I took my seat. I unfastened the bottle's wire cap, and popped the cork. "Ah, Pierre!" I grinned. "To the good life, *non*?"

His smile betrayed a mouth of ocherous, neglected teeth, stained with nicotine and wine. "Yes, yes!" he laughed, as I filled his glass with the bubbly effervescent essence.

As darkness fell, I wandered downstairs, only to meet Angleterre ascending the stairwell.

"Ah, Madame," I addressed her. "Thought I might wander up to the Boulevard Montparnasse for an apéritif. Would you care to join me?"

"O Professeur, *merci*, but I'm too tired," she replied. "Perhaps another time. But drink one for me." She raised her skirt and continued climbing the stairwell.

Outside, the night air felt warm and pleasantly balmy. As I walked along, it distressed me that I hadn't heard from Julene. I had their Alabama phone number, but not their Alabama address. Near Demetrius's latched up kiosk, I took a seat at a sidewalk café and ordered a cognac. As I sipped on it, a wave of remorse slipped up from my hidden self. It came on with intense immediacy. I had felt so calm, reassured; yet, there I was, struggling against a inner adversary, an introspection that sapped my mental resources of what should have been a pleasant experience. After all, I had conceptualized the final touches that my project would require. In addition, I had been of immense help to Claude. But the hounds of doubt were descending, and in fierce, heated pursuit. Nietzsche descried self-pity and ambivalence. Once I discovered his painful truth in his *The Genealogy of Morals*, I never wanted to indulge in self-misgivings again. But a curse on Nietzsche! Who among humanity hasn't slunk into his secret cave to seek a solace that only communion with the self can bring? I was determined to see my project through, published, and, then, plunge into whatever subject might captivate me next. But as I sat there it slowly began to dawn on me that, since my senior year in college, at which time I had formulated the goals I had to-date successfully pursued, that making *relationships* a legitimate goal had never been included in my inventory of objectives to achieve. I had lived for myself, dreamed for myself, even been a minister in search of myself, but I had never envisioned that at some point I would need, indeed, want, to bury my life in another's, that I would yearn to love another as earnestly as I longed to be loved. I knew Monique would call again. I knew I would melt like a hot puddle of wax when she did; that I would never be able to say, "No." Not to Monique. I loved her, or, if not loved her, burned with inordinate cupidity for her. I craved the fulfillment that her arms and thighs, lips and breasts extinguished when I was with her; that her face, her presence, her eyes, her smile, her laughter, her wit, her sarcasm equally provided. But I knew that Gibert was right. She was his wife, and I had no business "fucking" her. Yes, "fucking" her, I told myself. My God! *The Ethics of Virtue*? Why couldn't I instill in myself those virtues I knew to be right? How absolutely on target Aristotle was! We only become brave by doing brave deeds, just by acting justly, kind by showing kindness, chaste by being chaste. Dammit! Just or unjust, chaste or not, how I wanted Monique! I glared at the traffic and passers-by. Maybe it was time to go home. Back to the Shenandoah Valley. To hell with Paris and everyone! To hell with Balfour, Thiers, and Gibert! Down, down, I seemed to spiral, when, just then, I felt a tug at my elbow. I turned. It was Monique! She had drawn up a chair beside me. Her eyes glistened in the street's pale sheen. She wore a pink scarf pulled about her head, face, and neck; she had slipped her feet into a pair of black sandals and was dressed in a silky white blouse and pair of dark jeans.

"Your Madame Angleterre told me where to find you."

I leaned sideways, closed my eyes, kissed her, and reached for her hands.

"Jacques is gone again, this time to Strasbourg. He left on the six o'clock train. May I spend the night with you?"

"Have you had dinner? Would you care for something to eat?"

"No. No," she laughed. "I hunger only for you," she whispered, as we kissed again.

"Then, let's go. *Allez, allez, ma petite*!"

Hand and hand, we walked down the rue Bréa, crossed several others, darted between the taxis toward the pension, and slipped up the stairwell to my room.

"Monique! Monique!" I pressed her warm body against my chest. Our lips met and refused to part. Still kissing each other, we undressed, hugged amidst lovers' giggles, and rolled onto the bed. "Woman! Oh, woman!"

"Shhhhh!" she said in a low hush. "Just love me. Ummm! Just kiss me like that! Oh, my! Your shoulder! You have a scrape there. See!" she kissed it. "It's inflamed, no? Your fencing wound! Yes?"

"Yes. It'll heal, I'm confident."

"So stupid of you. So, so adolescent. You know, Jacques is quite good. He was a medalist in his twenties. Tried out for the Olympics. Lost in the last round. He was my hero. But, he is so different now."

"He loves you, Monique. He's jealous. Whatever his faults, you are still his *femme*, his devoted *Cherie*."

"How you say it in English?" she puckered up her lips, as she lay back and opened her thighs and clamped them about my hips. "*Boolle sheet*! No? He's a womanizer when he's not around me. I'm no fool!"

"But he still loves you," I repeated in French. "You're still number one. Remember what you said about French royalty and their favorite lustful pastime?"

"Enough of him. Ummmm! It is you I love; you I want."

"Would you marry me, if I asked you?"

"Why not ask?"

"Will you?"

"Let's not spoil the evening," she kissed my neck. "It's my turn on top," she whispered, as if in a trance.

We rolled to our right. As I settled back, I gazed up into her beautiful face and curly hair and cupped her small voluptuous breasts in my hands. "Smother me with kisses," I implored, as if in a dream, as she rocked back and forth between her soft, sybaritic moans.

"You are so hard and carnal," she sighed. "Oh, oh, God! Oh! Oh!"

I rolled her back over and pressed my mouth against her breasts. I don't remember falling asleep. I awoke her at five; we made love again, then she washed, dressed, and slipped quietly out of the room. "I'll call you soon," she whispered, as she closed the door.

28

I WAS IMMERSED IN Gibert's chapter on the Knights Templars, when Angleterre brought in my tea and mail. I had left the door unlocked, and she had simply opened it and walked in. After setting the tray down on my desk, she proudly handed me an *aerogramme, par avion*. "It's from the States? *Non*? Maybe good news? *Oui*?"

I glanced at the handwriting. It was Julene's. "Yes!" I blurted. "It's from the Sullivans! You remember them?"

"But of course! That little black girl was sweet on you. *Non*? I saw it in her eyes. And that man she was with? So glum, so overweight. Why does she want him? I think you liked her. *Non*?"

"You know too much."

"That's why I'm a good concierge," she curtseyed, with a half-smile. Suddenly, she sniffed the air. "*Alors*! You are approaching worthlessness, Monsieur, if I may say so. She was here last night, wasn't she? That woman! I can smell her perfume. You are going to get in trouble. Big trouble! Mark my words. That Monsieur Gibert, her husband, he tried to bribe me. Pay me if I'd spy on her when she comes." Her smile evaporated totally; a look of anger and admonition replaced it. "You are lucky I said, 'No.' 'Hire your own detective,' I said. Well," she smirked. "That's what I wanted to say. But, oh, I fear he's going to get you. Adultery is punishable in this country. He could make you pay dearly. So he told me." She shook her head with great disapprobation. "I don't like it. Why do you do it? Uh? I'm trying to be your friend? *Non? Votre amie*!" she stressed, with frustration.

"I'm sorry I disappoint you. I don't know why I do it, either. But, she pleases me. Immensely. I crave her presence, her love."

"Shhhosh! *Amour,* my foot! 'Lust,' is more like it. You just like to . . . to cohabitate. Like some *chien!* Some dog in the street. And you! You are so, so handsome, Monsieur. Tall! Desirable, *je crois*! It is time for you to marry. That's what this means! Ah! But your letter!" she clasped her hands with glee. "Tell me they're all right!" she bent toward me, in a more humble demeanor. "I have always wanted the best for people. *Non*?"

I opened the letter with my penknife, unfolded it, and ran my eyes down across Julene's beautiful, almost artistic, handwriting. "Uh, let's see! They've arrived safely. A delay or two here and there. But, her mother's dead. Died before they could reach her. Very sad, but their spirits are recovering. They buried her in the family cemetery overlooking the old plantation house. Uh! Carl is well. His book's been accepted. But he's drinking too much. Uhhhh," I raced past the more personal material. "Uhh! That's about it. Oh, '*Give your Angleterre a hug for us.*'"

"That is too bad about her mother. How nice of her to think of me." Angleterre sighed, turned about, and left the room.

I had made up the part about Carl's health and giving Angleterre the hug. Now I could read the letter in earnest and privacy and focus on the lines that Julene had doubtlessly kept secret from Carl:

> *All is not well! Carl has succumbed to long bouts of despair. We have wonderful sex, but his heart isn't in it. I guess it's not all that wonderful! Sometimes he sleeps past noon. The old place needs repairing if it's going to remain standing much longer. The columns out front need replacing. The odor of rot and mildew unnerves and saddens me. It hangs in the air and wafts through the house. It is Carl that is rotting. Something isn't right. But we have so much to live for. And he's so brilliant. His book had been accepted before we left Paris. But he's displeased with it already. Or maybe it's with himself. He is far more complicated than I thought. So, he's taken to the bottle. Oh, man! He drinks a pint a day. And wants only to eat pork. Side meat from the smokehouse! Ugh! I had enough of that as a child. And Mama! I miss her. Her caretaker was supposed to help Mama with her memoirs, but didn't, nor does she know where Mama left them, or kept them. Please write back. Give the Giberts our regards. When you return home, you must visit us. Then we can talk in privacy. Love, Julene and Carl.*

As I stared at the letter, my heart was lifted by the subtle innuendoes and enormous trust that Julene placed in me. A part of me burned for her with shameful hunger. As for Carl, I was not surprised. I knew I was far less blessed with acumen than he, nowhere near possessing his keen intellectual prowess, or sheer brilliance. Yet, his work had inspired my own, and I wanted, however selfishly it might have been, to probe his mind and personality for the real man, the real genius behind his eloquent words and perspicuous thought, not simply about Homer or the Greeks, but about earliest mankind and his understanding of Being.

In the days that followed, I wrote and rewrote numerous sections of my own project, revisited the national archives, and translated my favorite poets in the evenings. I longed for Monique. When would she call again, or just show up? I didn't dare call her. Plus, I hadn't written back to Julene and Carl, or even sent a condolence card, or called.

About that time, a self-styled American Buddhist , or "eclectic mystic," as he referred to himself, passed through Paris and stayed at our pension for several days. He was tall, slender, slightly bald, suffering from "atrichia," as he called it, yet with ample hair on the back of his hands and a thick sub-growth of black beard. He had deep-blue, penetrating eyes and fine lines that ran perpendicular down his thin face. He sat very erect, ate sparingly (a strict vegetarian diet at that), but liked cheese. At his first evening in the dining hall, I offered him a glass of wine. He responded with a frank but courteous, "No!" He eyed both me and Pierre with transparent superiority, especially when I returned to the table and filled Pierre's glass to the top. Whether he meant to or not, poor Pierre belched just as I completed my mission. We both burst into laughter. The "Buddhist" had published several books on spirituality and the inner life and had placed a copy of his most recent work, *On Solitude*, on a side table, as you entered the dining room. I had not read it, nor even cracked the cover to glance at its contents.

The following day in the park, however, I was afforded a second opportunity to reassess the newcomer. Soft shafts of citrus light sifted through the leaves of the overhanging plane trees and cast a lazy, but contemplative aura about the bench where he sat. Several silvery gray pigeons strutted about the path in front of him, and a large rose bush glowed aflame with velvet, beet-red petals. His hands were slightly folded in his lap; he was wearing jeans, sandals, and a light purple sweater.

"Good afternoon!" I greeted him. "May I join you?"

"Yes, of course!" he replied, as if he had been anticipating my acknowledgment of his presence. "Do sit down," he motioned, as he scooted to one end of the bench.

"Clayton Clarke," I introduced myself. "From Virginia. I'm on sabbatical. It's beautiful, isn't it?" I nodded toward the distant basin and the busy Boulevard Saint Michel, beyond.

"Sanghadhamma," he extended his hand. "That's my Buddhist name. I used to be a Catholic priest, Father Antonio d'Maricio of New Jersey. I'm on my way to a Buddhist institute south of here."

"May I ask what attracts you to Buddhism?"

"Everything and *nothing*," he smiled. "I'm searching for that *emptiness*, which the Buddha experienced. Then, who knows what will happen?"

"Why would a good priest want to convert to Buddhism?" I asked, playfully. "Isn't there a kind of *emptiness* already in being a priest, like the vows of chastity, poverty, and obedience? I don't mean to sound testy. Just curious."

He expelled something of a polite, but impatient sigh. "I could no longer believe in the doctrine of salvation: that Christ had died for me, or that Christ alone is my Savior, or that the Blessed Virgin is the Mother of God. Buddhism teaches that we are our own saviors, that no one else can save us. We must come to enlightenment on our own. It doesn't happen through someone else's experiences—however enlightening they may be. It's not something that someone else can do for you. 'You are your only helper,' says the Buddha. We must empty the self of thinking that it will come from anyone else. Once that happens, we are free. Free to accept reality for what it is. Free to see things as they are, and not as we wish they might be. The veils of illusion are lifted, along with the notion that 'I' somehow am independent from everything else, or that 'I' somehow will survive this existence as a conscious ego. Only the karma that I put into action will survive, whether good or bad, nothing more. That is the only thing that enjoys reincarnation. Forgive me, if I sound like I'm preaching, or being condescending," he smiled.

"I understand. In fact, much of what you've just said, I accept. But it sounds so idealistic, so intentional. Don't you think so?" I asked with some embarrassment.

"Yes, and No. Yes, the notion that we must empty ourselves of false ideas about the self and the world does sound metaphysical, if not programmatic. Still, the world is full of suffering, and that suffering is caused by cravings and desires that erode our possibilities for a richer self-fulfillment. To rid ourselves of those kinds of harmful desires and false hopes is surely a boon."

"But does going off to a temple, or ashram, or Buddhist institute, in the hope of experiencing enlightenment, or *emptiness*, or whatever you want to call it, help solve the world's problems? I don't mean to sound disrespectful, for my own sabbatical is a form of escape, a kind of illusion, I suppose. But I doubt if we ever get rid of most of our illusions, or extinguish our cravings and sufferings in ourselves, let alone the world."

"What a cupful!" he smiled, painfully. "Yes, it is possible. That's why going off to a sangha, or temple, or study-hall is essential. To break the chains of samsara, the cycles of rebirth, or your feeling of the impossibility of changing anything, requires *emptiness*, silence, and meditation. It requires an enlightenment that shatters our deceptions and opens the way to self-reform. Residence in a community of like-minded seekers is of enormous help. Between solitude and fraternity, it is possible to recover ones underlying being, as well as ones unity with the world. It's a way of experiencing anew the Buddha-essence. The renunciation of a craving self, and all that is wrong with it, is the first step toward that goal," he emphasized with satisfaction.

"Renunciation may have its value for a self in search of itself," I replied, somewhat hesitatingly, as I didn't want to offend him any more than I already had. "But isn't suffering endemic to life? And, somehow to me, it isn't the elimination of suffering that's the goal, rather—forgive me—the challenge lies in *celebrating* life, in spite of the suffering, in spite of all the bad karma that you and I are capable of causing. And that we *do need* to be saved from ourselves, and even forgiven—whether God exists or not—is surely equally true. Apart from that kind of transcendence, aren't we still caught in multiple strands of deception? Somehow to celebrate life and to help others do the same would not be a bad goal. Because, beyond that, I don't know what else to believe. But running off to monasteries, I know, isn't the whole answer. I tried that once ten years ago, less than forty miles southeast of here. It was a wonderful year, in fact healing. But after staying on for two more months, I knew I had to return to reality." I paused and glanced with no small uncertainty toward d'Maricio. "Sir, with all due respect, if we can't make a difference now, why suppose that we'll somehow make it in another life, or in a reincarnation? I don't mean to sound confrontational, as I really want to know."

The slender man appeared shocked. To say "annoyed" would betray his true feelings. His calm facial demeanor faded into a frown. A lump in his throat extended the soft tissue of his neck. He swallowed, then slowly regained composure. He deliberately sank into his inner-self, into the silence of the emptiness he sought.

Suddenly, I was jarred by the presence of someone, or something, behind me. I turned to behold the old woman I had helped at the Pantheon, whom I had covered with a raincoat in the dark and cold, and in whose hands I had stuffed my meager franc notes. I could smell her breath. The suffering in her eyes was unmitigated. I felt sick to my stomach, shorn of any idealistic blather. The man beside me jolted out of his silence and watched to see what I would do.

Why don't you help her? I wanted to retort. But I refused to break the silence. Whether his or mine.

I placed my face in my hands to conceal how I felt, or perhaps to hide. But from whom or what? I could hear Father d'Maricio of late, or his Buddhist alter ego, Sanghadhamma, snapping his fingers at her. As if for her to be off! Or was he snapping them at me? Whichever, the click was sharp and harsh, like a stern reprimand. I remembered that Zen Masters sometimes snapped their fingers to jar their disciples into reality. But what greater reality surrounded us than this woman's poverty and despair? I reached in my pockets and handed her a fist full of near worthless coins, as they were mere pennies and all that I had. She stared at them, then put them into her dirty skirt's left front pocket. She looked into my eyes, out of the dark pits of her own inflamed sockets, placed her hands on my cheeks, and kissed my neck. "*Merci,*" she whispered, as she hurried away. I turned back toward my new companion, but he had gone; he was nowhere to be seen. How could he have faded away so quickly? I sat there a long time, until it began to grow cool. I looked about. I realized that I alone was seated in the park.

Was it time to go home? Was it time to return to America? Time to say "Good-bye" to Paris, to gird my loins and repair to my classroom in the Valley of the Shenandoah, to teach philosophy however best I could, to say "Farewell" to Monique?

Should I call her? Should I call Julene, or Carl? Or write them? Or stay another month? What should I do? And what would my purpose be?

A gendarme's white cap caught my eye. He was swinging his Billy club out of boredom as he walked his rounds. He stopped in front of me, cocked his head curiously to one side, then brought his black shoes together in polite attention. "Are you drunk, Monsieur?" he asked. "One never knows about you Americans. Isn't that so?" He twirled his baton, as a wide smile creased his face. He glanced at his watch. I suddenly glanced at mine. It was almost seven.

"Thank you," I replied. "I was just daydreaming."

"*C'est bon*!" he retorted. "Don't we all?"

As he ambled on, I rose from the bench, wiped a tear from my face with my sleeve, and returned to the pension. I avoided supper altogether or, at least, the dining room. I hurried to my room, washed my face, slipped on a light jacket, and headed up to the Boulevard Du Montparnasse. I had no preplanned agenda. No place in particular to go. Aimless wandering was more like it. *Café d'Orion*! Yes! Why not go there? To Madame Evana's!

To my surprise, her place was crowded. The musicians smiled when they saw me enter. They were deliriously delighted, if not overjoyed, to be exact. They loved playing for a packed house. Madame waved and pointed toward a table near the kitchen curtain.

"Ah! You've come back! And alone! *Non*? Is it over? Did she leave you? This one, yes, she was beautiful. *Non*?"

"Who knows, you gorgeous widow! Maybe you're next!" I said, as I sat down.

"Ho! A Gypsy with you? Monsieur! I'm a woman of honor. I have a tradition to uphold! Besides, my husband's brothers would kill you, as well as me," she beamed. "But," she leaned forward, in a most seductive way, "a little *comme ci, comme ça*, who would know, save the Devil and his angels? Yes!" she pinched my cheek, as well as brushing my shoulder slightly with her right breast. "The works! *Non*?" she clapped her hands.

"No, no! Please! Just a little wine, and perhaps some cheese and bread. I'm in a contemplative mood."

"Monsieur! 'Contemplative!' my foot. You are more like sad. *Non*? When I come back, Evana will tell your fortune. *Bien sur*! That will cheer you up. I promise."

I doubted as much, but when she returned, she sat in the empty seat across from mine and looked gravely into my eyes.

"You're a Leo, aren't you? I'm never wrong."

"That's right. How did you know?"

"My secret! And gifts of the dark arts, *non*?"

"Go on."

"Leos are always friendly and kind, just like you. Courageous and generous. And accepting of others at face value. No? I think so," she smiled. "And that's the problem. Too generous! Gullible and easily hurt! And so you become despondent and sulky and harbor an air of contempt. You think you're better than the rest. *Oui*? Ah, yes!"

"You said you were going to make me feel better. That was a promise."

"Don't rush me," she glared, with roguish impatience. "You've still have a host of qualities. Like loyalty and a sense of caring to the point of self-sacrifice. That's you, isn't it? And it gets in the way of that elusive quest that's forever slipping away from you. Don't deny it. I know," she smacked her lips with cocky certainty. "I think I'll have some wine with you."

"Please, let me," I interjected, as I poured her a glass of the robust wine she had uncorked. "What about Monique? That luscious woman I brought in here? Do we have a future? Do you know?'

"I have to be honest. I don't know. Only you can decide that, along with her. But with a married woman? Who's to say? She is married, isn't she?"

"Yes."

"Don't be despondent. But I think she's a Capricorn. They are egotistical, critical, status seekers, unforgiving at heart. I could see it in her eyes. She's only having fun with you, Monsieur. Take my word. We're all capable of bad choices. But Capricorns love sex and will take risks and don't even cry when their partners are hurt."

"But what if I love her? What then? Would she leave her husband for me?"

"Maybe. Maybe not. Just be careful. Love is a wrenching thing, isn't it? We never fall in love with the right person. We're always drawn to an incompatible sign. Love is a turbulent power. Ah, yes, a soothing balm. Would that my own *mari* were alive!"

"Come, now! Cheer up! What's that old saying about wine? That there's truth in wine? *In vin veritas!*"

"True. But tomorrow, such truth is gone! I swore to make you happy. But, alas, we have made each other sad."

She leaned across the table and squeezed my hand. "There's a lonely girl in the kitchen, a German, if you want her. Ya?"

"You think of everything, don't you?"

"Yes or no. She needs the money. What's a little money for love? Even if it isn't love?"

"Please, Madame. I am vulnerable just now. I'd better not."

"Shall I call her to slip out?" she smiled. "You won't say 'No,' then."

I stared down at my glass, my hands. "Please, don't."

"Hanna!" she called in a hushed whisper, but loud enough to be heard. "Monsieur would like to see you."

A tall, slender, and shapely girl appeared at the curtain. Her eyes were black, like the sea at night, full of longing and uncertainty. She smiled, as she brushed her long, dyed, reddish blonde hair to one side. She had taken her apron off. Her hips were curvaceous and smooth, her breasts firm and noticeable beneath her damp, white shirt. Trickles of sweat glistened on her neck.

"There's a room in the back," said Madame. "For each other's sake, use it."

I scooted my chair back, stood up, and took the girl's hand, and followed her to a small room in the back.

It was late when I returned to the pension. For whatever reason, I paused by the dining hall and happened to stare down at d'Maricio's *On Solitude*. Out of curiosity, I picked it up. I climbed the stairs to my room, stood in the shower stall for a long time, bathed myself slowly until the musky odor of my flesh and the smell of Hanna's body were gone. Then I dried off and crawled into bed with my eclectic "friend's" book. The opening words stabbed at my conscience and consciousness with bitter irony:

> Every creature is alone. Man is no exception. Like a brilliant star, traveling through the darkest spaces of night, we dwell in isolation. Not only are we alone, but we know we're alone. That's what defines us as humans. We can't escape it. We can't prevent its recognition. It is there. Our solitude. And it speaks to us. Yes, it confronts us. It is part of our greatness as human beings. It both nurtures and haunts us. Theists know this silence as God; Buddhists as Being, as the inevitable truth beyond thought or words. In both traditions, it is that healing emptiness, that namelessness that fathoms us to the core. "Be still and know that I am God" (Psalm 46:10). "Nameless is the Great Tao. The name that can be named is not the Tao" (Lao Tsu). That is why we need solitude, time for meditation, moments in solitude alone with Silence. The silence of life, of no thought at all. No agendas. No theories. No musts, nor oughts. Only silence. The silence of Being. The silence of God. The silence that is God: that is Being. Which is why it heals.

I closed his book, set it on the floor by the bed, and fell asleep.

29

DAWN BROKE TO THE noisy, claxon wails of a police wagon or ambulance below in the street. The air vibrated with urgency and alarm; desperation and misfortune. All Paris's sirens had that effect, as if designed to shock the listener and make one rush from the street. The throbbing, pulsating sound grew louder and louder. My ears ached from the harsh, incessant blaring. Finally, the driver turned the siren off. I rose, walked to the window, and, after unlatching its large catches, pulled the double windows open, and peered down.

Someone had been struck by a car, or had collapsed in the street. The rear doors of an ambulance gaped open. Attendants had placed the injured person on a stretcher and were carrying it toward the ambulance. The victim appeared to be dressed in black. Probably a street person. I leaned out to acquire a better view.

"*Merde*!" one of the male attendants cursed. "This old woman should have died years ago."

"Watch your tongue! The poor thing's dead!" the second carrier added. "How would you like to have been her? What if this were your mother?"

Whatever the first man replied, I couldn't hear. His voice was laced with unequivocal anger, as if recovering such unfortunates annoyed him beyond measure.

A gendarme had stopped to peer at the woman's body. He was writing something in his police log.

A wave of sadness suddenly swept over me. It was the old woman they were carrying. I would have recognized her anywhere. Her lifeless form appeared all but dwarfed under her dirty, rumpled rags. From my vista above, her body looked like a dried up, discarded bone, under a soiled napkin.

They shoved her pallet inside the van, shut the doors, and climbed in the ambulance. The driver turned the claxon back on, and while its horrendous throbbing wails sang the poor woman's death song, the vehicle pulled away, out into the street, and off in the direction of the Boulevard Saint Michel.

After breakfast, I looked for Father d'Maricio, or Sanghadhamma, but he was nowhere to be found. Later I learned from Mme. Cueillier that he had departed for the south of France.

"*Oui*! He left here before breakfast." she said. "His type scare me," she rolled her dark eyes with uneasy disapproval. She let out a hushed sigh and ran her hands over her dumpy hips. "He never left a tip, you know. Not one measly sou! Who was he, anyway? That I should care!"

"Now, now! You have more dignity than that. And, I think you did care, or do care. No?"

She looked at me with droll shock. "Monsieur! Professeur Clarke! How dare you!" she all but laughed, as a huge smile spread across her purple lips. "Really? *Vraiment*?"

Determining how to reply to Julene posed innumerable conundrums. I couldn't write her directly without arousing Carl's suspicions, nor respond to her concerns openly. A general letter would have to do.

> *Dear Julene and Carl:*
> *I trust all is well at Sullivan's Landing. I was grieved to learn of your mother's death, Julene. Hopefully you'll be able to find her "memoirs" and discover the truth about her illness and whatever else she wanted you to know. When does your work require you back at school, Carl? I assume you'll reside at your home in Alabama until then. If invited, I would love to visit you and continue our chats on the Classics, Being, and whatever else no one can solve. I've about completed my own project. I still need to draw appropriate conclusions, provided I can figure out what those are. You would think I would know by now. The only thing I've resolved for certain is that the certainties we long most to know are beyond knowing with certainty. I suppose that is what makes us human and keeps us human. There are no epistemological foundations for resolving the tension. The calculations of science and logic are wonderful; the former produce theories that can be revised to do justice to the facts as we glean them. The latter provides us with unerring arguments and rules for testing fallacies. But no method thus far can prove the presence or absence of any underlying metaphysical reality that might establish some absolute*

about ourselves or our universe. Before my own project goes to press, I need you to peruse it, if you will. But enough of this nonsense!

How is your own book fairing? Julene says it has already gone to press. I await its publication with earnest interest, your conclusions with hope and terror. Terror, because I'm confident you're on to something that will force me to rethink my own prejudices. Well, enough of this! I'll probably leave here in another month. I'm overly fond of Monique, which Jacques fully knows. That's at least one certainty! She's sweet on me, too. How to end it with grace and class? Das ist Die Frage? Perhaps Goethe might know, or Rilke. The Shenandoah Valley is beautiful in the fall. Perhaps you can drive up and visit me? My house overlooks the Appalachians to the west; its back porch faces the Blue Ridge. The autumnal colors are spectacular, aglow with red maples and yellow hickories, tall noble pines, and graceful hemlocks in the coves. We must get together.

If I don't hear from you soon, I'll write again upon my return.

With affection,
Clayton

Paris's warm July rains kept me indoors most mornings. Two weeks had elapsed with no word from Monique. Jacques's *Le Futur d'un Grandeur Passé* enjoyed brisk sales in every book store. *Le Monde's* book editor had given it his resounding approval. "This is the France we have always loved, and the France we can be again, if our wills aspire to it," he crowed. "But it may require a humility that its author seems loathe to acknowledge. *On verra!* Yes, we shall see."

While returning from the park late one morning, I was surprised to find Thiers and Jacques seated at a café near the pension's entrance. It served mainly metro goers and cab seekers and was always subject to the noise and gray fumes of the area's traffic. They were obviously awaiting my return.

"Ah! There you are!" called Thiers. "The contracts are ready, and to your specifications, or close to them!" he smiled. "Please sign them," he beckoned for me to come over, "and let's get on with it. *Oui*?"

Jacques had risen to his feet. His white shirt was crumpled and stained, and he smelled a bit sour, as if he had been sleeping in his clothes for several days. His usual dapper demeanor had vanished, and, in its stead, a grim and exhausted figure wavered before me. He was trying his best to appear civil and alert. "I've just returned from another promotional trip," he allowed, as he offered me his hand. "My book has taken off, finally," he managed to smile.

"Jacques will translate your book and you his. The details are right here. I assure you, Monsieur, I've done my best to garner you a fair contract. Balfour has been most generous, and so am I. Please sign. I've marked all the places for you." An earnest and contrite spirit emanated from his voice and face.

"Of course," I smiled in response.

Thiers pushed his espresso cup to one side, smoothed out the sheets, handed me his pen, and pointed to the lines I needed to sign. He had already filled in his own signature on all the right pages, even on the copies designated for me.

He handed me my copies, along with a manila envelope. "We'll all be pleased with this in time. *N'est-ce pas*?"

"Yes. It'll be quite a labor of joy, and I'll look forward to reading my own work in French."

The three of us exchanged handshakes a second time.

"*Alors! Au'voir*!" Theirs said with relief. "My card and phone numbers are in the packet. Let me know when you can start."

"Give me a couple of months, and I'll be ready."

"Very good!"

"Same here," said Jacques. "I've a few more promotional jaunts, then I'll be settling down to your *Ethics of Virtue*." A slight glint of resentment gleamed in his eyes. I knew what he was thinking.

I kept my lips closed. How was I going to do it? What if Monique should call again? Was she a Capricorn? My resolve collapsed as I watched the two men slip away to hail a cab.

Upon regaining my room, I glanced through the contracts, then placed them on my desk. My interests had changed. Translating Gibert's work into English, or having my own translated into French, no longer appealed to me as it had a month earlier. My mind was simply elsewhere, although where, I could not say. That internal engine, or ego driving force, that had welcomed the opportunity, had stalled in remission. The thrill was no longer present. What did it matter if *The Ethics of Virtue* ever became *L'Ethique du Vertu*? In the grand scheme of things, who would know, remember, or care? And wasn't all virtue the consequence of years of choices and habituation that molded character and in turn was molded by character? As Aristotle had so aptly phrased it years ago: "*One swallow does not make a summer day, nor one day in the life of a man, blessed.*" One only becomes just by acting justly, noble by performing noble deeds, kind by kindness, and chaste by refusing to act promiscuously. I could not have been more promiscuous, nor did I hanker to cease. I craved Monique's presence, the scent of her perfume, the feeling of her breasts against my chest, the pressure of her tongue and lips against my own, her dark and sensuous eyes staring into mine. Should I call her, or wait for her to call me?

Following lunch, I slipped Carl's book, along with several others, into my shoulder satchel and returned to the park. I walked down the broad central sandy aisle to the spacious basin, then sought out the sequestered bench beside the Baudelaire statue. I took a seat. While flipping through Carl's work, his section on the Sirens caught my eye. It consisted of less than three pages. I could imagine him writing it with his eye on Julene, or his hand on her soft, light, cocoa-colored thigh.

> Who were the Sirens? We know so little about them. They were sea nymphs and possessed the power to charm all who heard their song. They lived on an island, some say near Sicily, others in the Aegean, and sang their irresistible song for passing mariners and sailors to hear. But woe-betide the crew who stopped to listen, or paused beside their oars to catch their song. Some leapt into the sea to drown, so intoxicated by their lilting melodies and haunting sounds. Others rowed their boats ashore, only to die in the surf, leaving their bleached bones to gleam ivory along the island's rocky beach. If it hadn't been for Orpheus's lyre, Jason's Argonauts would have perished on the Sirens' shores. With all his might and godlike power, he played his lyre and sang his repertoire of charming songs to lure them back from a certain fate.
>
> Even more alarming is the story of Odysseus. As his sailors approached the Sirens' island, Circe instructed Odysseus to fill his oarsmen's ears with wax, lest, like countless before them, they too should hear and fall prey to the Sirens' songs. But Odysseus went one step further, though out of wisdom, with thoughtful caution. He commanded his men to fasten him to the mast, to bind his torso in heavy ropes, before they passed the isle. But, unlike his men, he elected not to plug his ears with wax, for he so wanted to hear their magical song. Slowly the ship approached, the crew bent steady at their oars, while Odysseus listened for them to sing. The sea was calm. Over the waters came their ravishing music, its notes sinking into the hollow of Odysseus's viscera, into the heart of the great Seafarer's groin. He swept his long black hair from side to painful side. He struggled against his cords, clenched his

teeth, strained until his arms and chest bled. He begged his men to release him that he might plunge into the sea. But their ears were deaf to his pleas, their eyes fixed on the lapping waves and the gentle swells of green ahead. And so they passed the Sirens' isle to drift in the empty calm.

According to Hesiod, their parents were Asopus (an ancient river-god) and Sterope, or one of the Muses. Hercules, purportedly, battled with Asopus, breaking off one of the sea monster's horns. From its bleeding wound, the Sirens were born. Ancient vessels depict them with a bird's head, a woman's breasts and arms, and a lower body shaped like an egg. Some stories associate them with Persephone, the Queen of the Dead. The Sirens' task was to direct all wandering travelers to her court. Their music was intended to anesthetize their victims, thus alleviating something of the bitterness of death. Might the Apostle Paul have had them in mind, when he asked: "O death, where is thy sting?"

Can we be equally numbed? One hardly needs to be a depth-psychologist to fathom the Sirens' song today. Its ontological and aretetical dimensions are transparent. Aside from the peril of the sea, or fear of death, those bands of Greeks who first roamed the plains of Thessaly and crossed the Isthmus of Corinth, were haunted by life's inescapable enigmas that its quest requires. The song of life commands us to take risks. It is filled with enchantment and danger. Often the two go together. We are fascinated by the boundary of death, by the horror of the taboo, by what lies beyond the next rise, the distant hill, the terrifying wave. Even the entrails of the battlefield, the excrement of the dead, sing their Siren song of gore and sorrow. Come, see! Gaze upon horror! Its sweet song will fill you with the stomach of life. It is more than curiosity or gross morbidity. It is life! Its song comes to us everyday. Approach, but with caution. Never abandon your oar. Look! Look! But don't stay. Let your heart beat with terror! Tend to your oars; the storm of life will bear you on. Those who tarry perish in a thousand ways.

All this is in accord with Jung's own analysis. The conscious mind resists the unconscious. The human psyche could not have developed without such necessary repulsion. But our modern consciousness has strayed too far. The psyche is not of our design. Much of it is still unconscious and autonomous. Consequently, the approach of the unconscious induces panic and flight. Our individual experiences of the unconscious are incommunicable. Thus the power of myth and the richness of dreams, which come to us symbolized in feminine form, point to true nature of the unconscious. They come on fairies' wings, bathed in the light of angelic

> hosts, or in the Siren songs, heard by the ancient Greeks. Theirs is the power to infatuate and lead the lonely astray. Yet we must not fear the unconscious, for its hidden truths lead back to the realm of Being and the source of inner strength and peace. In the heart of Being, consciousness and the unconscious experience healing and renewed birth. That is why the Classics remain our truest and deepest source of self-renewal.

I knew Carl believed every word of that, though his own renewal had mired in a slough of odious doubt, brought on by his infatuation with his own Siren: his childhood sweetheart and supreme lover, Julene. My own Siren had left me wounded, too, and now another, Monique, had taken up her song, and no amount of wax could dim her call and song of sure destruction. Unless, unless, she might just leave her proud Parisian to his unchartered hopes and come away with me! But how unchartered and illusion-borne that fantasy seemed, even to me!

I replaced Carl's book in my satchel and slipped out Baudelaire's *Les Fleurs du Mal.* Better to imbibe a poet's dreams than storm an impregnable castle. I began flipping aimlessly from page to page, when his poem, "To A Creole Lady," caught my eye. Was this his own Julene? Baudelaire's true Siren? Or one of many paramours he loved and left behind? I began to read. I reached inside my satchel for my pen and pad:

To A Creole Lady

In a fragrant land caressed by the sun
I once knew a Creole of elegant charm
Whose crimson canopy shaded her arms
Under an indolent palm.
A brown enchantress of pale, warm tint

Her smile tranquil and eyes content
A svelte figure of grace and ease
A noble huntress, in a humid breeze.
If you should go, Madame, afar

To my native land, in its morning glow,
On the banks of the Seine or the verdant Loire,
Beautifully adorned in old chateaux,
Sheltered in the hollow of an ivied arcade,

Your presence would generate, in our poets hearts,

A thousand sonnets. For your eyes alone

Would render their arts, more submissive than all your slaves.

I replaced my pen, pad, and Baudelaire's book in my satchel and walked the score or more blocks to his burial spot, in the Montparnasse Cemetery. I stood by his grave and stared at its plaque. "You spirit of the gods, with the soul of Orpheus in your heart! With his lyre in your pen! What manner of genius you were and are!" His was the gift of Being, direct through his art, blending the conscious with the unconscious, unmediated, setting the soul free. No arcane epistemologies were needed to experience his dream.

30

ON THE EVE OF Bastille Day, I wandered far and wide across the Seine, up past the Garden of the Tuileries, the Place de La Concorde, and halfway along *Les Champs Elysées*. When I returned late that afternoon, Angleterre met me in the hall. She was coming from my room.

"Alors! There you are! Need I say who's called?" she waved her arms. A frantic quality resounded in her voice and accompanied her movements. "Monsieur! Monsieur! When will you learn? She's called again. You're to meet her at a Café Chanticleer, near L'Etoile, at seven. 'Don't be late,' she said. Call her, if you are."

I stared at Angleterre's face and into her fuming eyes. "You needn't be protective. I'm not a little boy, you know."

"You are a fool, Monsieur! Forgive me, but a fool! You have missed your lunch. Would you like some tea?"

"Yes. Thank you, I would."

"Very well," she sighed. There was an apologetic tone in her voice, though she rolled her eyes. She shook her head from side to side. "To be young again," she frowned. "But circumspect! I'll bring you some pâté and cheese as well. *D'accord*?"

"You are supreme. Where did you learn such grace?"

"From having to suffer fools!" A huge smile creased her lips. "You're like a son, you know. A younger brother. I have no one else who cares. At least you talk to me and let me talk to you."

I gave her a hug as she headed for the stairs.

I knew the café Monique had chosen, for I had dined there myself from time to time. It had a light air of intimacy about it, a high ceiling with a sparkling, lustrous chandelier, and a pale shell wallpaper of delicate pink and sandy flax. The latter was adorned with dolphins gamboling in a blue-green sea. The café's specialty was a dégustation of raw seafood, seasoned with chives and roasted garlic. I cared for neither, but I would go and meet her.

"May I sit here with you?" Angleterre asked, as she brought in the tray.

"Of course." I rose to pull back her chair.

"I'm going to miss you when you're gone. You know that, don't you?"

"Yes. Tell me what you know about French women. Do you think the Madame would leave Monsieur for me? Do French women do that? Should I even ask?"

"I can't speak for her, but I think not. Her soul is Paris. I've followed her *petites notations* for the past eight years. Avante garde France flows in her veins. She's every woman's envy, you know. She's just enamored of the moment, I'd say. You should take me. I'd go. I'd make you the best domestique you've ever had, or could ever want. My heart died long ago here. Would that work?" Her face glowed with unmistakable sincerity.

"I don't know. But you'd make one hell of a concierge for a professor. Isn't that so?"

"Well, enough of dreams! Just leave the tray at the door."

For a long while after she left, I rustled various pages of my forthcoming *magnum opus*. I stared at the mass of pages I had accumulated, somewhat incredulous that I had written so much about an epistemology of doubt while my own doubts remained. Oh, well! Wasn't all academia riddled with such slippery slopes of self-deception, of dreams of accomplishment that exceed ones noblest grasp? How vain and proud! How at home with Augustine of old, who stumbled upon the one absolute he could never evade—his own doubting heart! Thus, borne upwards on the wings of that one truth, his soul sought for those eternal certainties that his Neo-Platonism alone could provide. But Augustine's inner world of eternal ideas had died long ago for modern mankind. Certainly, it had for me. Yes, our minds have access to a world of noetic forms, of perfect patterns of excellence, such as "truth, beauty, and goodness." But that such forms exist independent of our individual minds in a realm of transcendent perfection, along with such independent realities as "God," or a "soul" that exists after this life, or a "heaven of celestial abode," has never been, nor can be, proven. Nor is there any way to know that it exists, nor any epistemology to verify it. It is only in that encounter of the self with itself, in the silence of itself, and in solitude with the beingness of the world, that one senses a "something" that has the power to innerve our present existence. Poets have fathomed this best, such as Rilke, and artists like the Impressionists, or Giotto in his masterpiece frescoes of St. Francis. Philosophers might call it "transcendence," or our capacity to question our existence. But if doubt, itself, possessed any reward, or virtue, it lay in sweeping the field clean of idle worldviews that our knowledge of the universe cannot justify, thus bringing us face-to-face with Being again. Carl was so right to explore that world in the form he had chosen: by returning to the Classics, to its heroes and myths, its gods and goddesses, to glean afresh whatever he could about ourselves, before that world of myth had become transmogrified and taken up into the phenomenon of Christianity. Not that Carl was an atheist, or an enemy of the Christ. But he knew one had to steal back in history before the Christ's time to ascertain what went wrong. What would his *Beyond Homer* reveal? What had he discovered? He had been so cautious. Not that I could blame him. I would simply have to wait and see. Probably by the new year, I would know. By then, my own book would have gone to press. But all that seemed so remote, as I shuffled through the numerous sheets, and thought about Monique.

A vast part of me wanted to end our affair. But an equally overriding part vetoed any such nonsense. Being with her fulfilled more than mere erotic desires. It was as if she had slipped into my world of the unconscious and was massaging it beyond pain. How was that possible? How could such a delectable affair be both cathartic and destructive? How could I be so deluded? What shred of evidence existed that made me think she'd leave Jacques for a life in America with me? Surely none! If anything, we were mutually caught up in self-denial, in some form of personality disorder that the affair masked on the one hand, while healing on the other? What would Freud have said, or Jung have advised? I both wanted and didn't want to know. Nor did my hormones. Yes, I would be there at seven! I would run this gauntlet to the end. I had to know how it would turn out. I would not leave France until I knew.

Promptly at seven, I arrived at the Café Chanticleer. The night air sang with desire. I could hear its Siren sounds. Their music pulsated in the throbbing red glow of the café's neon lights and in the hum of the restless traffic clogging the Champs Elysées. I waited for several minutes, first staring up the street, and then out across the wide avenue that lay bathed in the warm sweet rouge sunset of mid July. Workers were attaching large French flags to the avenue's light fixtures in preparation of Bastille Day.

Down the street, placards announcing the likelihood of de Gaulle's presence at the parade stared at passers-by from sections of grill work which were fastened about the bases of several trees. Should I attend? I had witnessed this national, mesmerizing ritual back in the late 'fifties and had even seen de Gaulle himself. That would depend on Monique, I thought, or how I should feel in the next twelve hours!

At last, I saw Monique. She was dressed very casually, clad in her black jeans and in a beige colored blouse, provocatively open at the neck. I could see her nipples beneath the blouse. She had not worn a brassiere. Her dark hair curled in soft ringlets about her ears. It framed her pale but resplendent face in the sunset's pink-lemon glow. A thin wisp of plum lipstick adorned her lips. She stepped directly into my arms and kissed me.

"I have craved you all day," she whispered. "Jacques is in Brest, and won't return until late tomorrow. I couldn't go another day without you." Her eyes drank in my silence, my mouth, my lips. She kissed me again.

"Monique! I am undone, whether together or without you. What are we going to do?"

"Eat right now! I'm starved. And nothing but the best wine! I'll make it up to you later."

"But aren't you known here? In your own backyard, so to speak? Won't someone recognize you? And inform Jacques?"

"So what if they do! Here, take my arm. It's too cool out here. We can sit in the back. What I don't need is for you to be a coward now." A fretful smile formed in her eyes, then slid away.

"Of course not, sweetheart. Good God, my darling! 'A coward?' How gutless do you think I am?" I took her by the arm, somewhat angrily, if not incredibly crushed. "*Bon Dieu, Chérie*. I'm in this, too."

"I know. That's what I like about it!" she said with a risqué glint in her eyes.

A waiter seated us toward the rear of the café. Most of the patrons were sitting outside, sipping wine or enjoying cocktails. I ordered a bottle of white wine. "Your finest," I said to the waiter. "Yes, Monsieur," he replied, as he handed us the menus.

Monique opened hers and held it sensuously in her hands.

"*Alors*, Monique, but you know how to destroy a man," I said.

"That's part of the pleasure. Part of the game. But you're just as bad yourself." She had slipped off a shoe and was stroking my right shin.

I had to smile. "Can you do that a little higher?"

"Later!" she grinned. "I have a voracious appetite. It knows no limits, you know."

"All too well, I fear."

"I'm having this breast of duck, smothered in garlic butter, with these crumb-topped tomatoes in salad oil. What about you?"

"I think I'll stick with cod and boiled potatoes, garnished with parsley and olive oil." I laid my menu aside and stared at her lips and eyes. She had applied a thin line of plum eye shadow under her eyelids. Silver earrings sparkled with tiny diamonds from beneath the dark ringlets of her hair. A softness had settled in her face. No mascara was needed to accent her eyelashes, or oils and lotions required to freshen the tiniest pores of her skin. Nor had she applied any. "You are so beautiful, Monique. I ache for you."

She had ceased rubbing my shin with her toes. A pleased smile spread approvingly across her face. She puckered her lips, as if to send me a kiss. "My darling," she whispered. "It's '*Mon-nique*!' Not '*Mo-nique*."

"Sorry! '*Mon-nique*!'" I repeated. "I'll get it one day."

"You're going to get *it* as soon as we've enjoyed this repast. I feel *decadent* tonight. As if my libido's unchained. Has risen right out of its lair." She glanced about and shrank her shoulders together slightly, as if to hunch down in her chair. "Don't you feel that way, sometimes?"

"Yes. Every time I'm with you I burn inside. A hidden flame immolates me. I feel hollow inside. You only see the dancing sparks, the glowing embers, that are flung off in passion's heat."

"My!" she shook her head with an expansive grin. "Let's get out of here, as soon as we eat. By the way, are you coming to the parade tomorrow? We can go together. I have to take notes for the paper, but that won't take long. Then maybe we can go to your place for a cozy nap? *Oui*?"

"Yes!" I replied, somewhat startled, but delirious with joy. "I want to marry you. My heart sinks in my chest without you."

"Now, now! Not so passionate, *mon petit*. Please don't spoil it! I love you! Truly I do. But, let's not talk about it anymore. I just want you to love me, like we've been doing. The summer will soon end." A tear appeared in her right eye and lodged in her eye shadow. It hung like a purple sparkle, a miniscule pearl, before she dabbed it away. "We have to be realists," she said, in a hushed whisper.

The waiter returned with our wine and poured each of us a glass, first mine, and then hers. "*Madame et Monsieur*, have you selected yet?"

"Yes, your duck for her and the cod for me." I handed him the menus.

"The potage is a *crème de sol*, you will like it, I think. I'll have it right out."

"*Bon. Merci beaucoup*! And your crustiest bread. *Oui*?"

He flinched, rather indolently, at my pronunciation of "*croûté*," then bowed slightly, before backing away.

Monique smiled amidst a hue of blushes. "That accent! *C'est terrible! C'est sauvage!*" Where did you learn your French, anyway?"

"Here! In Paris. Back in the 'fifties."

"Not here! You brought it with you. You must help me perfect my English. What if I were to say 'Yes' to you? Or go back with you to your America? You wouldn't want me to sound like some trollop off the streets, would you? Some *salope*?"

My heart raced with excitement. "I wouldn't care how you sounded. Nor would anyone else. They would love you as much as I do."

She stared at me in silence. The waiter returned, served our potage, and filled our glasses again. I listened as the wine gurgled out of the bottle. It formed a delicate ecru stream of pale gold, as it splashed into our glasses. Monique's eyes sparkled in its glow.

We sat silently, smiling and eyeing each other, as we sipped our potage. A dream world of hypnotic power had slipped over me, sunk inside me, and taken possession of my senses. Was that burning desire I had longed to have quenched, that enduring love that had evaded me since Leeta had left, was all that about to come true?

"Why don't we do something different tomorrow, if I spend the night?" I offered.

"Like what? I have to observe the parade, the different units and ancient costumes, even what the spectators wear. Then I want to cuddle down with you, in that musty pension of yours, with its dark hallways and your dismal room, and your Angleterre's odious sneer. There's something ruefully painful about it, morose and sad, like sinking into a cheap bed in a desolate bordello that's cleansing when it's over and comforting just clinging to you. It renews me as a woman. It makes me feel whole and wanted, like going home again. I don't know how else to explain it."

"You don't have to. Lying in bed after sex and holding you in my arms bears me also into another dimension. It's like being drugged, or recovering from an addiction."

The waiter brought our food and placed it before us.

My cod was slightly raw inside, but I ate around the edges and smothered it with slices of boiled potato and butter. I tasted Monique's duck, but my true hunger was for her. After eating bits of soft, crumbly camembert, I drained the bottle's last drops of wine into Monique's glass. I watched her sip it; then reached across the table to caress her hand. As my fingertips brushed across her wedding band, the cold reality that separated us came slinking back, like a scolded dog, quivering on its chain, and curling up in its box.

Monique detected the pallor in my face, the hesitation's touch in my hand. She placed her right hand on mine and pressed it hard. "Come on. Let's go, now!" she whispered. A longing of her own embraced mine.

I paid and left a handsome tip for the waiter. We walked out onto the sidewalk and walked the ten or more blocks to her house. A slight veil of russet clouds stained the northwest sky. They formed a sienna crown above the lighted Etoile. Dusk came quickly and darkened the streets. The last few blocks cast their cape of twilight about us. We paused in the lamplight to embrace. Darkness cloaked us in its silent secrecy as we approached her gates, unlocked the door to her house, and slipped up the stairs to the bedroom. Neither of us said anything as we undressed. I unbuttoned her blouse, kissed her luscious breasts, and lifted her into bed. O rapture, of rapture! *Decadent*, she had said. And decadent it was!

"O God, don't stop! O Clayton, Clayton. Yes, yes! My darling, my darling. Yes!"

We lay back in the bed, exhausted, drunk with delirium, in a euphoric state. I was just on the verge of falling asleep when I heard a motor's whine, a light bumping of tires over pavement stones, and an auto car's engine turn off.

Monique bolted, shoulders up, in the bed. "*Bon Dieu*! That's Jacques!" she whispered. She cradled herself awkwardly on her elbows. "You've got to leave. Quick! *Vite, vite*!"

I lunged out of bed, struggled into my clothing, and groped for my wallet, pension key, and other items I had placed on the night table. I could hear the car door open, then shut.

"Down the hall! There's a window you can climb out. It drops onto a side wall. There are vines you can hold to. Quick! O my God! You shouldn't have stayed. O *merde*! O shit!"

We both slipped out of the room and hurried to the hall window. Monique unlatched it for me as I straddled the ledge and peered down. I could see nothing, but I could feel the vines with my feet.

"Hurry! My God, hurry!"

I ventured out, holding onto the window's ledge, felt for the vines with my feet, grasped them with my fingers, and began lowering myself. I could hear Monique latching the window behind me. Below in the dark, from around the front of the house, I could hear Jacques letting himself in the front door. I waited for him to open it, but he had stopped. Had he heard my sound? I could feel the vines beginning to slip loose. A flurry of wings broke the inky stillness of night, as a pair of swallows swept out of a dark nest and flew to the corner of the house to the front.

"Ah, I have frightened you," called Gibert. "Forgive me for disturbing your rest." He opened the door. I could hear him shut it, as he entered the house.

I continued cautiously down the vines until my feet touched the wall. I stooped over, felt for it with my hands, and, clinging on for dear life, lowered myself slowly to the ground. Dirt and fine root hairs had sifted down the back of my shirt. I could feel the loose debris collecting around the inside of my waist. I took a deep breath and stole quietly to the front of the house. Monique had turned the light on in their bedroom. I bent forward stealthily, crept past the door, and strode quickly out the gates and down the street. A cold sweat trickled down my back. It caused the loose dirt on my skin to itch even more. I rubbed at my back as I reached the corner, turned and jogged in the darkness toward the boulevard near L'Etoile. I was panting when I reached it. My legs buckled like Jell-O when I stopped; I could hear my heart thumping in my chest. When I reached the main intersection at the Arc de Triomphe, I hurried toward the metro and caught the last train that night for my haven in Montparnasse.

How stupid! How utterly and purposefully stupid! How out of touch with reality could I be! What was I thinking? What if he had heard me? What if he "sniffed" something while climbing the stairs? Or had to smooth out the hot depression I had left in his own bed, on his own sheets? And how could any woman mask her odor, or cover her shame, while awaiting her husband's shadow to lengthen and enter the room?

I had to ring for Angleterre to let me in. Dufavre always locked the pension's door after two.

"*Monsieur! Vous-êtes bête. Complètement bête.* Where have you been?" She shook her unkempt hair with grim disapproval. Her face loomed in the shadows like a crinkled piece of brown paper. "*Alors*!" she sighed, as she brushed off flakes of dirt about my neck. "Tomorrow is Bastille Day, and look at you!"

There was nothing for me to say or do but to nod.

31

THERE IS SOMETHING REDEMPTIVE about the first light of morning. The mystery of its stillness, its sleepy and cold darkness that yields slowly to the fresh light under a clean, cerulean sky, with the smell of streets still wet with dew. I stared out the window, rubbed my eyes, and marveled at the purity of the delicate light. In the quietness of dawn, it spread ever so softly across the orange-tinted chimney pots and tin-roof tops of Montparnasse.

Soon, the city would be bustling for the parade. I watched Algerian street cleaners sweeping the night's debris away with their bristly brooms and dull metal shovels. They emptied the trash into shiny garbage cans. I could see a line of French tricolors beginning to flap in the breeze. They were all along the boulevard, perpendicular to the Rue d'Assan, in plain view. Dufavre had even displayed one from a balcony, at the corner of her building.

I had awakened so early. I had slept only fitfully. How had Monique fared? Had Jacques discovered anything? Suspected anything? Detected anything? Had I left anything behind? What if he should go to that hall window and open it? What if he should glance down at the wall? All by accident? Just by going to the window, would he notice the torn vines? Would he realize what had happened? Would he remember the panicky stir of the birds, and surmise the truth? He was no fool.

I showered, dressed, slipped down the five flights of stairs to the street, and wandered up toward Demetrius's kiosk. It was closed. A small café across the street, however, was open. I purchased a cup of *café au lait*, stirred in two lumps of sugar, and, standing at one of the tall serving tables, stared out the café's smoky windows. They were beginning to steam up from the warmth within.

The pension's dining room would be open soon, but I savored each sip, until I had emptied the cup. I left and walked slowly and thoughtfully down the boulevard toward the park. A numbness throbbed ever so lightly in my forehead. A bird sang sweetly from the top of a tree. It sounded like a chickadee, but the foliage was too thick to see it, plus I doubted if France had chickadees. Pigeons and sparrows, yes. And swallows, too. And certainly finches and hosts of others. But whatever its species, its song filled the morning with a cheerful, delightful lilt. I wandered on back to the pension, but by way of the iron grill work along the western edge of the park. Even there the hush of the morning prevailed. The gates had just been unlocked. I stopped and peered through the bars, near the corner of the street. I thought of Rilke's panther, pacing in its cell, turning so silently on the soft pads of its paws. I was that panther. I was in that cell. I clutched the bars. They were wet and cool. I was one with the morning, face to face with myself and that silence within, the silence of Being. That silence of silence that takes it all in and gives it all back. And I felt sad. Empty. Yet strangely at peace. Home! I wanted to go home. I was already at home. At home in my heart. As I grasped the bars I whispered to myself: "Good-bye, Monique. Good-bye, my love. I must leave thee now. It is time to go home." But the mere thought of her, the mere whispering of her name, negated my resolve. She just might leave Jacques, my heart argued with my soul. Wait! At least wait till the end of July.

After a breakfast of tea, rolls, and raspberry jam, I braced myself for the long walk down the Boulevard Raspail and through the throngs of crowds I'd have to pass on my way to the Grand Avenue to witness the parade. I took my stand just blocks from the Place de la Concorde, but my heart wasn't in it. Thousands of citizens and tourists alike clogged the Avenue. French flags waved from every building and every statue. A festive mood swept through the crowd. A troop of Mounted Lancers galloped past. Their silver helmets, crested with white plumes and shining spikes, caught the light of the warm sun. The riders' breastplates glittered with molten sparkles as their steeds raced by. The playing of "The Marseilles" stirred my own heart. After all, France had emboldened Washington's army and supplied and helped it. Its warships had saved the young Republic at Yorktown. I listened with grateful respect as the band lumbered by. Suddenly, cheers erupted all along the street and faces stared. Was it de Gaulle? I couldn't tell. "What is it?" I asked a bystander. He replied: "*Alors, Monsieur*! It's The Foreign Legion! The last symbol of our glorious past. Look, how they march! All of France loves them! *Non*?" Their guidons flapped in the breeze. Erect and tall, they marched past, their thumping boots echoing off the pavement. Jets streaked overhead, creating streams of blue, white, and red contrails. Dignitaries, in their passing vehicles, stood at attention. Polite applause accompanied their passing. However, no de Gaulle. But I could see him as I had remembered him in the late fifties: tall, somber, large and sagging of frame, as he towered over the crowd in the open limousine that bore him.

The metro was too packed to return to the pension by the subway. I settled for a Coke at a vendor's stand at the entrance to the Tuileries. I crossed the Seine by way of the Pont Solférino and, several blocks beyond, found a small café, tucked under a faded brown awning. There I enjoyed a brothy onion soup, wedge of crusty bread, beverage and cheese—all for five francs. I meandered on, strolling slowly through the side streets, until I came back out on Raspail and finally made it back to the pension around four.

"Would the *Monsieur Professeur* care for a gâteau and tea?" asked Angleterre. "*Oui*?"

"Might as well," I replied. "I can't imagine how far I've walked today. I gather you stayed here?"

"Yes. The best parade was following the Nazi's retreat. All of Paris turned out to greet de Gaulle and your GIs. There's never been another day like it!" she boasted with a patriotic gleam in her eyes. "*Alors*! It was magnificent!"

After she brought up her tray and left, I slouched in the chair at the desk, sipped on the steaming tea, and crunched hungrily on the dry, sugar-biscuits she'd arranged in a circle on a bright red tin dish. I hadn't realized how exhausted I was. I could have fallen asleep, had I let myself indulge in such a reprieve, or sought out the bed. But how could I? Monique would not leave my mind. Her image was engraved in every cell. It slipped across the miniscule gaps of every finite neuron. Instead of counting sheep, I would have had to count each synapse as it fired from gap to gap.

I picked up Father Sanghadhamma's book *On Solitude* and began thumbing through its pages. Midway, I opened it full-page and began to read:

> Silence does not always heal us immediately. To think that life is problem free, or that the world of suffering lies outside us, and torments only the poor and the ignorant, and not the enlightened as well, is to wander the maze of disillusionment and attached ego. We will never surmount all suffering. Illusion and falsity never

> give up. The ubiquitous presence of ambiguity ever hovers over us. What can help us cauterize the bleeding wounds within? Solitude, or silence. Let our stillness within become *le point vierge* for that inward inspiration that becalms and heals. There will be time for goals, for whatever our unique self discovers in emptying itself, while not letting its own predisposed self get in the way of Being. Yes, of that Silent Being within ourselves that unites us with all things, with all forms of suffering, and all who suffer. We will find peace, experience peace, renewal, hope and strength. But it will always be a daily peace, a hope in the present, and never a dogma. And each morning brings it to us anew, each hour, whether drinking tea, or reading a book, or fulfilling the work of our hands. To find peace in the present is to find it for eternity. Each dawn offers us the world of truth again, ever in relation to all other truths, and all other beings, and gives it back to us once more in the silent evening sunsets, and the darkness that blesses sleep, like the poet's snow that fell in the woods that evening while he still had miles to go. Call it God, call it Being, call it the Buddha-essence. Or call it Tao. But open yourself to it now, and let its presence purge your soul! As the Taoists know: "He who finds Tao in the morning, though he die that evening, shall not have lived in vain."

I closed his book. The only presence I felt was Monique's. Somehow I had to contact her before I returned to my own woods, nestled above the Valley of Virginia where they overlooked the college I had come to love. *Bon Dieu*! In less than five months it too would be lying under snow. I could feel trickles of sweat coursing down my neck. I had forgotten to open the window. Strangely, however, I didn't feel alone. For the first time, in a long time, I felt at one: at one with myself, at one with Monique, at one with home. Whatever might happen, it would somehow be OK. I rinsed my face in the sink, changed shirts, and went down to wander the park, before dinner.

I had scarcely seated myself in the dining room when I noticed the tall lean figure of Thiers, standing under the arched entrance to the area. He appeared awkward and uneasy, and was glancing about nervously. He spotted me and walked quickly to the table. By coincidence, Pierre happened to enter at the same time and sheepishly followed him, mocking his intent stride while smiling all the while. Thiers turned, which startled Pierre as much as himself. "Excuse me!" bowed Pierre. "No offense, Monsieur." Pierre smiled at me again and took his seat.

"Professeur Clarke, allow me to present you with this letter of *honneur*. I shall await your reply in the lobby," Thiers said coldly, while staring at Pierre.

I rose from my chair and accepted the letter. Thiers all but sneered at me. His eyes were filled with a stern but controlled air of defiance. He turned and walked toward the lobby and took a seat just beyond sight. I could see his polished shoes, but that was all.

"What's this all about?" asked Pierre. "Is he sick or mad?"

"Probably both." I opened the letter with my pocket knife and sat down again. A gold bordered sheet of crinkly brown parchment paper greeted my eyes. It contained an ornately crafted message in black ink. I read through the French text with shocked disbelief. It was brief and terse:

> Monsieur Jacques-Maria Gibert demands your presence on the field of honor in the Bois de Vincennes, in the Parc Floral, Saturday week, 6:30 A.M. promptly. Monsieur Thiers will serve as my Second. Your choice of a companion, if any, is up to you. As the offended party, I elect the epée. Under the circumstances, I shall provide one for you. A nod to the bearer of this letter will suffice. Your esteemed colleague, Jacques Gibert.

I let out a long, suppressed breath, rose slowly, and walked toward the lobby. Thiers stood, eyeing me coldly. I still held the letter and envelope in hand. "Tell him I accept," I said in a numb voice. Theirs nodded and left the pension. What else was I to do? What choice did I have? Leave Paris immediately? Apologize and beseech him to drop it? That would only incriminate Monique all the more and solidify Gibert's worst suspicions. How much had she told him? Probably, very little. In all likelihood, he had discovered some evidence of my having been there, and inferred the rest. I slipped the letter back in its envelope and returned to the table. I tried to smile at Pierre as I sat down.

"*Bigre! C'est sérieux, non*?"

"Yes. Serious enough, I suppose."

"You can't tell an old friend! Your old *ami*, Pierre?"

"In English we would say, '*Deep shit*!' I'm in *profond merde*, Pierre! Very *deep shit*, I fear."

"I've waded through my share. Come now, cheer up! I still grieve over Gaston. *Non*?"

"I guess so," I smiled. "That was bad, wasn't it?"

"Yes. As long as you're alive, my friend, there's hope."

I couldn't help but expel a nervous laugh. "Yes. As long as we're *alive*." I uncorked the day-before-yesterday's bottle of wine and poured the remaining dark purls of burgundy into our glasses. "*Salut*, my friend! To my noble and kind Frenchman, Pierre! May we ever endure!"

"*D'accord*! And here's to you, too."

We touched wine glasses, much to Mme. Cueillier's disapproval. "This is not a bar, you know! Some slum, working-class tavern! Your potage!" she grunted, as she set our bowls of warm, cabbage soup before us. "I'll bring the bread in a minute." She dried her wet hands along the sides of her apron. "*Salut!*" she repeated in a mocking voice. "*Salut, mon derrière*!" Suddenly, her face softened, and she winked at Pierre.

"There's your chance," I teased him, after she left.

"Too old, flabby, and a bit coarse. *Non*?"

"You could do worse."

While he sat quietly at his table, enjoying his soup, I reread Gibert's letter. The words, "*on the field of honor*," struck me as both insane and flamboyant, delusional to say the least. Would he consider a wound in the chest or thigh sufficient? Or was he after death? Had his own immersion in his *d'un grandeur passé* caused him to flip? Whatever, this honorable duel he desired was certainly, in his own mind, more preferable to his divorcing Monique, or humiliating her openly before some court. He well knew that and had probably been planning this for some time.

Who would I secure as a Second? I glanced toward Pierre. No! He was too peaceable. Mme. Angleterre? She certainly possessed the spunk to do it, but could I trust her tongue? Demitrius? What about Demitrius? Why not him? No. That would be putting him out, way out. Though he would do it, I thought, if asked. Whom did that leave? Evana of the *Café D'Orion*? Christine? The jailed Gloria, or Francine? Or her Belgian beau? He might do. But how would I ever find him? I realized how few people I actually knew. I had been in Paris for seven months, yet, I knew no one! *Personne*! Should I go to the Embassy? Seek out one of the counselor's at-large, with or without portfolio? This was no laughing matter. It was downright lunatic!

Oh, well! Whatever might happen, I needed to be calm. Calm, nothing! Practice! That was more like it. Get a sword and practice! Or at least a broom! Yes! A broom! Angleterre kept a closet full of them at the end of the hall. And they varied in length. And its door was never locked!

I could hardly wait to bound up the stairs after supper, sneak down the hall to the closet, and select a slender broom of epée length. I crouched, thrust, waved it about, and parried with it for close to an hour, all in the quietness of my room. Sheer lunacy! Absolute insanity, I concluded. I replaced the broom in its dark nook and closed the closet door. I had work to complete and preparations to make before departing Paris. I collapsed at my desk and turned to Sullivan's book. Achilles! Carl loved Achilles. Achilles would have known what to do. Along with Odysseus. I would console myself by reading about Achilles. But who was Achilles in this case? Gibert or I? What if one of us turned out to be Hector? That is, dead! I turned the back of the book up and laid it beside my journal and began pacing the room.

I walked to the window and peered out. The silent evening had spread its wistful cape of purple shades across the roof tops of Montparnasse. You can do this, Clarke, my inner self assured. Exercise, keep strong, be operose and diligent. And you will survive this. As for Monique, she must make her own choice—however much you love her, or she loves you. You have found what you came after. *Yourself.* Isn't that so? What other epistemology is there that can surpass it? The night air grew dark; twilight settled upon the streets; it mantled the stillness with its pale somnolence. The soft lights of Paris throbbed in the darkness, filling it with rainbow hues of neon light.

I settled back down in my chair, by the desk, and turned Carl's book upright again. "Counsel me, Carl," I whispered to myself. As my Second, if you were here, what would you have to say? I began reading his segment: "The Legacy of Achilles."

> Hail, Achilles! Son of Peleus and the sea-nymph Thetis! We owe you so much. Magnificent warrior, fierce in battle, fearless before your foe, how courageous, brave, indomitable, and awesome you were! Peerless in the arts of war! Save for your flaws. O proud man of rage! Sulking, vain-glorious, pampered hero! Why were you so spiteful and brutal? What did Homer have to gain by portraying you so? Was he merely following custom? Or fathoming something deeper in his quarrel with antiquity?
>
> Your mother dipped you in the River Styx, that confluence that separates all mortals from the realm of death, until the hour they are ferried over. But she held you by the heel. Such an innocent oversight of a mother's love. The centaur Chiron taught you the art of war, feeding you the marrow of wild beasts to give you

marrow of your own. The kindly Phoenix taught you eloquence, so that your fetes of strength might be matched by your gifts of speech—the two so vital for your time.

O how Thetis hoped to spare you from the coming Trojan War! Disguising you like a young maiden and sending you off to Lycomedes's Court. But shrewd Odysseus knew how to lure you from your mother's web. How crafty of him—placing weapons of war among the gleaming gems! And you fell for it. You slipped your hairy arm forward and clasped the spear with aching, eager fingers. Ah! Leader of the Myrmidons! You could not hold back! Your fate was sealed.

With what exciting valor you fought beside Agamemnon during the first battles of the war. How you loved your prize: Briseis! Young, voluptuous, graceful, passionate, desirous booty of war! But when Agamemnon was forced to return his mistress, he seized yours. And you withdrew from war. You refused to acknowledge your general's orders and prayed for your army's defeat. Your own Greek people's defeat!

Alas, girded in your own armor, your bravest friend of all, Patroclus, was slain by Hector's hand. Then you bolted awake, vowing revenge, and plunged with blood-lust into battle again. Down, down dropped the scales of life for Hector. Up, up rose your own. Hotly you pursued him. You split him with your swift bronze javelin. Down, down he fell. Angrily, you dragged him behind your chariot: once, twice, and thrice about the walls of Troy. Priam wrung his hands in horror, Andromache wept with grief. You brutal bastard! O feckless coward, uncouth barbarian! Even the gods turned away, vomit-sick with repulsion. Finally, the old king's tears mollified your heart, and you returned the blood-smeared carcass of the noblest man you ever fought to Priam's arms. At least you covered it with a long soft cloth.

But, oh, there was more. After Troy's best lay slain, Hector's sister caught your eye. The fair Polyxena. You took her to Minerva's Hall. Hand in hand you bowed before Athena's marble altar. "Grant me Virgin Goddess, but her love. Let it purge my hate-filled heart!" Then Paris, that craven cunning former shepherd boy, who named Aphrodite the loveliest of all, Priam's offspring and Hector's surviving brother, drew back his bow. He who had whined throughout the war and found protection beneath the skirts of Aphrodite, drew back the string. Hiss, hiss, the arrow flew! And stung Achilles's tendon. O sea-nymph mother who loved her boy, the hapless hero of Troy, now you may ferry him with tender sorrow across the River that flows by Hades' doors.

> No one escapes death. No armor immunizes from the final coil. Our own Achilles Heel gleams ever exposed. That is true both ontologically and aretetically of us all. Homer knew that. Do we? Our own worst enemy will always be the self. No inner anger can resolve the trauma of life. True, Homer's use of anger, of *ménin*, or mortal rage, was symbolic of his era's loss of Being. How he wanted to create a human who could transcend time's heavy burden, who, with a hero's courage, could lead the Greeks into a new age. But Homer couldn't do it. The meddlesome gods, who wallowed in their own slough of confusion, were no answer, either. Courage and valor, triumph and tragedy, without aim or insight, prove no anodyne. Thus Homer drenched his era with song and epic story of a past that was no more and a future still unknown. His glance was backward, into a time before Socrates and Plato, a time of war, when roving bands sought value in tests of arms and eloquent story. But he didn't go back far enough. And still today we are cursed by a loss of being, a failure to know who we are. Our unconscious still struggles to surface, like the sea-nymph Thetis, to open us to that hidden source of prowess, ocean deep, within ourselves. Call it animus, or anima, Id, or libido, it is there. Our true inner self, awaiting our approval. It cannot protect us from death, or Paris's arrow. But it can energize our life and unite with reason to recover our link with Being. That is Achilles's legacy. Transcending our rage of a meaningless world order and finding Being in ourselves. In spite of all the worthless immortal gods that myriads still cling to.

I closed the book and walked to the window. Below, in the Rue Bréa, prostitutes in a colorful array of silky blouses had taken up their vigil in the shadows of the street's hotel. Each waited her turn, as clients sauntered by. She would take her man by the arm and enter the hotel. Then the next girl in line would step up to take her place.

32

On the first Monday following Bastille Day, I took the metro to the Forest of Vincennes to revisit its park and chateau. I had toured it earlier, back in the winter, but had focused my attention solely on the chateau, its ancient keep, moat, and older castle. So many of France's ablest kings had resided here, or hunted in its vast woods, that the thought alone of so much royal history having taken place on the site was mind boggling enough. Philippe Auguste, Louis IX, Philippe VI, Charles V, Louis XIV! Of those five, Louis IX appealed to me the most. The very idea of his having chosen this woods, where he would sit under a mighty oak to adjudicate peasants' grievances, kindled my admiration. The tree was still out there, supposedly, or its stump, but my penchant for doubt created grave reservations.

The Parc Floral was relatively new. Continued landscaping appeared in progress. Graceful pines hid wooden pavilions, arranged to look out over crescent-curved lakes. Flowers of numerous species bloomed in majestic splendor. Flowering shrubs, delicate orchids, velvety azaleas, and spiny japonicas added to the luxuriant spectacle that bordered the pines.

So this was the setting Jacques had selected for the duel! The bright sunlight on the rows of magenta, pink, saffron, red and peach rose petals masked the dark side of this *place à mort.* But, if that is what he wanted, and I had agreed, was there a fairer spot to lay aside ones mortal robe? I felt resigned, trapped.

Upon returning to the pension, I wandered through *le Jardin de Luxembourg* to sit at my favorite benches in the shade of the park.

While ruminating on my pending fate, the large pigeon I had watched peck up the crumbly flakes of chocolate that had tumbled out of my pockets strutted in a gurgling, cooing fashion toward the bench.

"Ah, it's you again!" he chortled, smoothing out one of his feathers. "Why so glum?"

"Good question," I replied. "I might be dead here in another week."

"Here! In this park! On that bench?"

"No, no! I have misspoken. I mean, here in Paris. One of its citizens has challenged me to a duel, with swords. It's coming up this Saturday, in the *Bois de Vincennes,* in the floral park."

"Never fear! That's against the law now. The police will never allow it."

"But it's scheduled before dawn. They won't be around."

"Well, they'll be somewhere. Just call for help."

"*Non, merci*! My challenger means to cut me down. He'll grant no quarter."

"*Mon Dieu*! What did you do? Insult his wife? Uncover his *femme covert*?"

"Worse than that! I've been having an affair with her."

"*Alors*! It takes two to do that. Why doesn't he just kill her?"

"You've never been jealous, have you?"

"Not really. I always get what I want. But I talk the wenches into it. It's much better to be invited. You have more fun."

"Well, we talked a little, too."

"Who are you, anyway? I don't think we were ever properly introduced. As you know, the French—even we pigeons—are insistent on that."

"My name is Clarke. Professor Clayton Rogers Clarke. How are you called?"

He let out a series of coos! "Bavard!" he gurgled. "'Bavard, the Illustrious!' I know it sounds a bit presumptuous, but maybe you should try talking your way out of the duel. *Non*?"

"It's too late for talk. No palavering will save my *ass*, if I might say so?"

"Plain talk is all I ever covet," he cocked his head to one side. "*Ecoutez, Professeur*, you'll need a Second, won't you? I'd volunteer, but someone has to look after this park. I'm not really qualified for Vincennes. My ancestors are all from here."

"I've thought of everyone I know to ask. Do you know anyone I might have overlooked?"

"Yes, if you don't mind my saying so. Your Madame Dufavre would work fine. I've observed her coming and going through the park. She walks more like a man than a woman. Have you ever noticed her wrists, or shoulders? I'd choose her. You don't think she's a transvestite, do you, or some cross-dresser? I've been afraid to look up her skirt."

"You've taken the words right out of my mouth. I've wondered the same. But, no, I think she's wholly a woman. Just more animus than anima in her genetic structure."

"Why not ask her? I'll bet you a palm full of roasted chestnuts she'll say, '*Oui*.'"

I stared at my pink-toed friend with a smile. Yes, I thought. Why not ask her? But, then, there's her cousin, Daniel, the inspector. "I'll think about it. That's the most I know to do."

"Well, *bonne chance*. You've offered me nothing, and the daylight hours are beginning to fade. Fare-well!" he bid, as he flew off.

The thought of asking Dufavre had actually occurred to me, but I had been suppressing it, because of Daniel. After dinner, however, I moped about in the lobby, hoping to attract the Madame's attention. She often surveyed the dining room after guests had left. Perhaps she would do the same that evening. As fortune would have it, she did.

"Professeur, you're still here. Have you left something in your seat?" She was wearing one of her usually long skirts, in spite of the heat. It was dark navy blue and tight on her hips. Her white blouse also appeared too tight. The slight dimple in her chin on her large jaw gave her a mannish look.

"No, but I do need to ask you something."

"Oh!" Her gray eyes searched my face with a modest hint of pleasure.

O God! I hoped she wasn't a man! Surely, she was all woman! But I wouldn't have gambled my life on it, just then.

"Madame, I have been challenged to a duel. With swords. *Epées*. In the park at Vincennes, this Saturday. I need a Second."

"*Ah Bon Dieu*! You have to be joking. I've never heard of such a thing."

"Well, it's the truth!" I said, with imploring eyes. "You're the only one I trust."

She stared at me, half-smiling, half in shock. A strand of her dyed-red hair slipped over her brow. She brushed it back and glanced at me, as if she were sizing me up. "What do you know of dueling? Have you ever used an *epée* before? They are highly dangerous, you know. They don't bend. You could get killed. Who is your insane challenger, anyway? Or do I need to ask?"

"I think you know."

"Yes. I think so. Well, listen! Daniel must be informed. No, no, don't object! He'll surprise you. He's the fencing coach for his precinct's team. I'll ask him to be your Second and to instruct you, if I may?"

"Please do! Yes! But won't he tell? Won't he arrest the Monsieur and me? Or call it off? I really have to do this to live with myself and him. I think I can best the guy, or at least, not get killed."

"No. Gibert—if it's he—will kill you, or try to maim you. He's done this before. You won't be the first. Sometimes I think his wife sets the net for him. They work as a team, I think. Daniel has long been aware of them. He'd love to duel Gibert, himself. Not that he'd kill him, or that Gibert always kills his poor fools. It's a game with them."

I felt sick to my stomach. Betrayed! I didn't know what to say. "I fell in love with her," I mumbled. "I'm sure she loves me. Maybe this time, it's different."

"Perhaps, Monsieur. Still, let me call Daniel. Let him serve as your Second. Let him coach you these next few days. At least, let him do that. He won't divulge the duel. Sometimes we French may seem indifferent and weird, but Daniel would never disgrace you. Plus, he knows your own bent for courage. 'That Monsieur, that professor of yours,' he once said, 'he'd make a decent Frenchman, I believe.'"

"Very well. Call. I'll pace around out here."

She looked at her watch. "I'll have to wait till he's home, in his apartment. Their calls are monitored at the préfecture."

"I understand. I think I'd better get a drink."

"I wish I could go with you. I'll let you know what he says."

"All right. I can wait till the morning," I smiled. In truth, I felt somewhat relieved. But my heart still recoiled from what Dufavre had suggested. Surely, Monique's love had not been disingenuous! There was no way her lips and touch, her warmth and sighs, could have been insincere. If guilty of what Dufavre had charged, perhaps she was the one caught in her own web this time. As my chest sank into my viscera, I turned and walked away, descended the stairwell, and wandered up past the prostitutes, smiled at them, and sought refuge in a café-bar off Montparnasse.

As I sipped a martini, I played with the olives and stared out at the evening traffic. I must have had three martinis before I staggered back toward the pension and bed. A huge hole had opened in my soul, in my inner hiddenness, where only I could see. I tumbled onto the mattress and rolled on the bed.

33

AFTER BREAKFAST, MME. DUFAVRE broke the news. "Yes. Daniel will help. He'll come over tonight and demonstrate the use of the epée. He's quite excited, to tell the truth. But no one must know. You must think of a place to practice. We could use the dining room, but the concierge will hear. Mme. Angleterre cannot be trusted," she said with a prudent glance toward Angleterre's tiny office.

I doubted as much, but I refrained from replying.

For the remainder of the morning, I pondered a possible fencing place. Finally, it occurred to me that the alleyway behind the pension was the perfect secluded spot. It would be dark, but hopefully light enough to practice a few maneuvers. I would leave it up to Daniel to decline or accept.

In the meanwhile, I had ample to do.

I rummaged through my papers, began putting them in order, and stacked on the floor the few books I wanted most to package and mail home. I had accumulated quite a collection. Certainly, I would need all the Descartes, Pascal, and Rousseau tomes I had purchased. I also wanted to keep Baudelaire's *Fleurs du Mal*, Rilke's collection of poems, along with a book of Goethe's. An entire box of copied materials from the Bibliothèque would also have to go. Plus prints from the Louvre, the Impressionists' Museum, and several Chagalls. How could I leave those? And Gibert's book, as well. How ironic, I thought, as I picked it up and set in on the pile.

Toward noon, Angleterre knocked at the door. "Your mail," she called. "It's from the Sullivans. That wonderful black girl and her fat husband. I never cared for him," she said, as I opened the door. She handed me the mail and peeked inside. "You'll be leaving soon, won't you?"

"Yes. Probably in early August. A grand part of me doesn't want to go. How will I ever forget Paris? or what happened here? or how helpful you've been?"

"*Alors!* Let's not stretch the point," she crowed. "If you need help packaging your things, let me know. I'm good at bundling up boxes to ship abroad. We do it all the time. Besides, the post isn't that far from here."

"Give me another week or so, and we'll begin."

"*D'accord, Monsieur.*"

As soon as Angleterre left, I opened the Sullivans' letter. Slowly, I moved toward my desk and sat down, letter in hand.

Hello: Clayton:

Have we ever been busy here! During our absence, the caretaker ran off, or just left, though Carl had paid him six full months of wages in advance. So much for Northern Alabama help! He also stole some yard tools and rifled through Carl's mother's secretary, but nothing seems to have been taken. Just luck, I guess. Mold and mildew have been a true scourge. We have been airing out the old house and repainting the porch and its columns. We've had to hire a man to do that, but Carl and I have reworked the interior. We've hung new drapes, put up fresh wallpaper, and sanded the oak floors. Next week, we'll apply new varnish. I've redecorated the parlor, dining room, and two bedrooms. We are reserving one of them for you.

This past week, we mowed the yard (what an ordeal!), picked up apples under the orchard trees, and cleared briers out of Viola's Grove. Mama is buried there, along with all my own people, as well as Carl's ancestors. It was quite something, standing there with Carl—one of us white, the other black—together and married, and knowing that all our family are buried here in this quiet grove. We had to trim back the magnolia tree and clean out a number of cedars that have uprooted sections of the iron gate and rock walls. I want to tell you all about it when you visit us, and walk arm in arm with you down to the landing and back up through the woods.

When do you expect to leave? When do your own classes begin? Carl and I will be heading back to Tennessee the last week of August. Please let us hear from you. Carl seems in better health and spirits, though he still drinks too much and rocks on the front porch until late in the evenings. I've tried coaxing him to bed, but he seems to have lost his sex drive. He remains content just to rock and cuddle with me at night. O Lord! I've said too much. I do hunger to see you.

Please keep in touch.

Your affectionate, Julene

That afternoon, I decided I needed a change of view, so I took the metro up to Montmartre to revisit the hilltop and shops about Le Sacré Coeur. My heart wasn't in it, however, but climbing the steps to the cathedral, turning to stare out over the city, and walking about the square behind the church brought sufficient reprieve to distract me from acedia. A number of artists had set their works up for display. Many were worth purchasing, but I had reached my limit. I walked slowly about the square, examining the various canvases while trying to avoid their creators' eyes. Artists are like beggars, in so many ways. The beggar holds out his dirty hands, or looks up at you with his blood-red eyes and wipes his nose. The artist stands silently beside his or her work. Do you like it? Won't you buy it? Won't you affirm me? his eyes plead with you. Please, don't go by! Not so fast! Please, come back! Please, Monsieur, isn't there at least one picture you like? They try to smile. You are afraid to stop. But I do. I stare at one of his paintings. The artist has caught the square's inner spirit. His buildings and shops lean with the wind, filled with the breeze and the silence of this place. He has dipped his brush in just the right amount of pink, ruby, and pale gold for the awnings, white and gray for the buildings, and iron black for the shutters. A lone figure in a red scarf stands at the corner, capturing the loneliness that somehow haunts squares behind churches.

"Only fifty francs, Monsieur. I can wrap it for you. *Oui*?"

I admire the painting and glance back at him. I bend down and pick it up, where he has leaned it against an empty flower pot.

"Only forty, Monsieur. I know it's a little damaged on the edges. But I can touch that up. *Non*?"

"Yes. *Merci*. I'll take it."

I give him the full fifty francs.

"Thank you, Monsieur. I hope it will bring you many memories and much pleasure."

I know about the former, but the latter, I can't predict. I will hang it in my hallway, near my bedroom, when I get home, I tell myself. Now, it must be carried, until I return to the pension.

Thus the afternoon passed. After leaving Montmartre, I got off the metro at la République to wander the streets about the Canal Saint-Martin. Jostling the newspaper-wrapped painting under my arm brought little joy, but the lazy atmosphere about the canal and the Saint-Martin area more than compensated for any discomfort. I sauntered along its mile or more length of locks and foot-bridges and admired its Dutch appearance. A slender, tarp-covered barge floated past. It had been drifting sleepily in the channel's green waters while negotiating the long series of locks. I made more headway on foot than the quaint barge did by water. A spirit of restfulness came over me, followed me, befriended me. I wondered if Julene and Carl had ever visited this sector of Paris. I located a bustling café that seemed to be bursting with life. A group of tourists and their guide had assembled at a lock, opposite the square's restaurant. I paused to listen to the guide.

"Ah, my friends, take note. Just up the canal, past that foot-bridge," she pointed, "once stood a marvelous chapel and convent. Catherine de Medici, herself, laid the cornerstone in 1604. And not far from here, criminals and innocents alike were hanged. As many as sixty condemned people could be hanged at a time. Sixty! But in those days it was on the outskirts of the city, the Gehenna of Paris, when a Frenchmen's life was cheap and our dear Saint Louis was dead. And over here," she continued, but by then I had moved out of earshot and taken a seat at the café.

I ordered a beer and, while munching on a handful of pistachio nuts, stole a peek at the painting I had bought. It was worth it, I reassured myself. I re-taped the slight tear I had make, finished my beer, paid, and, clutching the canvas under my right arm, made my way to the nearest metro stop, and returned to the pension.

Pierre didn't show for dinner, for which I was grateful. Dufavre waited until all the guests had left, before approaching me. She glanced uneasily at Mme. Cueillier, who, picking up on the cue, retired to the kitchen.

"Good! Daniel will be here after nine. A little late. But he's coming," she whispered. "Have you thought of a place to practice?"

"Yes. In the alleyway. It'll be dark, but hopefully light enough." To my consternation, my hands began trembling, along with my voice. She noticed, but said nothing.

"I'll send him upstairs when he arrives. Or, better, why don't you come down around nine, and meet him outside, at the door. That way, no one will hear or see you. We must be discreet."

"Fine. *C'est bon*!' I said. "I'll come down around nine."

At nine, sharp, I reached the bottom step, but Daniel did not arrive until 9:45.

"Ah! There you are!" he greeted me abruptly. "*Ça va bien*? All's well? *Non*?" He was clad in a casual jacket, grey trousers, and black beret. Under his arm, he clutched the two swords, wrapped in a long, yellow oil cloth. "It doubles as a raincoat," he laughed. "So you are ready! *Bon*! Where to?"

"The alleyway. Remember it? Will it do?"

"Yes! *Formidable*! Let's go."

We left the pension and walked around the corner and down the Rue d'Assan.

"This is very grave, you know," he began. "I could have him arrested, and you, too. You know that, *non*?"

I nodded, in the affirmative. "I wouldn't do this, if I thought for a moment that his wife didn't love me. I have to find out."

"Love is a dangerous game. Sometimes, nobody wins. In the Monsieur's case, they've done this before. Or so we've heard. I must see it for myself. And I would like to be the one to hold the point at his throat. Oh, that would make a sweet twist, *non*?"

We found the doorway between Dufavre's pension and the building next to it. It was cocked slightly ajar. Daniel gestured for me to enter first; then he followed. The rancid smell of human waste and urine piqued my nostrils. Abandoned rags and soiled garments cluttered the narrow passage. We stepped our way through and over them to the rear. There the passage opened up, and one could see the night's stars overhead. The air was cool; the walls smelled dank; white starlight illumined our presence.

"Take this one!" Daniel said. "They're blunt. Strictly for practice. But don't jab too hard." He swished his about, making a swift, deadly sound, like the sing of a whip.

I did the same, but almost lost balance.

"Ah! It's like a dance, Monsieur. This art of sword play is really a state of mind. Remember that." He crouched, placing his left foot behind his right. "Feel the ground with your back foot. Rest on it with your toes, then your heel. Feel the spring? The spring's the secret. *D'accord*?"

"Yes, I feel that."

"Quickness! Like the lunge of a cat. A flirtation with death. You have to be aggressive. Limber. Supple. See?" He sprang forward. His blade barely missed my ear.

"I didn't even see that coming."

"That's because you were focused on the tip of my blade, rather than my hand. It's in the wrist as much as anything."

We began parrying and dancing about. I struggled to get a feel for the epée. It felt heavier than the foil and less limber.

"You must come after me, and not just at the tip of my sword," coached Daniel. "Yes, you have to watch it, and my hand, but my chest is the target. Not the blade."

Back and forth we parried, clanking and clunking the shining steel shafts. Their ringing sound reverberated in the narrow passage and echoed off the buildings' walls. In all that time, I constantly felt my body sustaining hits, while never once landing a blow on him. Finally, toward the end of an hour, with cold drops of sweat trickling down my back, I began to touch him. A shoulder point here, a chest nudge there, once even in the thigh.

"Good! Good! Very good! You are getting the hang of it. You are really better than I thought you'd be."

"I fenced on our fencing team in college, but never won a single match. I did score occasional points. But that was all."

"*Bon Dieu*! You mustn't think like that. You must duel to win! Do you understand? To win!"

"Yes!" I replied, as I landed another hit.

"Good! But keep a leaner profile. Turn your body away from my chest. Let me see only your arm, only your blade. Give me nothing to strike but the air."

On we practiced. We were both hot and wet, cold and tired.

"Enough!" he smiled. "Let's return to my cousin's and have a hot wine. A hot cup of wine will be best."

He wrapped the epées back in their oil cloth. We groped our way along the buildings' walls and re-emerged on the street.

I didn't realize how exhausted I was until I sank back in Dufavre's green armchair and sipped on the hot, red wine she served Daniel and me.

"A good lesson? Yes?" her eyes measured me. They were filled with shrewd hardness and a guarded twinge of doubt.

"Yes!" I answered. "I am in your debt."

34

FRIDAY'S MAIL BROUGHT YET another letter from Julene. I was quite surprised. A nervous Angleterre had delivered it; then left the room quickly. I completed several paragraphs toward my project that I had been perfecting. Finally, I picked up the letter. I stepped to the window and leaned out to peer into the street. A squabble of some kind had erupted below, but I could neither see nor hear anything to confirm whatever it was. I opened the letter and began to read.

> *Guess what? While cleaning out Mama's room, we found a packet of old letters and receipts from Dr. Wyatt Kingston. I can't remember if I told you about him, but he was Carl's father's physician. He would sometimes come by Mama's quarters and leave us medicine and things. Mama washed and ironed his shirts. The receipts were for the shirts, but the amount he left was for far more. He was including money for me! And notes, which Mama never gave me. "How's my little Honey?" he wrote on one of them. "I love the name you gave her. It was my mother's, you know." Again, "Please use these funds for Julene, our little girl. How I wish I could claim her!"*

I stared back out the window. A gendarme was arresting someone. It was Angleterre! I threw Julene's letter on the table and hurried down the stairwell. Dufavre was in the street, pointing a long finger at the handcuffed concierge. "Thief! After all I've done for you! Ingrate!" she hurled the bitter words at her.

Angleterre's sad eyes caught my own. She turned her face away, as she was assisted into the police van. "You could have paid more," she said in a teary voice. "Go look sometime in the attic where you force us to live! Monsieur!" she called to me. "Make her go up there and see how we live! What do you expect from the poor? That we should wipe your ass as well?"

Dufavre turned toward me with an embarrassed look. Her eyes, however, burned with anger and the hot rush of betrayal. "I trusted you!" she glared at Angleterre. "You are all alike! Just coarse swine! Just *cochons*. How you disappoint me!"

The gendarme closed the van's doors. I could see Angleterre's bent, scrunched form through the narrow oval windows as the van drove off.

"She had over five thousand francs on her. Rent money she was hiding in a jar," Dufavre groaned. "And I had trusted her, in spite of my suspicions!" she stated with grim lips. "Oh, *merde! Merde, alors*! Nothing is easy, is it?"

I returned to my room and read the rest of Julene's letter. Carl was just as stunned, but obviously pleased. Julene was ecstatic. "Now we can try for that baby I've always wanted."

I felt totally unfit to do anything. I stared at the books on the floor. Who would package them, now? Damn! That I should be so self-centered in light of Angleterre's arrest! How shameful could one get! Was there nothing I could do for her? I didn't even know Daniel's number. And tomorrow was Saturday. My own date with destiny.

Go take your walk, my inner-self whispered. Go down to the Seine. Do what Francine did and others before her, as well as what you have always done. Go to the Ile de la France, the heart of old Paris. Go to Notre Dame. Get up, now. Go!

I slipped into a light jacket, stuffed Baudelaire's *Fleurs du Mal* in my pocket, and headed for the Seine.

The long walk down Saint Michel distracted my burdened spirit, while the traffic's hum of motorbikes, buses, cars, and taxis, revived my zest for the city. What other world is like unto Paris? What other civilization unto itself? What other grandeur past or present? Did not its buildings and gay cafés cry to me on every corner, from every block, from every dormer, and every awning! How could I leave this behind? Would it not forever soar in my soul? Not *Fleurs du Mal*, but *Fleurs de Joie* was more like it!

I crossed the Seine and, next, the square and entered the ancient Gothic shrine. Mid-way down the central aisle, I took my seat. The votive candles flickered in the darkness. Mary never wavered at her vigil. Eternal mother of mankind's darkest hour. *Holy Mary, Mother of God*! That we should address our own last thoughts in whispered prayers to a Thou and not an It struck me as strangely wonderful. Evolution in love with

Mother Earth! A transcendence that even Carl would have understood. I wanted to pray, but what right did I have to pray? "Our Father, which art in heaven! Hallowed be thy name!" I muttered in a low breath. "Forgive me for calling on You so late. If You exist, you understand." The dark vault of Notre Dame's ceiling overshadowed me. I glanced up and back at the bright candles one last time.

After several moments, I struggled to my feet and returned to the pension. Whatever tomorrow should bring, I was ready. I took my meal in silence, in my room. Dufavre brought it up, herself.

"Here, now! At least eat this soup. It's a good potage, rich in chicken broth. You'll need it tomorrow. *N'est-ce pas*?"

I smiled at the big-boned woman and her thick wrists and homely jaw. "Thank you," was all I could say.

"It's the least I can do," she replied. "Maybe you should go out for a beer, or something stronger."

I hadn't thought of that. But, I preferred not to. A quiet evening, in silent reflection was all I wanted. I wondered if you met Tao in the evening, though you died in the morning, if Father Antonio's quote still held?

"You mustn't think like that!" Daniel had warned. I knew he was right.

"Merci, Madame. I think I'll stay here. Thanks again, for remembering me."

"How could I forget?" She studied my countenance momentarily; then left the room.

I read for a long while after that, mainly perusing Pascal. Toward midnight, I finally grew drowsy, undressed, and crawled into bed. "*All thy waves and thy billows have gone over me*," I remembered the line from the Psalmist. He, too, knew what it meant to be afraid. To be alone, yet to find strength in solitude. I turned on my side, reached up to turn off the light, and lay there in a curled position until, at last, I fell asleep.

35

The ridge rises slowly to break off in a series of jagged outcroppings. Large gray and orange sandstone ledges stand on end. Down slope, to the left, a flock of sheep (or is it a herd of Wildebeests?) runs toward a faintly, visible plain—green and lustrous—but far, far off. Dry, brown, thorn bushes form a riverbed of prickly obstacles through which they must pass. Behind them, lope wolves. They are silent and nipping at their heels. Back and forth, they harry the flock, herding it toward the distant patch of green. Soft columns of drifting clouds form dark shadows overhead. On the ridge, a lone male lion watches the spectacle below. His mane of scruffy brown hair ripples in the comb of the wind. Off to the right, a dull plain of acacia trees and parched earth stretches as far as the eye can see. Coming down the ridge toward me are three riders, each on an Indian pony. They are Native Americans. As they approach, their ponies neigh and rear their heads. The Indians see me. They have painted their faces for war. Red, black, and yellow patches decorate their solemn cheeks. The lead rider carries a spear. His black hair floats in the wind. Eagle feathers dangle from his coarse locks. The second rider lifts his bow to salute me. The two warriors gallop by. They hold their heads erect. I can hear their ponies' hooves slipping on the rocks and in the loose rubble. They do not stop, or bother me. The third has dropped out of sight altogether. I hurry down the slope, sliding in the dirt, past the large boulder on which the lion rests. Like a sphinx, he holds no interest in me, either. I have reached the green shade before the wolves. An eerie moans rises from the earth. I turn to stare into the sun. No! It's a light. Not the sun, but a light. Round and bright, irritating and riling, it gives me no peace.

"Monsieur! Professeur! Monsieur Clarke! Get up! It is time to get up." The light shifts; a hand touches me and shakes my shoulder. I recognize the voice of Dufavre. She has come into the room. She is shaking me. "It's five o'clock! Time to get dressed. Hurry now! I've coffee for you downstairs." She turns on the light switch and leaves the room. "Use plenty of cold water," she advises, as she closes the door.

I rose, slapped my face with cold water, dressed, and walked downstairs to sit at my place in the dining room. Dufavre had turned on only one light. Its rusty glow cast more shadows than its incandescence did to illumine the room. As I sat there rubbing my face with my hands, she brought me a cup of coffee and a little bread. Her worried look stared at me from tired eyes. "Daniel's not coming. There's been a homicide in his préfecture. He called early this morning, just before three, but I hated to tell you." She pulled up a chair and sat across from me. Her eyes never once looked away.

My stomach grew tight. A sinking feeling burned in my throat. I clenched my teeth. My right hand trembled. I sought to steady my cup, which was only inches from my lips. I had to set the cup down.

"Are you all right? Can you do it without him? I'll be your Second, if that's OK?"

"Yes. That will be fine. If I can just survive a rush, I think that would suffice him. Gibert's just angry, a little cocky and proud."

"You don't have to go. You know that," Dufavre reiterated, as she awaited my reaction.

"I know. But I'm up for this, and I love his wife. I think she'll come with me, if I can keep Gibert off. It's just a feeling I have, deep inside."

"Daniel has asked a partner to come for us. He's not a duelist, but he understands. He'll be discreet. If things go bad, he might arrest him. He'll pick us up around six."

I glanced at my watch. It was already 5:45.

"I need to go back to my room for a few minutes, then I'll meet you at the front door," I said.

Dufavre nodded her head and left the dining room.

Back in my room, I wrote a hasty note and placed it on my books and papers. It contained Carl's address. If anything were to happen, I felt Carl would know best what to do and would see that my project and notes were published. Time failed for me to write one for Monique.

A small car picked us up promptly at six. The plain-clothes driver said nothing. Or perhaps he said, "*Ah bon*!" He looked at me rather solemnly, then glanced away. He had that typical grey face of so many Frenchmen I had come to observe. Their dark eyes met yours, then looked away. Actually, I welcomed the silence. Dufavre said nothing, either.

It took a full half-hour to reach the walls of the park about the Bois de Vincennes. Mist from the River Marne drifted in pale wisps across the park and through the trees. The gates were already open, but the fog grew almost opaque as we approached the Flower Park. Our driver's amber beams illuminated the reflectors of a parked car just ahead of us. Thiers and Gibert were standing beside it. Henri gripped an epée in a gloved hand. Mine, I assumed. He was clad in a dark frock, gray trousers, and black boots. Jacques was wearing a lacy white shirt, with swooping sleeves, and black trousers. He held his own epée casually in his right hand. A woman stood behind him. I could see her legs. Her face was hidden behind a black shawl. A red cape was draped about her shoulders. It was Monique! Had she come on her own? Or had Gibert forced her to attend? Did she love me, or was it only a game?

Our driver stopped the car, and Dufavre and I struggled out. I never turned to see what the driver did, whether he remained or got out. Monique stepped back, but pulled an edge of her shawl to one side. I couldn't tell if she were staring, smiling, or crying. Wafts of mist enfolded us, then slipped away.

Henri approached and handed me the epée. "Examine it," he said to Dufavre. "It is strong and won't break. I have tested it myself." He turned and glared at me. "You have brought a woman!" he uttered with disgust. "There must be blood!" he said to Dufavre. "Do you understand?"

"Yes. Blood!"

"There will be no interference from either side. *D'accord*?"

"Yes. We understand," she replied.

He held a white handkerchief aloft. "Take your positions," he ordered Gibert and me. "Madame," he addressed the silent Monique. "Stay back."

She had something in her hands, but I couldn't see what it was. Was she for me, or against me? Would I ever know?

Thiers dropped the handkerchief. I sought a solid balance, as Daniel had taught me, and felt the soft ground beneath my feet. Gibert was on a pebbled path. He lunged, but I caught his blade and deflected it. I thrust in return. He swung his sword about and under and almost lifted my epée out of my hands. A wide smile broke across his mouth. "Simpleton!" he chided. "Fight for your honor. Fight for your life!" he laughed as he lunged again.

For the next five to six minutes, I danced anxiously about, dodging his blows, blade clanking and clinking off blade. Cool and vain, he pressed me back and backward, into the hedges, up a pavilion, and down into a row of roses. Sharp thorns bit into my legs. A seam of fog obscured us. I couldn't see him. I moved cautiously away from the thorns. I heard his feet slip on pine needles and the crunch of a fallen bough. I turned in the sound's direction. The fog had completely enveloped us. I could neither see nor hear anything. I felt suspended in a grisaille gauze. Suddenly a woman cried, "Behind you! Behind you! He's coming behind you." It was Monique's voice. A white flash of blade caught the edge of my shirt and nipped a rib. A tiny stream of blood trickled out. I sprang around and thrust toward the silver handle in the direction of his blade. But nothing happened. The fog lifted. With a triumphant gleam in his eyes, Gibert stepped forward and plunged his sword toward my side. It struck my belt and glanced off. I raised my right hand, gripped my epée's handle tightly in my fist, and smacked him in the face. Back, back he reeled. Blood splattered everywhere. The handle had opened his face with a single blow. He staggered on his feet, but lunged toward me again. I had thought he was down, out of the fight; that it was over. I had relaxed my grip. O my God! The pain in my side! The pain in my chest! It was his blade! His epée! Dark dirty blood gurgled out of my chest in spurts. Down, down, I fell. My legs crumpled under my body. My weight sank into the earth and into the fog. Someone was wrestling Jacques to the ground. It was Thiers. His hands were smeared with blood. Dufavre and the plainclothes officer were on top of them. A face appeared before my own. Tears watered my cheeks; lips caressed my bleeding mouth. It was Monique. She was crying. She was trying to say something. She was kneeling beside me and cradling my head in her hands. Back and forth she rocked. Suddenly, I felt weightless. I had no feeling at all. Nor pain. "My darling, my darling! O God, my darling. Please, O God, please!" It was Monique's voice. It echoed up, as if from a cavern, as from a far away and deep chasm. But I wasn't there. I was drifting somewhere. Drifting off. I wanted to tell her that I loved her. That I loved her more than anyone else in the world. I felt my mouth open, but no sound came out. I wasn't there anymore. I don't know where I was. Everything grew light. Suddenly, I had feeling again. But it was cold, icy, watery cold. And darkness was settling in. My head fell back, my eyes stared into hers. O light of light! Have I gone into shock? I heard something click, as the world fell away. Something was on my chest, something heavy. I couldn't breathe. Darkness! O darkness of darkness! Hector! Is that your hand? O Darling, Darling! The light is falling! I did love thee.

With all my heart, I did. I feel a rush, as if unseen hands bear me upward, then stop. The park becomes a red chiaroscuro of fading colors. Light! O Light! Why is everything so quiet? So still and calm? Monique! My darling, Monique! Momentarily, I feel her hands. If I could only sleep for a while, for just a minute or two. I blink, but my eyelids refuse to close. I am floating somewhere. I can see my body, but I'm not in it. I realize, I must be dead. "Monique! O, Monique! I must let thee go."

36

THE GREEN HILLS OF the distant forest undulate in gentle swells. Millions of years ago the earth's crust erupted with violent spasms in this place. Now, nubby Knobs are all that remain. I stand on the hill, overlooking the Knobs and down across the cedar-dappled meadows of the old farm, and marvel at the beauty of the rustic buildings where my father grew up as a child. I can see the granary, the barn—both under rusting red tin roofs—the outhouse, tobacco shed, sheep barn, and farmhouse, as they must have looked in his day.

Below rise the tombstones of grandparents and others I never knew. A central obelisk bears the family name: *Clarke*. An open grave awaits the arrival of my father's bier. The undertakers in town have promised to have it in place by noon.

The sun has climbed high into the sky. A brilliant white aurora shines out from its flaming core; it fills the blue vault of heaven with endless sunshine. Steers forage for new grass in the spring air. Wild blackberry tangles cover the ground, but the berries are still hard and green. Chickadees and tit-mice feed in the bramble. Grey doves peck for gravel in the lane below.

I know of this place only through my mother and my father's memoirs. I say "memoirs," but not really. They were the notes he left behind, the diaries he kept at Dufavre's. She found them after shipping his project and books to the Sullivans. They were in a corner of his armoire, along with an uncorked bottle of wine. He never knew of my mother's pregnancy, or of how much she loved him and loved me. She died at the turn of the millennium.

She remained faithful to my step-father, Henri Thiers, until his own death in 1985. Then she told me the story, the truth about my father, and how she wept at his death. She, Dufavre, and Theirs buried him in a cemetery near Senlis, where he had studied as a youth in the late 1950s. After my mother's death, I resolved to have him disinterred and reburied here.

The Sullivans will be coming soon. I met their daughter, Cyleste, three years ago. She and I are the same age, thirty-four. Like our fathers, we both have PhDs. Hers is in art history, mine, philology. After reading my father's journals, I knew exactly what I wanted to be and become. I could only imagine the last hours of his life. I cannot tell you how many times I have visited the Bois de Vincennes.

Cyleste and I plan to marry this fall. How do I describe such a beautiful creature? Tall, like her mother, lithe, nimble, the color of pale coffee, with brown eyes as large as chestnuts, glowing on the hearth of love. Henri and my mother raised me bi-lingual. Henri wanted me to translate my father's "journals" into French, but how could I? They belong to my mother and me and to our own hours of solitude. But I have inherited my father's love of poetry and have translated Baudelaire's *Les Fleurs du Mal* into English. I have also translated Sullivan's two books into French.

I was twelve before Henri told me about Jacques-Maria and what actually happened. Dufavre broke his neck! After she had wrestled him to the ground, she snapped his neck with her large hands and strong wrists. The duel was reported as an accident, although Gibert's paper badgered my mother for months for the complete details. Jacques's book slipped off the bestseller's list after that, according to Thiers, but its influence endured and still sharpens French feelings to this day.

It was Angleterre who confided in me the truth about Dufavre. Once out of prison, the concierge came to visit us at our home near L'Etoile. The truth? Dufavre's gender! Along with my father, Angleterre had had her doubts. But Dufavre was a woman. Just an unusually tall, thick-boned, and muscular female. Angleterre had the daring to spy on her during the woman's bath. "*Toute femme*!" she reported, with a sigh of disappointment.

It is so beautiful here, bucolic, restful, all so *au naturel*. I wonder if Daniel Boone ever climbed this hill and looked out across these same Knobs? They were probably dense with forest. But behind me, if one climbs higher, one can see Whitetop Mountain and the rumpled slopes of Mt. Rogers beyond. In fact, mother named me Roget—Roget Pierre Clarke. But whether my father was related to the famous George Rogers, we don't know.

How I should love to have known him—my father! Would he have been proud of me? Would he have loved me and bounced me about on his shoulders, as fathers do? Would my mother have come with him here,

here to this farm, or to his college outside Lexington? I think not, but I think my father would have loved me. It is in his poetry, in his kindness toward Angleterre, in his passion for Christine and my mom, in his solicitude for Francine, Demetrius, and the poor of Paris. Maybe he should have remained a minister, or become a priest. Whatever, I feel his presence inside wherever I go.

The hearse is coming. The men beside the grave have begun to move out of the way. I see the Sullivan's car, their limousine. It has stopped and Cyleste has stepped out. She is stunning in her pink dress and dark flowing hair. She waves to me, as does her mother, Julene. No wonder my father was attracted to her. She is dressed in modest black mourning clothes, but her large rose-red hat stylishly complements her graying hair and matching red sandals. Carl struggles with obvious pain from the opposite side of the limousine. He is almost bald, with a beard of silvery red. I have come to respect and admire him for all those qualities and ideas my father found so compelling.

I can hear a quail in the distance and the coo of a mourning dove. It is time for the service. I must come back here again. No wonder his dreams were filled with wolves! They were his connection to this land. My father's soul seems to haunt this place. I feel his presence. He is all about: in the sunlight, the grass, the breeze and this view. I lift my eyes to the light, the glorious light of life and power. Ah, Father! Some things are incommunicable. Yet, you are here. I am coming down to pay my last respects. May God ever bless this place! If it were not against the law, dear Father, I would offer a cock to Asclepios for you.

Finis

www.ingramcontent.com/pod-product-compliance
Lightning Source LLC
Chambersburg PA
CBHW070636310726
48982CB00001B/297
9781498250542